THE STORYTELLER'S DAUGHTER

VICTORIA SCOTT

Boldwood

First published in Great Britain in 2025 by Boldwood Books Ltd.

Copyright © Victoria Scott, 2025

Cover Design by JD Design Ltd

Cover Images: Shutterstock

The moral right of Victoria Scott to be identified as the author of this work has been asserted in accordance with the Copyright, Designs and Patents Act 1988.

Every effort has been made to obtain the necessary permissions with reference to copyright material, both illustrative and quoted. We apologise for any omissions in this respect and will be pleased to make the appropriate acknowledgements in any future edition.

A CIP catalogue record for this book is available from the British Library.

Paperback ISBN 978-1-83561-701-4

Large Print ISBN 978-1-83561-702-1

Hardback ISBN 978-1-83561-700-7

Ebook ISBN 978-1-83561-703-8

Kindle ISBN 978-1-83561-704-5

Audio CD ISBN 978-1-83561-695-6

MP3 CD ISBN 978-1-83561-696-3

Digital audio download ISBN 978-1-83561-697-0

This book is printed on certified sustainable paper. Boldwood Books is dedicated to putting sustainability at the heart of our business. For more information please visit https://www.boldwoodbooks.com/about-us/sustainability/

Boldwood Books Ltd, 23 Bowerdean Street, London, SW6 3TN

www.boldwoodbooks.com

For my amazing family and friends. Your support and love are a daily reminder of the good in the world.

PROLOGUE

'I knew it was you,' she says, wanting to make it clear, right now, that she knows he's been lying to her about who he is.

Then she notices that he is shaking. And so is she, because she knows who he is now. *What* he is. And she is frightened by this knowledge, and what it means.

Very, very frightened.

'You knew it was... me?' he says, his voice creaking. 'What do you mean, Nita?'

He's pretending to be frightened, to throw her off. He's so good at this, this pretending, she thinks.

She doesn't know how to reply. She's wary of provoking him. She thinks about what she has to hand to defend herself. There's a set of knives on the countertop in the kitchen. She wonders if she would have time to pull one out of the block before he came at her. He's likely to be well trained, though, isn't he? He'll be anticipating her every move. 'Who did you think I was?'

'Come inside,' she says, shutting the door behind him. As he follows her wordlessly into the kitchen, she considers her position. *He must know what I've found out*, she thinks. *He must. So why is he pretending he doesn't?* She wonders whether it might be a more sensible idea, though, to play along.

'Are you hungry?' she asks. It's the first thing she can think of that might extend her stay of execution.

'Yes. I am, as it happens.'

Nita nods and sets about making a sandwich from ingredients she'd already assembled on the counter, in anticipation of this meeting. He doesn't speak as she prepares the food. He just stands behind her, shifting his weight from one leg to the other. Nita finds the silence intensely uncomfortable. It heightens her senses. She can hear the grandfather clock ticking in the front room, wind forcing its way through the metal window frames, her own pulse hammering in her ears. She wonders what he's thinking, and what on earth he is going to say, or do, now.

She's relieved when the sandwich is prepared and she can place it in front of him. He descends upon it as if it's his last meal, swallowing faster than she feels she can breathe. She's about to turn around to offer him a drink when another noise enters the room. It's so faint that it's barely there, but they both hear it. Her eyes dart towards the door that leads into the sitting room, and his eyes follow.

In that moment, it's obvious he knows.

Their eyes meet for a second across the table, and then they both fly upwards and surge towards the door.

PART I

1

BETH

October 2008

It's a dank, sepulchral afternoon in late October when Beth Bineham creeps along the sunken roads of the Surrey Hills in her stupidly large company car, and, after spotting a half-obscured sign embedded in the soil bank, turns left and immediately brings it to a stop. In front of her are the wrought iron gates of Melham Manor.

She gets out and walks up to them. Beyond the eight-foot-high bars, a narrow road forks to the right and rises steeply, flanked by twin rows of trees which have over time leaned into each other, creating a natural tunnel as forbidding as one bored through stone. Anyone passing by would have no idea what sort of house to expect at the end of this driveway, and of course, that's why it suits Nita so well, Beth thinks. She has never liked prying eyes. Beth, meanwhile, has always thought it serves another purpose. This tunnel, she thinks, is a threshold. Melham Manor belongs to another dimension entirely.

She reaches for the gate handle and pulls down hard. It's been years since these were last oiled or maintained. She gives the gate on the right a sharp shove and it begins to fold inwards, the hinges creaking in protest. It's at least a minute before she's able to open them enough to allow her car through, and she returns to it slightly out of breath and already feeling the cold. The temperature this autumn hasn't yet dipped below freezing, but there's an insistent breeze blowing that has absolutely ripped through her thin woollen coat.

She fires up the ignition and turns up the heat as she inches through the gate, desperate to avoid scraping the car, which she'll have to pay to repair when the lease ends, and, given recent events, that's likely to be soon.

She will need to wash it, too. There's mud splattered all the way up both sides, which will make it a rare sight when she returns to the mean streets of Hampstead. There, the most common source of mud is when it escapes from the lorries of landscaping companies, hired to rid back gardens of real grass in favour of plastic turf. Their neighbour Jon had to visit the doctor last year when he slipped on his fake lawn and got some sort of burn injury. She wasn't particularly sorry to hear about it.

She exhales in relief when the car comes through the opening unscathed and puts her foot down so it can make easy work of the hill that follows. She enters the tunnel of trees and holds her breath, determined she won't be spooked by its dense, knotted branches, as she was on her visits to the house as a child. She had always felt they might reach down at any moment and ensnare her.

She's relieved when she reaches the top of the hill and returns to the daylight, such as it is on an overcast day like this. Just after the road forks left, she hits the brakes and pauses for a moment so that she can take in the view, which is as different to what's gone before as midsummer's day is to the winter solstice.

Beneath her the ground gives way steeply. At the bottom of the hill on this side, beyond Melham Manor's boundaries, is a tapestry of fields which surround Melham village, with its ancient church, thatched cottages, historic pub and cricket green. A pencil-straight railway line passes through the village, offering well-heeled city workers the perfect transport in and out of the capital every day.

When she was a child, Beth had liked to pretend that Melham was a toy village, and that she was its omniscient controller. Keen to avoid the strange atmosphere that was always present when the family were together, she'd sit at the top of the hill on warm days making daisy chains, imagining she was making the village church bells chime, the trains run, or the pub open or close. Now she's older and she knows more about the relationship her family have had with the area over the years, she finds the irony of this little game difficult to swallow. Nevertheless, it's a view that always brings her solace, and she's missed it. She wishes, for a brief moment, that she had brought Stanley, their Staffie, with her. He'd love zooming up and down this hill, she thinks, before remembering that she isn't here for fun. Stanley is far too joyful for moments like these.

When she feels she's absorbed as much peace from this view as she is capable of, Beth starts the car once more. She passes an enormous oak tree on the left, and then the house finally reveals itself, little by little, through its yellowing, increasingly meagre leaves.

Melham Manor, Beth thinks, is not a beautiful house. It wasn't even that extraordinary when this incarnation, a replacement for a Tudor house that had fallen into disrepair, was built in the seventeenth century. It isn't particularly sizable or grand, by stately home standards; it isn't covered in intricate flourishes or flying buttresses; and its twin wings that flank its Palladian-style entrance are regimented and unadorned.

And of course, it has now been neglected for decades. Its gravel driveway is weed-ridden and uneven. Rains and winds from the valley have buffeted and eroded the house's once elegant and refined facade. Paint is flaking from window frames, and dust, cobwebs and dirt are obscuring the glass. In short, Melham Manor is rather like Cinderella, if she'd never been visited by a fairy godmother and had instead grown old in the scullery.

Beth pulls the car up at the bottom of the front steps, noting that there's one other car on the driveway, a VW Polo. She realises it must belong to the nurse her efficient sister has hired. She steps out of the car, hauls her bag over her shoulder, checks her phone is in her pocket and walks up to the front door, watching her step in case any of the tiles are loose. She pulls the doorbell and hears the deep toll echoing around the hallway. She waits for a very chilly couple of minutes clutching her coat close, before she hears footsteps walking down a staircase. Then there's a rattle of keys, and a sharp whine as the door opens on its hinges.

'Hello. I'm Beth. Beth Bineham. Nita's great-niece?'

'Ah yes. They said you were coming. Welcome.' The nurse is wearing a grey striped tunic and dark trousers. She is in her sixties, shorter than Beth – she's about five foot four at a guess – has blonde hair and a welcoming, warm smile. Beth feels comfortable with her immediately, and she's incredibly relieved. The reason they are both here is very sad, and it helps to have another human to share it with her. 'Nita's in her bedroom. Do you want to come up?'

Beth nods and follows. They make their way up the creaking staircase to the first floor. They arrive at a large landing, with a tall window at the end of the corridor which should be providing light, but it's so covered in what seems to be a mix of bird poo, mould and algae that it feels like the sun has already set up here. Nita must have lived for decades in perpetual twilight, Beth thinks.

The nurse leads her into a large room at the front of the house. It has high ceilings and two deep-set rectangular windows with sills large enough to sit on. Unlike the other windows in the house, however, someone has wiped the glass clean. Through them, Beth can see the South Downs in the far distance, the village of Melham in the valley below, and far closer, the ancient woodland which surrounds the house and its gardens, a natural barrier that keeps outsiders away and insiders within.

'She's here, Nita,' says the nurse, and Beth's attention is drawn to the double bed against the back wall, and the woman lying on it. Nita had always seemed tall to a young Beth, but age seems to have shrunken her. *Mind you, it's been so long since I last saw her*, she thinks, remembering that she'd been no older than eleven the last time she'd stayed here for the summer. When you're a child, every adult seems tall.

She walks towards the bed slowly, embarrassed, in the way humans so often are, by proximity to death. It is so rarely acknowledged and almost never discussed. Certainly in Beth's family, anyway, although they say very little to each other of any substance on most topics that actually matter.

'Auntie Nita?' says Beth in a whisper, deciding that Great-aunt Nita sounds a bit too much like something out of Dickens. Auntie will do.

'You will have to speak up. She's gone quite deaf. And please do sit down.'

Beth nods at the nurse, who is tidying a tray filled with medical-looking items in the corner.

'Auntie Nita,' she says, louder this time. 'It's me, Beth. I've come to see you.' This is of course glaringly obvious, and Beth wonders why she bothered almost as soon as she'd said it. It does, however, have the desired effect. Nita's eyes open a little, and she turns her head very slightly in Beth's direction.

'Ah.' It's more an exhale than a word, but it's clear Nita is talking to her. But no further words follow.

'Dad is very sorry he can't come,' she continues, keen to fill the silence. 'He's so busy with the business. He says he'll try to come this weekend.' This is a white lie. Her father, Robert, has decided that visiting his aunt on her deathbed is not high in his list of priorities. The family property business, Stellar, demands constant maintenance, that's certainly true, but it seems to Beth that her father's decision says more about his own ambivalent, awkward relationship with his aunt than actual work pressure.

Her mother Marisa, meanwhile, is hard at work on edits for her tenth crime novel, which is being hotly tipped by anybody who's anybody in publishing to be another *Sunday Times* best-seller. Marisa could definitely take time off from this to visit Nita, but the fact is, she's never liked her. Marisa has never tried to hide this, and Beth suspects Nita knows and doesn't mind her absence. She's probably glad she doesn't have to tolerate some kind of saccharin, schmaltzy Hallmark movie-type scene just before her end, thinks Beth.

That just leaves Robert's sister Petra, who lives in Singapore now and has not yet bought a flight home to see Nita, and may never actually bother; and finally, Beth's sister Philippa, three years older than Beth and recently turned thirty-five, who is on holiday with her husband and two children in the Maldives. Philippa is the intelligent, high-powered sibling, the one her father clearly favours to inherit the business, and she'd definitely be here if Robert had told her to attend, because she has never refused their father anything. However, as she's currently snorkelling with sharks, polishing her chakras or saluting the

sunrise (or probably managing to do all three things simultaneously) she's out of the equation. So, there is only Beth left. And so
it is that the most unsuccessful member of the family, in both
financial and emotional terms, is the one here with Nita in her
final hours.

'I... don't want... this,' says Nita, her voice weak but defiant.
Beth looks at the nurse with alarm.

'It's not you, don't worry. She's been saying a lot of strange
things. That's quite normal for people when they're close to the
end. She hasn't been interested in food or drink for a while now. It
takes its toll. She's in her own world a lot of the time. But she can
definitely hear you. And sometimes she's really present. Just be
patient.'

Beth sits back in her seat and examines her great-aunt's face.
Her eyes are glassy. She appears to be looking at the ceiling, but
it's possible that she's not really taking anything in at all. Her lips
are dry and cracked. There's a pot of Vaseline on the table to her
right. She considers dabbing some of it on Nita's lips, before she
stops herself. She barely knows her now. That would feel like an
invasion of privacy, she thinks. And she has always been a private
person.

'I am not... ludicrous... dancing... Mother, no. I will not,' says
Nita, her face now a scowl.

'Lots of people seem to talk to their mothers at this stage,' says
the nurse, her voice cracking with obvious emotion. They both
know these are Nita's final hours.

Beth wonders whether she'd have the same instinct. *I'd be
more likely to call for one of my nannies*, she thinks. *I saw them
more.*

'Yes, if you think so... the woods... so cold.'

'Auntie Nita...'

Beth is about to launch into further lies about her family's interest and concern for Nita's health, when the old woman's eyes dart towards her.

'Beth? Is that you?'

Wherever Nita has been, she is now firmly back in the room.

'Yes. It's me.'

Beth instinctively places her hand on Nita's arm in greeting.

'You came then. Good.' She takes a deep breath, as speaking seems to tax her. 'I wanted to say...' there was another pause and another snatched breath '...there is a box in the attic. It has...' another long pause '...secrets.'

When she says this, there's a faint smile on Nita's face. Beth suspects she's having her on. According to her mother Marisa, Nita has in recent years made a habit of coming out with outlandish statements just for effect. This is just one of the many reasons she gives for not liking her.

'Secrets?' Beth replies, with a little laugh.

Nita's breathing becomes shallow.

'No! I will not, Mother. I will *not*,' Nita says after a pause. Her tone is different. It's clear she has returned to her dreams. Beth looks over at the nurse, wondering if she'd also heard Nita's strange statement about a box in the loft, but she is in the middle of sorting a pile of towels and what look like dressings, and her back is turned. If she did hear, she's not keen to chat about it. Unsure what to do or say now, Beth sits in silence, embarrassed both by her inability to feel comfortable, or at least, not uncomfortable, in the presence of someone who is dying. She considers trying to engage the nurse in conversation again, given that she's the only other conscious person in the room, but then realises she's come all this way to see Nita, not the nurse, and feels even more guilty about her embarrassment and the wider family's disinterest in their eccentric family member.

Beth's anxious thoughts come to halt when Nita jerks upwards without warning, as if she's been given an electric shock.

'Help. She's...' Beth says, unnerved because it appears Nita is trying to sit up. The nurse runs over to the bed and places another pillow beneath the old woman's head to raise her up. She seems placated by this. Her agitation subsides. She's quiet for a while, but then her eyes start to roam the room, and she takes another deep breath.

'I always wanted to tell you. *Always.*'

There is something about her tone that grabs Beth's attention. She seems to be present again. Quite conscious. Quite determined. When she's finished speaking, Nita's muscles relax and she sinks back into her pillow, her eyes closed. Beth wonders if she's talking to her, and if so, what she wants to tell her. Or perhaps, she thinks, she was talking to someone in her mind, someone from her past? Beth is wondering whether to ask her about it when the nurse interrupts her thoughts.

'I think she needs a rest. She's unsettled this afternoon, as you can tell. Why don't you go and get some food? There are some sandwich ingredients in the kitchen and the guest room across the landing is made up, I think. I'll come and get you if she takes a turn for the worse.'

Beth feels immense relief. This has been far harder than she anticipated. She feels incredibly unsettled, and the room is making her feel claustrophobic. She decides she needs to get out of here.

'OK then. I'll do that. Thanks.'

She stands up and pats Nita's arm, a sort of reflex which is supposed to convey *hello, goodbye* and *I'm sorry* in one swift movement. Then she makes her way down the corridor to the guest room.

She hasn't stayed in it for more than two decades, but it hasn't changed much. It's still sparsely furnished, with a fireplace in the corner and heavy velvet curtains in a deep burgundy framing a tall sash window overlooking the house's back garden. Beth looks out of it. The sun is setting, and the impending darkness means it's hard to make out where the garden ends and dense woodland begins. What she can see, however, are lots of raised beds full of what look like herbs and vegetables. Beth is taken aback by these, because they definitely weren't there when she was a child. She wonders how on earth Nita has been managing them. She knows she doesn't have any paid help. This kind of horticulture is way beyond an elderly, unwell woman, she thinks.

Beth turns around. There are two austere single beds here, traditionally made-up with sheets and blankets. Again, she thinks, this can't have been Nita, surely? Beth's father Robert – Nita's nephew – had apparently offered to pay for someone to visit, but this had been refused. So if not a cleaner, then who? Nita is an enigma all right, Beth thinks, as she sits down on the bed and pulls out her BlackBerry from her coat pocket.

When she unlocks it, her heart sinks. There's an email from her father asking her to attend a board meeting on Monday to 'explain her actions'. *Well, that'll be fun*, she thinks, before swiping the message away, filing it for a day when she can deal with it. This is not normal behaviour for her. That email is the sort of thing that her anxious disposition would normally brand into her consciousness in an instant. She would have tortured herself with it. *But how can I even begin to worry about that*, she thinks, *given the* other thing *that's at the forefront of my mind during every waking minute?*

That *other thing* is that David, Beth's husband of a decade, is leaving her.

She has known about it for a month. He, on the other hand, had apparently been thinking about it for at least a year, but it had come as news to her, and the weeks since she found out have been a living nightmare: trying to keep up appearances for the kids, who don't know this is happening yet; wrestling with the shame that this relationship, which began with such public intensity, is apparently now withering into dust; and clinging to quiet hope that it's not, actually, because they are still cohabiting.

But now it's the autumn half-term, and she is not on the family holiday with David and their two children that had been planned and booked back in February. Soon after he'd told her he wanted to separate, he'd also said he didn't want her to come with them on the trip to Dubai. He'd explained he felt uncomfortable lying to the children, uncomfortable pretending things were still OK between them. Strange that, she thinks, given that that's exactly what they're doing every day at home. Beth wonders now if he had ever booked her a place on the trip. She suspects not.

She lies back in the bed and closes her eyes, willing the faces of seven-year-old Raphie and four-year-old Ella to subside. Her heart aches to hold them, to listen to their stories and to get excited about their plans. She wants to spoon yogurt into them at breakfast and to sniff their damp heads after bathtime. She wipes away a tear – if she's being honest, several – and creeps under the covers, pulling the sheet and blanket over herself fully clothed. She can no longer cope with anything, she decides. She will not adult any more today.

* * *

Beth awakes with a start. There is a light, a ball of light, hovering in the room.

Her eyes dart towards the old-fashioned alarm clock on her bedside table, but it's so dark she can't read the time, because the light source is not illuminating it, and the windows, their curtains still pulled back, reveal only inky darkness. She looks back at the orb, disbelieving. It's about as wide as a football, and the light it's emitting is equivalent to a naked bulb. It's moving a little, but only in tiny increments, towards her.

Beth is initially too confused to be frightened. It's too unreal, too outside any kind of normal law, to even register. But her fears grow as it glides slowly towards her, and by the time she is fully cognisant of what she's looking at, she is petrified.

But then there is a knock at the door.

As soon as Beth hears the knocking, the orb shrinks into a tiny speck, changes direction and sweeps towards the window, before apparently vanishing into the night.

The door opens, and the nurse speaks.

'Oh, I'm sorry, I didn't realise you were asleep.'

Beth notices the room is in complete darkness again. She fumbles for the bedside light and turns it on. The nurse is pale and her eyes are red. 'But I had to come and tell you. I'm so sorry I didn't get to you before. But she passed away. Nita. She went quickly. Painlessly. Just now.'

2

NITA

October 1940

Nita unscrews the cap and pulls the piston all the way back, before dunking the nib into the ink and pressing the plunger. She hears it bubble as it fills the barrel. Then she tests it on blotting paper and holds it at a slight angle between her index, middle finger and thumb, just as Miss Bywater had instructed her to do. 'Ladies are judged on the elegance of both their handwriting and their poise when writing with a fountain pen,' her steely governess had said, far too many times to countenance.

Thank heavens that woman has gone, thinks Nita, pushing back a wayward, frizzy dark brown curl which has escaped the bun their long-suffering housekeeper Mary fashioned before breakfast. Nita's former governess, Miss Bywater, had been retained by her parents to help fill the apparently yawning gap between her half-hearted school years and the finishing school in Switzerland they'd put her name down for years ago, but which is now, thanks to Hitler, out of reach.

It didn't matter that Nita hadn't wanted to be 'finished', of course. It was just something she'd had to accept. It wasn't even her choice that her governess left. It was simply fortunate that Miss Bywater had seen an advert for a position at a boarding school which had recently relocated from London to the Surrey countryside to escape the bombing. Whether her teacher might also have found her wayward pupil rather too trying, she couldn't possibly comment.

Now that she's governess-less, Nita's mother Jane-Anne doesn't know what to do with her daughter. All of the 'amusements' – by this her mother means husband-finding activities – she'd normally have been subjected to have been halted due to the war. Nita is not unhappy about this. Pretty much every eligible bachelor of the 'right kind' is away fighting, anyway.

Unfortunately, the absence of marriage material has not changed her mother's outlook for her 21-year-old only daughter. The Bineham family has standards, Mother says, and these must be upheld. Bineham women do not work. Not in the past couple of generations, at any rate. And any mention of volunteering to help the war effort or finding paid employment is shot down immediately. Nita is the human equivalent of precious family silver kept hidden to prevent it from tarnishing.

Her pen hovers over the fresh sheet of writing paper. Writing, elegantly or not, is something Nita knows how to do. In fact, she takes refuge in it daily. She has notebooks stuffed under her mattress full of poems, stories and scribbled frustrations, none of which she has ever shared with anybody, and most likely never will. And yet, despite her affinity with the written word, she can't think how to start today's letter to her brother Frank. She writes to him every day, mostly to alleviate her boredom, but also because she is desperately worried about him and wants him to know he's missed. And she really does miss him. More than ever now she appreciates how well he provided a buffer between her and her mother's most heinous behaviour. She feels vulnerable without him.

She scans the daily newspapers for news of Frank's division, but there's been very little of late. He's serving with the British 7th Armoured Division in Egypt, and that's all she knows. He's not allowed to tell her anything more about what fighting they're actually doing, and she is beginning to suspect the newspapers and the Pathé newsreels might not be telling the absolute truth, either. It has been a fortnight since she last received a letter from him. She runs downstairs every day when she hears the post, grabbing the stack from Mary to see if there's one from him in the pile. She knows this lack of letters doesn't necessarily mean bad news. As post has to make its way to Britain slowly via ship, it has a tendency to arrive in clumps. Nevertheless, it makes her nervous.

She's about to write 'Dear Frank' when she hears the doorbell ring. Thinking it must be the postman, she leaps out of her chair and runs out of the room and down the grand staircase into the hall below. She gets there just as Mary is opening the door.

It's not the postman. Instead, it's a middle-aged man wearing a grey pinstripe double-breasted suit and a matching trilby hat. He has a thick moustache, a broad nose and ruddy cheeks. As she's examining him, her father strides out of his study.

'Thank you, Mary, I'll take it from here,' Ernest Bineham says, holding out his hand. 'Bridges, I'm so delighted you were able to make it. Do come through to the sitting room.' They shake hands. Nita is about to disappear upstairs to nurse her disappointment about the absence of post when her father spots her. 'Ah, Nita, just the woman. I've been telling Bridges what a keen writer you are. Why don't you come and join us for a while, before we start talking about business?'

Nita knows that while this is posed as a question, it is not optional. And anyway, she is fond of her father, and doesn't want to disappoint him any more than she apparently already has, with her refusal to be thin, quiet and to submit to marriage to a suitable man. She puts on her best smile and nods.

'Wonderful,' her father says. 'Mary, please could you bring us tea for three?'

'Yes, sir,' says Mary, shuffling towards the kitchen, which is at the back of the house.

Nita follows her father and the visitor into the sitting room. It's a large space to the left of the front door lined with bookcases and display cabinets full of trinkets, and furnished with two settees, a couple of winged armchairs and a large low table. There are three large windows with breathtaking views down the hillside towards Melham. On good days you can see the South Downs in the distance. But not today, unfortunately; it is damp and overcast and the village below is swathed in mist. Fortunately, Mary has lit a fire using logs their gardener has gathered from the woods, and it's doing its best to warm and dry the room's occupants.

'Do sit down, Bridges,' says her father, who gestures for Nita to sit down opposite the visitor on the other settee.

'This place is quite something,' says their visitor, crossing his legs. 'I've driven past the gates many times, of course, but I had no idea it was here.'

'Yes, we're very hidden, aren't we,' replies her father as he takes a seat in the chair nearest the fire. 'The chap who built this place in the seventeenth century wanted a place to entertain people without prying eyes. Don't ask me what he wanted to get up to. Not in front of a lady, anyhow.'

The pair guffaw. Nita maintains her best smile. She has no idea what they're referring to, although she has listened to enough radio dramas to have ascertained there are quite a lot of things her expensive education has not taught her.

'Well, it's certainly an impressive place. And a good size, I imagine? Not too large to run, but sizable enough for guests, et cetera?'

'Exactly. We also have a place in town, of course, but this is a great retreat from the madness. Especially now. It's wonderful not to have your sleep interrupted by air raid sirens.'

'Oh, absolutely. We are certainly lucky to be away from the worst of it.'

'Do you live far from Dorking?'

'No, we're near Box Hill.'

'Bridges owns and runs *The Bugle*, Nita,' says her father, finally bringing her into the conversation.

Her ears prick up. *The Bugle* is a local newspaper, and she reads it cover to cover every week. It arrives every Friday morning and she always spends a contented couple of hours reading about patriotic knitting drives, schoolboy geniuses and bumper vegetable crops in front gardens. It makes a nice change from the national dailies which are full of awful news. The intense bombing of England's cities and ports which began just a month ago has dominated every news bulletin. So many innocent lives had been lost – far too many for anyone interested in maintaining their equilibrium to think about too deeply or too much.

'Do you read *The Bugle,* Nita?' asks Bridges.

'Well yes, I do,' she replies.

'What's your favourite section? Let me guess. The fashion, I bet? Our ladies fashion pages are incredibly popular, especially the new make do and mend section. I am always amazed at what ladies can achieve with a needle and thread and some imagination.'

Nita feels like laughing. She couldn't care less about the

clothes she wears. Her outfits are all chosen by her mother, and they are usually specially made due to her measurements, which are not of a standard size. She is much taller than most girls, and far broader across the bust, waist and hips than her mother would like. She is regularly encouraged to eat less, but thankfully Mary holds no truck with 'slimming' and supplies her with tasty treats when her parents aren't looking. Nita adores Mary.

'I much prefer the news section,' she says.

Bridges looks perplexed.

'My little bookworm is keen on current affairs,' says her father, making her sound as if she's still eight years old.

'Are you? Wonderful. I had hoped you might be.'

Nita begins to realise she has been set up.

'Yes, Bridges has a proposal for you,' her father says, grinning.

Oh goodness, Nita thinks, her heart thumping. *He's not going to propose marriage, is he? He's old enough to be my father.*

'Yes. I rather wondered whether you'd like to come and help out at *The Bugle*?' he says as Mary pushes the door open and places a tray containing a teapot, milk jug and three china teacups on the table in front of them.

This pause gives Nita time to process what he's just said. She is incredibly relieved. So, this isn't going to be one of Jane-Anne's matchmaking efforts, at least. But a job offer? This is unexpected. Given her mother's determination that Nita should not cheapen herself by volunteering, making cups of tea or bacon baps, this opportunity is a huge volte-face. But then she looks at her father's expression, and she can see he is triumphant. Despite the success of his business, Stellar, and his standing in society, Nita knows it is her mother who rules the roost at home. In that moment she understands that in organising this for his daughter, Ernest Bineham has claimed a victory over his wife. And Nita is more than happy to let him do it. After all, *The Bugle* is a newspaper, and it's based in a nearby town, Dorking, and thus it represents an actual escape from the house, and a fairly exciting one at that. She nurses dreams of becoming a full-time writer, and this, she realises, could be her chance.

'Gosh. I don't know what to say,' she replies, wary of sounding *too keen*. Miss Bywater always cautioned her about the perils of appearing *too keen*.

'It would just be for a fortnight or so, initially,' says her father. 'And unpaid, as you have no experience. But Bridges says there's scope for you to stay there longer, with a salary, if you become fond of it.'

Nita doesn't care that it's unpaid. One thing she does have is a comfortable amount of money. What she doesn't have is freedom.

'Yes, the truth is we're rather short of staff. So many of our men have left to fight.'

'I would love to,' replies Nita, deciding that she's been bashful enough. She's tired of trying to be someone she's not.

'Well, that's excellent. Would you like to start on Monday?'

Just two days of boredom left then, she thinks, trying not to smile too broadly.

'Yes, I think that would suit,' replies her father. 'I'll get my driver to take her there. Eight o'clock all right?'

'Yes, perfect,' replies Bridges.

'Could you pour the tea, Nita?' asks her father, and she does so without question, as she has done so many times before. Except this time, she does it with a smile.

3

BETH

October 2008

It's 7 a.m. when Beth awakes. Motherhood has ensured her body clock is tied to the school run schedule, even when the kids aren't with her. This thought, which arrives unannounced just a few seconds after she opens her eyes, sends a sharp blow to her stomach. Raphie and Ella are probably eating an extravagant buffet breakfast with their dad right now, gazing out over a golden beach and a placid warm sea, she thinks, picking up her BlackBerry to see if David has emailed her the update he'd promised he would.

He hasn't.

That's four days now without seeing their faces or hearing their voices, and Beth feels as if her heart is going to break. They'd explained her absence on this trip by telling them Beth had to work. She wonders whether she should have at least tried to insist she should go with them, or perhaps persuaded David to cancel it. Instead, she had basically rolled over, telling him to go ahead because the kids had been so looking forward to it. She hadn't put her foot down about it, because she'd put the kids first.

That was the right thing to do, wasn't it? she thinks. *Surely it was,* even though it's causing her so much pain.

The plan – David's plan – is to tell the children about their separation when they return from Dubai. So this, she thinks, will be the last week the children will go to bed at night thinking they have two happily married parents. She's dreading telling them, partly because it will make it all more real for her. She has deliberately not thought about the reality of it much so far. It's just too painful.

Beth swings her legs out of the bed and walks towards the window, the floorboards chilling her bare feet. She pulls back the curtains. The sun is rising slowly over the woodland that backs onto the grounds, and this hasn't changed. But what has definitely changed is the garden, and the daylight makes its transformation into something of a market garden much easier to discern. Where there had once been a huge lawn to run around on, there are now rows and rows of raised beds planted with shrubs, roses, vegetables and herbs, and what look like several ramshackle sheds dotted around its edges. *I must ask Nita about this,* thinks Beth.

And then she remembers.

Nita is dead.

She chastises herself for that not being the first thing she thought of when she woke up. But then, she's self-aware enough to know that she has a lot of things going on in her life at the moment, and Nita hasn't been a part of it for a very long time.

But even so, how could she forget, even temporarily, the nurse breaking the news to her of Nita's death last night? Or the strange light she saw in the room just beforehand? That was... weird. Very, very weird. She decides she must have been overtired and overemotional. *When you're in that state, you can have crazy dreams,* she thinks. She turns back into the room and pulls clean clothes out of her bag and puts them on at speed, keen to keep the perva-

sive chill of the old house at bay. Once dressed, she opens her
door and walks down the murky corridor, pausing for a moment
outside Nita's bedroom.

She knows that she's still in there, lying in bed with her eyes
closed. The nurse had told her she'd arranged for the undertakers
to come and collect her today, and that they'd just leave her in
bed until they arrived.

Beth considers going in to see her, knowing she'll probably
look just as she did yesterday, except perhaps more peaceful. But
she doesn't go in. She has never seen a dead body and doesn't
want to start now. She'd rather go about her daily business and
never think about dying. *Like most normal people*, she thinks,
walking down the stairs and into the kitchen.

It's unexpectedly warm. She moves over to the ancient Aga in
the corner and realises it's still lit. This makes sense, of course;
unlike normal ovens, Agas are left on all the time, and the nurses
caring for Nita would have needed somewhere to cook their
meals and make their tea. She is incredibly grateful for this fact
this morning. She's dealing with multiple emotional loads, and
the warmth feels comforting.

Beth is familiar with Agas because her parents have one at
their weekend place in the Cotswolds. After she's absorbed a little
of its heat, she lifts the kettle off the tiled shelf immediately
behind the Aga, fills it from the tap, lifts up the lid on the left-
hand ring – the boiling ring – and places it down on it. Then she
notices one of the lower doors of the oven is open. She's about to
shut it when she sees movement inside.

She shrieks, convinced it must be a rat, or at the very least, a
mouse. But then she takes a few deep breaths and looks more
closely and sees a flash of red, realising with a start that what she's
looking at is the head of a rooster. And from what she can see, it's
asleep, safe and no doubt very comfortable in the warmth of the

Aga's simmering oven. *Goodness*, Beth thinks. She'd heard that Nita was an animal lover, but she hadn't expected to a find a live chicken sleeping in her oven.

Once she's recovered from the shock, Beth finds a freshly washed mug on the draining rack and a small box of tea bags on the countertop, another fortunate inheritance from the nurses who've been caring for her great-aunt, along with what looks to be a recently swept floor and a sink that has clearly been scrubbed.

These recent interventions mean that this room, along with the one Nita died in, are the tidiest and cleanest rooms in the house. The rest, including the guest bedroom she slept in last night, haven't been cleaned properly in decades, and most of the others are full of mysterious shapes draped with dust sheets. *It's going to be a huge job sorting this place out*, she thinks, retrieving a small bottle of milk from an almost empty fridge. The Binehams have owned Melham Manor for nearly two hundred years. There are layers and layers of family history contained within these walls. Nita's story is just the latest chapter of it.

When the kettle boils, Beth makes her tea and manages to cobble together a breakfast from the heel of a loaf of bread and some butter from the dish on the counter. Sated, she is about to walk back upstairs to pack her bag when she sees something through the kitchen window. At first she thinks it must be a squirrel or a bird, but then she realises it's too large for that. *It looks human*, she thinks, acting on her instincts and pulling back the bolt of the heavy oak door which leads to the back garden and pushing it open.

'Hello? Hello? Can I help you?' she calls out, wishing immediately that she was wearing a coat. For a moment she wonders if she'd imagined seeing someone. She looks about her, taking in the densely planted garden and the dark woodland beyond.

There's no one here, she thinks. *No one.* And of course, why would there be? Nita's dead, and the nursing agency knows that. No one else except the undertakers is due to visit today. And then she hears a sound, a clinking, as if someone's knocking something repeatedly against a pipe. It's coming from around the side of the house. Beth follows the noise along the paved path that runs the whole way around the Manor, her pace quickening as it gets louder and louder. And then she rounds the corner. And there is someone here, someone real and human. After the strange incident last night, Beth is almost relieved to find them there, even though she knows they must be trespassing.

'Hello?' she says again, very loudly this time, and the person turns round.

It's a woman. She's aged about seventy, Beth thinks, with a neat silver bob and wearing a green wax jacket, brown cord trousers and green wellington boots.

'Oh sorry, were you calling me for a while? I'd turned my hearing aids off. Let me just sort that,' says the woman, fiddling with something behind her right ear. 'Right. Here I am. Hearing properly again. Sorry.'

Beth is disarmed by the woman's smile and her general ease. She certainly isn't acting as if she's not supposed to be here.

'I was...' Beth is about to ask this woman to justify herself, when she has a swift change of heart. 'I was walking in the garden and I heard something. I wondered who else was here.' This is at least almost true.

'Ah, I see! Sorry. I'm Rowan Ringwood. I'm the gardener here. Well, I help Nita with the gardens and the animals, more accurately.'

'Animals? Like... the rooster in the Aga?'

'Oh, you've met Roger, then? I have a soft spot for him. And the numerous cats you'll see around the place.'

As she says this, Beth spots a ginger tom sitting on a windowsill nearby.

'Oh, right. How many cats are there?'

'Seven at the last count. Nita sort of collects them. People bring them to her, and other animals, too, all sorts – if they can't care for them any more.'

'So she ran an animal refuge?'

'Yes, basically.'

'Wow. Oh, I'm sorry, I should have introduced myself... I'm Beth. I'm Nita's great-niece.'

Rowan's face lights up. 'Ah, yes, she told me all about you.'

Beth doesn't believe for a second that this is true. She hasn't seen Nita for decades, and even then, she only visited when her parents dropped her off during the summer break, for a fortnight or so at a time. She'd be surprised if Nita could even remember what she looked like.

And then Beth realises this woman doesn't know Nita is dead. And she also realises she's going to have to tell her.

'Look, I... I'm sorry, I don't know how to tell you this...' she says, looking mostly at her feet. 'But...'

'I knew she'd passed away, I just knew it,' says Rowan. 'I felt it. Something shifted.'

These are strange and unexpected words. Beth analyses Rowan's face for signs she's having her on, but can find none. She decides to take her at face value.

'Yes. She died last night.'

'Goodness. What a journey she went on in life. She was a special one. Really special, Nita. One of a kind.'

Beth nods in agreement, although her father's description of his aunt is nowhere near as appreciative. In fact, Nita had rarely been spoken of in their home, except for the occasional reference to 'bonkers Nita', 'my batty aunt' and 'that strange woman'.

There's an awkward silence. Rowan is clearly lost in her own thoughts, although she doesn't look sad exactly; more reflective.

'Would you like to come inside for a cup of tea? I know it must be a shock,' asks Beth, feeling like it's the right thing to do in this situation. This woman had obviously known Nita far better than she had.

'No, you're all right. I think I'd rather be out here, in the garden she loved.'

'It's really impressive,' says Beth, looking around. 'I didn't know she was such a keen gardener. It wasn't like this when I was a kid.'

'Oh, really? I think she always loved gardening, but it was definitely something that bloomed in the last few decades, I reckon. If you excuse the pun.' Beth laughs politely, even though it feels strange to be laughing so soon after breaking the news of someone's death. 'Would you like a tour? I can show you what we have here, if you like?'

Beth nods out of politeness, even though she's feeling quite cold and she needs to go inside to get ready to head back into London.

'Great. Well, over here are our vegetable beds,' Rowan says, leading Beth over to the right-hand side of the garden. 'Obviously the summer crops have all come to an end now. I'm tidying up the courgette plants, cutting back the tops of the Jerusalem artichokes, and preparing to sow some winter crops – onions, broad beans – and plant some spring cabbages.'

'This seems like a lot of produce for one old lady,' says Beth.

'Oh, Nita didn't eat most of it. I've always taken it to the food bank in the village. They make good use of it there.'

'There's a food bank in Melham?'

'Oh yes. Shocking, isn't it? It operates out of the church hall once a week. There are lots of people around here who can't afford food, once they've paid their rent and their bills.'

Beth is astonished. She knows that food banks exist, of course, but it has never occurred to her they might need one in this apparently wealthy area of Surrey. Melham is so picture-perfect, she'd thought it might be immune to society's problems.

'Then over here we have our fruit – in the summer we have raspberries and strawberries – and here are our herbs. We have several beds of them. Nita knows... knew' – Rowan corrects herself after a pause – 'all of them by name. She had an amazing memory.'

'Wow. This is quite the enterprise. Do you work here full time?'

'Oh no. I'm not employed here at all, I should say. Nita never paid me. This is a hobby. I'm retired. I used to be a teacher. Head-teacher, actually, of Melham Primary, towards the end of my career. I do this for the love of it. Nita always said it was important to share the earth's bounty. And I agree with her.'

'Goodness. Well, well done you. It looks amazing.' Beth is not a gardener, but she means this. What Nita and Rowan have created is extraordinary. 'Well, I should probably be going,' Beth says.

'You're leaving so soon?'

Beth feels guilty, realising that it must seem rude for the only family member to visit Nita in her last days to run off with such speed.

'I'm afraid so. I have a meeting on Monday morning and I've got to get back to...'

'Oh yes, Nita said. You've got children, haven't you? Young children?'

Beth finds she can't respond to this immediately. She doesn't want to explain why her children aren't waiting for her at home, but she doesn't want to lie. And she's also amazed that Nita even knew she had children. She never brought them to visit her.

'I do, yes.' It feels the safest thing to say. 'I have Raphie – he's seven – and Ella, she's four.'

'Ah, they keep you busy, don't they. I have two of my own, grown up now of course, and four grandchildren.'

'Lovely.'

'But you'll be back soon, won't you?' says Rowan, smiling.

The truth is, Beth has no intention of ever returning to Melham Manor now Nita is gone. She has more than enough to do, trying to escape the enormous train wreck that is her private, work and family life. But she knows she can't tell her this.

'Of course,' she says, returning the smile. 'I'll definitely be back.'

4

NITA

October 1940

It's raining heavily when Nita opens the car door on Dorking High Street, thanks her father's driver and runs under the awning of a haberdashery shop for shelter.

Nita pulls her overcoat tightly around her. She'd thought long and hard about what to wear today, and eventually settled on a grey utility dress and a black jacket, hoping that this might help her blend in a little, despite her height and what her mother cruelly refers to as 'heft'. Unfortunately, that's not what she's wearing now. Her mother, still smarting, Nita suspects, from her husband's decision to let Nita volunteer at *The Bugle*, had taken one look at her outfit and made a face that could sink a thousand ships. Nita had been dispatched upstairs again immediately and had not been allowed out of the house until she was wearing her best girdle and bra, a red polka dot dress her mother had ordered from a Parisian fashion house before the war and a red jacket with brass buttons.

Any hope she'd had of appearing to be a normal, run-of-the-mill budding journalist is now blown out of the window. She looks more like a pantomime dame. Her jacket has a distinct whiff of mothballs, her girdle is cutting into her stomach and her ample breasts are now pointing towards the sky, like anti-aircraft guns.

The longer I can keep this coat on, the better, she thinks, as she eyes a sign hanging beside a neighbouring shop. *The Bugle* occupies the upstairs portion of several outlets along the high street, and the entrance is a doorway between the haberdasher's and Woolworths. Nita decides there's no moment like the present. She surges towards it, keen to avoid drenching her hair, which she's managed to tame into victory rolls, courtesy of step-by-step instructions in *Woman's Own*. She grabs hold of the handle, wrenches it open and walks up the short staircase ahead of her. When she reaches the top, she pushes open a white wooden door and walks through it.

The first thing she notices is the noise. The rhythmic clatter of typewriters, interspersed with the telephone bell and hum of intense conversations – 'Hi, *Bugle*!' 'Tell me more,' 'Is that so?' – is producing a beguiling symphony.

Then there's the smell. There's a thick fog of cigar and cigarette smoke hanging several inches below the ceiling, and there's the unmistakable but intoxicating scent of ink, too. She knows that smell from the newspapers she scours daily.

Lastly, there's the chaotic nature of the office. Three men are huddled over wooden desks in the centre of the room. The youngest is on the phone. Another, older, man is typing. The other one, of indeterminate age, is smoking and reading something he's presumably just written. Beside him is an overflowing ashtray. All three men are surrounded by piles of paper, not just typed scripts or newspapers but pages upon pages of what look to Nita to be incomprehensible scribbles. The office walls are covered in framed front pages, except for the frosted glass wall at the back, which has a door directly in the centre marked 'Editor'.

Nita walks towards it. As she does so, she expects to be challenged, but the men seem so absorbed in their work that they don't even look her way. She knocks on the door. A voice says, 'Come.' She walks inside to find her father's friend, Bridges, sitting behind a desk large enough for several members of staff. Despite the size of the furniture, he seems bigger here than he did in their sitting room. His smile is the same, though. It's the sort of smile people give a cat to distract it from a looming trip to the veterinarian.

'Nita,' he says, before pausing to take a drag of his cigarette, which, judging by the state of an ashtray nearby, is far from his first this morning. 'How lovely to see you. Do sit down.'

Nita takes a seat in the upright wooden chair opposite Bridges. 'Did you have a reasonable journey?'

'Well, yes, perfectly fine, thank you.' How could being chauffeur driven to work ever be anything other than fine?

'Dreadful weather.'

'Oh yes, dreadful.'

The polite formalities dispensed with, Bridges leans back in his chair and crosses his right leg over his left.

'So, Nita. I told you and your father we're getting rather short staffed here...'

'Yes, you did. And of course I quite understand that. So many young men have been called up. My brother Frank, for example...'

'Yes, yes. It's very difficult to run a successful newspaper in these times, you know. Very difficult indeed.'

'I am very happy to be able to help out,' says Nita, her excitement bubbling over into her voice. 'As I told you, I'm a keen reader and I don't know what my father said, but I'm a writer, too. I'm confident that I could turn my hand to...'

'Oh don't worry, my dear. Journalism is not a job for a lady of your social standing. I have assured your father I won't be letting you do any of that.' Disappointment surges through Nita, and then it's instantly replaced with rage. Miss Bywater always said ladies didn't show their anger, but Nita is dreadful at keeping it in. Her face turns red and she screws her hands into tight balls. She imagines they're grenades and that she's about to lob them at him. Bridges doesn't notice. 'No, the thing is, I've had to promote our former administrator, a young man called Joseph, to junior reporter. And that has left rather a gap. We need someone to welcome visitors, you see, to answer enquiries on the phone, to take notes in meetings. And your father thought you'd be perfect.'

So I'm to be a glorified receptionist, Nita thinks, clasping and unclasping her fists, her nails digging into her skin. This is not her dream. This is *far* from her dream. *And yet*, she thinks, remembering to breathe – and *yet*, this might still work. It's still a job outside Melham Manor. It's still at a newspaper.

Mighty oaks from little acorns grow, she thinks, and as she does so, her anger subsides. Her face returns to an ordinary colour, and she smiles; a big, keen smile, hopefully one Bridges will approve of.

'I'm sure I will be, sir,' she says.

'Excellent, excellent. Now, let me introduce you to the team.'

Bridges stands up. It takes him a fair amount of effort, judging by the strained groan he produces as he does so. Then he takes several deep breaths to regain his composure before he waddles through his door back into the newsroom. Nita follows.

'Phillips! Simpson! Miller! I want you to meet Nita.' The three men she had walked past earlier all stop their scribbling and reading and turn around to acknowledge their editor's call. Nita smiles at them, but none of them smile back. In fact, their facial expressions resemble more of a grimace. 'Nita here is going to help us out for a bit. She's taking your former role, Miller. As she's a lot prettier than you, I expect our visitors won't run away screaming any more.' Bridges laughs heartily at this, as do the two older men. The younger man, who Nita assumes is Miller, does not. He's a year or two older than her – twenty-three, perhaps – with blond hair arranged around a neat side parting. Nita isn't laughing either. On one hand, she's pleased to be described as pretty – no one has ever called her that, not even lovely Mary – but on the other hand, the idea of being decorative is infuriating. *My bloody mother and her stupid dress choices*, she thinks, trying to pull her mac around her.

'Well, I have a meeting to attend,' says Bridges. 'I'll leave you with Miller, Nita. He can give you a thorough briefing about his old job. We'll get you jump-started in no time.' He winks as he says this, and Nita feels queasy. The three men and Nita remain silent as Bridges turns and ambles towards the door. 'See you anon,' he says before turning and pulling the door closed.

'Thank heavens for that,' says the older man. 'Pub?'

'I don't think it's open yet, old chap,' says the middle-aged man. 'You'll have to wait until midday.'

'Damn it. Miller, could you make me a cup of tea, please?'

The youngest man looks at him with disdain.

'That's not his job any more, Phillips,' the middle-aged man replies with a slight smile. 'You'll be wanting to ask the editor's new bit of fluff.'

It takes Nita a split second to realise he's referring to her.

'I... I'm...' she starts, keen to defend herself, although she's not even sure what against.

'That's enough, Simpson,' says the youngest man, Miller,

getting up from his desk and walking towards Nita. 'I'm Joseph Miller. You can call me Joe.' He holds out his hand.

'Hello,' she says, shaking it.

'Come this way,' he says, walking towards the back of the room, where there's a white wooden door in the corner which she hadn't spotted before. He opens it and they both walk through it into a room that's full of bookcases and filing cabinets. It smells of dust. She follows Joe along the edge of the room and through another wooden door into a small kitchenette, which is lined with melamine cabinets with glass fronts and has a small portrait window that looks down over the high street. 'This is where we keep the tea and biscuits,' he says. 'It's also a great place to come to avoid the vultures in the newsroom.' Nita notices he's smiling. She smiles too, and some of the shame and revulsion from her recent encounter lifts. 'I often spend far longer than strictly necessary making tea,' he says as he retrieves a teapot from the draining rack beside the sink.

'How long have you been here?' she asks, standing awkwardly by the kitchen door, unsure what to do with her face, arms, hands, long legs and big feet.

'Oh, about six months. Not long.'

'Wow, that's wonderful, to be promoted so quickly.'

Joe raises an eyebrow.

'Well, more like bad luck for the men before me, I think. A couple of them volunteered, but the rest were called up, despite saying their roles were vital to the war effort – keeping up morale, spreading important information, etcetera. But they went anyway. Bridges didn't really have a choice but to let me do their jobs. I haven't been called up yet, you see.'

'Jobs? Plural?'

'Oh yes,' he says, filling a whistling kettle, placing it on the electric stove and turning on the ring. 'We used to have six full-time reporters on *The Bugle*. And a proper secretary.'

'What happened to her?'

'Oh. Bridges happened to her.'

It's Nita's turn to raise an eyebrow.

'Do you mean...' Nita doesn't really know how to finish this sentence. She doesn't really know what he means, but she does know how Bridges makes her feel.

'Yes. He's... too friendly, if we can put it like that. If you know what's good for you, I'd wear slacks and never have your back to him.' Nita's eyes widen. 'Oh, try not to worry. If you're careful, you'll be fine.'

'Doesn't his wife mind?'

'Oh, he doesn't have a wife. But if he did, I don't think it would stop him, frankly. He's notorious.'

Just the thought of Bridges begins to make Nita's skin crawl. *Perhaps I've made a mistake taking this role on*, she thinks. *Is it worth putting up with whatever Bridges is capable of doling out?*

'Goodness.' It's all she can think of to say.

'Sorry. I've probably put you off working here entirely. I don't mean to. Phillips and Simpson can be a bit like stuffed shirts sometimes, but they're nice enough. They can't be called up, by the way – Phillips is too old, and Simpson has epilepsy. And the paper is popular and I think what it does is important. So it's not all bad.'

'I agree,' Nita says, leaning against the nearest cupboard with what she hopes appears to be nonchalance. 'I read it every week. I love it.'

Joe's face brightens.

'Oh! Did you read the interview with the farmer who held that German pilot hostage after his plane crashed, with nothing but a spade and an angry bull? That was mine.'

'Yes, I did. I enjoyed it.'

His face is one big smile.

'That was one of my first proper stories.'

'That must feel amazing. I want to feel like that, too.'

'You want to be a journalist?'

'Yes. I do.'

There's an awkward silence for a moment, during which the kettle starts to whistle.

'Well, you're in the right place for it,' he says, turning round to retrieve a tin of tea from a nearby cupboard. 'Although I have to say I don't think there's ever been a female journalist at *The Bugle*.'

'There *are* women journalists. Nancy Astor, for example...'

'Yes, but they're also in London. Not out here, in the middle of the Surrey hills,' he says, spooning tea into a ceramic teapot.

'But things are changing...' she says, her belief in this tailing off as she says it. *Who am I kidding*, she thinks. *They might be changing on Fleet Street, but they sure as hell haven't changed at the Manor, and not in Dorking either, it seems.*

'Yes, I grant you, they are,' he says, pouring hot water into the teapot. 'There's talk of women being conscripted soon. For paid war work, not just volunteering.'

'Do you think they'll conscript all women? Even ones with husbands?'

'I don't know. Are you planning on getting married?' he says, placing a knitted tea cosy over the pot.

'No. No plans.'

'Just as well. It's bad enough having women working here, but Bridges would lose his head if you were married, too.'

'Oh, I'm not working here properly. Not formally, I mean. I'm volunteering. I'm not being paid.'

'Seriously?'

'Yes... I...'

'He's not even paying you?'

He shakes his head as he finds a tray and assembles a collection of porcelain cups.

'No. My father...'

Joe freezes. 'Who's your father?'

Nita's stomach lurches. *Me and my stupid mouth*, she thinks. 'He's a friend of Bridges'.'

'Ah.'

Nita hopes this is enough.

'Is he also in newspapers?'

'No.'

'Then he must know him through the Masons? I think he spends a lot of time down there.'

'Yes, that's right. They're both in the Masons.'

This is true, actually.

'He must have plenty of money, to agree to you working here for free.'

'He's doing all right. He just wants me out from under his feet, that's all,' she says. This isn't true at all, of course. Her mother would shackle her to the dining table if she could.

'Well, I wouldn't let Bridges take advantage of you like that,' says Joe. 'And I don't think your father should be letting him do that, either.'

Nita's face is burning. She's a dreadful liar. But she persists, because she also doesn't want this man to know that her father is the owner of the big house in the hills, and the boss of one of the area's biggest employers. She realises, for the first time, that if Bridges doesn't blow her cover, she has a chance here to strike out alone, to make a name for herself away from her father's far-reaching shadow. And she wants to at least try.

'No. I'll talk to Bridges about it. Just give me a few days to settle. I need to prove my worth first.'

'Fair enough. But don't let him get away with it for too long. He's not a man to be trusted. There are too many men in this area making far too much money out of their workers' labours.'

'Shall I help you carry the tea?' says Nita, perhaps a little too quickly.

'Yes, thanks. That'd be great,' replies Joe, apparently unaware of her discomfort. Nita pulls a tray from next to the sink and hands it to him. She watches him load it with cups, a jug of milk and the teapot. When this is done, she picks it up and they both walk towards the door. As they approach it, his sleeve brushes against Nita's jacket, and a bolt of electricity rushes through her.

This is new, she thinks, as she follows him back to the newsroom. *This is very new.*

5

BETH

October 2008

The rain is hammering on Melham Manor's windows, running in rivulets down the glass and forcing its way through rotten frames, creating miniature streams on walls and tiny lakes on sills and floors.

Beth has just stepped in one. She's wearing shoes – smart, polished black heels – but even so, she's managed to flick some dusty water up her skin-coloured tights. It's brownish black and looks like a string of pebbles running up her calf. She wonders how long it will be before her mother notices. Marisa has always been obsessive about appearance, to the point of standing beside the front door every morning before school with hairspray and a comb, in an effort to tame Beth's curly hair. And she'd won that battle, of course – but only for about half an hour, after which her daughter had usually decided to release it from whatever pony-tail, bun or plait her mother had achieved. Nowadays, Beth constrains her hair with the help of ceramic hair straighteners and spends a lot of time and money getting it highlighted every month. This is largely due to the employees she's been expected to manage at Stellar, the majority of whom are thin, fashionable women with impeccable hair. In recent weeks, she has been fighting the urge to dye her hair pink.

Anyway, Beth's keen to keep the offending stain on her tights away from Marisa until the funeral wake is over. She knows it's ridiculous to still care what your mother thinks about your appearance at the age of thirty-two, but that doesn't stop her. Beth wonders how old you have to be before you stop bothering what others think about you, and, in fact, whether that is even possible.

She retreats to the corner of the sitting room, picks a book at random from the bookcase behind her and pretends to read it. She likes this room. She used to come in here during her childhood visits and spend hours reading, touching and smelling the books, picking up random facts along the way about things like the birdlife of Great Britain, the development of the railways or the workings of the human body.

They are gathered in here because it's the only room downstairs, apart from the kitchen, that is even remotely clean and tidy enough to host the embarrassingly small gathering that's now taking place. Why they're holding the wake in the house, and not at a smart local hotel or restaurant, Beth doesn't really understand. When she'd asked, her father had muttered something about suitability, family heritage and history, but Beth suspects it's more about privacy. The family who own the big house on the hill are always a local curiosity, and she reckons her father is embarrassed about the isolated, disorganised, alternative lifestyle his aunt had chosen. And so they are here, a tiny family group of five – her father, Robert, her mother, Marisa, her sister Philippa and her husband Nick, and Beth herself – all putting on a ridiculous show of unity for the one non-family guest, the local vicar, who, judging by the eulogy, had never met Nita and knew almost nothing about her, and the two catering company staff hired by Philippa, who are distributing finger food and English sparkling wine. This seems a ludicrous extravagance to Beth, who'd have been happy with a sandwich platter from M&S, but Philippa never does anything by halves.

'I think, sadly, I must be going,' says the Reverend Bishop, a rotund gentleman in his late sixties who has a formidable moustache. He's sitting on the sofa next to the fire, with Marisa to his left and Robert, Philippa and Nick on a sofa on the opposite side of the coffee table. 'I have to visit a parishioner in hospital this afternoon, and I mustn't be late. But it's been wonderful to meet you all and remember Nita. She certainly sounds like a wonderful lady.'

Marisa, who has been making polite conversation with the vicar for at least an hour whilst chucking back the wine, hides her relief at this news well. Beth suspects this Anglican priest hasn't yet worked out that Marisa is a fervent Catholic, and also hopefully hasn't twigged that she wasn't at all fond of the deceased.

'She was, yes,' she replies, her face shining.

The vicar returns the smile, clearly captivated, as most men are, by her mother's charm.

'Yes, yes,' he says, hoisting himself up to stand. 'Oh, and I very much look forward to reading *The Voice Over the Waves*, Marisa. It was such an honour to hear about it before publication.'

Her mother's face bears the expression Beth has seen at many a book signing or talk; an unholy mixture of false modesty and inner brilliance.

'Now, let's see if we can find where the staff put your coat...' says Robert Bineham, rather more overtly keen to be rid of their guest than his wife.

'I'll get it,' says Beth, keen to escape the oppressive atmosphere in the room. She doesn't wait for anyone to disagree with her, heading out of the door and into the hallway without a backward glance. She finds the vicar's practical green anorak hanging up on the wonky coat stand next to her sister's Burberry mac, lifts it off and goes to stand by the front door to wait for their guest, like a butler.

'As I said, we're holding a fundraiser for the church tower next month,' says the vicar, emerging from the sitting room and accepting the coat from Beth with a smile and a nod. Her father Robert is at his side.

'Ah yes,' says Robert, leaning across to open the door.

'If you'd like to pay us a visit to find out more, that would be wonderful...'

Beth cringes inwardly at the priest's understandable play for a donation from her father. He is incredibly rich and her family's links with the village would mean, historically, that such a donation was expected. But she also knows that her father hates being cornered like this and asked for money. He's far from a philanthropist.

'I'll ask my secretary to check my diary.'

'Excellent,' replies the vicar as he pulls on his coat.

'Take care,' says Robert. 'Safe journey back.'

'Thank you. Lovely to meet you all. God bless,' he says, turning and walking through the door. Beth is sure she hears him exhale as he walks down the front steps. As her father closes the door, she wonders whether the priest might be just as pleased to be leaving as the family are to see him leave.

'Have we paid the caterers to clear these things away?' asks Marisa as Beth walks back into the sitting room. She's finally given up her warm, comfortable seat by the fire, and is brushing imaginary dirt from her figure-hugging black suit.

'Yes, I thought of that,' says Philippa.

Beth is not surprised. Her sister thinks of everything.

'Wonderful. Then shall we all push off then, Robert?' says Marisa, glancing at her husband, who's hovering by the door, checking his phone. He doesn't respond. 'Robert?'

'Oh, yes, of course. I'm happy to,' he says, with an eye still on the screen.

'Great. Nick, let's go too,' says Beth's sister to her husband. 'The nanny wants to leave at six thirty today. She's got Zumba.' They both stand up immediately and head off towards the hallway to reclaim their coats.

Beth watches her sister and brother-in-law leave and realises it's now or never. She's been hoping not to have to tell her parents about the mess she's apparently made of her marriage, given the other mess she also recently made at work, but David is making things difficult now, and she feels she has no choice. She needs to speak to them both, face to face, and this is the first time she's seen them properly for months. The appalling board meeting just after Nita's death, at which her father had of course been present, didn't count, Beth thinks. Robert had not acted in a paternal capacity at all then. In fact, in his worst moments, he'd acted as if he didn't really even know her.

'Your actions have brought the company into disrepute,' he'd said to her, in front of the other board members, who'd included Philippa and many well-known, well-respected business people.

'I was under pressure...' she'd said, trying to defend herself. She had been about to explain that her role as a spokesperson for Stellar had been thrust upon her and that she had never felt up to it and that she was prone to anxiety and going through a hideous time at home, but then she realised her efforts would be about as useful as trying to bail out the sea with a bucket.

'Beth, your answer to that question has been in every news-paper and on every news channel worldwide this week,' one of the other board members, a woman called Lorna, had said.

She'd sounded like a jaded schoolteacher. 'We have people pulling out of deals all across the country. This is serious for us.'

Beth cringes both inwardly and outwardly at the memory. She'd been appearing on *Fab Brunch*, a popular daytime TV chat show. She'd been booked to contribute to a discussion about the housing crisis in the UK and had been all teed up to talk about Stellar's vital role as a private landlord – providing quality, well-maintained, reasonably priced housing across the UK, or at least, so went the script. But then the other guest, a woman from a housing charity, had told her and everyone else watching that she'd once paid more than £1000 a month for a Stellar flat that felt like living in a shoebox.

Beth had been completely wrong-footed. She just hadn't expected it at all. And so she'd responded with an appalling attempt at humour which, however she looked at it now, couldn't ever be considered funny.

'Let's be honest, there's lots to love about living in a small place,' she'd said, with a stupid grin on her face to try to mask her nerves, which Beth knows made her look unbelievably smug. 'They're cosy, minimalist, and perfect for, I don't know, existential dread?'

Existential-bloody-dread! Why the hell had she said that? She might as well have sent in her resignation letter on the spot.

The end result had been an indefinite suspension from Stellar, rather than losing her job entirely. As the daughter of the boss, it had been unthinkable for them to sack her, although she kind of wishes they had. It would have given her a reason to run away and hide. Instead of that, she has to keep turning up to family events, pretending that she's spending her days absolving herself of her sins and becoming a better spokesperson, a better business person, a better daughter.

But she can't think about this now. She needs to focus on getting what she needs from this particular conversation.

'Mum... Dad... do you have a few minutes?' she asks when she's certain her sister is safely out of earshot. 'There's something I need to ask you.'

Her mother shoots her a look of concern, and her father stops looking at his phone.

'OK,' Robert says, his eyes darting towards his wife. 'Marisa?'

'Yes, of course,' Beth's mother replies. 'Yes. Of course.'

At that moment, Beth's sister and brother-in-law burst back into the room to say their goodbyes. Air kisses are exchanged and plans to meet up soon mooted, and within a couple of minutes, the front door is shut and their car, an Audi Quattro, is roaring off down the drive, gravel flying in its wake.

'I can't get you back in the office for at least a few more weeks,' says Robert Bineham, putting his phone into his pocket, walking to the sofa and taking a seat next to his wife. 'I need to be able to show that...'

'It's OK, Dad. It's not about that. It's fine. I know things need to... settle down.'

'Yes.'

'How are you doing after... the incident, Beth?' says Marisa. Her face is full of concern, although she didn't call or message her after it had happened, so Beth wonders how concerned she really is.

'I won't lie. I've had a few sleepless nights.' This is a massive understatement, of course, although it's hard to separate the twin reasons for her insomnia.

'I can imagine.'

'If it's not about Stellar, what is it?' asks Robert Bineham.

Beth thinks she sees his eyes flicker towards his watch. She takes a deep breath.

'I need to talk about David and me,' she says, staring at her hands, which are clasped in her lap. 'We are... he has... he's talking about a... separation.'

It's at this moment the caterers come into the room to retrieve the trays and cups and empty glasses. Beth is almost glad. It gives her parents a minute to absorb what she's told them, and means she won't be subjected to a knee-jerk response from her mother, which historically could be anything from 'Oh, good,' to 'Would you like some of my diazepam?'

When the caterers are gone, her father speaks first.

'I'm sorry to hear that,' he says, and Marisa nods. 'What happened?'

'Honestly, I don't know. It felt like it came out of the blue,' she says, running her hand vigorously across her forehead. 'One day he just came home from work and told me he needed time away from me. Us. At first I thought it might blow over, but now he's saying he wants to make it permanent. He's looking for a rented place. He says he wants us to go to mediation to work out a settlement and he wants the kids to come and live with him half the week and I...'

'Mediation? Goodness me, no,' says Robert. 'You'll be getting a lawyer. I'll ask one of the company lawyers to recommend one.'

This suggests he'll foot the bill, which is a relief, even though she also knows he's probably primarily motivated by a desire to protect family assets, because David hadn't signed a prenup. Technically, this means he could try to claim some ownership of Stellar in the divorce settlement. Her parents had put pressure on her to get him to sign the agreement, and so she had asked him to, but he'd refused. And she had loved him so much. They had loved each other. So she'd been fine with that.

'Yes, you mustn't let him take anything that's not his,' says Marisa. 'You need a proper lawyer who can fight your corner. I bet he's got another woman,' she says, picking up her glass again and swigging some more sparkling wine.

'Marisa...'

'I said, didn't I, that he wasn't right for her. I said so, and here we are. Here. We. Are,' she says, apparently furious on Beth's behalf.

Beth is reminded of the awkward weekend visits to the family home David had endured on her behalf in the early days, when she'd tempted him away from their university halls in Manchester, where they'd met, with promises of proper food and London nightlife. He'd been a duck out of water; a middle-class, hard-working, well-educated lad from the north of England cast out in a sea of entitled southerners who had no need to even consider their future, because it was predestined and served on a silver platter. He'd hated it, but he'd done it for her.

'Marisa, I don't think this is helpful.'

'He's so... separate, isn't he? He's never wanted to really join our family, has he? It's like he was planning this all along.'

Beth is now wondering whether her mother is angry for her daughter's sake, or her own.

'Marisa... I mean, Beth...' says Robert, clearly exasperated. 'How are the children taking it?'

Beth is grateful for once for her father's ability to focus on the business at hand at the expense of everything else around him.

'They're OK. The thing is...' she says, keen not to be diverted from what she needs to say. 'The thing is, he wants to keep the house. After we – you know' – she is struggling to get the words out – 'after we separate. And what with being suspended from work, I'm worried my salary isn't going to be enough to get a mortgage on somewhere else in the area, even if he buys me out. It's so ridiculously expensive.'

David and Beth live in Hampstead, about a ten-minute walk

from the heath, in a semi-detached house with three bedrooms that is now worth more than a mansion anywhere north of Watford. They were able to buy it, in very poor condition, in the mid-nineties due to David's impressive career trajectory and Beth's senior job at Stellar. The children are settled at an excellent local school, with a pre-school attached. Beth knows David will expect her to find another house or flat in the area so that the kids can stay where they are, but she has no idea how she'll fund that, especially with her job hanging in the balance. The only other real asset she has is a shareholding in Stellar, and her father would go mad if she sold that, handing significant control of the business over to an outsider.

'You are not leaving that house,' says Marisa. 'And you are keeping your children there, too. With full custody. Don't give him an inch, Beth. And we will of course help you with any money you need, won't we, Robert?'

Beth examines her father's face. She can see he's debating tempering this very generous offer from his wife, but thinks better of it.

'Of course we will. We will make sure you have whatever you need. But... don't let this be known when you return to the office. You know how...'

Beth nods. Yes, of course she knows this. She has to be seen to be disciplined for her recent misdemeanour. She's heard the whispers behind her back about nepotism. There's no way in hell she'd be in such a senior job without being born into it. She's self-aware enough to know that.

'I know. I won't say anything,' she says, almost embarrassed by how grateful she feels.

'Good,' he says. 'But please do let us know what we can do to help. I'll get that lawyer's name to you soon.'

Beth sees her father glance at his watch again. She's aware that her audience with him is finished.

'Thank you. I'm really grateful for your help.' And she is. She really is. Having her heart ripped out is hard enough, but going through it while worrying about where she'll live – that's just one worry she doesn't need. Her parents may have let her down in other areas over the years, but they have always provided her with a financial safety net.

'Oh, darling, I was meaning to ask you earlier,' says Marisa, standing up and smoothing down her skirt. 'Now you've got a bit of... time on your hands... I wonder whether you could take on the necessary jobs here?'

Beth is flabbergasted. Does she mean she wants her to renovate it, or something?

'Jobs? Here?'

'Yes. Just the clearing of Nita's things, really. And we would like to identify anything that might fetch a good price at auction. You could do that for us.'

'You're going to sell things from the house?'

Marisa shoots a glance at Robert, and in that moment Beth understands that this is definitely something that was decided long before the funeral. Perhaps, she thinks, even before Nita's death.

'Yes,' replies Robert, who is also preparing to leave. 'The fact is, my father was far too soft on Nita. He allowed her to keep living here alone, stuffing this place to the rafters, mostly with tat.' Beth knows that Nita didn't actually own the house, but that her grandfather, Nita's brother, had arranged for a special family trust, which required that she be allowed her to remain in it for the rest of her life. 'There are, however, quite a few objects that pre-date her tenure that would certainly sell well. And we don't need them.

We have houses full of beautiful things in London and the Cotswolds. It's just taking up space here, all of this' – he looks around at the room, at the books and dark wood furniture – 'stuff.'

Beth is annoyed. Although she hasn't been a regular visitor at Melham Manor for almost two decades, she feels an unmistakable attachment to the house. She spent every holiday here until she reached secondary school. She likes the fact that you can find an interesting trinket on every surface, a first edition of a novel in a box, an old oil painting stuffed down the back of the sofa. But she can also see that the house needs a lot of work to make it properly habitable again, and it will be hard to do that with all of this clutter everywhere.

'I see.'

'Yes,' says Robert, walking into the hallway to retrieve his coat. Beth follows, noting that her father has already taken his phone back out of his pocket.

'So will you come back in a couple of weeks and sort this place out for us?' Marisa asks, also donning her coat. 'I've found an antiques dealer who can come down and value things, but we just need you to identify anything that's worth looking at.'

'But I...'

'And when it's done, you can come to dinner with us and we can talk about your long-term financial set-up.'

Beth knows when she's being strong-armed into something. There is no option for refusal here, that much is certain, not if she wants their help finding somewhere else to live in one of the most expensive places in the UK. So she nods, gives her parents a perfunctory air kiss goodbye and closes the door. Then she inhales deeply, sweeps her hair back and sets about helping the catering company clean up the mess her family has left behind.

6

NITA

November 1940

'I need those notes, Nita,' says John Phillips, his cigar hanging out of the corner of his mouth. 'I've got to get the story filed by three o'clock.'

Nita grimaces as soon as his back is turned. She hates typing up interviews he's made her take notes for, particularly because she knows he can write shorthand, and doesn't actually need her. It's all about making himself feel important, she's sure of it. And it's not her job.

She's been at *The Bugle* for three weeks now, long enough to understand what her role is supposed to be, and what it isn't. She's now a dab hand at making tea and buying biscuits; dealing with complaints from local business people whose adverts haven't made it to press, or if they have, have spelling errors in them; and she's even found that her role includes writing the wedding and engagement column. The latter is a wonderful and unexpected opportunity for her to actually interview people on the telephone and write up what they say, even though she's limited to waxing lyrical about the kind of flowers they chose, the colour of the bridesmaids' hair ribbons or the spread at their reception venue. What her role shouldn't involve, however, is sitting next to John Phillips in the local pub while he has interminable conversations with 'sources', which seem mostly to involve drinking beer and smoking a great deal, with him occasionally turning towards her and pronouncing, 'Take this down, please, Miss Bineham.' She is not a secretary. She is an *administrator* – a junior journalist, in fact, like Joe was – and should be treated as such, even though she's female. And unpaid. She still hasn't worked up the courage to ask Bridges for a wage, mostly because she thinks her parents would be embarrassed if she did, and also because she still feels like a fraud. But unpaid or not, she is *not* a secretary. Her anger about this increases, until she cannot contain it. It's that failing of hers again, that she can't contain her indignation at injustice.

'Actually, Mr Phillips,' she says, and he turns around to face her. 'Actually, I don't think I can attend any more of your meetings. I'll type this one up later, but I...'

Instead of issuing a retort, however, John Phillips just laughs.

'You will do what I tell you, young lady,' he says, turning and sitting down at his desk, his back to her.

His lack of engagement means Nita's fury needs another outlet. Without thinking, she turns and strides towards the editor's office and raps hard on the door. There's a lull in activity in the newsroom as she does so. Clearly the rest of the staff would like to hear the conversation she's about to have with Bridges.

'Come in,' he booms from behind the door. Nita turns the handle and enters, swiftly closing the door behind her, even though she knows it doesn't block out much noise.

'Mr Bridges...'

'Yes, Nita?'

'I cannot and will not be treated like a secretary.'

'I see. Do you want to take a seat?' he says, his expression bullish.

'No,' she says, her fingers tingling, as if her anger has reached the tips and is desperate to escape. 'Mr Bridges, I am volunteering here...' she starts, and he looks startled.

'Do take a seat, Nita,' he says, beckoning for her to come away from the door. His tone is different, quieter, and there's a smile on his face. Nita, however, is not keen to sit down, but she does move a foot closer to him as a concession. 'All right, then,' he adds, acknowledging her position. 'So tell me – tell me what it is that's upset you.'

'Mr Phillips has been asking me to attend his interviews to take notes,' she says, her breathing shallow. 'But I'm already very busy with reader enquiries and advertising issues, not to mention the marriage column... And I know my father is keen for me to get more hands-on experience of the way the newspaper is run...' This isn't strictly true. In reality, her father is probably just delighted she's not cluttering up the house, but she doesn't think there's any harm in embellishment in this instance. They are friends, after all, and surely, she thinks, he wouldn't want to upset a friend?

'I see,' says Mr Bridges. 'Well, I'll certainly have a word with Phillips. There has obviously been a misunderstanding.'

Nita starts to breathe more easily.

'Yes.'

'So, you said you want more hands-on experience.'

'Yes.'

'I have just the thing,' says Bridges, hauling his girth up to standing and waddling towards her. She moves out of his way as he approaches the door and opens it. Suddenly, the journalists in the newsroom spring into life.

'*Miller*,' he shouts from the doorway. 'Could you come in here for a minute?' Joe stops typing and leaves his desk. 'Miller, you know that story I was going to send you out on? The one about those crazy women in the woods?'

'Yes,' says Joe, his face a picture of tolerance, despite Bridges' obvious disregard for his ambition to be a 'serious' journalist. Nita wishes she also had this skill.

'I was thinking, you know, that Nita might be a good fit for it. She's also... female, after all. They might relate to her better.'

Nita is not entirely flattered that some 'crazy women' might relate to her, but she thinks she's probably said enough for one day already, and also, reporting on an actual story? She would be prepared to go out and report on the world needle-in-a-haystack challenge if it involved getting out of the newsroom and speaking to people.

'I see. Yes, well, that's fine, then,' says Joe, clearly a little confused by this turn of events. 'I'm busy anyway helping Phillips with the break-in at Millward.'

Nita has heard the men talking about this. The Millward factory, a major local employer, manufactures car parts. At about five o'clock this morning, a security guard raised the alarm after he found a window smashed round the back of the building. Police are being cagey, but there's a rumour that an office was turned over and that the factory floor is in disarray. No one is saying yet if anything was stolen.

'Ah yes, well, in which case, my idea is fortuitous. This forest story is a nice bit of light relief, so we should definitely still cover it. I propose we send Nita to cover it and you and the other chaps can focus on the break-in.'

My own story, thinks Nita, her anger now forgotten. *My own story!*

'Can I leave you to brief her, Miller?' says Bridges. He doesn't wait for an answer. He's back in his office with the door closed before Joe can even reply.

'Well, you've done well,' he says. Nita detects a note of sarcasm, or perhaps frustration. She understands. He's only just been given reporting to do himself. He must be annoyed that she's managed it so easily.

'I—'

'Come over to my desk, and I'll tell you what you need to know.'

Nita is glad he interrupted her, because she hadn't actually known what to say. After all, she's just managed to somehow shame the boss into sending her out on a story. She follows Joe back to his desk in the corner of the newsroom, where he picks up a notepad from his desk and reads from it.

'The woman you need to speak to is called Harriet Morgan. She lives on the edge of Melham. I'll give you the address.'

'So what's the story, then?' Nita asks, trying her best to sound like the professional journalist she dreams of becoming.

'It's a mad one, to be honest.'

'Something about witches?'

'Yes, believe it or not. Harriet is apparently part of a witches' coven...'

'A coven?'

'Yes. I told you it was mad. Yes, a coven, a modern-type of coven, she says, and she and her witchy friends are planning to hold a special ritual in the woods near Melham to try to stop Hitler invading us.'

'Goodness. Right.'

'Bridges reckons it'll make people laugh. He's probably right.

We have enough grim stories in the paper everyday – why not something a bit crazy?'

'Quite,' says Nita, pretending she already has some understanding of editorial decision-making.

'Well then, off you go,' says Joe. 'There's a bus to Melham that leaves on the half-hour.'

* * *

The bus smells of body odour and fish paste. Nita knows this is at least partly her fault. This is actually her first ever bus trip – not that she was going to tell Joe that – and she'd initially got on the wrong one and ended up speed-walking back to Dorking. That effort had produced a great deal of sweat. During that walk she'd also felt a bit hungry and had given in and bought a sandwich from the baker's. She's grateful the bus isn't very busy, as she's doubtful that anyone would want to sit next to her at the moment. Then the bus driver calls out, 'Melham End.'

This is her stop. She walks down the aisle gingerly, trying to avoid whacking someone in the face with her bag or her hip. She's always been spatially unaware and has been known to walk into door frames after misjudging the width of her body.

The driver closes the doors and the bus pulls away. Nita looks around to get her bearings. She's familiar with Melham, of course, although she rarely visits this part of the village, which borders the dense woodland that also surrounds the Melham Manor estate. The cluster of houses here are old cottages – possibly, she thinks, once tied to the big house, and the agricultural land that once came with it. The buildings are typical of the local area, made from red brick and tile. She checks the piece of paper Joe gave her, noting that she's looking for a house called Bramble Cottage. She walks down a lane for about a hundred and fifty metres, noting that the trees are becoming more dense with each step, and the houses more and more spaced out, before a rough wooden sign nailed to a gate tells her she's found what she's looking for. She pushes the gate open with some difficulty because it's sagging off its hinges, and then walks up an overgrown path flanked by beds full of luscious-looking plants towards the front door. She knocks.

The woman who answers is not who Nita is expecting. The rustic cottage, its wooded surrounds and the story she's been sent to cover have all prepared her to meet the sort of witch you find in scary stories. She was expecting a pointed hat, a warty face and a black cat at the bare minimum. What she finds instead, however, is a smartly dressed woman in her late twenties with a sharp, smart haircut and a made-up, wart-free face.

'Hello,' says Nita, determined to appear as professional as she can manage, given that she has no idea what she's doing. 'Are you Harriet Morgan? I'm from *The Bugle*.'

'Ah, wonderful,' says the woman. Her voice, like Nita's, is distinctly upper class. 'Do come in. Would you like some tea?'

'Yes please,' says Nita, who thinks it might be best to drink something to swill down her fish paste sandwich.

'Take a seat. I'll be with you in a moment.'

Nita takes in her surroundings. Despite the cottage's worn external appearance, its inside is warm, comfortable and inviting. A fire is lit in the hearth – Nita notes the absence of a cauldron – and there are two comfortable chairs either side. Harriet has gone to a small kitchen which is visible through a door to the rear, and there's a further room adjacent to it which appears to house a single bed, a lot of books and a very busy-looking desk. A rickety wooden staircase runs along the wall opposite where Nita's sitting, presumably leading up to a further bedroom and a bathroom.

'Here you are,' Harriet says, returning with cups and a teapot on a tray. 'It's actually herbal tea – chamomile – I hope you don't mind.'

'Sounds lovely,' says Nita, who has never tried it before but does not want to upset her interviewee.

'I grow the plant myself,' Harriet says, sitting down opposite Nita.

'I could see coming up the path that you like to garden. Are you digging for victory?' Nita says, referencing the now-famous campaign to encourage householders to use every bit of outside space to produce food. A furrow appears between Harriet's eyebrows as she places a cup down in front of Nita and pours.

'Well, I'm not sure chamomile would count as food. I grow for pleasure, mostly, and for health too, but also, yes, to eat.'

Nita realises she has offended her, so she masks this by picking up her cup and taking a sip. A gentle floral aroma fills Nita's nostrils, and the taste, she decides, is not unpleasant.

'I'm sorry...'

'Don't be. I just dislike this edict we're all living under that says we can only grow food. There's a great deal of benefit, you know, in the beauty of nature, and in the medicinal qualities of plants.'

'I'm sure,' says Nita, reaching into her bag and pulling out a notebook. 'Do you mind if I take notes?'

'Please, go ahead.'

'Can I start with your full name, age, and what sort of work you do?' asks Nita, copying the opening gambit of the journalists she's observed at *The Bugle*.

'Of course. I'm Harriet Morgan, I'm twenty-nine, and I'm a university lecturer.'

Nita stops scribbling. She is taken aback. She had always wondered about going to university, and what that might be like.

Given the world she has been brought up in, where women are only taught things in order to snag a decent husband, the idea that a woman might be at university teaching other women, and perhaps even men, seems extraordinary to her.

'Lecturing? What's your subject?'

'Oh, English, at King's College London. And in the rest of my time, when I'm not in college, I try to write poetry.'

'Have you had any published?'

'Not yet. But one is in the pipeline. It should be published next summer.'

Nita is liking this woman more and more.

'How wonderful. You must tell me more about it after this,' she says, glancing at her watch and realising she only has about three-quarters of an hour before her bus leaves.

'I shall.'

'So, Harriet – I'm here because I'm told you're part of a... coven? A witches' coven?'

The words sound quite mad coming out of Nita's mouth, and she examines Harriet's reaction to them. She expects her to tell her there's been a mistake – after all, how could this professional, intelligent woman be a witch? But she doesn't. She pauses for a while instead and fixes her gaze on Nita.

'Yes,' she says, finally. 'Yes, I am a witch. Although we prefer Wiccan, actually. It's an ancient name for a witch.'

'We?'

'Yes. I'm in a coven. We're a group of witches – both men and women, before you ask – but we're not the witches who ride broomsticks. They simply don't exist, even though the men who mercilessly persecuted women during the witch trials would have liked you to believe they did. You know, most of those women who were called witches then were just scapegoats for the ills of society, just because they looked different, or were interested in herbal medicine, or just because they hadn't married or had children, or had rejected the wrong man.'

'Are you married?' Nita asks, before censoring herself for firmly putting her foot in it.

'No.' Nita can't bear to look at her, but Harriet's tone is thankfully not as chastising as she deserves.

Not having a spouse or children is still considered unusual in today's society, Nita thinks. Are women who fall outside this norm labelled as witches even now, just because society's scared that they're different? she wonders. Still pondering this, she decides to try to steer the interview back on course.

'So... Wiccan? Can you tell me more about that?'

'Yes, of course. I suppose you could categorise Wicca as a sort of religion. Our roots are in the Witch-cult, which goes a long way back into history – long before Christianity, you know. You can read all about our history in Charles Leland's *The Gospel of Witches*. After centuries of persecution, Wicca was thought to have died out, but we're back now, as Wiccans, and increasing in number. Have you heard of Gerald Gardner?'

'No. Should I have?'

'I suppose not. He's important in my world, however. He's a writer. He's travelled a lot, most recently to Ceylon and Malaya, and he developed an interest in magical practices there. When he came back to England he became interested in the writings of historian Margaret Murray, who wrote about the origins of the Witch-Cult. That changed everything for him, and he decided to bring like-minded people together to revive our ancient religion.'

'What do you believe, in this religion?'

'At the heart of it is a belief that nature is divine, that there's God in every living thing. We believe that harming nature harms ourselves. We live our lives by the earth's calendar – we have eight festivals throughout the year, which mark the changing of the seasons.'

So far, this doesn't sound as outlandish as Nita had expected it might.

'And you use magic...?'

'Yes. We believe that through ritual, we can connect with God and use nature's power to influence things for good. Not for bad, I think that's important to say. We are not in the business of cursing people.'

'And you want to use your magic to somehow help us win this war?'

Nita observes Harriet's reaction carefully. This is an extraordinary intention, by anyone's measure. But Harriet doesn't flinch.

'Yes. I know what you are thinking,' says Harriet, her gaze fixed upon Nita. 'I do live in the real world too, you know, as much as you might think I live with the fairies, or whatever. But I work in London and I read the papers and listen to the wireless. I know how bad things are and I know what people think about magic.'

'I didn't say...'

'I know you didn't. But you were thinking of it. Everyone is. But that's why I agreed to this interview. I want people to know we are not... mad.'

'I see.'

'Yes. So, it's like this. We are going to perform what we call a Cone of Power. We won't be telling you where or when, for obvious reasons, but with this ritual, we hope to be able to affect Hitler's thinking, his power, to bring him down, to stop him trying to invade England.'

This is now sounding quite, quite mad, thinks Nita.

'How will you... get inside his mind?'

'The Cone of Power is a secret ritual, and I won't be sharing details of it with you. But suffice to say that the Witch-Cult has used it successfully twice before, first in 1588 against the Spanish Armada and again in 1805 to see off Napoleon.'

'Right,' says Nita, swallowing hard to try to mask her instinct to laugh. Harriet had almost convinced her, until she'd started talking about winning wars with rituals. Nita wonders how on earth she is going to write her article. This sounds like madness. 'How many of you will be performing this... Cone?'

'We do not share our membership. But there will be enough witches there to make an impact. And it will be soon.'

'Right,' says Nita, deciding that there is no point continuing this interview with someone who is clearly several sandwiches short of a picnic, despite her apparent education and intelligence. 'I should be off now...'

'Before you go,' says Harriet, her demanding tone reminding Nita of her governess.

'Yes?' says Nita, momentarily abandoning her efforts to pack up and leave.

'I need to tell you something else,' Harriet says, refilling her cup from the teapot and taking a sip. 'I need to warn you.'

'Warn me?'

'Yes, I need to warn everyone around here. That's the other reason I agreed to this interview. I don't just want to tell you about the Cone of Power. I want to tell you about a darkness that's far closer than the continent.'

'Go on,' says Nita, although her doubt is obvious in her voice.

Despite this, Harriet continues, 'There's someone around here who is closely linked to Hitler. I don't know who it is – that's for the authorities to find out – but I'm certain there is a Nazi spy in our midst.'

'In the Surrey hills?' says Nita, who can't imagine why anyone would ever bother doing anything clandestine in such a boring place as this.

'Yes. In the Surrey hills.'

'And how do you know this?'

Harriet pauses.

'I have been told this.'

'By whom?'

'I can't tell you, I'm afraid.'

'Goodness,' Nita says, reckoning that Harriet has most likely been told this by a wisp of grass or a talking squirrel. Nevertheless, she writes 'SPY?' in big block capitals in her notebook before slamming it shut and putting it in her bag, for no reason other than to not appear rude. 'Is that the time? I need to catch my bus.' She's absolutely discombobulated by the turn this interview has taken, and she wants to leave, now. She's at the front door within seconds. 'Thank you for your time,' she says.

'It was a pleasure,' says Harriet, apparently unruffled by Nita's response to her story and her extremely quick exit. In fact, she looks absolutely serene – confident, even, and this unsettles Nita.

How can anyone be that certain? she wonders, as she walks down the path to the gate and back along the lane in the direction of the bus stop. How can she be so certain of something so... outlandish?

Then something brushes Nita's face.

She looks down and sees there's a perfectly clean, fluffy white feather resting on her chest. It's about four inches long. She looks above her to see where it might have come from. There are no birds in the sky and no trees overhead. There isn't even much of a breeze. Instead of brushing the feather off her clothes, as she would normally do, something makes Nita pick it off and hold it.

It feels warm.

And then something shoots through her, from her toes to the

top of her head – a frisson of something, a flash of light. It's gone almost as soon as it came, but it was definitely there.

She puts the feather in her pocket and continues walking, determined not to be wrong-footed by one strange moment. But as she pulls her head up high and walks with purpose in the direction of home, Nita finds herself patting the pocket, making sure the feather is still there. Because something is telling her she needs to keep hold of it.

7

BETH

November 2008

'Where shall we start?'

Beth has been at Melham Manor for several hours already today, and she's tempted to tell Tim, the antiques dealer who's visiting at her mother's request, not to bother. Not because there's nothing to find – there must be, given her family's wealth – but there's just so much of everything, it's overwhelming. Nita had stacked boxes everywhere, and a lot of them seem to have functioned more as waste bins than storage for important items. Closer inspection of the furniture reveals similar behaviour. Beth had opened a cupboard in one of the downstairs rooms and found herself almost swimming in dried flower heads which had been stored in there, loose.

'How about the dining room,' she says. The room is at the rear of the house, overlooking Nita's impressive gardens, and she heads there now, with middle-aged, moustachioed, slightly portly Tim in hot pursuit. On the way, she bats away a large cobweb which is dangling from the ceiling in the corridor. 'There are a couple of display cabinets in there with nice-looking stuff in them.'

'How long had your great-aunt been living here?' he asks, stopping to free his cord blazer from the clutches of an upturned hatstand.

'Oh, all her life. She was born here in 1919 and grew up in the house. But if you mean living here by herself, I think since the end of the Second World War, or thereabouts. My father tells me his grandparents got bored of living in the country and preferred their house in London, so they left Nita here, holding the fort.'

'And she never married?'

'No.'

Beth realises as she says this that she has no idea why this was. It wasn't the sort of thing she'd have thought to ask her when she'd been a child, and her parents have never said a word about it. She'd always assumed, given the family narrative, that Nita was a loner who didn't want any company, male or female, but she's now rethinking this, given her recent conversation with Rowan, the woman who helped Nita with her garden. Beth is realising how much she didn't know about her great-aunt.

They reach the dining room. Shiny, tobacco-stained paint is peeling off its walls. There's a long, polished wood dining table in the centre, and on top of it there's a mishmash of old saucepans, empty jars, dusty glasses and margarine tubs full of elastic bands and old labels. Around the edges of the room are several rickety-looking chairs and, as Beth had already said, some glass-fronted cabinets full of figurines and crockery.

'Oh, yes, these are interesting,' he says, going straight for a cabinet which contains silver plates and jugs. 'I think they're Victorian.' He opens the door and pulls out a plate. 'And the engraving is exquisite. Can I take photos? It'll help me price everything up.'

'Sure, yes, whatever you need to do,' says Beth, leaving him poring over the family silver. She spends the next ten minutes writing and then deleting a text message to David. Before she left the house this morning, she'd told him she was going to use the lawyer her father had recommended rather than going through a mediator, and he was furious. She's quite glad that she's here, actually, as he's working from home today, and given the mood he'd been in when she left, they'd probably have had a hideous row. At least now he has time to cool off, to think about why she might be feeling in need of robust legal advice.

It's only been a month since he first told her he wanted to separate, but in that time she's felt like everything she'd previously been certain of has been rendered null and void. A few days ago, he'd told her that he wondered whether they should ever have got married at all. The idea that what remains the most important day in her life was anything other than unfiltered joy, is now poisoning a new part of her psyche with every day that passes.

Her state of mind has also not been improved by losing most of the friends she'd thought she had. Her best friend, of course, is – was – David. The withdrawal of his support has probably been the singularly most hurtful, most difficult part of their separation so far. And then there are her female friendships, formed mostly in their close social circle in their local area, a circle she's latterly realising had David as its lynchpin, and not her. She's sent a few messages to friends in the past couple of weeks and had very sparse responses. No one has offered to meet up or invited her round to their place to drown her sorrows. She wonders whether her recent faux pas on TV has anything to do with it. The idea she might now be considered an embarrassment to be seen with has crossed her mind more than once.

The one good thing is that, despite her mum's proclamation,

David still insists there's no one else. If this is true, she's relieved, because the thought of him touching someone else, being intimate with someone else, is frankly vomit-inducing. The downside of his innocence, however, is that he's leaving her with no one else to go to, which, like an employee resigning with no job offer to hand, strongly suggests there's something fundamentally wrong with their relationship. Beth's brain is now a twenty-four hour cinema screening of every high and low point of their relationship, and she has examined these images – their meeting at university, David's proposal, their first serious argument, the birth of their two children, her miscarriage in between those two children, their holidays in the sunshine full of laughter and good food, their chaotic, rushed dinners at home with the kids – and she still cannot see those moments how David now sees them. She wonders what she's missing, what she hasn't seen, in all of their years together. What is it, she wonders, that he finds unlovable? What about her has changed?

'These are worth something,' says Tim, bringing Beth back to the present. She walks over to the cabinet and sees that he's holding two porcelain figurines. 'These are Royal Doulton statuettes. There's one for each month.'

'Which are they?' she asks about the pair he's holding, feigning interest. Her mind is not on the task today.

'March,' he says, looking underneath for the label, 'and October.'

'Great,' she says, moving on and looking at the other cabinet. 'Let us know what they're worth. By the way... I wondered about these vases?' There are two of them, angular and colourful. Beth thinks they're art deco, and she rather likes them, unlike most of the other stuff in this room.

'Oh yes! These are Clarice Cliff. They're stunning,' he says, his eyes bright. He's probably thinking about his commission, she thinks.

'OK, good. Well, just let us know,' she says. 'Look, can I leave you to it for a bit? I've got... something else to do.'

This isn't actually true. Her entire purpose here is to facilitate his visit, to make sure that everything worth any money at all is removed from the Manor before the house clearance firm come to take the rest. But she just cannot work up any enthusiasm for this task when her life is falling apart around her. She needs time to think, and she can't think when she's helping Tim unearth buried treasure.

'Sure. That's fine. I'll just make my way around the rooms down here.' He seems relieved, if anything.

'Great. I'll be... upstairs.' She had planned on going outside, but she's noticed it's raining again, and she doesn't have a raincoat with her. She walks up the creaking staircase and stands on the cluttered first-floor landing trying to decide where to go. A second later, she walks back into Nita's room. When she enters, she glances over at the bed, as if she's expecting her great-aunt's body to still be in there, which is, of course, ridiculous. The undertakers removed her the day after she died. It does feel wrong, though, for her to be in Nita's room without Nita.

Even though she'd been very young when she had last done so, Beth still remembers her great-aunt's warm, soft hand holding hers; the sun on their faces when it broke through the leaf canopy; dandelion pappi floating around them like summer snow. Yes, Nita had been such a *force*. Such a strong personality, and so much part of Melham Manor that it feels impossible that she's no longer living here. If there is such a thing as a ghost, Beth thinks, there's no doubt Nita will come back and haunt this place.

Beth walks towards the window and looks out. It's still raining heavily, and the village below is obscured by low cloud. If you didn't know differently, you'd think there was no other house for miles around. The only living things she can see are a wood pigeon pecking away at the grass and a squirrel running along a low wall. She turns to face the bed once more, thinking she'll go and take a look at the room next door, when she remembers what Nita had said to her when she was dying. She hasn't had much time to think about it since her death, given the nightmare she's living through in her personal life, but it returns to her quite clearly now.

What did she say exactly? Yes – 'There's a box in the attic. It has secrets.' Now that Beth is back in this room, it's like she can replay the scene from a recording. Yes, that's exactly what she said, she's certain.

And then she's seized by the need to find out if it's true. Frankly, she needs to do something, anything, to distract herself from her personal problems, and why shouldn't that be looking for something Auntie Nita told her to find? she thinks. After all, she's here to look for things. And so, what had originally seemed like a crazy idea now seems sensible and logical.

Yes, that's what I'll do, she thinks. *I'll go up into the attic and look for that box.*

* * *

The only light in the attic comes from a small, oval window in the eaves. The weak rays of sun which are managing to pass through it reveal a wasteland of dust and detritus. Beth hauls herself off the top of the ladder and onto the nearest bit of floor, and such physical activity in this long-abandoned place unleashes a cloud of dust, making her cough.

She pulls herself up to standing, dusts herself down and looks around for a light switch, eventually finding one on a wall behind the loft hatch. It's a wonky, old-fashioned black fitting and she wonders for a moment whether she might risk electrocution if she touches it. After a moment of deliberation, however, she decides this is unlikely, and a bare bulb hanging from a cord in the middle of the room surges into life.

Beth's heart sinks. Like the rest of the house, the attic is absolutely rammed with boxes.

She curses her mad old great-aunt under her breath – she has always imagined Nita might have been the type to swear quite a lot behind closed doors anyway – and begins her search. The first ten boxes contain a random mixture of Christmas decorations, childhood toys, odd-ends of wallpaper and dried pots of paint and many, many moth-eaten clothes. Nothing is properly packed and several items begin to fall apart on contact. A red blazer in one open box appears to have provided a home to an extensive family of mice.

An hour later, she decides it's time to give up. Tim the antiques dealer will be wondering where she is. And then a beam of sun, perhaps the only one that day to burst through the dense clouds lurking over Melham Manor, pierces through the circular window behind Beth and lands upon a battered box a few feet away.

She is not a superstitious person. She doesn't avoid walking under ladders and she doesn't ritually greet magpies. But, despite this, something makes her walk over to this box, which is momentarily basking in unseasonal and frankly entirely unexpected sunshine.

She sits down next to it and her eyes fall on two words, scribbled on its side in pencil, in capital letters: 'FOR BETH'. She assumes this is Nita's handwriting, and the fact she must have done this some time ago, before she became too infirm to climb up here, makes Beth smile. She wonders how long ago it was, and why she'd done it, come to that. Yet again, she is amazed that her great-aunt had even thought about her, given how absent she'd been from her life for so long.

Beth pulls back the mottled cardboard leaves which partially cover its contents. Given the light that guided her to it – rather like wise men to Jesus, Beth reflects – a small part of her expects, or perhaps just hopes, to find something significant inside. Maybe an amazing antique which she could persuade her parents to let her sell to fund her divorce, she thinks, before catching herself.

Divorce.

She hadn't even thought that word yet, let alone said it, but now she's thought it, she realises she can't unthink it. And actually, the thought of it makes her feel ill. *We can't be heading that way, can we*, she thinks, absent-mindedly pulling a couple of grey cardboard files from the box. The very idea of divorce seems like madness.

When they'd first met at the tender age of nineteen, they'd promised each other that no matter how difficult things got, no matter how annoying they found each other, they'd always work hard to find their way back to each other, back to the magic.

How naive they'd been. They'd thought the first flush of love and obsession would see them through anything, that their intense passion would power them through whatever life threw at them. But real life, it turned out, was far more prosaic. All it had taken in the end was the passage of time, two children, a difficult family dynamic and two stressful careers. The reality, she thinks, as she flips one of the files open, is that the shield of love you build around yourselves in those heady days is barely strong enough to withstand even the most mundane of blows.

Beth's attention is drawn away from her thoughts to the contents of the file on her lap. There are hundreds of yellowing newspaper clippings in it, all from *The Bugle*, a name she recognises. She thinks it still might exist. Beth picks up the one on the top of the pile. It's dated November 1940. The headline is 'Local Witches' Coven Plans to Take on Hitler'. Beth has a vague recollection of being told Nita had worked as a journalist in her youth, but has never thought to ask more about it. She wonders whether these clippings are all her great-aunt's work. She pulls out another. This one is an article about a craft fair being held in a church hall. Then there's one about a new bus route to Guildford, another about women campaigning for better treatment at a local factory, and another about someone vandalising a cricket pavilion. Some of them actually have Nita's name on them. Beth assumes the others were probably linked to her too, but her name isn't included either for space or because she hadn't written all of it. So this, then, is Nita's collection of memories from her time as a reporter. Are these the secrets she was hinting at? Beth wonders. If so, they aren't very secret at all, or very exciting. Maybe in her isolation she has built this brief foray into newspapers into something it never was, Beth thinks, leafing through the stories on her lap at some speed. And if that's the case, how sad...

Beth's train of thought stops abruptly, because one of the stories looks very different from the others. Instead of being a small clipping, it's a full-page story headlined 'Police Link Factory Break-in to Nazis in our Midst'. The byline is Joseph Miller, but underneath it says, 'with additional reporting by Nita Bineham'.

But the story itself isn't the really remarkable thing. What catches Beth's attention is the writing that is scrawled all over it. 'WHO IS X?' is written in capital letters across the top. 'Is he in Germany? Is he in Surrey?' Then she turns the page over, and sees that Nita – well, she presumes it's her – has doodled the letter X all over the back of it, some large letters, some small, some curly and cursive, some in block capitals. But all X.

Beth's curiosity is now piqued. Whoever X was, Nita thought about them a lot, that's for certain.

She peers into the box to see how much is left in there. There's another cardboard folder at the bottom, which she lifts out and opens eagerly. There are no newspaper articles in here, however. Instead, there are pages and pages of notes. Some of them are legible – they are most likely notes for stories, Beth reckons – and then there are pages of what look like scribbles but what might be code. She wonders what on earth these are. Was her great-aunt involved in some kind of espionage? Really, the mind boggles, she thinks, but her interest isn't sufficiently piqued to enquire further about them.

That just leaves two things. The first is a white feather, a few inches long, and still remarkably intact. Beth leaves that in the box. And then there's one final item – a piece of white card. In fact, it's the only piece of card in the box. Written on it in large letters is a long string of numbers. The only words are in capital letters across the top. They say, clearly: 'WHERE IS X?' She wonders what the numbers underneath represent. A phone number, perhaps. No, it's too long for that. A key for something, maybe?

Beth returns the piece of card to the box. She checks her watch; she's been here far longer than she meant. Keen to return to the antiques dealer, Beth makes a snap decision, and picks it up.

There's something about the box and its contents that has drawn her in. Nita had said there were secrets in it. Beth's not sure whether she was having her on or not yet, but what she does know is that the answer to a mystery far closer to home is contained within it. This box will tell her far more about her great-aunt than her father ever will. In just the small amount of time she's spent with these documents, she already feels closer to

Nita than she has in years. Perhaps, she thinks, this box will explain why Nita never left Melham Manor, and why her family essentially disowned her. And for this reason Beth, whose own parents and sister are currently flirting with disowning her, feels a sense of sisterhood with her great-aunt.

As she walks with the box towards the attic entrance, Beth wonders whether Nita ever found X, the person who clearly dominated her mind, for a short while at least. *If you did, I hope he got what was coming to him*, Beth thinks, carrying it awkwardly down the steps. I really hope he did.

The following morning, Beth wakes before dawn. But it's not the unfamiliar bed in a very cold room that is stopping her from sleeping. It's the noise. She hears footsteps. *There's someone in the house.* As adrenaline jerks her into consciousness, she realises they will be here to steal. They think the house is empty, she realises, and they must know that Nita, or at least her family, had money. Easy pickings.

As she lies there in the inky darkness, she tries to formulate a plan. It would be best to call for help, she thinks.

But then, the footsteps stop. What does that mean? Beth wonders. Are they looking at something? Or standing still and listening?

She needs to call the police, that's certain. But she'll have to speak to them if she does, and then whoever's in the house might hear her. *And what if they're violent?* she thinks? They might be. And she doesn't have a weapon. But then she remembers there's a fireplace in her room, and that hanging up beside it is a long, heavy metal poker.

It's on the other side of the room, however, so she needs to move quietly. She picks up her BlackBerry from the bedside table, peels away the sheet and blanket and sits up slowly, a shiver running through her as her feet meet the bare wooden floor. She can feel goosebumps all over her skin, and she's unsure whether it's fear or just the chill that's the cause. She's only wearing her pyjamas, and it's freezing in here.

Then her ruminations about Melham Manor's lack of central heating end, because she can hear the footsteps again. It's now or never, she thinks. She needs a weapon if she's going to face them. She stands up and begins to move. With each tentative step, the floorboards seem to whisper. Have they heard her? She stops near the fireplace and listens. The only sounds she can hear are the ragged rasp of her own breath and the ticking of the grandfather clock in the hallway. Hoping against hope she's still undiscovered, she reaches down and picks up the poker.

Beth feels better when it's in her hand. It's heavy and solid and it emboldens her. She's about to dial 999 when she hears what sounds like the front door shutting and then footsteps walking across gravel. Whoever it might be is leaving, she realises. With what, she doesn't know, but she needs to find out.

All attempts at silence are abandoned. Still carrying the poker, Beth runs to the bedroom door and wrenches it open. Then she flies down the disordered hallway, narrowly avoiding tripping on numerous objects, dust taking to the air every time her feet hit the ground, before she pelts down the stairs, her right hand grasping the bannister for support.

She is at the front door in seconds. She grabs hold of the handle and turns it, expecting it to fly open. But it doesn't, because it's locked. She's incredibly confused. If they didn't leave through this door, then which one did they use? she thinks. She had definitely heard them walking on the driveway. She doesn't have time to think about it now, however. She needs to confront them. Beth flicks the light on and grabs her keys, which she keeps on a hook in the hallway. Then she unlocks the door quickly, ready to face them, whoever they are. She surges forwards, down the front steps, the poker held aloft like a sword.

But there's no one there.

It's still dark, of course, but the moon is bright and her eyes gradually adjust to the twilight. She can see as far as the woods on either side, and a good way down the hill towards the village, and she can't see anyone at all. *Even though it took a few seconds to unlock the door, they can't have had time to get into a car or even onto a bike*, she thinks. *So where are they?*

Beth stands at the bottom of the steps for a long, cold minute, her brain refusing to accept what her eyes are seeing. Finally, however, the freezing temperature wins out, and she turns and walks back up the steps into the house, shivering. When she closes the door behind her, however, she turns on the light in the hallway, and then every light she can find until she is back in her bedroom. Because she simply cannot understand what just happened, and she knows instinctively that what she needs now is light and warmth.

So, instead of heading back to bed – sleep will not come easily now – she builds a fire in the hearth in her room and then pulls up a chair, draping the blanket from the bed over her shoulders. And, because she desperately needs to do something to distract her brain from overthinking, she reaches once more for the box she retrieved from the attic and continues to try to make sense of the fragments of Nita's past contained within.

8

NITA

November 1940

'So, what was she like?' Joe asks as Nita walks over to the desk she's been allocated in the far corner of the newsroom.

'Not at all what I imagined,' she replies, exhaling loudly as she sits down onto the wooden chair, glad to have survived her first foray on public transport. She enjoyed meeting Harriet, mad as she was, but she's also glad the adventure is over.

'Not on a broomstick, then?' he says, leaving his own desk and standing next to hers.

'Not even close. She was... normal. Posh, even.'

'One of your lot, then.' Nita eyes him, trying to work out if he's taking the mickey or if he's being serious. She knows her accent and her clothing set her apart. She decides to give him the benefit of the doubt, because there's a twinkle in his eye.

'Well, she's definitely well educated. I'd wager, better than me, actually, Joe,' she says with a raised eyebrow. 'She's a university lecturer.'

'Goodness. But she lives in a little cottage in Melham?'

'She does. A very nice little cottage, mind you.'

'But she must be funny in the head, surely? All this rubbish about casting spells to send Hitler packing?'

Nita picks up her bag and pulls out her notebook.

'Honestly, I'm not sure what I think,' she says, flicking to the notes she took during the interview.

'This sounds a lot more serious than the light column-filler Bridges sent you out for,' says Joe. 'Want to come out back to make a cuppa?'

She agrees and follows him, glad that he's understood her need to talk about the conversation she's just had with Harriet.

'So tell me,' he says as they enter the room, 'what's spooked you.'

'Do I look spooked?' she asks, heading towards the sink and filling the kettle, the steps required to make tea for her co-workers now tattooed into her consciousness. She's aware, however, that she's doing everything too quickly, and the kettle collides with the taps as she tries to fill it.

'You do.'

'It's silly really. I feel silly.'

'Tell me.'

'She... Harriet... She told me there's a spy... a Nazi spy... around here.'

'In Dorking?'

She's still filling the kettle, but she can hear his smirk.

'Yes, I know. That's why I feel silly.'

'What would they be spying on? The village fete? The butcher who keeps some of the nicest rump under the counter for a special price?' He seems to be enjoying this idea.

'Well, lots of important politicians have weekend homes here. And we do have a few factories locally making parts for weapons and aircraft and cars and all sorts of other things for the war effort, don't we?'

They are silent for a moment, because they are both thinking about the bombing of the Vickers factory in Brooklands, also in Surrey, in September. Neither of them needs to mention it by name, because the loss of life there – almost ninety deaths and four hundred injured – is etched in the minds of everyone in the county.

'Yes, I give you that. But why would this batty woman know anything about it? Where did she say she heard about this... spy?'

Nita takes a deep breath and pulls the cups out of the cupboard.

'She wouldn't say. Look...' she says, trying to pre-empt what's surely coming, but it's too late. Joe is already laughing. 'Look,' she says, more firmly. 'I know it sounds crazy.'

'It sounds... well...' He doesn't sound as though he's laughing now, at least, she thinks. 'Well, I suppose there may be something in it.'

'But if there is, the police will be on the case, won't they?'

'Yes, I assume so.'

'So there's no point in us looking into it... ourselves?' says Nita, finally putting into words the thought that's been swirling around her brain for the past few minutes. What if... she thinks quickly, what if she took this on, as her own story, her own investigation? Because that's what real journalists do.

There's another momentary pause while Joe considers his answer.

'We could, I suppose,' he says. 'But where would we start looking?'

Nita realises she is very out of her depth.

'I'm not sure,' she says, spooning tea into the pot and pouring the hot water over it. 'Do you have any ideas?'

'We could perhaps start with enemy aliens who live locally?'

'Those who haven't been interned already, you mean?'

At the beginning of the war, the British government had set up a tribunal system which aimed to identify and deal with all German, Austrian and Italian nationals living in England. They had been divided into three categories: Category A were held in special camps, known as internment; Category B were not detained but subject to special restrictions; and Category C were exempt from both.

'Yes. There will be some here, I'm sure of it, but no doubt they're keeping their heads down.'

'But you think they might be... spying?'

'Well, that's why the government is interning people, isn't it? It's a risk. You never know. Maybe one slipped through the net.'

Nita feels excitement building in her chest. This could be something, she thinks. Maybe she will be able to find something out that really makes a difference locally. Perhaps she could actually stop something awful happening, like those hideous bombings that have taken so many civilian lives. Or maybe she could stop some vital information about the British war machine reaching Germany, and potentially save the lives of soldiers, soldiers like Frank. And if she did that, there's a chance it could really make her name as a journalist. She wouldn't need to rely on her parents or an arranged, dreadful marriage. She'd be able to stand on her own two feet. Just the thought of this makes her heart soar.

'You're right.'

'I have been known to be right,' says Joe, smiling.

'Will you help me with this?' she asks, tentatively.

'I will certainly try. I'm quite busy with other stories but... yes, why not. Maybe we can look into this after work today?'

Nita is expected home straight afterwards, but she's not going to let that get in her way. She'll call home and say Bridges has asked her to stay behind to do some filing.

'Yes, that's a great idea,' she says, her spirits lifting.

'Let me help you carry the tea,' he says, and together they bring the teapot, cups and milk back into the newsroom, where they distribute them to the other journalists, who barely acknowledge their existence. 'We'll talk later, then,' says Joe after their task is done.

'Yes, let's.'

Nita walks back to her desk and sits down on her chair with much more enthusiasm than she had just half an hour earlier. She takes a deep breath, picks up her pen, and opens her notebook. She turns over a new, clean page and writes clearly at the top, in block capitals:

'WHO IS X?'

* * *

When she arrives home that evening, Nita's mind is buzzing with ideas. This could be her big break, she thinks. People in the area are scared, understandably, and it would be truly awful if there really is a German living in their midst, stealing secrets to feed back to Hitler. She's been feeling guilty for so long that it's just Frank who's out there, fighting in the war. Well, this is her chance to do her bit, she thinks. She could do something worthwhile for a change, rather than trying and failing to look pretty at horrible society functions.

'Ah, Nita, you're back.'

Jane-Anne is standing in front of the staircase.

'Hello, Mother.'

'I was hoping they wouldn't keep you too late today. Your

father has a guest and we thought it would be nice if you joined us for an early supper.'

Nita tries to think of an excuse, but fails. And she's also hungry. She's always hungry.

'Why don't you go and get changed, and we'll see you in about ten minutes?' says Jane-Anne, the subtext of her request clearly understood by Nita. What she's wearing is not acceptable. Her mother moves away from the stairs so that her daughter can pass.

Twenty minutes later – Nita has to score her points where she can – she enters the drawing room, where her parents have gathered for pre-dinner drinks with their guest.

'Ah, finally,' says Jane-Anne. 'We thought you'd got lost. Darling, this is Peter Sanders. He's a friend of Daddy's.'

Nita examines the man who's sitting in one of the armchairs in front of the fire. He's about forty, she thinks, with brown hair peppered with grey, separated in a side parting and pasted down with Brylcreem. His skin, like his hair, is also greying, as if he spends a great deal of time working in darkness. It's also covered in a sheen of sweat.

'Hello,' she says, sitting down on an armchair opposite him. She doesn't shake his hand, because she feels a bit sick about its inevitable warm dampness, and her mother bristles.

'Well, hello,' he says, casting his eyes up and down her, as if she were a cow at an agricultural show.

'Peter runs a large firm of undertakers, darling,' says her father.

Ah, that explains his skin, at least, thinks Nita. And the reason why he hasn't been conscripted.

'Yes, we're the largest firm in the south-east,' says Peter, puffing out his chest.

'Oh,' replies Nita, not knowing what to say to this.

'We're expanding locally, actually, this month. We've just

taken out a lease on a property in Dorking. The operating profit of an undertaker is significant. And our customers never argue with us!' Peter guffaws, and Nita decides she's rarely met a more disgusting man.

The evening that follows is one of the most excruciating of her life. It becomes clear that, improbable as it might seem to her, her parents consider Peter to be a prospective suitor for their daughter. His clumsy attempts at small talk and his obsession with explaining aspects of his business that nobody has asked are both incredibly irritating, but it's his hungry gaze that really makes her want to vomit. Her forays into the world at the newspaper have taught her a few valuable things in recent weeks, one of which is that all women are not – despite what her governess had told her – adored and protected.

Nita leaves the dining room as soon as dinner is over, refusing her father's invitation to 'join them for after-dinner drinks'. She does not care what her parents think about this behaviour. One more minute of time in Peter Sanders' company would be one too many.

9

BETH

November 2008

'When are you coming home, Mummy?'

'Tomorrow. Just one sleep, and I'll be back.'

'OK. Do you promise?'

'I promise. Now, go on, get to bed. And don't wake Ella when you go upstairs. It's getting late.'

'OK. Oh, Daddy says he wants to speak to you. Goodnight, Mummy. Love you.'

'Goodnight, Raphie. I love you, too.'

There's rustling as Beth's son passes the phone back to his father.

'Hello? Beth?' David sounds slightly hassled. Beth assumes the children have been their usual demanding selves. She allows herself a small smile.

'Yes,' she says.

'When are you coming back? I thought you said you'd be back tonight.'

'Tomorrow. I was hoping to come back today, but the guy that Mum asked to value stuff said there was so much, he'd have to come back tomorrow. And someone has to be here to let him in and check he doesn't nick anything, or whatever.'

'And naturally, that person has to be you?'

This tone is familiar. It's the one he uses every time her family annoys him. It's something that happens regularly. She rolls her eyes, even though they're on the phone and they can't see each other.

'Yes.'

'Couldn't you drive back up tonight and go back down tomorrow?'

Their house in Hampstead is only about thirty miles away from Melham as the crow flies, but the capital's choked road network means it might as well be on the moon at all times of day, except the dead of night. The train journey, meanwhile, is almost two hours long, with a taxi journey required from Dorking. Anyway, Beth has her car here, so she's committed to driving back. The journey usually takes at least an hour and a half in stop-start traffic, and she really doesn't want to have to do that twice in just over twelve hours. David knows this, of course.

'No. It's too far and I'll be knackered.'

'But I have to be in Oxford by nine tomorrow morning.'

As awful as their current predicament is, and however much Beth is missing being with her children tonight, the deep irony of David's statement makes her smile. He's a partner in a surveying firm that specialises in commercial property. His work takes him all over the country, and he's often away for several days at a time. She has always accepted this and just dealt with it, fitting the school runs, shorter pre-school hours, parents' evenings and after-school activities around her work for Stellar, often risking the disapproval of both her colleagues and her father when doing so. And so she isn't particularly bothered that David might be late for work tomorrow. She wonders whether he's thought about how he'll deal with childcare when they separate. Because it will be much harder than this for him then, she thinks. *Much harder.*

'Oh dear,' she says, trying not to let him hear her schaden-freude. 'I should be back by school pick up tomorrow.'

Beth hopes this is true. She wonders how long an antiques dealer can actually take. Surely not another entire day.

'That's good,' he says, clearly irked. 'I'll have to call and let the team know I'll be late.'

'Yes.'

There's a pause.

'So I'll see you tomorrow evening, then.'

'Yes.'

'Bye.'

'Bye.'

Beth makes sure the call has disconnected before throwing her phone down on the bed behind her and letting her head sink into her arms. *How on earth did we come to this*, she thinks, *scoring stupid points over our amazing children?*

It's just before 9 a.m. and Beth is washed, breakfasted and dressed by the time Tim's car pulls up on the driveway. She's been awake for hours after a restless night, although this time it wasn't strange footsteps that roused her. Her brain was far too active to sleep. She's grateful that it's now time to put the plan she's been hatching all night into action.

'Good morning,' she says as the antiques dealer extracts

himself from behind the wheel of his vintage Jaguar. 'I've left a pot of tea on the kitchen table for you. I'm just popping out to the shops. I'll be a couple of hours. Will you be OK here by yourself?'

Beth anticipates he'll say yes. She reckons he's probably desperate to get on with sifting through generations of goodies without her peering over his shoulder.

'Ah, yes, of course. Fine,' he says, barely concealing his delight.

'Excellent. I'll be back by lunchtime,' she says, walking towards her car. When she turns around, she sees he's made his way towards the front door with almost indecent haste.

Beth feels a weight lift from her shoulders as she drives away. As much as she is drawn to the house, *by the house*, she knows its spell can sometimes be overwhelming. This morning, she needs some normality. She exhales with relief as she drives through its gates, before asking the satnav to take her to Dorking. The car's satnav springs into life, and a confident female voice tells her to turn left, a route which will take her through Melham.

When she reaches the village, she slows down to the requisite thirty miles per hour and takes in sights that had been familiar to her in childhood: the village shop, where she'd been allowed to spend her pocket money; the local primary school, St Mary's, where Rowan had apparently been headmistress; the cricket green that plays host to a popular fete during early summer, which the eldest male member of her family has always opened; The Jolly Farmer pub, which she remembers always held a Christmas community lunch every year, something her parents had been known to sponsor but never to appear at; and finally, the parish church, whose tower, according to a sign erected outside, is badly in need of remedial building work.

When she had been young, Beth had always admired – and, frankly, been jealous of – Melham's sense of community and the calm, happy, normal lives its residents seemed to lead. Her life, despite the comfort her parents' wealth had bestowed upon it, had not been – to her mind at least – happy, calm or normal. Her parents had quarrelled regularly, and the poisonous atmosphere this had produced had infected everyone in the household. Her mother's creative brilliance, moreover, had not lent itself to brilliance at parenting, and her father's responsibilities in the family firm had meant he had been almost entirely absent. She had actually wished, often, that her parents had decided to send her to boarding school instead of the exclusive private day school she had attended – endured – where all of the girls had private ski instructors, a chauffeur to pick them up every day, and eating disorders.

Beth arrives in Dorking twenty minutes later. Her early morning research has told her that *The Bugle*, the paper Nita used to write for, still exists and has its office opposite The White Horse on the High Street, which she locates without difficulty. She finds a spot in the St Martin's Walk car park and walks the short distance to the Georgian building that houses the paper. It has three floors, the ground floor of which is currently occupied by a bookshop and a pharmacy, and there's a glass door between these and a staircase behind it leading upwards. She pauses for a moment, however, because she'd expected to see a large sign above the door announcing the newspaper's presence, or perhaps etching on its glass, but there's neither. Eventually, she sees there's a scrap of paper squeezed into a plastic panel next to the doorbell, with '*THE BUGLE*' written in blue biro. She presses it. There's a hiss of static from the speaker above it and some unintelligible words, and then she hears the door unlock. She pushes it, walks up the stairs and opens the door at the top.

The sight she's greeted by is not what she expected. She'd imagined a busy room full of tired old hacks bashing out copy on PCs or wittering away on the phone, in a room still stinking of

cigarette smoke, even now, a year after the indoor smoking ban
came into force. But what she can see instead is boxes. Piles and
piles of them, some of them open and some of them taped up.
There are, however, a few gaps in the piles and it's through these
that she sees there's a desk in the corner, and from what she can
make out, there *might* be someone sitting at it.

'Come in,' says a man she can't see. She proceeds carefully
through a narrow space between the boxes – it wouldn't do to cause
a landslide – and bit by bit, the person behind the desk is revealed.
He appears to be in his mid-forties and is wearing a crumpled blue
check shirt and baggy jeans. What's left of his hair is being held at
bay by a number two all over and his two-day old stubble suggests
I-can't-be-bothered rather than I'm-a-hip-gangster. In front of him
are an empty bag of Skips, a half-drunk coffee in a mug emblazoned with the logo of a local second-hand car garage and the skin
of a banana. What a sorry looking breakfast, thinks Beth.

'Hello. I'm here because... well it's sort of a long story,' she
says.

'Well, we're in the business of stories here,' says the man. 'I'm
Steve, by the way. I'm the editor of *The Bugle*. Why don't you take a
seat?'

'Thank you,' says Beth as he moves past her to lift a pile of
paper off a chair on the other side of his desk and puts it on the
floor. When it's clear, she takes a seat. 'I'm Beth.'

'Great,' he says, sitting back on his own chair. 'So, what can I
do you for?'

Beth realises then who he reminds her of: David Brent from
TV show *The Office*. Not in looks, perhaps, but certainly in
mannerisms. Now she's thought of this she can't unthink it, and
she tries desperately not to appear too amused.

'Well, as I said, it's a long story. I'll try to make it brief. My great-aunt used to work here. She was called Nita. She worked here during the Second World War. Anyway, she died recently.'

'Oh, I'm sorry to hear that.'

'Thank you. Yes, so she died, and I have been sorting through her things, before we sell the house. And I found this box yesterday...'

'Oh, I love these sorts of stories. Our readers are mad for them.'

Beth is momentarily put off by this obvious glee, but decides to persist.

'Yes, so there were lots of articles in this box. Old *Bugle* articles.' Steve now looks less interested. She wonders what other people have found in boxes in their attics that had excited him so much. 'They were all from when she wrote for the paper, and on all sorts of topics, but there was something she wrote about in particular – a search for a Nazi spy in the area.'

Steve's right eyebrow is now slightly raised.

'Go on.'

'She calls him X. To be honest, from what I've read, she was absolutely obsessed with finding him, but I can't find out what happened in the documents I've read so far, and I'm a sucker for a mystery.' This is true, to a point. Beth loves reading crime novels and watches *Poirot* to relax, but this is the first time she's decided to pursue a real-life mystery. It's a very useful distraction from her own worries.

And then there's the fact that her great-aunt's death has shaken her more than she'd care to admit. Beth realises she feels deeply guilty that she was completely absent from Nita's life for the past two decades. Not that it was Beth's fault, particularly; she had only gone where her parents had told her to go, or not go. But how must it have felt, she wonders, to be ostracised by your loved ones like that? To live such an isolated life, rattling around that huge, dusty, creepy house?

'So you want us to write a story to see if anyone can help solve your mystery? *Claudia!*' Steve shouts, so loud that Beth jumps in shock. 'Claudia, can you come in here a minute, I've got a little job for you.' There's a whine as a door is pushed open and shuffling as someone makes their way through the obstacle course of boxes, chairs and empty desks, before a young woman wearing a pink hoodie and jeans comes into view. 'Claudia, this is...'

'Beth Bineham.'

'Yes, Beth Bineham... Hang on a sec. Bineham? Are you one of the Binehams from up on the hill?'

'Yes, I am. My great-aunt was Nita Bineham.'

'Well I never. So that means your mother is...'

'Marisa Bineham.' Beth says this with a sigh, because when people find out who her mother is, the conversation always ends up being entirely about her.

'So she is! Claudia, you have here the daughter of one of the bestselling crime novelists in the world. I'm a big fan. I always take one with me to Tenerife every year.'

'Great,' says Beth.

'Well, well,' he says, beaming. Beth wonders whether he's considering asking if she can get him an exclusive interview with Marisa. It's happened before. 'Do you write, too?'

'A little bit.' This is a lie. Beth writes a lot, and has always done so, but none of it has seen the light of day since she was a child, when she'd read one of her poems out loud and her mother had simply said afterwards: 'How sweet, darling. Have you finished your maths homework yet?' Since then, writing has been a clandestine activity. She has an unfinished novel saved on her laptop. She's called it 'Shoppinglist.doc' to put off anyone who might accidentally come across it.

'Well, anyway, Claudia, as I say, this is Beth,' says Steve. 'She's come in with a reader's story she wants us to put out.'

'I...'

'Claudia here is on work experience and this sounds to me like a perfect job for her.'

Beth is bemused. She hasn't even told this man what she's come to ask him yet. 'Shall I leave you two to get on with it, then?'

Claudia's expression suggests she's just been asked to produce the perfect cappuccino from the world's most complicated coffee machine with zero training. Beth realises she has to save her.

'Actually, I'd like to write it,' she says. This had been her original plan, anyway.

The editor, who had been in the process of vacating his desk for the startled Claudia, sits back down.

'Oh, do you? That's fine, yes. A lot of the content we publish these days is written by clients with very little editorial input. We don't have the staff, frankly. Well, as you can see, it's just me, and... Claudia.'

'You don't have anyone else?' says Beth, momentarily distracted by this sorry state of affairs.

'No.'

'Oh.'

'I used to read *The Bugle* when I visited here, when I was younger. You had quite a big team then, I seem to remember.'

Steve shuffles in his seat.

'Yeah. Sadly pretty much everyone has been let go. Occasionally we advertise and we get a junior reporter who's just finished their NCTJ diploma and needs a first job, but they never last long because we can only pay them the minimum wage. But luckily we have lots of great work experience kids who come through here and lend a hand...'

Kids, Beth thinks. *Kids?* When she was younger, she remembers that everyone they'd visited in the area had had a copy of *The Bugle* on their coffee table. She wonders how it went from that to this so quickly.

'That's such a shame,' she says, meaning it genuinely. 'So, is it OK? Are you fine with me writing the story?'

'Yeah, yeah, fill your boots.'

'Great,' says Beth. Now, time for part two of her plan, she thinks. 'I'll also need to look in your archives, to see whether there are any answers in there. To help with the story?' Her early morning internet search into spies in the area had turned up nothing, leading her to realise she needed to search offline sources instead.

'You've come just in time,' says Steve. 'Claudia has been helping us... me... sort out what needs keeping from our records room, because we're vacating it. It's being let to some company that sells mobile phones. We can no longer justify the rent.'

'Oh.'

'Yeah, so that's why all these boxes are in here. Most of this is going to the tip, when I get around to getting the clearance firm to come and collect it.'

'Right. So could I look through them before they go...'

'Be my guest,' he says. 'Claudia, it's OK, I don't think you're needed in here right now. You can go back next door and carry on with whatever you're doing.' The teenage girl appears relieved, and walks back from whence she came, having never uttered a word.

'I have another thing to ask,' says Beth when she's left the room.

'Shoot.'

So David Brent-y, she thinks, before trying desperately to put this image out of her mind.

'Yes, so there is a string of numbers on one of the documents in the folder. It seems like an important piece of paper. She's written "Where is X?" at the top. I wanted to ask whether it's some sort of journalist code...'

She reaches into the bag she's brought with her and brings out the page with the string of numbers first.

'Nope. No clue what that is,' he says.

Beth is slightly disappointed, even though she hadn't really expected him to know what they were. *I mean*, she thinks, *why should he?*

Then she places two pages of unintelligible scribbles from Nita's box in front of him.

Steve smiles broadly.

'That's Teeline,' he says. Beth looks blank. 'It's a kind of short-hand. Journalists are still taught how to write it, for court reporting purposes, mostly. Yeah, I can read that.'

So that's what it is, she thinks. Of *course* it isn't some kind of Secret Service cipher.

'Could you tell me what it says?' she asks.

'Yeah, all right,' he says, holding it nearer to the lamp on his desk. 'This is a transcription from an interview with someone called Mary. It says she's a school receptionist. It's asking about... hang on a sec... yeah, about whether any enemy aliens work in the school. What records they keep on them. That sort of thing.'

Beth can't help but be impressed that he can read it so easily.

'Do you think you could translate some more of the documents for me?' she asks.

'That depends.'

'On what?' she says.

'On whether you scratch my back, if I scratch yours.'

'In what way?' She wonders if he's angling for money. This place, she thinks, clearly needs it. Or maybe he wants that interview with her mother, after all.

'I've had an idea. I need a writer.'

'Oh.' This is not what she had imagined he would ask. 'I can't ask my mother for any favours. She's so busy, you see...'

'No, love, I meant you. I mean, I'm used to whipping even the worst writing into shape. Some of the teenagers who come here can't even use capital letters. And you're clearly from a writing family...'

'But I work in PR...'

'Don't we all, sweetheart. I seem to do far more PR than journalism these days. And frankly, I'm sick to the teeth of it. It's absolutely obvious to me that the paper is going down the toilet and I'm going down with it, but before it's replaced entirely by social media, I want to have one last hurrah.'

'So you want me to... write stuff for you?'

'Yeah. Between me and you, Claudia isn't really any great shakes.'

'She's about seventeen...?'

'Yeah, she's doing A levels and all that, but she has no style and no news sense. You, on the other hand, come from a family of journalists and authors and frankly I need someone else to help me fill the paper. There's only so much I do with press releases and agency copy, and I can't really go out and leave the office with only Claudia in charge.'

'But you don't know me.'

'I know you've got time on your hands.'

The penny drops. *Of course*, Beth thinks, *how naive of me*. He's a journalist; *of course* he will know about her very public gaffe and subsequent suspension from her job.

'Look, I'm not here to be laughed at,' she replies, colour flying to her cheeks. 'My mistake. I think I'll go now.'

'Look, love. I didn't mean it like that. We've all said unwise things. Me more than most.' Beth can see he's remembering something painful. 'What I meant was, I know, from what I've read, that you're at a loose end at the moment. And you've come here trying to do research for what to me sounds like a great story. Your instincts sound spot on.'

'Right... so I...'

'Yeah, so the deal would be, I let you come in and rifle through our archives for whatever it is you want, and you write me a couple of articles this month. You know, actual news about the actual local community. I can even pay you a little bit. Not much, admittedly. But something. What do you reckon?'

'And you'll help me translate the notes?'

'Yeah, I will. If you buy me a pint.'

Beth winces.

'I'm married,' she says, and her voice catches a little as she does, as she knows she may not be married for much longer. 'I don't want you to get the wrong impression...'

'I'm only messing with you,' he says, his manner suggesting he might not have been. 'I wasn't serious. Yes, of course I'll look at them, but if there are masses it may have to wait a bit. So shall we say I give you one story a week?'

'I don't live locally.'

'Where are you? London? You can drive down here easily, can't you? Loads of people commute into town from here.'

'It's north London. But yes, I suppose so.'

'And I'm only asking for a few articles. And in return I'll give you a key and you can come and look through our archives whenever suits.'

Beth weighs up this offer. David would like her to be at home for the kids, of course, but then, he also wants her to move out of his life. Why should she do what he wants? And she can probably manage to do most of the reporting during school hours and be back in time for pick-up if she's clever, along with the odd overnight stay at the Manor. Just to keep an eye on the house. And why shouldn't she write again? Why shouldn't she do something new, something different, just for herself? And why shouldn't she find out more about a woman she'd been close to as a child, whose own story she now, for reasons she has yet to properly understand, feels compelled to understand and to tell?

'OK,' she replies. 'I'll do it.'

10

NITA

November 1940

'Are you sure you want to go in alone?'

'Yes,' Nita replies, not at all sure she does, actually, but knowing that she's going to have to learn how to do this by herself if she's ever going to be a proper reporter.

Joe and Nita are standing outside a house on the outskirts of Dorking. It's an ordinary-looking house – a semi-detached red-brick cottage with a small front garden that's currently hosting a vegetable patch, windows criss-crossed with tape to prevent bomb damage, and a wooden front door painted in bright green gloss paint.

'All right, then. I'll head back to the office, if you're sure.'

'Yes. See you in a bit,' Nita says, and she waits for him to turn and start walking down the street before she pushes open the gate in front of her – which is also painted green – and walks up to the front door. She knocks twice, as firmly as she dares. She doesn't want to give anyone the impression that she's nervous, even though she most definitely is. She's gone through what she's going to say many times, and Joe has given her lots of tips, but she knows this is going to be an awkward conversation. After all, she's pretty certain her interviewee will have kept their identity hidden from everyone.

She looks around her as she waits for someone to answer. There are children playing in the road and a woman several houses down is scrubbing her doorstep. A curtain twitches in the front living room of the adjoining house. She wonders what these people will think when they read the story she's going to write. They won't like it, that's certain. Not when they discover who they have living in their midst.

She hears footsteps and the latch is pulled back on the door. Then it opens, and she's glad to see her timing is good. As she'd hoped, her interviewee has just got home from school.

'Mr Brown? Mr Matthew Brown? I'm Nita Bineham,' she says, trying to speak slowly and with confidence.

'Yes?' he says, his face stern and expectant. She imagines he looks at the boys he teaches in a similar way. It reminds her of her old governess, and not in a good way.

'I'm from *The Bugle*.'

'Oh? Is it about the fundraising we're doing at school? I know the headmaster wrote to the paper about the bring and buy sale we are planning – but now is really not a good time. Can't you come to see me at work?'

'It's not about that, Mr Brown. Can I come in?' she says, noticing a neighbour peering out of a nearby window.

'As I say, it really isn't a good time.' He looks behind him, his expression concerned, or maybe agitated. *Perhaps he doesn't want someone in there to hear what I have to say*, she thinks. Well, we'll have to have this conversation here instead, she decides, knowing that she may only have one chance to ask what she needs to ask before he slams the door.

'It's about your real name, and where you come from,' she says, gaining in confidence.

'I said, not now...' he says, his eyes wide and his voice cracking. He is panicked. Nita realises she must be on the right track. She continues. 'Your real name is Matthias, isn't it, Mr Brown,' she says loudly. 'You were born in Germany.'

He opens his mouth to reply but he doesn't get the chance to speak, because suddenly there's a bloodcurdling scream from inside his house.

'Martha! Martha, my dear, it's all right, I'm still here.' Matthew – Matthias – Brown abandons Nita at the front door and bolts back down the hallway towards the rear of the house. There is very little natural light in the corridor, but she can just make out the silhouette of a person standing in the doorway of a kitchen. 'You had better come in,' he shouts. 'If you absolutely insist.'

Nita enters the hallway, still keen to pursue this story, the product of hours of combing through old *Bugle* stories for any reference to German immigrants in the local area. It had been Joe's idea, and it had been a good one, if rather time consuming. Two evenings after hours in the archives room had uncovered a story about a German artist, his wife and two children moving to the area in 1930. Matthew Brown's father had been fairly well known in the art world, it seemed, and had even exhibited at the Royal Academy in London. His children had gone to school in the area and his son had trained to be a teacher. Nita and Joe had discovered he was still living in the area and working at a local prep school. The spelling of the family surname had been changed from Braun to Brown soon after they arrived in England, and Matthias had become Matthew soon after that.

'I just want to ask you some questions, Mr Brown,' she says, shutting the door and inching down the corridor, not entirely sure about what she will find at the end.

'As I have been telling you repeatedly, now is absolutely not the time,' he says once more. And as her eyes begin to adjust to the darkness, she understands why. He is on his knees in the doorway, clutching a young girl who Nita estimates to be about eight. Although it's now five in the afternoon, Martha is wearing a nightdress, and Nita can see that the front of it is soaked through. She initially thinks this might be water or tears, but then she notices the little girl is dribbling. She also seems agitated. She has her hands clasped together and they're wringing with an intensity Nita thinks might even induce pain. And then she screams again, and it's just as shocking a noise as it had been the first time, except of course Nita is closer to its source this time.

'Ssshhh, Martha, ssshhhh,' says Matthew Brown, stroking her arms and shoulders in a slow, repetitive motion. 'Mummy will be home soon. She's just popped out to the shops. She'll be back. Let me take you back into the parlour. We will put on the wireless. Let's find you some music to listen to,' he says, his focus entirely on the little girl. He's so focused on her, in fact, that he seems to have forgotten Nita is there, and when he eventually manages to persuade Martha to leave the kitchen, he walks towards the front room with her, his arms never breaking contact with her shoulders. Nita does not follow.

It is several minutes later when the radio is turned on in the front room and Matthew Brown returns to the hallway. *He looks exhausted*, Nita thinks. *Beaten.*

'I'm sorry. I'll come back later,' she says, realising now really is not the time to ask Matthew Brown why the world at large is unaware of his German heritage.

'She's... not well,' he says, wiping his hand across his forehead. 'Martha. She's... the doctors don't know why... but she's not well. My wife looks after her all day. She likes to get away in the afternoon for a bit when I get back from work, just some time to herself, you know.'

Nita nods, although she really has no idea what their daily lives must be like.

'Look, as I say, I'll come back another time,' she says again, although she now feels completely differently about Matthew Brown's past being her ticket to front page glory. There's real pain here, she realises, real angst, and she doubts very much that this man has the time or energy to devote to spying for Hitler.

'You wanted to know about my family,' he says, pulling himself up a bit and busying himself by the sink, washing some plates and glasses which his wife had presumably left there after lunch. 'Well, I'll tell you. You can print it in your paper if you like. My father was a great man, a man of principle. He refused to fight for Germany in the Great War and the authorities sent him to a mental institution for a while, because it was easier to believe he was mad than that he really believed that war achieved nothing. When he got out, he met and married my mother, continued with the art he had loved since childhood, and eventually was able to move here twelve years after the war ended, when I was just ten, because of his talent. He died last year, far too young. He never really recovered from the way they treated him in the mental institution. So yes, I am German, if you say so. But I have a special exemption because of my political views and my father's background, and that is why I am still working here in a school, and not interned in a camp for enemy aliens. I have paperwork to prove it. Does that answer your question?'

'Yes.' It's all Nita can find to say, and she knows it is absolutely insufficient. 'I'll go now,' she says, her voice barely even audible. 'I'm sorry for taking up your time.'

11

BETH

November 2008

'You're going back down to Melham Manor again?'

David rubs the back of his neck as he says this. He always does this when he's annoyed, but trying to pretend he isn't. Beth sees this and puts her hands down on the kitchen counter, hoping that some physical stability will help stabilise her mind, too. They had another hideous row last night, and she is still processing it.

'Yes, I am.'

'So soon? Why?'

'I'm doing some freelance consultancy work,' says Beth. This is only a white lie, really – her agreement to do ad hoc work for *The Bugle* isn't far off that – and she's decided that her quest to uncover her great-aunt's secret is not her wannabe ex-husband's business. She also knows he'll find it hard to be annoyed at the prospect of her actually working, which of course she hasn't been doing since she was suspended from Stellar. David has a serious work ethic and she suspects he views her current predicament, suspended on full pay, as abject idleness. Which is ridiculous, given how much work she has always done looking after the kids and the house, on top of her job. Work he has never noticed.

'Oh,' he says, his surprise clear. *Yes, there you go*, she thinks. Her working always seems to make him happy.

'I'll probably be back for school pick-up. Raphie has football club after school anyway, and I can always ask if Marika can pick Ella up and take her to their place for a bit...'

Marika is the mum of one of Ella's classmates. Before David's announcement, they had hung out as a couple with Marika and her husband Paul about once a month, enjoying dinners in each other's houses. It had felt friendly, funny, grown up, to have mutual friends, and a relief, too, because she has gradually let her school and university friendships wane. Now, however, Beth has noticed she's getting far fewer messages from Marika. From a lot of her friends, in fact.

'No, no, it's fine. I'm working from home today anyway. I can get them.' So, he's cross that she has somewhere else to go, even if he doesn't, she thinks. Beth wonders, again, whether he's really thought this separation through. How will he cope when he no longer has a say in what she does with her time? This thought makes her feel lighter.

'Are you still angry about last night?'

'Yes,' she says, deciding there's no point in lying. After dinner last night, David had told her he'd instructed an estate agent to value their house, so he could find out how much he'd need to borrow to buy her out. He'd simply mentioned it in passing, as if he was telling her that the milkman had cancelled or that he was planning to change energy providers.

'It would have been so much better if we could have talked about all of this in mediation,' he says.

'It would have been better if you'd actually talked to me about it first.'

'You know I want to buy you out,' he says, clearly frustrated. 'It's hardly a surprise. And I didn't know you were so worried about finding somewhere else to live. As I say, we could talk about this in mediation, if you'd just agree...'

'It wouldn't make any difference, would it? You would still be doing it. You don't care how any of it makes me feel. If you did, you wouldn't be doing this at all.'

Tears are flowing down Beth's cheeks now. She has always done this when emotion overcomes her. Crying is like her pressure valve. One of the worst things about David's decision to end their relationship is that, previously, he was the person who would embrace her and calm her down when she cried. Now the person who was her solace is the source of her pain, and it's absolutely discombobulating.

'You mean I wouldn't be wanting a divorce?'

'Yes,' she says, gulping.

'We've talked about this. I've explained, as best I can, that I just don't feel... the way I felt before. Something has changed. I just can't see us spending the rest of our lives together any more.'

'Is it because... I made such a mess at work? Are you embarrassed to be with me? Ashamed?'

'Don't be ridiculous. No. I don't give a damn about the stuff going on at Stellar. For what it's worth, I think they put you under too much pressure and don't give you enough support.'

Beth pauses.

'Do you have someone else?' she asks, for what is probably the fourth time since David told her he was leaving her, her mother's comments about the likelihood of this still ringing in her ears.

'No!' says David, his voice defensive, as if she's just accused him of theft. 'How many times...'

'So it's just that you don't love me any more?'

'Don't do this, Beth.'

'Did you ever love me?'

'Don't. You don't want to have this conversation. It'll only make you feel worse. Why are you so keen on self-flagellation?'

'Did you?'

'You know I did. I wouldn't have married you if I didn't.'

'So what happened?'

'I don't know. I don't. But all I can tell you is that I don't love you now. It... faded. I wish I could change things, I really do, but our marriage is not making me happy any more.'

'But the kids... Don't they make you happy? Our family, doesn't it...'

'They make me happy, yes. But the time we spend together doesn't. I don't know how many different ways I can say this...'

'Don't. I don't need to hear that again,' she says, realising that he's right: this conversation is doing her absolutely no good. 'Look, I'm going to go now,' she says, setting off at pace for the front hall, where she retrieves her coat from a hook on the wall and her handbag from over the bannister.

'I'll see you later,' says David, who is now standing just behind her. In the past, she'd have turned around and hugged him, revelling in his warmth and reassurance. But this time it's like there's some kind of force field around him, repelling her.

'Bye,' she says, opening the door and pulling it shut behind her, without a backward glance.

* * *

Despite her concerns about the length of the drive to Surrey, Beth is grateful for it today. It gives her the time she needs to regain her composure. She channel hops between radio stations, singing along to her favourite songs at the top of her voice, making the most of her isolation. By the time she reaches the address she's been given in Dorking, she's feeling considerably better. She takes a moment to check her make-up in the mirror – her nose looks a little red, so she applies some concealer from a tube in her bag – and then opens the email Steve has sent her on her BlackBerry.

Dear Beth,

Thanks for agreeing to do this today. I owe you one – on that note, pop into the newsroom when you're done and I'll give you a key to the office so you can come and comb the archives for whatever it is you're looking for.

Anyway – so yes, I'd like you to go and meet a local councillor, James Connors, who emailed me a while ago about a new social housing project in the Surrey hills. We haven't had any bandwidth to get out to him yet but affordable housing is getting to be a real rarity in these parts, so I reckon it'd be good to find out what he has to say. He wants to show you some local council houses first – I'll text you the address of where he wants to meet you – and then if you have time he also wants to take you to the land he's persuaded the council to buy to build some new houses. Just make sure you get the key facts and a couple of good quotes. I'll send our freelance snapper out later to get a picture of him. Email me the copy when you've written it, no huge pressure, it's not breaking news.

Oh, and if you want me to 'translate' that shorthand for you, maybe leave it on my desk when you pop in. I can't guarantee I'll get to it quickly but I will try to do it, I promise.

See you anon,

Steve

Beth stashes her BlackBerry in her bag and gets out of the car. She's in the car park of a community centre in an area of Dorking she has never visited before. She drove through a warren of narrow streets of terraced houses to get here, each lined with cars straddling the pavements, making it unlikely that a wheelchair user or a parent with a buggy would be able to get by. This car park, meanwhile, has stern warning notices on each wall about the penalties for leaving a car there illegally. Beth has been warned about this. Her interviewee has promised to organise a permit for her.

She walks to the community centre entrance, clutching her bag to her chest as a kind of armour. She's more nervous about her first journalistic assignment than she cares to admit. Beth enters the centre and sees there's a woman sitting in an office to the right. She knocks gently on the open door.

'Hello. I'm looking for James Connors?'

'He's in the small hall,' says the woman. 'Down there on the left.'

Beth thanks her and follows her instructions.

She hears James before she can see him. He's sighing loudly, or perhaps even grunting, as he stacks large boxes in the corner of the room.

'Oh, hello,' he says, noticing Beth as she enters. 'Are you from *The Bugle*?'

'Yes, I am,' she replies, realising that she really is from *The Bugle*. She feels a tiny frisson of pride.

'Great to have someone come to cover the project eventually. I was losing hope,' he says, running his hands through his hair, which has got a bit dishevelled during his labours. James Connors is in his early forties, Beth thinks. He's tall and fairly slim, with brown hair that's receding slightly, peppered with grey. He's wearing a smart pair of rectangular steel-rimmed glasses, a red checked shirt and chinos and a scuffed pair of brown leather shoes. There's a hint of stubble on his chin. 'Sorry, I know that's not your fault. Shrinking funds, etcetera. Right. Just, give me a second. I thought I'd spend a bit of time tidying up after the food bank while I waited for you.'

Beth is almost about to tell him that her great-aunt had donated vegetables to his cause, but then she stops herself. She doesn't want to be known forever as just one more member of the family from the Big House, so she says nothing about Nita.

'Anyway, I took on a bigger task than I meant to, clearing up, but all good now. I'll just go and grab my coat and a car parking permit for you and we can head out. The houses I want to show you are only on this street, so we can walk.'

Beth waits for him to return with his coat, and then follows him back out into the car park, where she puts the permit behind her windscreen and locks the car.

'The people who run the centre had to introduce permits because so many locals were using this area for free parking,' he says. 'I mean, you can't blame them, have you seen how little space there is on these streets? These houses were built before everyone had cars, and of course most local people have to have them now, given how appalling public transport is around here.'

'You're not in charge of transport at the council, then?' Beth asks, realising that she should really have done some research into James Connors before coming to meet him.

'Goodness no. I stood as an independent, actually. I'm not aligned with any party. I'm not sure I could be. I'm politically homeless, if you like. I just do my best for the local community, in whatever way I can. I do regularly push to keep local bus routes open but there's only so much money to go around and when demand drops so does passenger revenue, so services become unviable – it's a vicious circle.'

'Do you have a day job?'

'Oh yes. I couldn't survive on the allowance we get. When you see how much it is, you realise why so many councillors are retired, wealthy people. It's a joke.'

'So what do you do?'

'Me? Oh, I'm a social worker, part-time. It keeps the wolf from the door, and it also means I'm always in touch with local people, and what their lives are really like.'

'I can imagine,' says Beth, who realises she has little idea how people outside her immediate circle live. She feels embarrassed to even admit this to herself.

'It's just here,' says James, stopping abruptly outside a house with a front door covered in peeling black paint. He sees Beth looking at it. 'You can always tell which of these houses are still rented as social housing, because they don't have decent doors,' he says. 'The officers in the council housing department tell me they have a waiting list for improvements that's years long. Decades, in some cases, for really expensive stuff. Right, let's see if Alice is in. She should be. She sent me a text earlier telling me she'd wait in for us.'

James Connors knocks on the door and moves back and waits. Beth goes to stand at his side, realising that standing behind him is probably not something a proper journalist would do. A few seconds later, a woman opens the door. She's in her thirties, wearing a smart pair of blue jeans and a yellow jumper, and her face is artfully made-up, framed by a neat red bob.

'Oh, hi, James. Glad you could come.'

'Thanks for having us. This is Beth, from *The Bugle*.'

'Lovely to meet you, Alice,' says Beth as they both cross the threshold and walk into the house's front room, which opens directly onto the street. The room's small but tidy. There's a large plastic box of toys in one corner, a baby bouncer near the two-seater grey sofa, and a small flat screen TV perched on a small low table.

'Can I get you a cuppa?' asks Alice.

'No, don't worry. We won't keep you,' says James. 'I just want to show Beth what's going on upstairs, if that's OK?'

'Sure thing.'

Beth follows James up a steep staircase. She notices that the carpet is worn through in several areas.

'These houses were built more than a hundred years ago and are really showing their age,' says James as he climbs the stairs and walks into a room on the right-hand side. 'They didn't originally have indoor bathrooms so there's a tiny one sandwiched up here in what used to be part of the second bedroom. And the rooms up here are... well, you can see for yourself.'

Beth gasps, and immediately regrets her outburst. But what she's looking at is shocking. Almost a whole wall of the room they're in, a room that seems to be a child's bedroom, is covered in mould. 'Yes, I know. It's horrible, isn't it?' says James.

'What's causing it?'

'The council came and did a survey and they started off telling Alice that she needed to open her windows more to let condensation out. She tried that for a bit, despite the fact it meant her house was cold and she's short of money to heat it, but it didn't work anyway. Long story short, another surveyor came and said that it was the gypsum plaster the council used on the walls here in the sixties. It stopped the walls "breathing" and well, you can see what's happened since. Alice tries to keep it at bay with bleach but it just keeps coming back.'

'And a child sleeps in here?'

'Yes. Well, I think when it's this bad, he sleeps in with Alice. She only left it like this so I could show you. She'll clean it off later I expect.'

'How long has it been like this?'

'Ever since Alice was housed here, definitely. So a few years.'

Beth is so taken aback, she doesn't know what to say. 'Oh, and Alice is a food-bank user too, by the way.'

'Is she?' *What a stupid thing to say, Beth*, she thinks. *Stop sounding like an idiot.*

'Yes. She works part-time as a carer but because she has her son to care for, she often doesn't have enough money left after bills to pay to feed them both.'

'That's awful.'

'Yes. And really common.'

James walks into the other bedroom, which houses a small double bed. She notices a stuffed dinosaur and a large brown fluffy teddy are propped up on the pillows.

'So why hasn't the council come and fixed the source of the damp?'

'Well, it took them a long time to get to the bottom of what the problem was. And there's not enough money to fix all the council-owned houses on this street. It's just throwing good money after bad, really. The best solution, in my opinion, is selling these on to private owners, and building new, purpose-built, energy-efficient social housing. Which is why I want to take you to Hazel's Field.'

* * *

'So how many homes would there be here?' asks Beth, surveying the muddy field in front of her.

'About eighty. Some apartments in low-rise buildings, and the rest small houses. Obviously this is a very pretty town and a rural area and people don't want hugely modern design here, so the architects have designed something that mirrors what's around us – rows of cottages, you know, and buildings that resemble barns. There would also be a sort of village square, plenty of parking and a playpark for kids. They'll all have solar panels and they are made using lots of prefabricated parts so they're quick to build and pretty economical.'

'Sounds great,' says Beth, writing the details down in her notebook. 'So what stage are you at with the planning?'

'Well, that's just it. That's why I need you. I am aware that local people don't like change. Don't want new houses built, especially on the green belt. I'm hoping that your stories will be able to explain why we need this new development on Hazel's Field.'

'I can't imagine it'll be easy to get it through planning permission either…'

'Well, it might be tricky, but as I say, if we can get the local people behind us, the council reckons it can apply for a loan from central government to build it all. It's rare for them to be doing this – for years it was just housing associations who built social housing – so it's a big deal to get them this far. We really need to get this across the line so that other places follow.'

Beth remembers a hugely popular online petition signed by almost everyone on their street the previous summer, against the planned redevelopment of disused garage into affordable housing. That was mostly about a lack of local resources, though, she thinks – not enough GP surgeries, school places, things like that.

'Won't it put a strain on local facilities, though?' she asks.

'Well, the local primary school isn't actually full, so that's OK. The GP surgery needs another doctor, however. But is that a reason not to do the right thing and build homes for people to feel safe and secure in? After all, there are hundreds of houses being built in this area right now by private developers and sold for a huge profit, and no one stops those, just because the GP surgery can't cope.'

Beth cringes internally, because she knows that Stellar, her father's company, the one she is technically still employed by, is in the business of building and selling such homes all across the country. She's very glad that she's here as a journalist, and that he has no idea who she really is.

'Thank you for bringing me here,' she says, turning away, keen to move on from a situation which is now making her feel awkward. 'I'll put something together as soon as I can.'

'Great,' says James, following her. She notices that he has two dimples in his cheeks when he smiles. She smiles back, despite how uncomfortable she's feeling. 'Thank you for your help with this,' he adds. 'I know it will make all the difference.'

12

NITA

November 1940

Nita is having a surprisingly good day. With the help of a borrowed textbook and occasional tutoring from Joe, she is learning shorthand. She has been practising it whilst on the phone to newly married couples and making a decent stab at it.

But everything is about to change.

She's pushing the kitchen door open with her elbow after yet another tea run when she hears the two older journalists, Simpson and Phillips, talking.

'The poor man has graffiti on his front door?' says Phillips.

'Yes. Apparently someone heard the conversation he and Miss Bineham had on the doorstep, and put two and two together.'

Nita is stopped in her tracks. Her stomach lurches.

'What does the graffiti say?'

'"Krauts Out".'

Fearing she's about to drop the tray, Nita retreats back into the kitchen at speed, the door slamming behind her. She doesn't care that they will have heard it. She feels sick. She slams the tray down on the surface and runs to the sink and puts the tap on. The sound of running water will hopefully hide her cries.

Oh my goodness, she thinks. *That poor, poor man.* She knows this is entirely her fault. She'd been motivated by a stupid desire to make her name in an industry she knows nothing about. It had been her own ego that had led directly to Matthew Brown's current situation. And knowing what she now knows about him and his family's troubles, she realises she's compounded their misery.

Her tears are in full flow when the kitchen door opens and Joe walks in.

'Nita?'

'Yes.' She sniffs.

'Are you all right?'

'Not really.'

'What's the matter?'

'It's fine, I really don't want to talk about it.'

'Don't be silly. You're very upset. Please tell me. I might be able to help.'

He's now standing directly behind her. Nita knows she must look a terrible fright, even worse than usual. She doesn't want Joe – friendly, handsome Joe, who she realises she likes more than is strictly proper – to see her like this. She decides that ignoring him is rude, so she will talk to him with her back turned instead.

'You must have heard what they just said,' she says, reaching for the tea towel that's hanging off the hook to her right and using it to dab her eyes.

'I did think it might be that, yes.'

'It's my fault! All my fault. Poor Mr Brown. He's got a special exemption and everything and a handicapped daughter and now he's going to feel hounded out of his hou—' Nita is so upset she's beginning to swallow words.

'Oh, Nita. Don't be like that. You weren't to know. You had a good idea and it could have paid off. And you didn't write about him and put it in the paper, did you? You came back and refused to write it up. That shows backbone.'

Nita sniffs and turns the tap off.

'But I've ruined his life.'

'I think that's probably pushing it. Look, I've been asked to go and write a story about the graffiti. I'll make sure I write about how nice he is and how he has an exemption and everything. It'll be all right, I'm sure.'

'Do you really think so?'

'I haven't been a journalist awfully long, Nita, but what I do know is that today's news will be tomorrow's chip shop wrappings. It's a cliché, but it's true. It'll pass. He'll be fine. Chin up.'

Nita stops dabbing her eyes and turns around to face him. She has finally stopped crying.

'I must look a dreadful state.'

'Well, I think you look lovely.'

Nita blushes.

'Thank you. I appreciate it, even though I know you're just being kind. Do you really think it'll be all right? Honestly, I feel like a liability sometimes. Mother is right, I think. I should just get married to some crusty old man and save the world from more of my bright ideas.'

'Come, now. That's not fighting talk! You're a journalist, Nita. You need to buck up your ideas.'

'I'm not a journalist.'

'You are. You work for a newspaper, writing things. You're a journalist.'

'Oh. But do I write anything more important than wedding reports and stories about blimmin' witches?' She laughs, despite herself.

'You do, actually, as of this afternoon. I was due to go out on a story, but I've been diverted to report on Mr Brown's front door. And I reckon this story will suit you down to the ground.'

'Why?' Nita asks, doubting that any story will ever suit her, ever again.

'Because this one is about women. A group of women, actually. And I rather suspect they'll be far more comfortable with you asking them questions than me.'

'Oh. What's the story?' she asks, tentatively.

'I only have the basic details, but essentially it's a group of local women who are working in a factory for the war effort. They've started a childcare cooperative so they can care for their children and cope with shift work.'

'Goodness. I see. Well, I could try, I suppose.'

'Oh, come on, Nita. You know you'll be fine. Why don't I pour you a cup of tea,' he says, noting the abandoned tea tray on the surface, 'and then you can head out to meet them.'

* * *

This time, Nita successfully navigates the local bus networks and half an hour later finds herself standing in a street of terraced houses on the outskirts of Dorking.

The houses are red brick and each has its own door facing onto the street, where children, newly released from school, are playing hopscotch. Nita seeks out the house she's looking for, number thirty-five, and raps on the door.

It's opened within a few seconds by a woman in her early twenties. She's wearing a housecoat over a day dress and stockings. A small child, who Nita judges to be a few months old, is balanced on her hip.

'Hello. I'm Nita, from *The Bugle*?'

The woman looks like she's about to speak, but then yells into the dark hallway behind her.

'Arthur! I said no! Stop it! Sorry, would you mind?' she says, handing Nita the baby. Nita takes the child awkwardly. The truth is, she's never held a baby before. She has no nieces or nephews yet, and no friends with children. She simply doesn't know what to do and ends up holding the child out at arm's length like a naughty cat. It doesn't seem to mind too much, however. In fact, it breaks out into a broad smile, and then chuckles. Nita relaxes for a moment, and pulls it closer to her, surprised at how sturdy it feels, how strong its little lungs are, through the rise and fall of its chest. And then the woman comes back, and as she does there's a rumble and something akin to an explosion around the baby's bottom. Nita jumps with alarm.

'Oh, Annie! I'm so sorry. She will need changing.' Nita hands her back with some relief. 'Sorry about that. Arthur, Mary's son, is an absolute devil. He can't be left alone for a second. Come in.'

Nita walks into the front room of the house. It's furnished with a battered leather sofa, a tall standard lamp with tassels and a low table made from dark brown wood. Net curtains offer privacy from prying eyes on the street. A coal fire burns in the grate behind a metal guard. The floor is strewn with spinning tops, tin toy soldiers and tiny model cars, and a boy, who she presumes must be Arthur, is sitting among them.

'So you must be...' Nita says to the woman.

'I'm Irene.'

'Yes. They told me you were in charge of the... collective?'

'Ha, I wouldn't say I'm in charge of anything. Let me change Annie, and then would you like a cuppa?'

Nita nods and sits down on the sofa while Irene sorts out the baby and makes tea in the kitchen. She watches Arthur playing with his toys on the carpet. He's so completely involved with his game of make-believe that he is apparently unaware that she's there, looking at him. Watching him reminds her of her own childhood, of the hours she'd while away playing house or school with her dolls or building miniature houses for fairies in the woods out of bark, grass and sticks.

'Here we go,' says Irene, returning with a tea tray and placing it down on the low table. She sits down on the sofa next to Nita, the toddler now on her lap.

'So is Annie yours?' asks Nita.

'Yes, she's mine. She's my youngest. I have an older one, Thomas, but he's playing out with his friends. You probably passed him when you walked up to the house.'

'Yes, I saw some children playing,' Nita says, feeling a tinge of regret that Melham Manor's isolation meant she had only ever had Frank to play with, and then, only for part of the time. He'd been sent off to boarding school at eight, so she'd only had his company in the holidays.

'It's easier having them out there at this time of day. It gives me time to make supper without them bothering me every second.'

'So how many children do you look after at a time?'

'It varies a lot. There are four of us in the collective at the moment, and we're on lots of different shifts and we have a mix of days off. Some days it can be up to three little ones and another four outside school hours, and others it's just one or two. And obviously we only do this when we aren't at work ourselves.'

'Yes, my editor told me you all work at a factory?'

'Yes. We're at Wendels in Leatherhead. Do you know it?'

Nita freezes. She knows it well, because her father's company, Stellar, owns Wendels. Stellar owns several factories, in fact, and is also now branching out into housing. Nita knows that before the war, Wendels used to make clocks, but now it's been repurposed to make munitions.

'Yes,' she replies, instinctively hiding her link to the place. 'It's a bit of a distance from here. How do you manage to get there?'

'There's a bus for the workers that comes through here in time for the shift changes. It's free. That's one good thing about Wendels, I'll give them that.'

'Are you all working full time there?' Nita asks, concentrating on the notes she's making on her pad.

'Yes, there's no other option.'

'And none of you have family locally who can help?'

Irene pauses.

'Nah.'

And then she pauses again. It's clear she's uncomfortable about something.

'I'm sorry, I don't mean to pry. It's just I think I'll need to explain to our readers why you need to help each other out.'

'My husband was killed. Six months ago.'

'Oh I'm sorry. I'm so sorry. I...'

'No, it's all right, that wasn't why I wasn't saying anything. It's the others.'

'The others?'

'Well, as you know there are three others. Betty's husband's fighting, out at sea, he is, and she doesn't have anyone nearby to help, because they moved here from Kent for her husband's job before the war. It's fine, you writing about Betty. And then there's Elsie. Well, please don't write this bit... her husband, he hit her and she's had to leave him and rent somewhere else for her and her kids. He's not giving her a penny, and yes, her family don't live round here either.'

'I won't say anything about that, if you don't want me to.'

'Good. Thank you. I only agreed to do this interview so we can tell other people how difficult it is to work and look after children, with everything being as it is. I don't want it causing any of my friends any trouble. Yes, so, then there's Mary, Arthur's mum.' Irene nods in the direction of the little boy playing in front of the fire. 'Between you and me,' she says, whispering, 'she wasn't married to his dad.'

In Nita's limited experience, every child has married parents. Maybe not happily married parents, of course. But legally wed, anyway.

'Yes, I know,' says Irene, seeing Nita's shock. 'Please don't write that, either. Can you lie and say he's serving overseas or something? Mary tends to say that when people ask. She came down here when she was expecting. She used to live in London. Her parents threw her out.'

'Goodness.'

'The only way she can keep shoes on his feet and food on the table is through work. So she needs the job at the factory. However blooming hard it is.'

'Is it? Really hard?'

Annie squirms. Irene puts her down on the floor and hands her a toy car to play with.

'It's absolutely exhausting, to be completely honest,' she says, rubbing her eyes. 'We work eight-hour shifts around the clock and it's so hard to sleep during the day. Sometimes we work six days a week. And it's so dangerous, what we're making, using all of the TNT, and we get hardly any training. Sometimes it feels like we're sitting ducks, just waiting for something awful to happen.'

They sit there in silence for a minute. Nita is feeling so much guilt about the money her father makes from these women's labours that she's temporarily unable to think what to ask next. Instead, she watches Annie and Arthur play companionably side by side on the floor. And then she is seized by an idea.

'What would it take, to make things better for you?' she asks, still looking at the children, and not at Irene, who, she worries, might be able to see her discomfort.

'Oh. That's a question. Well, the war being over – that would do it.'

This, Nita certainly cannot do. But there might be something else she can try.

'No, seriously. Tell me what smaller things would make a difference,' she says, turning over a new page on her notebook and holding her pen poised. 'That seems like a good place to start.'

* * *

'So some of the women have actually had to leave their children alone at home in bed, with a milk bottle propped up against the side of the cot, because they can't afford to pay for someone to come and babysit their child.'

'I see.'

'And do you know what? The manager of the factory turned down their proposal for an on-site nursery without even thinking about it. Just turned them down flat.'

It's dark when Nita and Joe leave the office and walk towards the bus stop for Joe to catch his bus home. There are no street lights due to the blackout, so they are picking their footsteps carefully, using what moonlight there is to light their way. Nita doesn't actually need to walk anywhere. Truth be told, she needs to find a payphone to call home and ask for someone to come and pick her up, but she doesn't want to tell Joe this, so she's pretending she needs to get a different bus.

'Goodness, Nita, you're really serious about this.'

'I am, yes. I think we should help them.'

'We?'

'*The Bugle*. I think we should run a story about the plight of these women and shame the owner of the factory into improving conditions for them.'

'And you want me to pretend I've written it? Why?'

'I just... feel it'll be taken more seriously if it's by a man.'

'Come, now. That doesn't sound like the Nita I know.'

She pauses, before deciding that it's time to tell him the truth. She hates lying to him, even by omission.

'No, you're right, that's not it. It's because... my father owns that factory,' she says, glad of the darkness. She doesn't want to see his reaction. She waits for his answer with trepidation. 'He runs Stellar. They own factories, and properties.'

'Oh, I see.'

She can't work out what the tone of his voice is telling her. Is he angry? Disappointed? Surprised?

'I'm sorry I didn't tell you before.'

'Why didn't you?'

She's still not sure what to make of his response. 'I was afraid of what you might think of me.'

'Oh, I see.'

'Do you think badly of me now?'

There's a pause.

'I'm a bit sad you felt you couldn't tell me the truth, Nita, but no. He's your father. He's not you. And after what I said when we first met, about unscrupulous employers abusing their staff... I'm not surprised you didn't want to tell me.'

'So you're not angry with me? You don't mind still being friends?'

A bus passes them in the darkness. Neither of them says anything until it's driving away into the distance.

'No, you silly thing. No.' He reaches out and pats her arm, and relief floods through her.

'Thank goodness.'

'Do you have any other secrets you're not sharing with me, though? Are you actually a copper, or a Fleet Street journalist come to write an exposé?'

Nita laughs. 'No. More's the pity.'

'Well, then. All's good.'

'So will you write it then? The article, for me?'

'No. I still can't write it, Nita.'

'Why not?'

'Look, I know you feel guilty about what happened to that German teacher, and I think this is probably your way of trying to make amends. But this story... Think about it. Your father is friends with Bridges. Bridges isn't going to let us run a story rubbishing his firm's war work.'

'*Oh...*' Beth wants to scream.

'Honestly, it's not worth that. It's only a story.'

If only he knew the truth. She feels so horrendously guilty about what happened to Mr Brown; embarrassed about her family and the money she has always enjoyed and never really acknowledged. And then there's her self-hatred for her lumpy body and her plain face and her lack of grace and all the other things her mother chastises her for. The sudden dashing of an idea that had given her a small hint of possible salvation brings all of these things to the surface. But he's right. Her father and Bridges are friends. Why didn't she think of that?

'I'm sorry. Really I am,' she says. 'I must go...'

'No, stay a while. Let's find a cafe...'

Nita has to get home soon or her mother will send someone out to get her. She can't stay here long without calling someone.

'No, it's all right. I'll get myself together in a minute.'

'If you insist. Look. I think you're probably going to have to write a jolly piece for *The Bugle* about a group of plucky young mothers clubbing together so that they can all work hard to hold off the Hun,' he says, and Nita winces. 'But I do have an idea. I'm a member of a group. A group of socialists. We have a newspaper we write, in our own time. It's distributed for free at rallies and meetings. We could write a piece together for that instead? Neither of our names would be on it, but it would certainly get it out there, wouldn't it?'

'That's a wonderful idea. Thank you.'

'My pleasure. I do admire you, you know, for wanting to stand up for what's right.'

'Thank you. Oh, thank you.'

And then something very strange happens.

Nita is so delighted about his idea, so relieved that he has given her a way forward, that she forgets who she is, who *he* is, and where they both are. This frumpy, bookish society refusenik reaches out for the handsome young journalist, the darkness emboldening her.

The aim is to give him a brief hug of thanks, the same kind of hug she gives their housekeeper when she's made her a lovely dinner. She has been imagining what he feels like to touch for some time now, and she realises this may be her only chance.

It doesn't work out this way.

She reaches for his upper torso first, and that's fine, that's part of the plan, but then he reaches out, too, and all of sudden they are embracing much more firmly than she'd ever imagined, and then his cheek is next to her cheek, and he smells of tobacco and ink and something musky, and his fingers are running up and down her bare forearm and they feel like feathers, and then they are in the small of her back and walking up her spine, and his right hand is clasping the back of her head and he is pulling her towards him, and oh my goodness, oh my goodness he's so close now and oh my those are his lips, and they're on hers. They are on hers!

Nita almost springs away in disbelief but then she realises that, whether it is a dream or not, this will probably be one of those moments that features in the secret picture book in her memory bank of her life's most show-stopping moments (a minuscule publication, so far), and so she knows she must capture it. Immerse herself in it. So, she kisses him back. And for what feels like hours but is most likely seconds, she stands in the blessed darkness consumed by a desire so powerful she simply does not recognise herself. Her most private imaginings have not prepared her for this force. These sensations. This magic.

And then there is the sound of an engine.

Joe pulls away.

'This is my bus,' he says, still holding her by the waist. As the bus approaches, its lights, dimmed and dipped due to the black-out, light up their legs and feet. 'Goodnight, Nita,' he says, as he walks away to board the bus. 'Will you be all right, finding your bus stop by yourself?'

'I'll be fine. Goodnight, Joe,' she says, surprised she can still speak.

'See you tomorrow,' he says, as the bus door closes, and he is driven off into the inky darkness. Nita turns and walks back towards the office, knowing there's a phone box nearby she can use.

But she's not walking. She's floating. Because whatever happens next, she thinks, whatever Joe says tomorrow, even if he tries to pretend it never occurred – tonight *happened*. It definitely happened, and no one is ever going to take that away from her.

And this thought, the memory of the magic she has just experienced, will stay with Nita forever.

13

BETH

November 2008

The explosion's so loud, it makes Beth jump. And then there's another one, and another, and four-year-old Ella, who's on her shoulders, shrieks with delight. Seven-year-old Raphie, meanwhile, is standing against the cordon, watching intently as the pyrotechnicians light the fireworks with flares, one by one.

'It's brilliant, isn't it,' says a woman who's standing next to her, accompanied by her husband and grandchildren. 'It always is.'

Beth nods in agreement, although she hadn't been at all sure she should come back here, bringing her own kids. She has such special childhood memories of Melham's annual Guy Fawkes' celebration, with its gigantic bonfire and extravagant firework display, that she thought returning might tarnish them. After all, the world has undoubtedly changed since the eighties, and not, she thinks, demonstrably for the better. Those years, before her family had drifted, perhaps, surged away from here, never to return, had seemed to her to be a time of innocence and joy, and of freedom. But then, perhaps that's what everyone thinks about their childhood. Adulthood obscures even the most iridescent of experiences.

She needn't have worried, however. The villagers are still putting on a great show. There's bitter bonfire toffee to buy in striped paper bags that threatens to remove your fillings; hot dogs served in twisted foil stuffed with mellow mustard and caramelised onions; and a myriad stalls offering the chance to win a mystery gift bag, rubber duck or chocolate bar in return for a donation to the church spire fund or the local food bank. Everyone in the village seems to have turned out tonight, from the newly born to those nearing the end of their days, each one of them buoyed up by that special sort of infectious joy that can only be found where large groups of people are all enjoying the same special experience in close proximity to one another. Beth tries to take a mental snapshot of where she is at this moment, not just visually but with her other senses: the soft, warm grip of Ella's hand on her fingers; the yielding earth beneath her feet; the scent of sulphur and burning wood; the taste of spun sugar on her tongue. She does this because this moment is the closest to happiness she's come in quite some time now. She's glad she told David she was bringing the kids with her for this visit. He'd protested, but only half-heartedly. It's a weekday, it's half-term and he's working long hours. He's hardly going to be at home to be able to miss them, anyway.

'Are your kids in the school?' the woman next to Beth asks, continuing their amiable conversation during a temporary lull in the firework display.

'Oh, no. We live in London.'

'Ah. Relatives here, then? Grandparents?'

'No. Well, there were. My great-aunt, Nita. But she died.'

'Nita? Goodness me. You're not a Bineham, by any chance, are you?'

'I am, yes...' says Beth, stuttering. Where is this going? she wonders. No one, either family or from the local community, has been to visit Nita for decades, she reasons. 'Sorry... I didn't know anyone around here even knew her.'

'Oh, we're friends with the vicar. He told me he'd conducted the funeral, and we all know about the Bineham family around here, of course.'

When Beth had been younger, she'd have felt pride at this statement. But now, not so much.

'I see.'

'Yes, I'd heard that family members had come up for the funeral. I didn't know any of you were still around, though.'

'Yes, we all live up in the city now. I'm just down sorting through Nita's things. And I thought I'd bring my kids here. I always loved Bonfire Night here when I was little.'

'Are you going to take possession of the house now, now that she's gone?'

Beth doesn't know how to answer this. She has no idea what her parents plan to do. She suspects that the answer is, *not very much*.

'Not sure. I'm just focusing on sorting things out,' she says, letting her daughter down onto the ground, where she walks over to her brother, who reluctantly holds her hand.

'That must be a big job. It's quite... run down now, isn't it.'

Beth raises an eyebrow in the darkness. It's impossible to see the house from the road, so her knowledge of the house's condition suggests this woman has been trespassing. Interesting, she thinks, that she's not even trying to hide this fact.

'It definitely needs some TLC,' says Beth.

'Nita was such an interesting woman.'

This lady's position as chief gossip of the village is now becoming very clear.

'Did you know her, then?'

'I didn't know her particularly well. But I saw her a fair amount, mostly at a distance. I walk my dogs in the woods. I know that's Melham Manor land,' she says, clearly hesitating, 'but it was known, among the villagers, that she didn't mind us doing it, you understand. She liked animals, didn't she?' Beth thinks of the very cosy cockerel and the cats, and nods. 'But yes, she was certainly an unusual woman...' she adds, as a rocket explodes above their heads, showering the earth with green stars.

'Unusual?'

'Yes...' says the woman, loudly, so Beth can hear her over the fireworks. 'I know people who said they'd seen her wandering around the garden talking to herself, and then there are those stories...'

'Oh, hello, Jean,' says another woman, who Beth hadn't spotted before. It's hard to see in the darkness so it takes her a moment or two to realise that Rowan, the woman she'd met in the garden the morning after Nita had died, is standing right beside her. 'How nice to see you. How are you and the family keeping?'

The woman Beth had been speaking to, Jean, embarks on a monologue about her arthritis, a financial crisis at the local WI and her daughter requiring her to provide childcare for grand-children due to her new job. Beth is relieved her strange aunt is no longer the woman's focus, and instead tries to enjoy what's left of the fireworks with her children. She ruffles Raphie's hair. She is pleased she brought the children, even though it had made her initial plan for the afternoon – not clearing out Nita's house, as she'd told Jean, but in fact going through the archives at *The Bugle* in search of the mysterious X – very difficult. She *had* gone to the newspaper's office, and endured some more conversation with Steve, who was very pleased with her first article for him. She'd even received the princely sum of fifty pounds, cash, for her trouble. He had also translated a few more pages of shorthand notes for her, all of which had been transcriptions of interviews Nita had done, mostly about weddings. She was beginning to wish she hadn't bothered to ask him to do it. When she'd finally managed to get him to stop talking, she'd attempted to start looking through the archive room, and that's when everything had started to unravel. Raphie had quickly grown bored of the few toys she'd brought him, and Ella had deposited half-eaten snacks all over the floor. Researching with children in tow is not to be recommended. Beth's thoughts are momentarily distracted by an enormous cacophony as several rockets explode in quick succession, making Ella jump. Afterwards, the crowd erupts into applause.

'Well, wasn't that lovely,' says Rowan, who's still standing beside her. Beth notices that Jean has walked away, relieved, perhaps, not to have to make polite conversation with a relative stranger any longer.

'Yes. Lovely,' she says, letting Ella down.

'I told you you'd be back,' says Rowan.

'I have always loved this place,' says Beth, surprising herself a little as she says it. Because it's absolutely true, of course, but she realises she's tried to suppress how good she feels here, how free she feels, how *different*, for a long time. But she doesn't want to do that any more, she thinks. Her whole life is falling apart, anyway. There is no longer any point in pretending. The Manor and Melham *do* make her feel good. They always have. And that, she realises, is part of the reason she's come back. It's not just about her mother's orders or her niggling desire to find out the solution to this puzzle that her aunt seems to have set for her. Not at all.

'Yes,' says Rowan.

That's all she says. No more. And yet Beth understands there's meaning in it. Rowan seems to know what Beth's thinking, and oddly, she doesn't even mind.

'I didn't see you at the house today when I went to feed the animals,' says Rowan, picking up a soft toy which Beth didn't realise Ella had dropped, and handing it to her daughter, who takes it, then chuckles.

'Oh. No. I wasn't there. I've... started working at *The Bugle*.'

'You're a journalist?'

'Oh, not really. A sort of trainee, I suppose,' she says, aware that saying this, at her age, must sound ridiculous. 'I was supposed to be... working there, but I had the kids with me and it was a complete nightmare. I was trying to find a document I need...'

'Goodness, yes, that must have been tough.'

'I'll just need to come back in a few more days, I suppose,' says Beth, realising as she says this that David is unlikely to let her come down without the children, as this means he'll have to provide the childcare. 'I mean, I've got a key. Maybe I can come back one evening or something...'

'Why don't you go now?' says Rowan, who has just produced a sweet from her bag. 'Are they allowed toffees?' she asks. 'I know some parents don't like sweets...'

'Goodness, yes. They love them.' The children both beam and accept the sweets. 'But I'd have to take the kids again, and it's nearly their bedtime, so...'

'Well, how about I take them back to Melham Manor for you?' says Rowan. 'We can hang around here for a bit, and then I've got car seats in my car that I use for the grandchildren, so that's all taken care of. I could stay with them there until you get back. Would that work? How much time do you need?'

Beth is astonished. No one, even her mother, has ever offered to take the children off her hands, even for a few minutes. But she doesn't know this woman, well, not apart from one short conversation, and surely she can't just leave her children with someone she hardly knows? But then she was a teacher, wasn't she, Beth thinks, and also her great-aunt's trusted friend.

'Look, I'll give you my number,' says Rowan, holding out her phone. 'You can call or text me at any time. And I'll call you if they give me any trouble.'

Beth is about to say no, but then she sees that Ella is already holding Rowan's hand. She looks so comfortable, she might have known her for years.

'Are you absolutely sure about this?' she asks Rowan. 'Oh, and I should warn you, our dog, Stanley, is in the house. He's very friendly but likely to kiss you to death.'

Rowan laughs. 'Noted.'

'OK then.'

Beth is beginning to relax. She instinctively trusts Rowan and she realises that it would be wonderful to go and do this research unencumbered. She needs to satisfy her curiosity. Scratch this annoying itch. And it shouldn't take long.

'Are you sure you'll be OK with them all?'

'Of course. I love children. And dogs. We're going to have a grand time,' Rowan says, as Raphie looks up at her with adoration. 'Aren't we, kids? Someone told me they have hot dogs over there,' she says. 'And there are fresh doughnuts for afters. We could get some before we head to the car.'

'I'll give you some money for it all,' says Beth, as they exchange numbers.

'Oh, no, my treat,' says Rowan, her smile broad. 'I love being around kids. Honestly. As you know, I used to be a primary school teacher. And even that didn't put me off.'

'Thank you,' says Beth, really meaning it. This is the first kind thing anyone has done for her in a very long time, and her brain doesn't quite know how to process it.

'No bother. Just come back when you're done,' says Rowan.

Beth stands for a while and watches as the older woman and her children disappear into the crowd. The kids are having such a good time, they don't even turn around to look for her. Satisfied, she turns and walks towards her car. She'll be at the office within twenty minutes.

* * *

It all happens very fast.

Beth opens the door to the newsroom. Flicks on the lights. And then there's a crash, a shout, and someone comes barrelling towards her, holding a large object above their head.

'Get out. Get out. There's nothing in here for you... to... stea—'

'Steve?'

The editor of *The Bugle* is standing in front of her. Except he doesn't look like he normally does. He's wearing a crumpled T-shirt with some sort of stain down the front and a pair of baggy grey tracksuit bottoms, and he's holding a large plastic bottle of what looks, on closer inspection, to be supermarket own brand cider.

'Beth. Oh... sorry... I thought... someone was breaking in.'

When he speaks, Beth is enveloped in a cloud of boozy odours. Steve is very, very drunk, she realises.

'I've got a key.'

'Oh... yeah... I gave you one, didn't I?' he says, retreating in the direction of his office.

'I've come back to just take a look at the archives again, before they are all got rid of. I still want to see if there's anything in there that corresponds with that string of numbers I found in Nita's file...' Steve doesn't seem to be listening. Instead, he walks slightly ahead of her and closes his office door with undue haste. As he does this, he wobbles.

'Steve... are you OK?' she asks, maintaining a safe distance in case he vomits. He certainly doesn't look good.

'Yeah, yeah, why wouldn't I be?' he says, standing right in front of the door.

'You seem... drunk, to be honest,' says Beth. She knows he could decide to 'fire' her for this, but given she's basically only being paid enough to cover her expenses, she's prepared to risk it.

'I've had a couple. Only a couple.'

A couple of bottles, I reckon, thinks Beth. She knows what alcoholism looks like.

'Right. What've you got in your office you don't want me to see?' she asks, as ugly scenes from her childhood replay in her mind. She's seen this before, and she's not inclined to let it go.

'Nothing.'

'Then let me in.'

'No.'

'Let. Me. In.'

She lunges past him and opens the door. He tries to stop her, but he's so unsteady on his feet, he loses his balance and falls forwards onto one of the other desks. Meanwhile, she flicks on the light and walks in.

Usually, in her experience, there would be a hidden stash of alcohol in here, perhaps behind some books or between some files. Instead, she finds a bed roll, a sleeping bag, a yellowing pillow and in the corner, an open backpack, some of its contents spilling out onto the floor.

'Oh my God. You're sleeping here?'

'Yeah. I...'

'Why?'

'Why do you think? I haven't got anywhere to go, sweetheart,' he says, walking past her and sitting down heavily on his office chair, which is now pushed against the back wall. 'My wife and I are having... artistic differences.' He opens the half-drunk bottle of cider and takes a large swig.

'Oh, Steve. I'm so sorry.' And she is, because of course she knows exactly how he feels.

'Yeah. It's crap. Very crap. She's kicked me out. She's at home with the kids and I hardly see them. I miss them... oh crap. I miss them...' He takes yet another drink, and she can tell he is close to tears.

'Are you getting divorced?'

Steve nods.

'Yes. Well, apparently we are. She's appointed a lawyer and I've got to do the same. I went to see a lawyer here, in Dorking, for a free hour the other day. They offer you one before you book them, you know. He told me that I'll be better off when we've come to an agreement. That I'll be able to afford to rent somewhere. But how far will my money stretch, with my puny salary? It's such a bloody mess.'

Beth wonders whether she should tell him that she's also being divorced against her will, but decides against it. She doesn't really know Steve and he might think she's coming on to him, telling him she's available. The idea makes her feel slightly nauseous. But she does feel sorry for him, really sorry. She feels sorry enough for herself, after all, and she has her family's financial backing. She doesn't know how much editors of small local newspapers earn, but she doubts it's enough to support two households in such an expensive part of Surrey.

'Something will come up. I'm sure you'll find somewhere to stay.'

Steve looks at her incredulously.

'I doubt that. All of my mates have families and no one wants a washed-up, emotionally compromised middle-aged man on their sofa.'

'At least you can stay here,' she says, scrabbling around for something to say. 'You're the boss, after all.'

'Yeah, as long as this place still exists. It's dying, *The Bugle*. The current owner's looking to sell, but I doubt he'll find a buyer. Local newspapers are tanking across the board. Unless you're prepared to just churn out clickbait riddled with ads. If you can even sell the ads...'

'Really? It might close?'

'Really,' replies Steve, sinking further into his chair.

'That's really sad.'

'Isn't it. That's why I was glad when you walked in the door. You're doing some actual journalism for me. If this paper is going to go down the tubes, I want it to go down fighting, producing actual local news. News that people in the area need to know about. Jesus knows, there's plenty of it. People deserve to know what their elected representatives are doing with their money, for a start.' Steve is so passionate about this topic he even seems to be sobered up a bit.

'Well, I'm glad I'm helping a little.'

'Yeah, you are. So how's this story about your aunt's spy search coming on?'

'Not much progress so far. I just want to check the archives, as I said...'

'Yeah, sorry, of course. I'm sorry for almost attacking you. No one's ever come in after hours before.'

Beth decides it's time to leave Steve to it.

'It's OK. Look, I'll go next door now. Pretend I never turned up. I won't say anything about you being here. I don't have anyone to tell, anyway.'

'Thanks,' he says, his face a picture of defeat. 'I appreciate that.'

Beth opens the door into the archives and exhales loudly as

she shuts it behind her. Blimey, that was unexpected, she thinks, taking in the dusty, cluttered room that she'd tried and failed to search earlier when she'd had the kids in tow. It's unsettling to think that she and Steve are going through something so similar. But actually, she thinks, are they? David hasn't talked about getting a divorce for weeks now. They're still cohabiting, managing the kids as they've always done, sharing meals. There's a chance, she thinks, that it all might blow over. The thought calms her, and she sets to work opening each file in turn, trying to work out what sort of cataloguing system the paper uses for its archives. She has a theory that the string of numbers on that document of Nita's might be a reference to a document or an old copy of the paper, and if so, it might be in here.

It takes half an hour for her to realise that she's wrong.

Nothing in the archives is catalogued using numbers. Instead, everything is alphabetical – there are files on local businesses, schools, churches, fires, crashes etc., all labelled according to their name or the type of event. Beth scans these files but realises they're unlikely to be helpful, and given that she needs to get back for the kids soon, there's far too much to examine in detail.

There are also stacks of boxes with years printed on them, holding copies of every paper printed in each of those years. After reading a text message from Rowan saying the kids were safely back at Melham Manor, Beth takes a snap decision and finds the box relating to the year she knows Nita was working at the paper – 1940. She sits for a while and leafs through the papers, spotting several of Nita's bylines, some of which she's already seen in the cuttings in the box in loft. There are others she hasn't seen, however, including a series on women doing war work in the local area. They're interesting and well written, but definitely unrelated to Nita's hunt for a Nazi spy. Beth puts them back in the box, shuts it, and is about to put it back when she reconsiders. Will Steve miss this? Isn't all of this being junked anyway?

Beth rises, still clutching the box. Then she turns the light out, saying a brief goodnight to Steve, who's still slumped in the chair in the corner. When she reaches the street, she sends a text to Rowan telling her she's on her way back. She finds her car and places the box safely on the passenger seat.

She's not sure why she's taken it, particularly, but she feels like Nita's work deserves to be read again. And if nothing else, she thinks, it might be nice to put it all together in a scrapbook or something.

Nita has gone. She knows that. But these stories were hers. She cared about them. And somehow, it feels like it's Beth's duty to take them home for her. Home, to Melham Manor.

14

NITA

November 1940

'Nita, I need you.'

Joe is so close to her she can smell his signature scent of cigarette smoke and paper.

'What do you need?' she asks, her voice unnaturally light. Almost squeaky. He only kissed her last night and she is doing a terrible job of pretending it isn't the most amazing thing that has ever happened to her. It's the middle of the afternoon, so they've been in the same room for at least six hours now. She's been trying not to look at him all day in case other people notice, and also in case he now regrets what he did. However, every time he passes near her it's like he's some kind of heat source and her cheeks flush and she starts to sweat. She's been mopping her face with a handkerchief so often her colleagues probably think she has the flu.

'Bridges wants us to go and cover a job together.'

'Oh. Right. Well.'

Just say a proper sentence, she thinks. *You can speak, girl, so speak properly.*

'Shall we go now?'

'Yes,' she says, standing up and putting her notebook and pencil in her satchel. She still tries not to look at him and sucks in her stomach on her way to the coat stand so that she doesn't accidentally brush against him and cause herself to spontaneously combust. She pulls on her overcoat in a couple of seconds and is out of the newsroom and halfway down the stairs to the street before she hears him follow her.

'Nita, is something wrong?' he asks, pushing the door open to the street about ten seconds after she had done so.

'No... no,' she says. Her fingers rubbing the leather on her bag strap. 'I just didn't want to hold us up.'

'Well, that's a shame, because I was rather hoping to enjoy a quiet moment alone with you on the stairs, where no one could see us,' he says, and she almost melts.

Oh my goodness, she thinks. *He doesn't regret it at all. He actually might kiss me again. Me. The too tall, too broad, too bolshy girl from the house on the hill.* Just thinking about this is amazing. She beams at him, all thoughts of trying to contain her joy forgotten.

'Oh... Christ,' she says, and starts to laugh. She is not one for taking the Lord's name in vain, but this extraordinary turn of events seems to call for it.

'Never mind. There will be time later,' he says, with a glint in his eye. 'We haven't got much time now, anyway. We've got somewhere to be.'

Joe puts his hand gently on the small of Nita's back as they walk together towards the bus stop and she tries to give him her full attention as he explains what they've been asked to do. He tells her the police now think the break-in at the Millward car parts factory was the work of a Nazi spy. This news is enough to break Nita out of her romantic spell, and she actually stops walking for a moment.

'A spy? Genuinely? Why would they break into the car parts factory?'

'Rumour is, they're checking all the factories locally, searching for top secret weapons, anything they can send back to Germany to give them a better chance of beating us. Obviously this one was a bust. But from what I've heard, it seems the police think this may be just the first in a series... So your crazy witch woman was more on the money than we thought. I doubt it's Mr Brown, though...'

Nita remembers that horrible misunderstanding and wishes the ground would swallow her up.

'No.'

'But anyway, the police are holding a press conference and I need you there because I may not be able to take notes well in the scrum, and I know you've been working on your shorthand. Anyway, Bridges was fine about it. He says he'll let your father know.'

Nita has only heard of scrums in the context of rugby but she imagines that if similar were to happen at a press conference, notes might indeed be difficult to take.

'Where's it being held?'

'At Scotland Yard.'

'In London? But it's already 5 p.m., and the trains are all tremendously unreliable now. And it's hard to get around after dark.'

'I know. That's why I persuaded Bridges to put us up in a hotel.'

Nita turns to look at Joe. He's grinning like a Cheshire cat.

'I see,' she says, feeling an invisible force pushing her towards the bus stop, despite the incline. 'I see.'

* * *

'So was your first press conference what you expected?'

Nita and Joe are tucked in the corner of the hotel restaurant, eating an unremarkable supper of cottage pie – 95 per cent of which seems to be potato – accompanied by tinned peas.

'No,' replies Nita, shovelling food in at pace. Then, realising that ladies are supposed to eat daintily, she puts her knife and fork down and regrets it immediately, because she's starving. 'Although, frankly, I didn't expect anything. Until I started at *The Bugle*, I'd never given press conferences much thought.'

It had been very warm in the room, which had been packed out with men, all of whom seemed to want to ask questions simultaneously. They had flapped their hands repeatedly to try to get the police superintendent's attention. It had reminded Nita of the time her parents had made her come with them to the horse races.

'Fair enough. It was unusual even for me, to be honest. Nothing much happens in our patch, usually.'

While the police officer had been delivering his statement, the braying pack of journalists had remained silent, except for the scribbling of their pens and pencils. Nita had sat on a chair in the far corner and taken copious notes throughout. The details had been scant but stark. The break-in at the factory had apparently been too sophisticated to be petty theft, and evidence they'd found at the scene had suggested an enemy agent's involvement. The reporters had pressed the police for more detail on this but had been refused. The superintendent went on to say it was likely the agent was scouting around for factories working on secret prototypes for new weapons or aircraft. This first factory wasn't engaged in business of this kind, he said, but they were concerned that for this reason he or she might be plotting further attempts on local factories, or even one of the nearby RAF bases. Security would be stepped up as a result, he said. He also warned that it might not be just one Nazi spy; that there could actually be a 'cell' of them operating in the local area. The general public had been warned to be on its guard, to report any suspicious activity and to avoid being loose-lipped about war work with anyone, even close family members.

'Do you think they'll catch them? And, you know... do you think they're right? That there may be more than one? And that they might be plotting other things?' asks Nita, giving up and picking up her cutlery once more. Joe, she notices, is also eating hungrily.

'I don't know, in all honesty.' He looks pensive.

He's probably still thinking about what they saw on the way back to the hotel, she thinks. She certainly is.

At first it had just been broken glass. They'd just emerged from the tube station at Westminster and turned into a side street, and the ground had been littered with tiny shards. But then she'd looked up and realised that an entire building, most likely housing residential flats above and a shop beneath, had been reduced to a pile of rubble. It had clearly happened recently, perhaps the night previously; rescue workers were still sifting through bricks, wood, glass and dust, occasionally placing personal items they'd found on a small pile on the pavement. Nita had spotted a woman's court shoe, a smashed wristwatch, a grubby porcelain doll. She hadn't been in the centre of London for at least three months, and it had been a shock to see the reality of the Blitz. Everywhere – the streets around their hotel, and around Waterloo train station, around Scotland Yard – is littered with jagged holes where shops, homes and businesses had once stood. The immense damage, both physical and undoubtedly emotional, is plain for all to see.

These spies, she thinks, whoever they are, want to make the whole country suffer even more. They want to pulverise it, obliterate it so that they can invade and Britons won't have the energy to fight back. This thought makes her feel wretched.

'Nothing usually happens in Surrey,' Joe continues, after a pause. 'But these aren't ordinary times. I suppose we are just going to have to get used to that. Our jobs will certainly get more interesting, I expect.'

'What do you mean?'

'Oh, I should think every Tom, Dick and Harry will be reporting their neighbour for being able to speak German, for having blond hair, that sort of thing. And I doubt your Mr Brown will have an easy ride of it.'

Nita puts her fork down. Thinking about the poor teacher and his handicapped daughter, and the horrible graffiti on their front door, makes her feel sick.

'It's not your fault, Nita. This allegation would have made things difficult for him anyway. Lots of people at the school already knew his parents were German.'

She's grateful for this attempt to make her feel better, even though she is still racked with guilt. She stares glumly at her half-eaten dinner.

'Look, let's finish eating and then we can go up to my room and file this story. Bridges is expecting me to call it in by eight.'

Nita nods and eats a few more mouthfuls, before taking a swig of the tea she'd ordered. She has never drunk alcohol outside of Melham Manor, and a work trip doesn't seem like the time to start. Joe followed her lead and is also drinking tea.

'I'm ready when you are,' she says, keen to get to work, to avoid thinking any more about poor Mr Brown.

'Excellent,' he says, as he finishes his last mouthful. 'Let's go.'

It's only when they're climbing the stairs to the second flood that Nita realises she is about to be alone in a room with Joe. He'd talked about filing the story in his room, of course, but she'd been so consumed with guilt and so discombobulated about being away from the house, and without her parents, that she hadn't really taken it on board. Then, all of a sudden, he's turning the key in the lock and she's following him into a room which is furnished with a desk, a chair and a double bed, and nothing else. Joe stands while she enters and gestures for her to sit at the desk, for which she is grateful. Even with her limited experience, she knows that sitting on a chap's bed is not the done thing.

Seconds later, however, he sits down on the bed. Nita is nervous. Very nervous. She has no idea what happens now. So she does the only thing she can think of, and reaches into her bag to retrieve her notebook. Joe, meanwhile, opens his travel bag and pulls out his typewriter, which is contained in a smart leather carry case, and for a focused, energised forty-five minutes, they work perfectly together, assembling the facts in the right order, for a story destined to be the lead in tomorrow's paper.

'So the headline is, "Police Link Factory Break-in to Nazis in our Midst",' says Joe, typing as he says it. 'By Joseph Miller...' and then he pauses '...with additional reporting by Nita Bineham.'

Her eyes dart towards his. 'Really?' she says.

'Oh yes. Absolutely. You came to the press conference. It's your notes we used. You deserve the credit. And goodness, your father will need to see your name there, for proof that you're not on some kind of terrible assignation.'

'Imagine that,' she says.

Nita can't help it. She blushes bright pink.

'Yes, imagine that,' he says, packing up his typewriter and placing it back in his bag. And then he pulls something else out of it; a bottle of whisky, and two glasses. 'Now, I think we should propose a toast to your first byline in *The Bugle*. No wedding write-ups for you today.' Nita beams. 'And I think you're doing a good job, by the way. You're working long hours. You could be sitting at home and knitting socks for servicemen or something, but you're not. And it's not easy in the newsroom, is it? Bridges certainly doesn't make it easy.'

'No,' says Nita, half laughing. 'He doesn't.'

'Well, then. Toast?' he says, opening the bottle and pouring two-inch-deep whiskies.

'Why not,' she says, even though she's never tasted whisky before. She's had sherry a few times, and small glasses of white wine during formal dinners, but whisky has usually been reserved for her father and her brother, and their male guests. He hands her a glass.

'To you,' he says.

She smiles and takes a sip. Her mouth is immediately warm, and so is her throat. It's an unexpected taste, but not, she decides, a bad one. She takes another sip, and then another. Soon, the warmth is spreading out into her limbs and up to her head.

'Like it?'

'Very much.'

'Excellent,' he says, placing his own glass down on the bedside table, and standing up. She thinks he may be about to head out to the shared bathroom at the end of the corridor, but he stops when he reaches her.

Nita suddenly finds she can't breathe.

He places his hand on her shoulder. She turns towards him. He takes her hand and pulls, and she allows herself to stand up.

They are nose to nose now.

It's Joe who leans forward first, but only because Nita is too afraid of rejection, of this moment being fiction. She is alone with a man she would never even have dreamed of previously. In truth, she would have kissed him the very minute he'd shut the door of this room, if she had been brave enough to do it.

Then his lips are on hers, and a surge of adrenaline runs through Nita, as she realises that their first kiss hadn't been a mistake, or a dream, or an embarrassment. And as his hands set off to journey around her body, Nita surrenders herself to him. With each caress, he brushes away a cruel jibe thrown at her by a schoolground bully, a cutting aside delivered by her mother, a muttered rejection from a potential suitor. In this moment she is a woman, a woman who is wanted. And when he lays her down on the bed and she feels his weight and his heat, she does not even consider whether this is the right course of action. Frankly, this is the only course of action, she thinks, in between short, frantic breaths. This, yes, this, yes, is all the world, right here, yes, in this bed, with these hands and this body. *Yes.*

15

BETH

November 2008

Beth opens the creaking, heavy door that leads out into the garden from the kitchen and discovers that frost has enveloped Melham Manor overnight. The berries on the shrubs nearby glitter in the early morning sun and the grass crunches underfoot.

Stanley, their six-year-old Staffordshire bull terrier, runs past her eagerly, desperate for his morning pee. He's also probably on the scent of a squirrel or a rabbit, she thinks, both of which he will thankfully fail to find. He'd be a terrible hunting dog, but he's a gorgeous family pet – definitely a lover, not a fighter. He hasn't shown any interest in the numerous cats that roam the garden, or in Roger the rooster, who Rowan has thankfully returned to his large, secure run in the garden for the duration of their stay.

Beth pulls on her coat and shuts the door behind her. Her breath is visible in the freezing air, and there are two little clouds apparently floating above both Raphie and Ella, who are making their way at some speed across the grass, towards the woods.

'Come on, Mummy! Come on!'

Beth had mentioned at breakfast that she'd once played on a large swing strung from one of the large oak trees in the woods, and the children had seized upon this idea and refused to let go. She has fond memories of swinging on it for hours, alone. Philippa had never wanted to play outside, and Beth hadn't really minded. She had enjoyed the solitude. She doubts the swing will still be there, but she's so enjoying the children's laughter and their joy at being outside that she doesn't much care. Their tiny London garden has hardly any room for them to play. So this morning, this glorious autumnal morning, Beth is determined to take full advantage of the space Melham Manor provides. If they don't find the swing, she thinks, perhaps they can make a den out of fallen branches and leaves, or hunt for bugs under rocks in the stream that runs at the bottom of the hill. Anything, frankly, to prolong their time out here, away from screens, away from London, away from David and the hinterland of their separation.

'I'm coming.'

Within minutes they've left the lawn and the raised beds behind, and the children are barrelling down a path that wends its way into the woods.

'How far is it, Mummy?' asks Raphie, slowing down, his cheeks rosy red.

Beth looks around her. There aren't too many landmarks around, but she remembers that the tree with the swing comes just after a fork in the path, and she can see one ahead.

'It might be just over there,' she says, picking up her pace, the children's enthusiasm rubbing off on her. And she's right. Just twenty paces later, she's standing in front of a small clearing, and at its heart is a large tree with low branches. Hanging off one of them is a large wooden swing, big enough for an adult to sit on.

'It's here!' shouts Raphie, making a beeline for it, with Ella in hot pursuit. Beth foresees an argument when they both want to try it out first, so she jogs towards them, reaching the swing when they do.

'Why don't you both get on it? There's room enough,' she says, and they agree. She lifts Ella up onto it. 'Hold onto her, Raphie, OK? Don't let her fall backwards.'

'OK,' he replies, eager to get going.

Beth pushes them, and they shriek with delight.

'Higher, Mummy. Higher,' they shout, and Beth obliges.

And then she remembers something.

She can hear Nita's voice.

'Come with me, child,' she'd said, and Beth had done as she'd been asked. Young Beth had adored Auntie Nita. She'd allowed Beth to play with things her parents disapproved of, and let her run wild in the garden, far from her father's disapproving eyes. Not her mother's, however, because Marisa would never have been looking her way. If she'd been at the Manor at all, rather than on some kind of literary tour, she'd have always been tucked away in the library, writing, with a negroni by her side. She'd never seemed to enjoy her visits to the house. But yes, Beth remembers now; Nita had brought her into the woods on more than one occasion. She wonders whether her great-aunt had ever pushed her on the swing. She doesn't remember that, but she does remember something else: the warm earth beneath her, a candle flickering in the breeze, Nita's hand in hers, and a feeling of warmth and safety.

A flash of colour catches Beth's eye and brings her back to the present. It's something red. At first she thinks it might be a bird, perhaps a robin, but then there's another colour, pink this time, and then orange. As she pushes her children back and forth, she realises they're coloured ribbons, tied onto the tree's lower branches.

'Ah, you've found the clotties.'

Beth turns and sees that Rowan is standing a few metres away. She hadn't heard her approach.

'Sorry, I didn't mean to startle you,' the older woman says, reacting to Beth's obvious surprise. Then she waves at Raphie and Ella, who wave back happily.

'Oh, I was in a world of my own,' replies Beth, still pushing her children on the swing. 'Sorry. Clotties – is that what they're called?'

'Yes.'

'What are they for, do you know?'

'Each ribbon represents a prayer,' Rowan replies. 'It's believed that the spirit that lives in the tree – in the trees – will answer them.'

'Who leaves them here? I thought this was Melham Manor land?'

Beth wonders, a bit late, whether the ribbons are Rowan's doing.

'Well, the woods aren't really private now, not like they were when you were young. People walk their dogs here, and bring their friends and their lovers. You know how it is. There isn't much of a fence, anyway.'

'Ah, yes. That woman I was talking to at the fireworks said she walked in these woods.'

'Yes, it's quite a popular option, locally. That's happened really since Nita started taking in local animals. People got to know she wouldn't mind if they brought their dogs here.'

'So much has changed,' Beth says. 'In some ways, I feel like a stranger here now.' She pauses. 'Oh, by the way, I meant to send you a message earlier, but I got sidetracked. I wanted to say thank you for last night. It was so kind of you to bring the kids back for me.'

'Honestly, any time. We had fun. They're lovely kids. Was it useful time?'

'Oh, no. Well, it did help me look at the archives, but I didn't find what I was looking for.'

'Is this for a story you're working on for the paper?'

'No. Well, maybe. It's about... something I found in the attic. Something of Nita's.'

'Oh?'

Beth wonders whether she should tell Rowan. After all, Nita had kept that box hidden from everyone, hadn't she? And she'd said there were secrets in it. But then, she's dead now, and who will she tell? And also, Beth realises Rowan knew Nita far better than she had ever done. It occurs to her that perhaps she might know something about her great-aunt's search for a spy.

'Before Nita died, she told me there was a box in the attic she wanted me to look at. She said there were secrets in it.'

'Goodness.'

'Yes. I know. So I went up there and looked through it. There were lots of clippings from when she'd been a journalist, during the war. Most of them were just run-of-the-mill stuff, but there was a separate folder called "X" and in it were lots and lots of notes, some of them in shorthand, about suspicions there was a Nazi spy, or spy ring, operating in the local area. She'd helped to write stories about it, and it seems it became an obsession for her. She called this potential Nazi "X". She'd written "Where is X?" and "Is he still in England?" over articles from *The Bugle*. But the really interesting thing was what was written on a piece of card, in large, clear writing, at the front of the file. It was a string of numbers, with "Where is X?" at the top. It was like she left a clue for me to follow, you know? I had thought maybe it was a reference to something in *The Bugle* archives. That's why I was there.'

'And was it?'

'No. Their files are all in alphabetical order. I looked for anything numerical – dates of publication, stuff like that – but nothing worked.'

'Curious.' They stand in companionable silence for a minute or so, listening to the children's shrieks of delight and the rustling of the leaves in the tree canopy overhead. 'Have you tried the library? The local library, I mean?'

Beth raises an eyebrow.

'No. Not yet. Will they have newspaper archives and stuff?'

'Yes, they might, and local history books, things like that. I volunteer there one day a week. A group of us campaigned to keep it open a few years ago. Anyway it's a lovely little place, near the church. It wouldn't hurt to try.'

'Wow, thank you. That's a great thought. I'm assuming it's not open today, though, it being Sunday?'

'Yes. Sadly, it's actually only open for half of the week. But if you can make it down on a Tuesday or Thursday morning, Friday all day or Saturday morning, I'm sure whoever's on shift there will be happy to help.'

Beth files this information away. She has a long-dreaded dinner with her parents to deal with first, but she definitely wants to discover what the numbers mean. Because for some reason, Nita's quest has now become her own.

16

NITA

5 December 1940

It's a bright, cold morning and Nita has a spring in her step as she walks down the high street towards the offices of *The Bugle*. It's her second month at the paper and although she's still not being paid, her parents are now allowing her to 'volunteer' five days a week. Although it's been a steep learning curve and she's still essentially a secretary with some writing privileges, she's never had freedom like this before. It's intoxicating.

And then, of course, there's Joe.

He is an entirely unexpected, extraordinary part of her life now. In fact, if you were measuring impact based on the amount of time her brain spends thinking about him, you could argue that he is now in fact the *main* part of her life. It's unbelievable, frankly, that their relationship is still a secret. She is surprised other people can't tell how she feels about him, and what they have been doing together in the park at lunchtime – and, with some careful planning, in the room he's renting from an elderly lady – from her behaviour and her expressions. Surely she must have changed outwardly, she thinks, given how much she's changed inwardly. As she strides along the street, taking in the Christmas displays in the windows – slightly toned down due to the war and the shortage of paper, but still there in defiance – she feels like the way she walks, the way she now holds herself, must give her away. She's finally beginning to love her body, and what it is capable of.

Joe hasn't just taught her about her body, of course. She's learned so much from him about journalism, too. They've been working together on stories about the search for the spy, or spy ring, in the area. There's been no real update on the police hunt so far, and a great deal of worry among local residents. The paper has been receiving multiple letters every day from people convinced their neighbour, friend or colleague is a spy, even if there's no German heritage anywhere in their bloodline. There have also been a few other break-ins which may be linked – or may in many cases, Nita suspects, simply be local ne'er-do-wells taking advantage of this Nazi spy hysteria to commit crime. The paper has been putting out stories designed to reassure local people, at the encouragement of the local police, who Nita knows have visited Bridges on several occasions. It doesn't do to cause panic in wartime.

As well as reporting on these stories, Joe has also been helping her with her shorthand, which she works on every evening after dinner. It's a fabulous excuse to avoid having to talk to her parents. She's also learned how to write in short, snappy sentences; that you should always put your first quote in the third paragraph; and that news stories are like inverted triangles. You put the most important information at the top, and by the bottom of the story, you're getting to the 'interesting to know' things, not the 'need to know'. She's also now more confident about talking to people she's never met before, of whatever class they happen to be. She can feel her years of trussed-up mock aristocracy starting to fall away from her. *And that*, she thinks as she walks past a dress shop playing Christmas carols on the wireless, *is a wonderful feeling.*

'Good morning, Miss Bineham,' says Bridges as she pushes the door open at the top of the steps, and walks into the newsroom, casting her eye around for Joe, who she can see isn't in yet. He's the first person she always looks for. 'Would you mind coming into my office when you've hung up your coat?'

Nita is taken aback. Bridges hasn't wanted to see her in private since her little rant about not wanting to be treated as a secretary. She wonders what she's done wrong. She leaves her satchel by her desk, hangs up her coat and follows him into his office.

'Take a seat, Nita,' he says, dropping the 'Miss Bineham' as soon as they are alone. She finds this unpleasant, as if he's unilaterally decided they are now close acquaintances. Nita does not want to be close to Mr Bridges, ever.

She sits in silence, waiting for him to say whatever he feels he needs to say. Perhaps she's made a mistake in one of the engagement or marriage write-ups or let an error in an advertisement slip through the net. *Whatever it is, I can take it*, she thinks. *I'm a different woman now. A stronger woman.*

'I have good news for you,' he says. She's suddenly more alert. This is not what she expected. 'I've spoken to your father and he has agreed to me offering you a salaried position here at *The Bugle*, as a junior reporter.'

She can't believe what she's hearing. This is beyond her wildest dreams. Two months ago she was calcifying at home, barely able to choose when to breathe, and now she's being offered a proper professional job. A chance to be independent and perhaps to achieve the dream of dreams – to have her own place where she can be in control of her own destiny.

'Goodness. I don't know what to say.'

'Well, I do hope you'll say yes. After all, we'll be one short when Joseph Miller leaves us, so we'll need you.'

All of Nita's joy dissipates in an instant.

'Joe... Mr Miller is leaving?'

'Yes, I'm afraid so. I knew he'd be called up eventually, of course. He's rather lucky it's taken them this long to get around to him. I know he did write to them telling them his position here should be protected, but I understand the authorities are less and less inclined to agree.'

Nita feels a wave of nausea crash over her. She needs to get out of this room.

'I... have a story to write.'

'Ah. yes, of course. Mustn't distract you from the job in hand. But do I take it it's a yes?'

Nita is already standing up.

'Yes... yes,' she says as she turns.

'Excellent,' he says, just before she shuts the door.

She walks towards the back of the office on autopilot, through the door which leads to the staff toilet. It's not somewhere anyone would ever want to spend too long. It's dusty, there are suspicious sticky patches on the linoleum floor, and there's at least one resident spider. But, at the moment, it's the only place where Nita can cry in private, so she walks inside and bolts the door.

Her tears of confusion, frustration and devastation are already falling by the time she sits down on the lowered toilet lid. She wonders why she had to find out like this. *Why didn't Joe tell me himself?* she thinks. *And more importantly, what on earth am I going to do without him?*

* * *

'Nita? Are you in there?'

Joe has arrived. He's talking to her through the toilet door. Nita isn't sure how long she's been crying in here, but it's certainly been at least five minutes. Long enough for her colleagues to notice her absence, anyway, and perhaps to work out that she's upset.

'Ye-es,' she replies, her voice breaking slightly.

'Are you all right?'

She takes some toilet paper and blows her nose, lifts the lid to drop it in the toilet, and pulls the long handle to flush. While she waits for this to happen, she grabs more paper and dabs around her eyes, trying to clear up the worst of the damage. She doesn't mind him seeing her like this – after all, he has seen her in the raw now, absolutely vulnerable. She does mind her colleagues seeing her like this, however. Especially as she's now about to be brought onto the staff. She slides the bolt back across and opens the door. He is standing in the tiny corridor outside, beneath a single bare bulb.

'I'm...' she says, intending to tell him how she feels about him leaving and him not telling her about it first, but she finds she can't get the words out. 'I'm...'

'I'm so sorry, Nita. Bridges told me he offered you my job, and that I'd been called up. I'm so sorry you had to hear it from him. I meant to tell you yesterday, but I had to go out on a story, as you know, and then the bus was delayed this morning and I didn't get in as early as I'd hoped...'

'You're leaving,' she says, realising she cares far less about how the news was delivered to her and far more about the reality the news brings with it. 'You're going away.' She starts to cry again, unable to contain the feeling of wretchedness that's overtaking her, because this man has become everything to her. He represents her new-found freedom, and all that's good and exciting.

He's unlocked a hidden world of joy and euphoria, and she knows that if he leaves her life, he'll take it with him. Perhaps forever.

'I've got to go, Nita. They've written to me now. I can't refuse it. But, my darling, you know I don't want to go. I never want to leave you, ever.' He pulls her to him, and despite the fact they are in the office and anyone could walk in on them at any moment, Nita allows it to happen. She sinks into him, her tears soaking into his green woollen jumper. 'Look, I'm sure I won't go far,' he says, as he runs his hands through her hair. 'It's the Army. They'll send me to a training camp first, and that will be in England. I'll write every day. I'll get leave. It will be fine. We will still see each other, I promise.'

Nita wants to believe this, desperately. But she also knows that when he leaves the paper, they will no longer have a ready excuse to be alone together. There will be no more press conferences necessitating overnight stays, no stories that she needs to accompany him on as part of her 'training'.

The irony of this situation is devastating, because she will be working here at the paper, finally doing a job she's long dreamed of, but she will be doing it with a broken heart. And despite the promises they are undoubtedly going to make to each other, she knows that things will simply never be the same again.

17

BETH

December 2008

It's 6 p.m., and another long winter night has begun. The twinkling Christmas lights and the elegant festive window displays in the upmarket boutiques on the King's Road are doing their best to fight it off, however, and there's the odd blast of 'Last Christmas' and 'Jingle Bell Rock' coming out of shops and restaurants as Beth walks past.

This is an area of London Beth knows well, because her parents live here, still occupying the house she grew up in. Beth pulls the hood of her coat up to ward off the drizzle which has just started to fall and continues to walk down the road in the direction of Albert Bridge, then takes a side road to the right.

A few minutes later, she arrives outside an elegant Georgian townhouse. Warm white lights are strung around the columns of the portico and wrapped elegantly around topiary so well trimmed, it could be fake. Beth knows it isn't, of course. Her parents spend a fortune paying a gardener to trim it twice a week.

Said gardener probably also put up the Christmas lights, she thinks, approaching the door, or perhaps they've found some ludicrously expensive designer to do it for them instead. It wouldn't be the first time. In fact, that sort of thing is de rigueur in Chelsea.

She rings the bell and waits. A minute later, her mother answers.

'Darling! Do come in.'

Beth leans in for the expected air kiss and catches a whiff of gin on her mother's breath. She is not surprised. Marisa Bineham shuts the door behind them and Beth is hit by an onslaught of Christmas.

An expensive candle is burning in an alcove to the right, infusing the hallway with the scent of frankincense and myrrh. Immediately behind it is a hand-crafted nativity scene. Straight ahead of her are elegant stairs adorned with ivy, and to the left of the staircase sits an eight-foot real pine tree, lit with warm white lights and decorated with glass baubles. Her mother has really gone to town. She does so every year, in fact. Her Catholic upbringing combined with her love of parties makes Christmas her favourite season.

It's only when Beth follows her mother into the kitchen that she realises something is wrong. Her father is sitting at the table nursing a very large glass of white wine. There are two issues with this picture. One, he's usually in his office at the top of the house unless food is actually being served, and two, he rarely drinks.

'Dad?'

Robert Bineham looks up at his daughter.

'Hello, darling.'

Beth sits down opposite him, as her mother places another glass in front of her and starts to pour.

'What's up?' Beth asks.

'Your father had some bad news at work today,' Marisa sits at the end of the table and gulps down the wine she has just poured for herself. Robert shoots a withering glance at his wife. 'What? You need to tell her. She'll find out soon enough, anyway.'

Robert now has his head in his hands. His two thumbs are going back and forth across his forehead, rubbing vigorously.

'Yes... so... the shareholders aren't happy,' he says, after a pause.

'Are they still unhappy with what I said...' Beth's shame and guilt over what happened are still bubbling under the surface.

'Goodness, no, we're way beyond that. Don't you read the papers?'

Beth shakes her head. She feels chastised, as she often does by her parents. He does have a point, however. She hasn't kept up with either the newspapers or the TV news since David told her he wanted a divorce. She's had enough drama in her own life to deal with, without welcoming the rest of the world in.

'Property prices are dropping,' her father says. 'The markets are in chaos. Our share price has tanked.'

'Oh.'

'Yes, *oh*.'

'What does that mean?'

Robert gives her a withering stare.

'It means we could be in real trouble.' He takes another sip of wine.

'I see.'

'Do you?'

'Yes,' says Beth, frustrated at his blatant lack of faith in her knowledge. After all, she's worked in the business since university. 'Yes. I assume the value of our assets have tanked, we're laden with debt and we're going to have to take some pretty hideous measures to stay afloat.'

'Yes, that's about it.' He slumps in his chair.

'I'm sure it'll get better,' says Beth, but her attempt at optimism is met with silence.

'Perhaps.'

They sit in silence for a moment, until they're interrupted by the doorbell.

'Ah, dinner has arrived.' Marisa gets up to answer the door, her eagerness at escaping the kitchen quite obvious. She wobbles slightly as she stands, before regaining her equilibrium.

'Your mother is back to her old tricks,' says Robert, as soon as she's out of earshot.

Beth raises an eyebrow. Her mother had been drinking at the funeral, too. This is not news. Marisa's relationship with alcohol is cyclical. She spends months, perhaps years, ramping up consumption, then reaches an abject low at some stage, followed by AA meetings and a period of monastic abstinence, during which time she finds she can't write. And then the drinking begins once more.

'And you too, by the look of it.' She eyes her father's glass.

'Only tonight. Special occasions only,' he says with a hollow laugh.

'Are you coping OK, both of you? Aside from the problems with the business?'

'Oh, well, your mother's writing continues to bring in a very healthy income, if that's what you mean.'

'It's not what I mean. I meant – are you two OK?'

She has always known that her parents' marriage is permanently balanced on a tightrope. Marisa is mercurial; brilliant, funny and beautiful, but also unpredictable, depressive, and given to an anger that occasionally spills over into violence. Beth and

Philippa were often sent to bed at night to the soundtrack of flying plates and unrestrained rage.

'Yes. Well, to be perfectly frank I've hardly been here for the past couple of months, so it's impossible to say.'

'Here we go! The very best the Bluebird Cafe has to offer.' Marisa surges into the room bearing two large, ornately decorated paper bags and thumping them down on the kitchen surface.

This takeaway is not an unusual affair. Marisa rarely cooks, and Robert never does. Beth suspects they are on first name terms with all the delivery drivers in the area.

'Lovely,' says Beth automatically, walking over to the cupboards and retrieving plates, cutlery and serving spoons.

'So how are things with you and David?' asks Marisa, taking a seat with a clunk.

'Oh, the same. He's still angry I took your – my – lawyer's advice about not going to mediation. I understand he's trying to get the money together to buy me out of the house. We're barely speaking.' Beth places plates down and doles out food, because it's clear neither of her parents are going to do it.

'And how are my two wonderful grandchildren?'

Beth smiles. This topic at least is not too painful.

'They're doing well, despite everything.' They had sat them down as planned, a few days after their return from Dubai, and explained that Mummy and Daddy were going to live in different houses soon, but that they still loved them. Perhaps because of their very young age, neither Raphie nor Ella have seemed too worried about it. Or at least, not yet. 'I suppose they haven't noticed much change so far,' she says, as a flash of a potential future appears in her mind, of a different, smaller house, and of many nights spent alone in it, the children's beds empty. A shiver runs down her spine. 'Yes, they're both really happy at school,' she continues, her voice unnaturally light.

'That's good. You must bring them to visit.' Marisa always says this. It doesn't occur to her that she could also come to visit them in Hampstead. It's hardly another continent, Beth thinks. If she asks Marisa why she doesn't come to see them, she always mutters something vague about edits, or a new draft, or a meeting with an editor. Beth suspects that the reality is that while Marisa likes the idea of being a parent and a grandparent, she finds the actual practicalities of it rather boring.

'I will,' Beth takes the path of least resistance, as she always does.

'How's that lawyer we found for you?' asks Robert.

'Oh, he seems good,' says Beth, although in truth, she hasn't warmed to him. He's certainly efficient and suitably ruthless, but she's found she doesn't want to tell him what she really wants.

'Excellent.'

'Oh, I forgot to tell you, darling,' says Marisa. 'We heard back from the antiques dealer. He found quite an inventory of inter-esting things during his visit to Melham Manor, so thank you for facilitating that. It will be good to get that shifted, ahead of us putting it on the market.'

Beth is halfway through taking a sip of wine, and splutters so hard she almost chokes.

'You're going to do what?'

'Oh, I thought you realised. We're going to sell it,' says her father, who's chasing a piece of chicken around his plate with his fork. 'It's time to get rid. With the state of the markets, it's frankly a good time. We need to realise some assets.'

'But it's our home. Our family home.' Beth puts down her knife and fork and takes a few deep breaths. This news has hit her hard.

'Hardly. We're not landed gentry! It's only been in the family a couple of generations. And none of us have spent any time there for absolutely years, have we? And it's in a dreadful state, anyway. You saw that for yourself.'

'But it's... special to me.' Memories of time spent there populate Beth's mind; of bonfires in the woods, of blowing dandelions on sultry days, of skipping through the corridors, carefree.

'Oh, come on, darling. I thought you'd be over that by now,' says Marisa.

'Over what?'

'Your childish love of that place... It was always ridiculous.'

Beth is nonplussed. She had no idea her mother looked on her childhood experiences in this way.

'You never liked Nita, did you, Mum?'

'Nita was mad, darling. Absolutely mad.' Robert doesn't contradict her. Beth knows that her parents disapproved of Nita, but she's been thinking of her a lot recently and she remembers a kind, funny woman. A woman she enjoyed spending time with.

'In what way was she mad?'

'You've seen the state she let that place get in to? That's like a visual representation of her mind. She lost touch with reality, with sense, a long time ago.'

'If you say so.' Beth knows from experience that there's no point arguing. 'So... Do you have someone lined up to buy the Manor, Dad? I assume you do. You always have a plan.'

'I do, actually,' he answers. Beth notices that his cheeks are now both bright red. 'A developer I know wants to turn the house into apartments and build a small, exclusive estate of executive houses in the grounds. They'll clear a few of the trees, and then they'll all have fabulous views over the valley and a great deal of privacy. I expect they'll fetch a tidy sum, even in this market.'

'Houses? Apartments?'

'Of course. You didn't expect it would be sold as a private home, did you? Not when it's got so much land. It's worth too much broken up. And anyway, we all know that we need to build more housing in this country. It's obscene, one family owning that much property just for itself.'

Beth knows that her father doesn't mean this at all. He's trying to sound socialist and appealing – a mode he trots out for newspaper interviews – but really he's just thinking about the bottom line. They'll make much more money if the estate is developed into lots of small units. Not units for locals or people on lower incomes, of course, she thinks. 'Executive' homes are not for the poor.

Beth thinks about the single mother whose mouldy home she visited, about the users of the food bank in the village hall, about the patch of land the counsellor she interviewed is hoping to use for a local housing project. What will those people make of the news that Melham Manor will soon be for sale to the highest bidder? And then there's Rowan. What, she wonders, will she think when the raised beds are dismantled, and flowers and trees uprooted? And what would Nita have thought? Beth shudders. Just thinking about it is painful. It feels like a terrible betrayal.

And then she has an idea.

'Do we have to sell it? Why can't Stellar do the development instead? We could retain control, make sure that the house is sympathetically refurbished. We could reserve some of the units for local people on average wages, couldn't we? What do you think?'

Marisa and Robert don't reply immediately. They're staring at Beth as if she has two heads.

'Bloody hell, girl,' says her father, after another glug of wine. 'No wonder your department head is making noises about moving you on. You've got no idea about business, or life in general, come to that. Absolutely no idea at all.'

Beth is not normally given to anger. She's anxious enough,

without thousands of angry exchanges replaying daily in her head. She's learned over the years that life is much easier for her to deal with if she avoids confrontation and aggression.

But not today.

She has spent her entire lifetime doing pretty much whatever her parents have told her to do. They'd allowed her a small rebellion, taking English Literature at A level rather than Economics, but apart from that she had done the required Business degree (passing with a low 2:2); joined the family firm as expected; danced attention upon her parents when required; and played second fiddle to Philippa with very little complaint. The only thing she has ever actually done against their advice, she realises, is to marry David. Not that that's worked out, of course, but she refuses to regret her marriage or the children that resulted from it. Yes, apart from that, she's always gone along with what her parents want because they hold all the purse strings. And also, she realises, she just wants to please. She hates upsetting people, hates them thinking bad of her.

And she knows it's this behaviour that has brought her here, into this kitchen with her two very drunk parents. She has a failed relationship, is essentially unemployed, and scared about what the future might bring. But she is also angry. And that's what gives her the confidence to do something she has never done before. She bites back.

'I know far more than you give me credit for, Dad.' Beth pushes back her chair and throws her napkin onto the table. She is no longer hungry. 'I know that your marriage is deeply unhappy. I know that Mum is an alcoholic. I know that you are a workaholic and that you'll probably work yourself to death. And believe it or not, I *do* understand economic theory, I know what a recession is and I understand its implications on the family business. But you know what? I don't care. I don't care about any of it.

I'm going home now, and when I get there I'm going to write a letter of resignation. You'll have it by first thing tomorrow morning. I'm leaving Stellar.' She pushes her chair back under the table and walks at pace towards the door. 'Oh, and Happy Christmas.'

18

NITA

18 December 1940

It's 6 a.m. and still dark when Nita silences her alarm clock, turns on the lamp on her bedside table, wraps herself in her wool dressing gown, walks over to the small desk in her bedroom and sits down. She needs to leave at seven thirty to get to work on time, but she has a letter to write first.

Melham Manor
18th December 1940

My darling Joe,

It's been a fortnight since you left, and I feel so wretched about it I'm amazed I am still able to breathe. I can't help but dwell on the way it felt to have to say goodbye to you in front of our colleagues. I had to fight the urge to grab your hand, to hold you. The few minutes we managed in private together that afternoon in the kitchen were never going to be enough, but

*they are all I have, and so I am going to cling to them as best
I can.*

*How are you doing, my love? Your first letter was such a
tonic to receive.*

Nita pauses and pulls out a folded letter from a compartment
in the desk. The paper, presumably Army issue, is particularly
thin and she's been very careful to store it out of harm's way. She
unfolds it slowly and reads it. She knows it by heart now, but
holding something Joe has also recently touched gives her
comfort. It's dated 8 December, just two days after Joe left Surrey
for training.

It begins:

Hello, my love,

*I do hope you're keeping well and not missing me too
badly. I must say I'm missing you a great deal. This place feels
like a different world to the one we've been inhabiting together.
The journey up here was lengthy – you know how unreliable the
trains are at present – and I was utterly exhausted when I
arrived. But there has been no rest for the wicked...*

He goes on to detail his uncomfortable sleeping quarters, the
exhausting and frustrating drills, the men he's met already and
their shouty sergeant major. And then at the end, there is her
favourite part.

*I am finding it impossible to stop thinking about the moments
we've shared. They were so special to me. Your love has transformed me and made me see things more clearly. I promise.
Nita, I absolutely promise that when this is all over, we will be
together. Forever. You have my word.*

All my love,
Joe

Nita folds the letter back up and clasps it to her chest for a moment, allowing the power of the message it contains to recharge her heart. Then she returns it to its hiding place and continues to write her own letter.

I was so pleased to hear you'd arrived safely in Yorkshire at the training base. I hope you've been receiving my letters? I've been writing every day. I'm not sure how efficient the military post is. I have been desperately hoping to receive a reply from you every morning, but I imagine that they are keeping you busy, and perhaps they don't give you time to write in the first week. It was like that when Frank was sent to boarding school. They wouldn't let him write to us until the first half-term, which I thought was absolutely brutal.

Things are going along here as well as can be expected. I'm turning up at work each morning at the paper and going through the motions. We are still running lots of stories about suspected German spies, although none of them seem to be our mysterious X so far. I am still looking, however; still asking questions of everyone I meet and keeping copious notes. We must find him, or them, even. People around here talk of little else. They suspect the spy to be behind everything. Someone broke into the Melham cricket pavilion a few days ago, and they even think he's somehow responsible for that! I can't imagine what secrets they think might be kept in there.

Anyhow, I must go and eat breakfast and prepare myself for another day. I am thinking of you always, my darling. Write soon.

All my love,

Nita

Nita puts down her pen and folds the letter carefully. As she addresses the envelope and places it inside, she reflects that she now has two men in her life to write to and worry about. Frank, her brother, and now Joe. At least Joe is in Britain, for the time being at least. Frank, meanwhile, is still out in north Africa and the news from that part of the world is scant, and his letters are achingly rare. They are just grateful no telegrams have been delivered to their house with news. No news, as they say, is good news, in this hideous war at least.

Nita eats her breakfast in the dining room in blissful silence. Her parents are rarely up at this time, and this is a huge relief. Her mother has been talking about potential husbands again, something that Nita is even more violently against now than she ever was. She knows the only man she will ever marry is Joe. His letter to her makes his intentions clear. She knows accepting him will mean her parents will cut her off completely, but this thought excites rather than worries her. She has never fitted into this family and its expectations, and she has a profession now, a proper profession and she is certain she will be able to make her own way in the world with it.

This thought carries her through her morning of work, which involves interviewing a butcher who thinks he may have served a German spy the previous week due to his pronunciation of the word 'yes' as 'yaas' and writing a piece about the drive to recruit local women as Land Girls, helping to keep farms going now so many of the men have been sent off to fight.

At lunchtime, she wraps up warmly and heads out to the bakery down the street to buy a sandwich. Despite rationing, the shop still smells of the twin seasonal spices, cloves and nutmeg, and there are paper chains wrapped around the till.

'Nita! How wonderful to see you. Ham and salad?'

She's become something of a regular and the woman serving her, Mrs Schofield, knows her by name.

'Yes please,' she replies, aware that due to the shortages, there will be vastly more salad in it than ham. She digs into her purse for the money she needs, but in doing so drops several coins all over the floor.

'Argh, why am I so clumsy?' she exclaims, and bends down to pick them up, only to find there's another woman down on the floor, helping her.

'There you go,' she says, handing her two coins. Nita is surprised to see it's Harriet Morgan, the woman she'd interviewed about the coven and its attempt to thwart Hitler.

'Oh, thank you,' says Nita. 'And it's nice to see you again.'

'You too,' replies Harriet, smiling.

The two women wait companionably while Mrs Schofield makes their sandwiches, before walking out together into the weak winter sunshine.

'I meant to thank you, Nita, for the article you wrote for *The Bugle*,' Harriet says when they're safely outside the shop.

'Oh! Thank you.' This is something new Nita has discovered. People now sometimes talk to her about stories she's written, and it can be either exhilarating if they've loved it, or intensely awkward if they haven't. But Harriet clearly falls into the former camp, thank goodness.

'Honestly, I had worried you'd do a hatchet job about warty faces and mad old women, but you reported it straight down the line, which I admired.'

'Goodness,' says Nita, her cheeks undoubtedly glowing, and not just with the cold. 'Did you do it? The Cone of Power?'

'We did.'

'And Hitler still hasn't invaded,' says Nita with a smile.

'He hasn't,' replies Harriet, her matching smile hard to read.

Nita wonders whether Harriet really believes that she's somehow repelled Hitler, or whether she's prepared to accept the role of chance.

'I had been meaning to ring you, actually,' says Nita. 'Do you remember you told me about a darkness closer to home?'

'I do.'

'I wasn't sure what to make of it... I apologise for not asking more about it at the time, about what you meant. But it did stick in my mind and now that we are all looking for this German spy, I wondered... How did you know about it?'

Harriet is still smiling, but she has a look in her eye, and Nita finds her hard to read.

'Why don't you come round to see me at my house some time, and I'll tell you what I meant,' she says.

'All right, I'll do that.'

'Just call me up when you have time to spare. After Christmas, perhaps. You have my number.'

'I will.'

'Goodbye, then,' says Harriet, waving goodbye as she walks in the opposite direction, up the street.

'Goodbye,' replies Nita, wondering, as she takes her first hungry bite into her sandwich, what this enigmatic, clever woman wants to tell her.

19

BETH

20 December 2008

Beth is singing along to 'Stay Another Day' on the radio in her car when her phone starts to ring, cutting both the song and her singing voice off in their prime.

'Hello,' she answers, through her hands-free kit.

'Beth. It's David.'

He's away on another work trip, somewhere in the north of England.

'Yep,' she says, not at all bothered that he sounds angry. Because she's also angry, very angry, and she's decided that it's time to stop caring how he feels about everything. It's time, she thinks, to focus on how *she* feels. She wonders if he ever gives her feelings any consideration at all now.

'You left early. Where are you?'

'I'm driving down to Melham. I need to do some research.'

'For what?'

'A project I'm working on.' Beth has not told him the real reason: that she's trying to find out more about Nita's secret mission to locate a Nazi spy, and that she's also reeling from her parents' decision to sell Melham Manor. She feels the need to visit the house again, to soak up its atmosphere, to immerse herself in the woods, to spend time there just being, not doing.

'Right. And this would be... for Stellar, would it?'

'No, as you know, they suspended me.' David doesn't know she's resigned yet. She's trying to find alternative employment and she doesn't want to tell him until she finds it. She hasn't had any joy yet, but she *will* find something, she thinks. Eventually.

'Is this project something you're being paid for?'

'Not much at the moment, no,' she replies. 'Which is why I sent you the message this morning telling you I need more money to buy Christmas presents for the children. I don't have enough, since you excluded me from the current account.'

'I've been giving you an allowance every month for the kids' sundries.'

'Well, let me tell you, that doesn't buy many Lego sets, David.'

'So you haven't bought the kids anything for Christmas yet?'

Beth suppresses a laugh. The fact he's only just thought about the kids' Christmas lists now, less than a week before the big day, is a brilliant example of his selfishness. Why, she wonders, is it that a mother should always be the one to think about this, to do the leg work for it, even if she's just as busy as her partner? He absolutely could have done it, but he hasn't.

She's actually been buying presents since August and has quite a number secreted away, but she's not going to tell him that.

'No.'

His announcement two days ago that he wanted the kids to spend Christmas lunch at his parents' house, without her, had been the final straw. She'll get to see them in the morning and the evening, apparently, and this is supposed to be sufficient. Her heart aches just thinking about it.

'For God's sake, Beth. We promised when we started this that we wouldn't take it out on the children.'

This time, Beth does laugh. How, she thinks, is refusing to let their mother spend Christmas lunch with them *not* taking it out on the children?

'And they will have presents,' she replies. 'If we sort this. I have a whole load in my Amazon basket ready to check out. I just need some money from you for them. We can go halves if you like.'

'How much?'

'About a hundred quid should cover your share.'

She hears him swallow. *Probably an expensive flat white*, she thinks.

'Fine. I'll give you the cash later.'

'Good.'

'I'll see you when I get back tomorrow.'

'Right,' she says, and clicks the call off before she rants at him about being away again and taking her ability to do the school pick up today and childcare tonight entirely for granted. He'll find that out soon enough, when he's living by himself.

* * *

About half an hour later, Beth pulls into the small car park next to Melham library. It's a utilitarian, brown-brick, single-storey, eighties building, constructed by the local council after the previous site, Edwardian and purpose-built, was sold for development. She locks her car and walks up to the entrance with care, as an overnight frost has made the pavement hazardous.

She opens the door and is greeted by the sound of children laughing. She looks over to the corner of the small library and sees that story time is in progress. A group of parents and small children are gathered on bean bags in the corner, and a woman is reading a book Beth recognises – *Father Christmas Needs a Wee*. It's one of her kids' favourites and she stands near the unmanned front desk listening to it, enjoying its gentle, peculiarly British humour which focuses on all of the drinks Father Christmas is given in everyone's homes, and the inevitable human need to find a toilet. Because, of course, Father Christmas is human.

'It's a clever one, isn't it,' says a female librarian who Beth thinks must have just emerged from the back room. She had been too busy listening to the story to notice. 'So funny and such lovely pictures, too.'

'Yes, my kids make me read it every night at the moment. That, and *Santa's Suit*.'

'Well, children enjoying books is very much our purpose in life, so I'm glad to hear that,' says the librarian.

Beth smiles.

'I was hoping you might be able to help me,' she says, drawing in closer to the desk, keen for her voice not to distract the children's reading session. 'It's a bit of a strange one...'

Beth pulls out the sheet with 'Where is X?' at the top and the string of numbers underneath it and explains briefly what she's trying to find out, and that her friend Rowan had suggested the library might be able to help work out what the numbers relate to.

'Well, Rowan is right,' says the librarian, taking the sheet of paper from Beth and placing it down next to her keyboard. 'We do have a numerical system. Let's see if this corresponds to any of the books we have in the district.'

Beth waits while the librarian taps the numbers into the online catalogue.

'Aha,' she says, a minute later. 'Yes, it does actually correspond to a book we have. It's even in stock here. But it's not about World War Two or anything like that, though. It's about... plants.'

Beth's reaction goes from euphoria to confusion in an instant. She had imagined that if it referred to a library book at all, it would be one about local history or a collection of old newspapers. But... plants?

'Oh. I see.'

'Well, shall we go and get it anyway? I can see it hasn't been taken out in a very long time,' says the librarian. 'I always feel sorry for books like that.'

Beth follows her to the far corner of the room, on the opposite side to the children's section, where there's an area for reference books.

'Yes, here it is,' says the woman, pulling out a large leather-bound book, and blowing dust off its cover. She takes it over to a small table by the window, lays it down for Beth to see and stands back.

Beth examines it. The title, *A Book of Traditional English Plants*, is embossed into the brown leather cover. It's tall and thick, about the size of one of the Encyclopaedia Britannica books her parents had bought when she was a child. She turns the first page and sees there's an old library card on the front, last stamped in August 1996. Then she turns over to the index, which is at the front of the book, and sees that someone has written on it in pencil. Beth's heart quickens.

'Someone's written something in here,' she says to the librarian.

'Have they? Goodness, that's not good,' she says, coming to take a look. 'What language is it though? That's not English.'

'No. Well it is, but not as we know it. It's shorthand. And I know someone who can translate it for me. Can I borrow this book?'

Beth knows that Steve is having a pre-Christmas break with

his kids at the moment, but she decides to take the book to him as soon as she can after the festive season is over.

'Of course, dear. Just come up to the front and we'll set up an account for you. Do you live locally?'

Beth ponders for a moment.

'Yes,' she replies, with an unexpected new confidence. 'I live at Melham Manor.'

PART II

20

BETH

A fire crackles in the grate. Beth twists in the armchair to check on the children. She can see that Raphie and Ella are finally asleep, tucked up in a musty double bed under a pile of blankets. Stanley is curled up by her feet. Beth feels her shoulders drop and her body sinks into the chair. Knowing they're all safe and sated after a busy day gives her a sense of achievement, particularly given the circumstances.

She's never particularly liked the empty period between Christmas and New Year, but she absolutely despises it now. She came down to Melham on impulse because she simply had to get away. She'd barely survived Christmas Day, which, after the children had left the house to go to David's parents' place, had disappeared in a haze of Prosecco, chocolate and tears, and the forced frivolity she has made herself channel whenever they've all been at home together – her and David and the kids – has been utterly exhausting.

Yes, coming here was the right thing to do, she thinks. *Definitely.*

It's been incredibly cold and damp of course, given the complete absence of heating in the house, but the kids had been excited about the building of fires and the need to snuggle under blankets while they watch Nita's ancient television. They and the ever-loyal Stanley have also enjoyed running around the grounds, as she'd known they would, and Rowan had visited this afternoon and spent a couple of hours showing the children how to make garlands from winter greenery and dried flowers. Once a primary school teacher, forever a primary school teacher, quite clearly.

Beth is about to get up and head to her own room next door when she hears a noise. Stanley does, too. His head snaps upwards and he emits a low growl.

She wonders what it could be. Squirrels in the roof, perhaps, or, she thinks, with a shudder – rats? The house is definitely infested with mice, so she knows there might well be larger rodents.

Then she hears another noise. It sounds like a door shutting.

She knows it's probably just the old house creaking or the wind blowing a door closed, but she remembers the unidentified person who was in the house last time, the one who ran off before she could get to them. This time, she thinks, she mustn't let them get away. She needs to check, just in case. She gestures for Stanley and he obeys, trotting along beside her as she leaves the bedroom and sets off down the cluttered, dimly lit corridor. She wonders if he'll start growling again, but he's surprisingly quiet, as if he's on edge, too.

She pauses outside each room in turn, listens, and then throws the door open, ready to face whoever might be inside. All that she finds, however, are large pieces of furniture shrouded in dust sheets and many, many plastic bags filled with knick-knacks and newspapers. She relaxes. It seems as if there's no one in the house who shouldn't be there. She walks to the window in one of several guest bedrooms and looks out at the front drive and the village below. Most of Melham's residents will have drawn their curtains against the biting cold, but the village's street lights are forming a swirling line, tracing its winding, silent streets. The moon is shining in a clear, cold sky, and a layer of ice has formed on her car windscreen, making it gleam. Ice is also forming on the inside of the windowpane. It's freezing in here too, she thinks.

'Right, one more room on this corridor,' she says to Stanley, feeling relieved. As she walks out of the guest bedroom, however, she hears another slamming noise, apparently coming from the next room. The dog growls.

Beth feels her heart quicken, and realises she has no choice but to go and investigate. Again, she knows it's most likely nothing, but she won't be able to get to sleep if she thinks there's an intruder in the house. She takes a deep breath, turns the handle, throws the door open and flicks the light switch.

For a heart-stopping few seconds she and Stanley check behind the door, beneath covers and under tables, before concluding that the room is empty.

Then – *slam*.

Beth's head swivels just in time to see the fanlight above the main windowpane banging against the frame. It isn't shut, and it isn't propped open. She walks over and closes it. Odd, she thinks. She had come up here briefly during her search for objects for the antiques dealer to sell, and she hadn't noticed it was loose then. She wouldn't necessarily have spotted it though, she reasons. She'd been in a rush, keen to get the job done and get out of Melham Manor.

'Just the wind,' she says to the dog, patting him on the head. He's stopped growling now and seems relaxed. He leaves her to sniff his way around the room.

As she waits for him, Beth realises she hadn't really questioned during her last visit what sort of room this is. It's on the first floor, but there's no bed in it. She lifts a dust cover nearest the window and finds an old wooden desk, the kind that folds out. It's a kind of office then, she thinks, wondering if her grandfather had used it when he lived here. She opens the desk and finds an old manual typewriter. Apart from this, however, she finds only faded receipts and unused envelopes. Next, she lifts a cover and discovers a bookcase. There are some classics on its shelves – *Wuthering Heights*, *A Room with a View*, *Persuasion*, *A Passage to India* – and a large collection of romance novels by the very popular author Josephine Rees, one of her mother's favourites, on the quiet. Marisa always tells journalists she's an enormous fan of whoever recently won the Booker, but Beth knows she prefers romantic, commercial fiction when she's off duty. Beth wonders who these particular books belonged to. If they were Nita's, she realises this unexpected affection for romantic literature is yet another part of her great-aunt's personality she hadn't anticipated. She reaches down and picks one at random from the bookcase, to take to bed with her. If Nita liked it, she thinks, perhaps I will, too.

Finally, Beth lifts a cover next to the room's fireplace and discovers a high wooden table. Unlike the other furniture in this room, its surface is rough, not polished, and she can see there's something on top of it. She tugs at the cover so she can see it more clearly.

What she finds puzzles her. There is a pile of what looks like ash in an old tea plate. Cigarette ash, perhaps, she thinks, wondering whether Nita had smoked. She sniffs it. It doesn't smell of tobacco. It's far more fragrant than that. She realises that it's incense. She wonders who in this house would have been burning incense sticks. It's impossible to tell how long the ashes have been there, but she doubts they'd pre-date Nita's occupation of the house. It must have something to do with her, then, surely. Had Nita liked the scent of incense while she worked? Curiouser and curiouser, she thinks.

Beth pulls the dust sheet back over the table, calls for Stanley to come to heel, and heads back in the direction of her bedroom. She climbs into bed with reluctance. Sleep hasn't been her friend in recent months. And so it's unusual that tonight, in this freezing cold, damp, dusty and slightly spooky house, she falls asleep almost immediately.

* * *

'Will Daddy be there when we get home?'

'Da-da, da-da,' choruses Ella.

Raphie and Ella are sitting next to each other in the back of the car, watching the hedges and the trees give way to open fields as they drive to Dorking under steely skies.

'He should be, darlings. Yes.'

In truth, she has no idea what her soon-to-be ex-husband's movements will be today. He is more distant than ever now, far worse than he was in the weeks leading up to the bombshell that he wanted a divorce, and worse even than he had been in the month or so after that. Perhaps he's simply unable to pretend to like her now, and this thought stabs at her very core. How can he not even like her, after all these years? A brief memory of the stupid mind games she'd played with him about the children's Christmas presents flashes into her conscience, but she dismisses it quickly. She doesn't have the energy today to engage in self-flagellation.

'Where are we going now?' asks Raphie, when they turn into Dorking High Street.

'Well, as I told you earlier, we're on our way home and should be back in time for dinner, but I've just got to stop off at *The Bugle* offices to do a quick work thing.'

'Will Rowan be looking after us while you do it?'

Goodness, they do love that woman, Beth thinks.

'No, not this time. We'll only be a few minutes.'

'Ohhhhhh,' says Raphie, his disappointment clear.

Beth pats Stanley on the head and tells him they'll be back in a few minutes. She is really hoping that Steve will be in – she knows that most workers take leave over the Christmas week, but she suspects journalists aren't able to – and also that he'll be more sober than last time. She needs him to take a look at the shorthand on the book of plants she's borrowed from the library.

Many shops on Dorking High Street still have their pre-Christmas decorations up, while others have large red signs advertising sales that are clearly not bringing in the madding crowd, judging by the ease with which Beth finds a parking spot near the office. There's almost no one about, bar a few people stumbling out of the pubs after a long and boozy Twixmas lunch. As she unclips the children from their car seats, it starts to snow.

'Quick, quick, let's catch as many snowflakes as we can on our tongues,' Beth says, throwing back her head to stare into the dense clouds above, and feeling a frisson of cold as one lands in her mouth. The children copy her, and for a moment they all look in awe at the constantly changing, dotted artwork above their heads. Then Ella shrieks with laughter as she sways uncertainly on her feet, and Raphie runs around in circles, believing, Beth suspects, that speeding up will encourage the snow to seek him out as a target.

As she watches their joy she remembers something from her own childhood, something she hasn't thought about for a long time. She remembers spinning around in the garden at the Manor, the dense trees at its border blurring into haze. She'd gone so fast she'd fallen to the ground panting, moss cushioning her fall. And then she remembers someone else being there, helping her up afterwards. She wonders who it was. Had her mother been there, perhaps? She realises that she can't have been. Marisa never came out to play with her. She decides that it must have been her sister Philippa. More fond of TV and her CD collection than the natural world, the snow must have been just enough to persuade her to take a rare outing outside. Beth tries to remember more, to conjure up what must definitely be a rare happy family memory, but it escapes her grasp.

When the novelty of the snow finally wears off and the children start to feel cold, they run together hand in hand towards the office entrance, where Beth rings the buzzer and a muffled male voice answers and admits them. Steve is at least in, then, she thinks.

'Hello,' she calls as she opens the door.

'Come through,' calls Steve from his office. Beth and the children weave through the piles of boxes – there seem to be even more of them than before – and find Steve fully dressed and clean shaven, at work in front of the computer on his desk.

'Hi there,' says Beth, suspecting her surprise and relief are showing on her face.

'Nice to see you. This is unexpected. I haven't given you some work I've forgotten about, have I?'

'Oh, no. Nothing like that. Although I'm happy to do more.'

Steve smiles.

'But actually I wondered if you might be able to quickly tell me what this says.' Beth pulls out the book of plants from the library, walks over to Steve and opens it at the page with the shorthand on it.

Steve's brow furrows as he reads.

'Right, so I don't really know what this means, but I can certainly tell you what's written here,' he says, and Beth nods.

'OK, so the first one is calendula. Dunno what that is.' Beth isn't sure either, but she writes it down and decides to google it later. 'Then there's Larkspur, Arctic... yes, King, Arctic King, and the last one is... White Lisbon. Jesus, these all sound like cryptic code words James Bond might use,' he says, laughing, and Beth laughs too, partly because he might actually be right. Or, of course, they might just be plants. Beth finishes writing the list down and puts the notepad away.

'Thanks so much for that. We should be off now,' she says, noting the kids are getting restless. 'I don't want to take up any more of your time...'

'No, that's cool. Always nice to see you. By the way, I would love you to write something more about that housing project the councillor wants to get going. There's a meeting in a month or so you could go to.'

'Great. I'd love to go,' says Beth, meaning it. She had really liked the counsellor and she'd really bought into his vision. His bad feeling towards developers like Stellar makes her nervous, however.

'Awesome. I'll drop you a line.'

'Great. Come on, monkeys,' she says and ushers the kids in the direction of the door.

'Happy New Year, when it comes,' he calls out as she opens the door to the stairs.

'You too.'

* * *

It's four thirty in the afternoon and already dark when Beth draws up outside the smart Victorian semi-detached house she has lived in with David since the year after they married. Her parents had given them a large down payment towards their mortgage as a wedding present, a fact her mother has reminded her of several times since David announced he wanted a divorce. Marisa certainly wants to make sure Beth leaves the marriage with that money, and Beth imagines her father does, too, although she knows it's small fry compared to the amounts he deals with every day in the business. Despite this, she really hopes her lawyer manages to get it back, as it'll certainly help with securing somewhere else to live within the school catchment.

There's a light on in the living room, and someone's turned on their Christmas tree. Its lights are twinkling through the front window. David's home, then. Once unstrapped, the children and dog leap out of the car with relief after the confinement of the journey and run to the front door, where the kids press the doorbell repeatedly, eager to see their father. Meanwhile, Beth busies herself picking up empty snack packets from the back seat and emptying the boot, keen not to endure standing awkwardly by the door while David lavishes attention on the kids. She only finishes hauling the two bags out when they've had their fill and run inside. When she locks the car and looks up at the front door, she's surprised to see David still standing there.

'Hi,' he says.

'Hello.'

'I didn't know when you'd be back.'

No, David, you didn't, she thinks. *But you didn't tell me when you'd be back home, either.*

'The traffic was dodgy,' she says, even though this is untrue.

'Oh, right. Look, Beth, I wanted to have a chat with you.' He looks hunted. Her stomach lurches. *This cannot be good*, she thinks.

'Oh?'

They stand looking at each other for a moment, a thousand different questions swirling in the vacuum between them.

'Come inside. It's cold out here.'

She does as he asks, noting that this is the sort of thing you say to a guest, not your spouse. She waits while he turns the TV on for the kids and joins her in the kitchen.

'Do you want a drink?' he asks. This is unusual. He hasn't made her so much as a cup of tea for at least a month.

'No.'

'Fair enough,' he replies, and she watches in silence as he walks to the fridge, retrieves a bottle of beer, finds a bottle opener and pours the beer into a glass. Then he pulls a pack of posh crisps out of a cupboard and opens them, pushing them towards her. She adores crisps. He knows that.

She doesn't take one.

'What's this about, David?' she says, running out of patience with this obvious attempt at buttering her up.

'I've got something to tell you.' He shoots a sideways glance at the door into the lounge, which is slightly ajar. They're both aware the children are in there and might be listening. Beth puts her hand on the counter to steady herself. She's hoping her expression appears bullish, but inside her guts are churning and her legs are beginning to shake. She doesn't answer. She's not going to make this easy for him.

'I... I've met someone,' he says.

And just like that, the bottom drops out of Beth's world.

21

NITA

February 1941

Nita's walking down the High Street to the post box and yet again, she is amazed that passers-by can't tell how changed she is, how different she is now, in both her mind and her body.

This time, however, it's not her passionate encounters with Joe she's surprised people can't detect. Instead, it's something else that's consuming her every waking moment, and, she suspects, most of her dreams, too.

She runs her right thumb over the ridges of the envelope she's clasping in her right hand. She had written it and rewritten it in her head throughout most of the early hours, and finally put pen to paper at dawn. She can't delay sending this any more. She is very certain now, or at least, as certain as she'll ever be. She knows the letter's contents off by heart.

Dear Joe,

I hope this letter finds you well. I am thinking of you daily. More than daily, in fact. I am still hoping to receive a letter back from you, perhaps a huge pile of them, caught up in the Army postal system, which I understand is not the most efficient. I miss you terribly, my love, more than you will ever know.

The reason why I'm so anxious is that I have something important to tell you. You may not even be surprised. I know you took precautions when we were together, but I'm afraid we were not successful. I've not had my time of the month for eight weeks now, and along with some other symptoms I feel too embarrassed to share here, I am now as confident I can be, without the confirmation of a doctor, that I am to have a baby.

I know this will come as a shock. I'm shocked too. I've endured many sleepless nights worrying about how I will manage, and when I will have to tell my parents. I'm praying you will receive this and reply long before I have to disclose my secret to them, because I fear what they'll do with me when I do.

My love, if you're reading this, please reply soonest and let me know that we'll marry as soon as we can. I think it really is the only way for us to keep this baby. I don't care what my parents think about me marrying you at all; we will be fine together, both working. We will cope. I just need to be certain that we have a plan, and then all will be well.

All I want, absolutely all I want, is to be with you, Joe. I love you. Please write to tell me you are all right.

With all my love,

Nita

Nita takes a deep breath and posts the letter, before turning back up the road, in the direction of the bench where she waits nightly for her father's driver to pick her up and take her home. She sits down and pulls her coat tightly around her in an attempt to ward off the chill in the air. The skies above her are dark. The forecast suggests it might snow.

She wonders how Joe is coping with the cold, wherever he is. She wonders whether soldiers are given proper warm clothing when they are training outside. Perhaps, she thinks, she should knit him a scarf. The thought of doing something positive for him buoys her. She can't shake the niggling fear that something awful has happened to him. And if it has, she knows no one would think to tell her, because she's not his official next of kin. He could be seriously injured in hospital, or even dead, she thinks with a shudder, and she'd never know.

The driver arrives, and she gets in the car, grateful for its warmth. As they wend their way through the narrow, high-banked lanes that lead to the house, Nita reflects on the conversation she's going to need to have at dinner. It won't be about her pregnancy. She's not naive enough to drop that particular bombshell over gristly gammon and mashed potatoes. She needs to be certain that they have a solid plan to marry before her parents find out about her predicament. No, the conversation will be about the fact she's still 'working' at *The Bugle*, and her mother's increasingly vocal concerns that her new-found profession is thwarting her chances to find a potential husband. Jane-Anne has been away in London for a few days, but is returning tonight, and something tells Nita that she won't be able to avoid this particular conversation for much longer.

And so it proves.

Two hours later, Nita has changed for dinner and is sitting down opposite her father at the dining table, when her mother launches the first salvo of her attack.

'Doesn't Nita look wonderful tonight, darling,' says Jane-Anne. 'Her complexion is exquisite.'

'Yes, she does,' says Ernest, smiling broadly at Nita. Whether he is aware of what his wife is about to propose, Nita has no idea. She doesn't know how well they communicate in private. She suspects not very.

'There's a ball in Chelsea in a fortnight,' says Jane-Anne.

Here we go, thinks Nita.

'Is there? You should go along,' says Ernest.

'Yes. I was thinking I would take Nita with me. It's being arranged by a woman I know quite well, whose daughter also didn't get a proper Coming Out party due to the war. It's a sort of second chance for all the girls who haven't yet made... connections. I think it would be wonderful for Nita.'

'Well, whatever you think, dear,' says Ernest, chewing on his meat. He is not meeting Nita's eye.

'I can't go,' says Nita, even though she knows what she's about to say is going to be shut down by a million verbal missiles. 'I have to go to work.'

'Won't it be at a weekend?' Ernest asks.

Oh, you naive man, thinks Nita.

'Well, I'll need to get her up into town earlier than that for a dress fitting,' says Jane-Anne. 'I was thinking anyway that this work experience spell at *The Bugle* has gone on for long enough. Surely Nita has learned all she's going to learn from such a provincial publication?'

'I like my job, Mother.'

'It's not a *job*, darling. Heavens. Bineham women don't have *jobs*.'

'I'm not coming. I just won't. I don't want to come. I don't even like dancing.'

'You will come to this party, and that's the end of it,' says her mother.

Nita looks pleadingly at her father, but he's not meeting her eye.

'Fine. I'll come. But only for a few days, and only as long as I can stay at *The Bugle*. And I need to tell Mr Bridges I'm not going to be there.'

'I doubt he'll mind, darling. But you'll call him about this, won't you, Ernest?'

'Hmm, hmm, yes,' he says, still chewing.

Nita starts to eat her own meal, seething quietly. At least this will probably be the last party she ever has to attend, she thinks. Once she's married to Joe, she'll most likely never be invited back to Melham Manor, let alone to a society party. The thought of the latter makes her rejoice. The former thought, however, does give her pause. She knows her days in this house are numbered.

Nita makes a silent promise to try to enjoy them while they last.

22

BETH

January 2009

Beth is woken by the sound of a creaking door. Given that she's the only person currently staying at Melham Manor, this should cause her alarm, but she is so numb and so exhausted, she hasn't the energy to get out of bed and investigate. *If someone's arrived to steal something, go ahead*, she thinks, *I don't care. I don't care about anything any more.*

'Beth? *Beth?* Is that you?' It's Rowan.

That makes sense, Beth thinks. She has a key. Beth mumbles in reply under the covers, but it's barely audible, even to her.

'Beth? Are you in here?' The door to the bedroom opens. 'Oh, you are. Sorry, I saw your car. But I didn't think you'd still be asleep.'

Beth doesn't respond. She doesn't know how to.

'Are you OK? Are you ill?'

Beth turns over and pulls the covers down far enough so that they can see each other.

'Oh goodness. Shall I call a doctor?'

I look that *good then*, thinks Beth, wryly. 'No. They couldn't do anything for me, anyway,' she says, finding the energy to speak.

'Shall I go?' asks Rowan.

Beth looks up at her friendly, concerned, familiar face, and realises she's actually quite glad to see her.

'No. Stay,' she replies, her voice creaking.

'OK. Can I sit down?'

'Sure.'

Rowan opens the velvet curtains a few inches, allowing a shaft of weak winter sunlight into the room, and sits on a wooden chair next to the window.

Neither of them says anything for a minute, and Beth would usually feel awkward about this kind of silence, but for some reason, she feels at ease instead. It's the first time she's felt at ease in days.

'Shall I make you a tea?' says Rowan, finally.

'There's no milk.'

'Oh, I meant herbal tea. I make my own. Would you like one?'

'OK.'

Beth sinks back under the covers after this exchange, and only re-emerges when Rowan enters the room and places a cup and saucer on the bedside table.

'Here you go. It's lavender tea. From the garden. It's a bit of an acquired taste I suppose, but it's very soothing. For both the body and the soul.'

'Thank you,' replies Beth, pulling herself up a bit so that she can drink the tea without spilling it everywhere. She lifts the cup up and inhales its aroma. She has a flashback to a baking summer's day, to warm, bare feet on freshly mown grass, to hands grasping plants that are as high as her waist. She takes a sip and swallows, feeling the warm liquid soothe her throat, which is hoarse from crying so physical, her chest actually aches.

'You don't have to tell me anything,' says Rowan. 'I can just sit with you, if you like.'

'No... no. Look, I'm sorry for still being asleep in the middle of the day. I'm not my usual self, as you can see.'

'Yes, I can. I'm sorry.'

'You're not responsible for my husband's new girlfriend,' she says, the bitterness catching in her throat. Beth takes another sip of tea to try to flush it away.

'Oh, I'm so sorry. That must be a shock.'

'Yes. No. I don't know. I suppose I knew, really, but I thought... I thought... maybe we might get back together. Which is ridiculous. He wanted a divorce. But I thought maybe with time...'

'Is the girlfriend very new?'

'You mean, was she around before we split up? He says not.' Beth can't remember much after he told her about *Anna*, except the pain and the shouting and the tears, but she does remember him insisting she hadn't been the reason he'd wanted a divorce. He had repeated this many times, but she wonders if he was protesting too much. Her presence would explain a lot.

'I see. It's hard to know what to believe in a situation like this, isn't it.'

Rowan's tone suggests experience.

'Yes. Are you divorced?' Beth realises she has never asked Rowan whether she has a partner.

'Yes. I was married, but unfortunately we didn't last.'

'I'm sorry to hear that,' says Beth, responding with instinctive compassion to the other woman's pain, despite her own.

'Yes. It was tough for a time. The children felt it, too. But it was right, in the end. We weren't good for each other.'

Beth wonders whether the same applies to her and David. She'd thought for a long time that they were well suited, but maybe, just maybe, she'd just been wishing that, towards the end?

She remembers, with a new clarity, the barbed comments he'd been making about her career at Stellar in the past few years and his growing intolerance at her messiness, something he'd once regarded as an endearing, quirky part of her personality.

'Yes. Yes,' says Beth, sipping more tea. She doesn't have the energy to say much more.

'Where are the kids?'

Rowan's reference to Raphie and Ella shakes her out of her stupor.

'They're with him. Well, with my mother-in-law, probably, while he's working. She's come to stay. To help him.' Beth waits for Rowan to say something in response, but she doesn't. 'I know you're probably thinking how awful it is I've abandoned them. I know. I'm thinking it myself. But I just couldn't... manage. I just couldn't plaster on a coping face and carry on. I'm... knackered. I'm too knackered to try to pretend I'm OK when I'm not.'

'I think that's very sensible, to be honest. You have come here, where you feel safe, to recover. You'll return stronger and ready to care for them and deal with whatever happens next, then, won't you?'

Beth blinks a couple of times and inhales deeply, processing what Rowan has just said. Yes, she does feel safe here, she realises. She'd originally thought it was simply the absence of other people that had brought her back to Melham Manor, but now she realises it's much more than that. The house, the gardens, the woods: they comfort her. They always have. She is amazed that somewhere along the way, she'd forgotten that.

'How do you know I feel safe here?' says Beth. It occurs to her that most people might feel unnerved by mouldering Melham Manor, with its rooms cloaked in decades of dust, and the dense woodland surrounding it that threatens to encase its inhabitants.

'Oh, Nita told me.'

'Did she? But I hadn't visited in years.'

'I know. But she told me you loved this place as a child. That you and she used to spend a lot of time in the garden together, and in the woods. You used to follow her around, she said, doing whatever she did. It was obvious to her that you were at home here. And it's a special sort of place, isn't it? If you love Melham Manor, you'll always love it. It gets into your blood, into your soul. I feel that way about it, too. But not everybody does.'

'Like my parents, do you mean?' says Beth, raising an eyebrow.

'I couldn't possibly comment.'

The two women smile at each other.

'They stopped coming here when I was about eleven,' says Beth. 'So I stopped coming too, obviously. And by the time I was old enough to come on my own I think I was just far too interested in university and boys and travel and stuff and my parents said Nita was mad, anyway. Oh sorry... I know you were friends.'

'We were. And it's OK. She was certainly eccentric.'

'That woman I spoke to at the fireworks said as much.'

'Oh, yes. Well, she didn't actually know her. She just knows that a couple of local people had spotted Nita walking around after dark, talking to herself. That sort of thing. Yes, Nita was definitely a little eccentric, but I loved her. She was a wonderful woman.'

'Yes, she was. That's why I came to see her, at the end,' says Beth.

'I'm very glad you did. I know it will have meant a lot to her.'

'Would it?'

'Yes.'

'Oh.'

Beth remembers Nita's warm hand encasing hers. She wonders, with a start, whether she had been the person who'd been with her in the garden that day when it had snowed? Maybe, she thinks. Maybe it had been Nita, after all.

'How long are you planning to stay here?' asks Rowan.

'Oh God, I don't know,' says Beth, rubbing her eyes and forehead. 'I just don't know. I'll need to face it at some point. All of it.'

'Yes, when you're ready. There will be a lot to discuss. Are you in mediation? I know former colleagues who used a mediator and it seemed to help a lot, where kids are concerned in particular.'

'No. I've got a good solicitor on the case, though.'

'Well, if it's working for you. Mine was a bit combative to be honest. I don't think he helped much. He even made *me* angry.'

'Well... David's definitely angry I didn't want mediation. But my parents are concerned about the impact on the business. I have shares in it, you see...'

'They'll be worth less at the moment...' says Rowan, before catching herself.

'Why?'

'Look, it doesn't matter. Would you like another cup of tea?'

'Tell me why.'

'I suppose you haven't looked at your phone this morning?'

'No.'

'Well, someone has to tell you, I suppose. Stellar has collapsed.'

'Collapsed? The share price has fallen?'

'I don't know what to tell you, Beth. The firm has... folded. It's the latest casualty of the financial crisis. It's all over the news.'

'But why?'

'Something about being exposed to too much debt, and plummeting house prices.'

Beth pulls herself up sharply and leans over to where her BlackBerry is plugged in, recharging. She unlocks it and sees that she has at least twenty messages. The top few are from her mother and her sister – 'call me when you get this' in various guises – and then sundry friends who she hasn't seen for years, but who clearly now want to share a piece of the drama.

'Oh, crap.'

'You didn't know it was coming?'

'Well, I knew there were issues. But I haven't been working there recently...' Beth wonders whether she should tell Rowan about her suspension, but then she realises that she probably knows, anyway. The whole of Britain enjoyed her gaffe for at least a week. 'And I resigned before Christmas.'

'Oh, I didn't realise. That must have been a big deal... I mean, it's the family firm.'

'Don't you mean *was*?' says Beth, throwing the covers back and reaching for her coat, which she'd slung on the floor the previous night. The house is as frigid as ever.

'Sorry...' says Rowan, standing up. 'I realise I've just given you some very bad news, and you're having such a dreadful time. I'll leave you. I'm guessing you have calls to make.'

'No, no, I don't,' says Beth, sitting on the side of the bed with her head in her hands. 'I don't. I mean, I probably had a part to play in this, didn't I, making Stellar a laughing stock on TV. I doubt my parents have anything to say to me and I no longer work for the company, anyway. Who would I call?'

Beth is utterly overwhelmed by the utter quagmire she's in, and the intense isolation she's feeling. She can't even call David. Then she thinks about Anna, and she feels much, much worse.

'It'll be all right, Beth,' says Rowan, suddenly by her side, rubbing her back like a mother reassuring a sick child. 'It'll be all right. I know you can't see your way out of the darkness at the moment, but I promise you, you'll find a way through it.'

23

NITA

Early March 1941

'Why haven't you left yet? I thought you had to be in town today for that vitally important event in your social calendar.'

Bridges has been enjoying Nita's father's request to allow her time off to attend the ball rather too much.

'I don't know how the men of London have managed without you for so long,' says Simpson, and this sends Phillips into a fit of laughter which makes him sound like a vomiting cat.

Nita ignores them. She's used to them being rude about her now, and their behaviour has got even worse since Joe left. They obviously had no idea that Nita and Joe had become intimate, but they knew they were friendly, and they respected Joe, she thinks, so they eased off a little on her when he was around. But it seems they have no respect for her at all.

'How's the story about the break-in at the post office going, Simpson?' asks Bridges.

'Oh, well, sir. I've got two solid quotes from the girl who works there on the counter, you know, the one with...'

'The short skirts,' says Phillips, sniggering.

'Yes. And I am expecting a call from the police superintendent at any moment.'

'The superintendent, eh? They *are* taking this seriously.'

'It's crawling with police out there,' says Phillips. 'They've sent a whole lot down from Scotland Yard. They seem to reckon this has something to do with this spy they're looking for. Well, it must have, mustn't it? I can't imagine they'd put this much manpower into investigating a normal break-in.'

'Absolutely, yes. Well, good work, Simpson. I shall leave you to it. And you, Miss Bineham, apparently have a train to catch. Happy... breeding ground,' he says, smirking as he walks away.

* * *

Bridges' words are still ringing in Nita's ears as she gets into a taxi outside her parents' house in Chelsea. She sits down next to her mother and father and automatically smooths down the pale blue dress she's wearing, which actually belongs to her mother. Jane-Anne had naturally attempted to buy something new, but Nita had been incredibly relieved when they'd found nothing worth exchanging for eleven clothing coupons in all of the shops they'd tried – a rare occasion when her mother's haughty dress sense had come in handy. So, they'd raided her mother's extensive wardrobe instead, and the chosen dress had been picked apart and re-sewn by a clever seamstress.

A *very* clever seamstress in fact, thinks Nita, given she's a dress size larger than her mother and now definitely swelling around her middle. In fact, she'd heard the dressmaker inhale rather too deeply when she'd been doing up the back of the dress this afternoon. Whether she thought Nita had simply been eating too much or whether she suspected the truth, she will never know.

They set off, and Nita passes the time looking out at battered, bruised London. Windows are criss-crossed with tape, road surfaces are uneven after hasty patching-up, and there are signs for bomb shelters around every corner. When they drive through Parliament Square, she's relieved to see both Westminster Abbey and the Houses of Parliament are still standing, despite several bombs over the past year which have caused them significant damage. They are two of her favourite buildings in the capital and she knows it would damage morale terribly if they were to be lost to the Blitz.

'Here we are,' says her father a few minutes later, as they pull up outside a large neoclassical building with an elegant portico lined with fluted columns. 'The Athenaeum. I must say, it's handy they're holding this at my club.'

'Well, Joanna's house is now being used for some kind of war work, so I hear,' says Jane-Anne. 'She and Bertie still have the apartment near Kensington Gore, of course, but it must be a hardship. So yes, they had to choose another venue.'

'It's a good one,' says Ernest Bineham, holding out his hand to help Nita out of the vehicle. She smiles at him.

'I must say, darling, that you look lovely tonight,' he says, and she is taken aback. Although she definitely has a more stable relationship with her father than her mother, he's usually wrapped up in either the business or the newspaper, and not given to what he would usually refer to as inconsequential details.

'Thank you,' replies Nita, still holding onto his arm as they walk up the stone steps towards the front door, which is being guarded by a smartly dressed man with an inscrutable expression.

'Straight through to the drawing room, please,' he says, and opens the door, through which warm light briefly bursts out into the street, its pre-war regalia dulled by the blackout. The door shuts behind them and Nita and her parents walk through into a large room with an ornate recessed ceiling, a patterned carpet and deep green drapes. Nita assumes this room is usually furnished with sofas and comfortable chairs, but all of the chairs are now lined up against the walls, and there's a pianist playing a grand piano in the corner, and a band seems to be setting up next to her.

A waiter walks up to them with a tray of what Nita suspects might be champagne. She takes a glass, mostly so she has something to hold. She wants to avoid being asked to dance, if at all possible. In fact, as much as this location is beautiful and most people would be absolutely delighted to be surrounded by treats many are struggling to get hold of due to the war, Nita is not most people. She has become embarrassed by her privileged upbringing, for a start. Her months as a reporter have taught her much more than how to write shorthand and ask a good question. She thinks of the people she's met who are struggling to get by. The plenty around her now feels obscene. And then there's the fact she feels awkward at parties, has two left feet, and anyway, she's going to marry Joe. There's no one here who is of any interest to her at all.

'Ah, Bineham. How lovely to see you here.' Nita hears a voice which sounds familiar and looks across to see who's talking to her father. Her stomach lurches when she realises it's Peter Sanders, the man who runs the undertakers, and, more importantly, the man her parents seem to think she should marry.

'Peter, how wonderful. What a surprise,' says Ernest, shaking his hand vigorously, and her mother follows suit. Then he holds his hand out to Nita and she has no choice but to take it. His palm is clammy, as she had imagined it would be, and he holds her hand for several seconds too long.

'I hope you'll join me for a dance,' he says.

'Nita would love to,' says her mother, jumping in before she can reply herself.

'Excellent,' says Peter. 'I'll see you when the band strikes up.'

'I don't want to dance, Mother. You know I don't like dancing,' says Nita to Jane-Anne, when Peter has walked away. 'This is ludicrous...'

'Don't be silly, dear. It's only polite. You can't turn the poor man down, once he's asked you. And he's a nice chap, Nita. He's got a successful business, and he's lonely. His first wife died, you know. Cancer, I think. He has two small children at home. They need a mother.'

Nita feels a small amount of sympathy for him then – no one should have to endure the loss of their spouse so relatively young – but she absolutely refuses to be guilt-tripped into essentially becoming someone's unpaid nanny.

The evening progresses as Nita had known it would. She is resolutely ignored by every eligible bachelor in the room except Peter, who rarely leaves her side, even though she gives him zero encouragement. She agrees to dance with him only once, a speedy foxtrot, a dance she hopes gives little excuse for skin contact. She spends most of it trying not to trip over her own feet, which is a helpful distraction from Peter's unwavering gaze.

Afterwards, he follows her to the corner of the room, and sits down next to her.

'Thank you for that dance, it was wonderful,' he says.

'Yes,' replies Nita. 'But you know, I feel rather hot. I think I'll step outside for a spell.' She doesn't wait for his response. Seconds later she's up and walking down the hall and pausing as the doorman opens the door onto the street. As the cold air hits her, she takes a big breath in and exhales slowly, as if she's pushing Peter and the party away.

When her eyes adjust, she can see that she's not alone on the pavement outside the club. There are people walking past, slowly, and carefully, some with dim torches. Then a double-decker red bus passes her, its headlights covered with stickers which cast their light down onto the street. Nita finds this ordinary, everyday activity comforting. It's easy, when you're in an uncomfortable situation, to feel like no other reality exists, but here she is, just a matter of feet away from this ridiculous meat market of a ball, back in the real world, and she feels so much better.

Or at least she does, for a while.

'There you are,' says Peter, who obviously decided to follow her outside. More's the pity.

'Yes.'

'Look, Nita. I know we haven't known each other very long, but there is something I've been intending to ask you.'

Oh my goodness, she thinks, *surely you can't be so numb to the feelings of those around you that you haven't picked up on how I actually feel about you?*

'I've been talking to your father and he and I both agree that we are well suited. I like to write in my free time too, you know. I have some poems I'd like to show you. Anyway, I was wondering whether...'

Nita doesn't stay to hear the rest. Whether it's marriage or simply a series of interminable dates he's about to propose, she doesn't much care. Both would feel like hell. She spots a taxi and runs towards it, holding her arm to flag it down. She's inside it within a minute, and thankfully, this time, Peter doesn't follow her.

She gives the driver the address of her family's London home and sits back in the seat, taking stock of what she's just done. Her parents are going to be furious. And disappointed, although she suspects she's already so disappointing to them, it can't get much worse. She wonders whether they will retaliate by telling her she can't work at the newspaper any more. Despite Joe's call-up, the thought of leaving *The Bugle* makes her feel nauseous. She's going to have to fight to stay there. At least until Joe gets in touch with a plan. She knows they won't have a huge amount of money but she hopes it will be enough to rent a room somewhere for her and the baby, while Joe is away.

The taxi pulls up outside Nita's house. She pulls out some cash from her purse, thanks him, walks up to the door and knocks. She waits a couple of minutes – far longer than she would usually expect to wait – until the door is opened by one of the housemaids.

It isn't until she's inside in the warmth and the light that she realises something is awry.

The maid looks frightened.

'I'm sorry, miss. I know it's late and you've been out enjoying yourselves, but I... We... We received a telegram earlier. I think you need to read it.'

Nita gasps when the maid hands her the telegram. It's from the Army. They both know what this means. She tears it open, her heart in her mouth.

24

BETH

January 2009

'Just hold it gently by the stem, and, using the secateurs, cut it on the diagonal, just above any signs of new growth,' says Rowan. 'That way the water won't linger on the cut and make it rot.' Beth does exactly as she suggests, although she feels nervous about severing one of Nita's beloved roses. 'It's OK. I know it seems brutal, but roses really do need cutting back properly every year to really flourish.'

Beth soon finds a rhythm, and they spend a companionable half an hour tending to Melham Manor's rose garden. There's something immensely comforting, she thinks, about the fact these bare twigs will, in just a few months, be longer, stronger and full of life and colour. She has always loved spring, even in central London. Every new shoot she sees on the trees in the park, every daffodil, always raises her spirits. Watching nature perform its miracles, year on year, according to each season, is a source of joy.

'That's it, I think,' says Beth, making the final cut in the final plant in her section of the garden.

'Great. Thank you. Having you around has been a huge help.'

'I doubt it. I'm a very amateur gardener,' replies Beth.

'Don't be silly. You're a natural. I can tell,' says Rowan, walking up to her, carrying a trug loaded with garden tools and gloves. 'Put your gloves and secateurs in here, and let's head inside.'

Beth follows Rowan into the kitchen, where they both take off their boots and wash their hands, and Beth puts the kettle on the Aga.

'Tea or coffee?' she asks Rowan.

'Oh, tea, please. And I've brought something for us to have with it.' She pulls a plastic container from her bag. 'I made these yesterday. I thought you might like one.'

Beth looks inside and sees four beautifully decorated cupcakes, with icing that resembles petals.

'They're amazing. They look too good to eat.'

'Don't be silly. Half the joy is in the eating. You make the tea, and we'll sit down and have them.'

Beth finds some cups and saucers, makes a pot of tea when the kettle boils, and joins Rowan at the kitchen table. She picks up a cupcake and takes a bite. It tastes of cinnamon, nutmeg and something floral.

'It's absolutely delicious.'

'Can you taste the rose?'

'Is that what it is?'

'Yes! I thought it was appropriate.'

Beth nods and smiles, because the cake is delicious and because, against all odds, she has actually enjoyed this hour of gardening with Rowan. Given what's going on in her life – the collapse of the family firm, and her impending divorce – it feels like something of a miracle.

'Thank you,' Beth says, pouring two cups of tea. 'Thank you, for giving up whatever you're supposed to be doing, to spend time with me, given how I am at the moment. I'm not fun to be with, I know that.'

'Don't be silly. You were a huge help. I promised Nita I'd carry on looking after her garden and animals until someone told me to do otherwise. And no one has, so here I am, still doing it.'

'I'm glad you are. I'm sorry no one is paying you for it.'

'Oh, don't be. I don't need the money. Anyway... How are things with you? You don't have to tell me if you don't want to, but I've been worried about you since I came over and found you yesterday...'

'That's OK. I'm so embarrassed you saw me like that, to be honest.'

'Don't be. We've all had days where we wanted to stay hidden under the duvet.'

'Probably not as epic as mine, though.'

'Well, you are definitely dealing with two very tough things at the moment. If I was going through that I doubt I'd get out of bed at all. And here you are, fresh from the garden. That's quite the achievement.'

'It's made me feel better.'

'Nature always does,' says Rowan.

'Yes. It's really helped. And to answer your question – well, things haven't changed much. I've told David I'm going to stay here for a few days to clear my head, and he's had to accept it. My mother-in-law is doing the school run, as I expected. I miss the kids like hell, so I can't stay here for too long. But I can't yet face him and... her.'

'I don't blame you. And the business? Have you spoken to your dad?'

'We had a phone call,' says Beth, the memory of what he'd said to her emblazoned on her mind. 'It was difficult. He's... not coping with it very well.'

This is an understatement. Her father had been drunk when she'd spoken to him, and her mother too, judging by the shouting in the distance, partly aimed at Robert, and partly, Beth thinks, at her. Both of her parents feel she should be with them in London, helping them make decisions, although why they feel this when they've never taken her opinion seriously before, she cannot fathom. And Philippa is there, anyway, and she's the golden child. What is playing on Beth's mind, however, is Robert's repeated assertion that his plan to sell Melham Manor is even more important now. The family isn't personally liable for the company's losses, according to her father, but the company's collapse does mean they will no longer be able to draw salaries from the business, and they will have to manage with the assets they already have. Robert is also making noises about raising capital to start something else, which seems insane in a recession. But then, what else does he know, Beth thinks. Business has literally always been his life.

But selling Melham Manor? Beth feels sick at the thought. She can't bring herself to tell Rowan about it, or any of the people she's recently got to know in the area. She imagines they wouldn't be heartbroken by the idea of the house being sold – after all, so few of them have ever even visited it – but she knows the woodland around it is much loved by walkers, and that locals are concerned about the strain recent housing developments have had on local services. The kind of development her father has in mind would involve cutting down trees and definitely would not offer much needed housing to local people looking for a rung on the ladder. Instead, it would bring in well-heeled Londoners who would probably commute into the city and contribute little to the local area, and he's told her that he plans to fence off the grounds properly, to 'offer privacy'. No more dog walking in the woods for Melham residents, then, she thinks.

'I'm not surprised your father isn't coping well. His whole life has changed overnight,' says Rowan.

'Yes. And so has mine. I mean, not about the business, because I'd already left – although God knows who I'll get to employ me, but yes, at least I was already unemployed. But David and me... I have no idea what to do. How do I handle this? I need to call my lawyer but I just can't bring myself to...'

'Can I tell you something? About my own divorce?' says Rowan, pushing a second cupcake towards Beth.

'Of course.'

'When Michael and I parted ways, it was messy. And it was my fault. I'd had an affair with a fellow teacher, someone he actually knew. He was furious. And so was I, full of the righteous indignation of a woman who felt she deserved so much more than he'd been prepared to give me. We went to war. I found this lawyer in Guildford who'd originally worked for some big City firm and he and my ex-husband's equally bombastic lawyer went into battle and my goodness did they enjoy themselves, and charge us for it. By the end, the legal fees had eaten through a huge amount of the equity we had in our house. When we'd finished I barely had enough to afford a small flat, and Michael ended up with the same. The kids had to share bedrooms in each. And then after all that, after all the acrimony, he and I ended up becoming friends again. Not the best of friends, admittedly, but good enough to attend family weddings and funerals at the same time without fisticuffs, and most importantly we were able to parent our children well, together. I deeply regret I fought him so hard, that I wasted so much of my energy feeling angry. Life is too short. Honestly.'

'So... what do you think I should do? Fire my lawyer? My parents are paying for it and I need all of my savings for a new house...'

'Well, mediators don't cost as much as lawyers, and you can pay for it out of your joint funds. I don't want to tell you what to do, my lovely, but what I do know, from all of the years I've lived on this earth, is life is too short to spend it full of rage and regret.'

'You may have a point,' says Beth. 'But I think I might still be too angry to talk to him. I just feel... too hurt.'

'I get that.'

'I'll give it some thought.'

'Good.'

There's a brief silence while the two women eat their second cupcake.

'Oh, I wanted to ask you something, actually,' says Beth, washing down a mouthful of cake with more tea.

'Yes?'

'Do you remember you suggested I ask at the library about that string of numbers on Nita's document? Well, you were right. It corresponded to a book at the library, and I borrowed it, and I got excited when I found some words in the margin in shorthand, which Nita clearly knew how to use. But I got them translated by the editor at *The Bugle*, and it was just these words,' says Beth, unfolding a piece of paper from her handbag. 'I've looked them up online, and I think they're just a list of plants. Do they mean anything to you?'

Rowan takes the piece of paper from Beth and dons her reading glasses.

'Let's see,' says Rowan. 'Calendula – that's a plant, yes. You'd know it as a marigold. Larkspur is another name for a delphinium. They're gorgeous and tall, great for borders. Arctic King is a kind of lettuce. Chervil, otherwise known as French parsley, is a herb. And White Lisbon is a type of spring onion.'

'So they're all really different. But they're all plants?'

'Yes, they're all plants.'

'Oh. A dead end, then. Maybe it was just a shopping list for her, or something? I know she liked gardening, so...'

'Hang on a second. There is something they all have in common, actually.'

'What's that?'

'They are all best planted in August.'

'August?'

'Yep.'

'So they could still just be a shopping list, couldn't they?'

'Yes, they could. But I don't know why she'd write that in a book, rather than on a separate piece of paper. It might be more than that. Maybe she was trying to tell someone that something important happened in August?'

'I don't know. Maybe?' If that was the case, Beth thinks, what might Nita have been trying to say?

'Did she leave a diary or something? You could look up August in there.'

'No, no diary that I've found. A lot of journalism, though. And some notes.'

'You could look at the dates on those, though, couldn't you? See if anything stands out?'

'Yes. I'll do that later,' says Beth.

'And you could maybe ask at the local museum, about important things that happened locally then? There's one in Dorking, open most afternoons for a few hours.'

'Good idea.'

'You already look brighter, you know,' says Rowan with a smile. 'You look like a woman with a plan.'

Beth does feel better, it's true. There's something about following this story of Nita's, this personal project, that's a brilliant distraction. And doing it makes her feel connected to her great-aunt, and she's gradually realising that she's missed that feeling a great deal. She feels now that Nita's absence from her life may have done her harm.

'I do have a little plan at least. Thank you.'

'Don't thank me. Thank Nita. She always knew what to do when someone was hurting. Always.'

* * *

Later that afternoon, Beth sits down in the drawing room and stares at her BlackBerry. She's feeling a little deflated. She's been through every single document in the box she found in the loft, and she can't find anything remotely important or interesting that happened in August. She doubts a local cricket match and a bring-and-buy sale at the village hall are important clues to the whereabouts of a Nazi spy. Perhaps Rowan's right, she thinks. Perhaps the answer lies at the museum. She will visit it tomorrow.

With this decided, she can no longer put off the thing she absolutely must do.

Now.

She picks up her phone and dials David.

'Hi, Beth,' he says. He sounds resigned. Worried even.

'Hi. Look, I've been thinking...'

'And...? Are you going to stay down there forever?'

Beth looks around her, at the musty curtains, the peeling walls and the cluttered floorspace, and despite all of this, she knows that right now, the answer would be yes. Melham Manor, despite all of its faults, is truly balm. But that's not what she needs to discuss with David.

'I'm sorry I left with so little notice,' she says. 'I will be back up in London tomorrow, or the next day at the latest.'

'OK.'

'I don't know if I can come back and stay in the house...?'

'Don't be ridiculous, Beth. It's still your home. I'm not going to move... move her in or anything. We've only just met. I'm not that heartless. Give me some credit.'

'Right. Yes. OK.'

'Look, I *am* so sorry... This timing is dreadful but I just didn't want to lie to you...'

'Yes, I get it.'

They're both silent for a moment.

'Look, shall we get together again and try to talk about it all properly this time? I feel like last time we were both too upset.'

'Yes,' says Beth. 'In fact... I'm wondering whether we've been doing all of this wrong. And that's my fault. I'm wondering if we could... try mediation after all?'

As she says this, she feels her body letting go of tension she had until now been unaware of.

He doesn't respond immediately. She wonders if he's angry it's taken her so long to change her mind.

'Sure. Let's do that,' he says, finally, clearly relieved rather than angry.

'OK. There's someone in Finchley I saw online...'

'Yes, I saw them too. Shall I see if I can make us an appointment?'

'Yes. Please.'

'OK, good. I'll see you soon, then, shall I?'

'Yes.'

'Goodbye, Beth.'

'Bye.' She puts down the phone and feels unexpectedly calm. That was the most effective communication they have managed in months. Maybe this will be all right, she thinks. Well, not all right, but maybe this won't be a disaster. And then she starts a new message, this one to her lawyer, explaining that she will not need his services during the negotiation. He'll be cross, she thinks. He'd probably chalked up the fee as payment for his annual skiing holiday in Chamonix.

* * *

'Hello. Can I help you?'

'Oh... yes please,' says Beth, taking in the slightly tatty, yellowing displays of the museum as she does so. She walks over to the information desk, behind which an elderly man is waiting. He has white hair neatly separated at the side and a well-trimmed moustache. 'This is going to sound a bit mad, but bear with me...' Beth tells him about her great-aunt's collection of newspaper articles about a potential spy ring, and the string of numbers that had led her to the book at the library, and the connection with August. 'I'm not sure what I'm looking for, to be honest. But some sort of event?'

'I see. Do you know which August, by any chance?' the man asks. Beth notices he seems far more alert now than he was when she'd entered. She supposes there probably aren't many visitors here, and far fewer who actually have a mystery to solve. She's glad she's made his day more interesting, anyway.

'No, not really. Except it's likely to be during the Second World War.'

'Yes, that makes sense. Well, let's head over to our "Surrey in the War Years" section, over there, and we can see if there's anything of particular interest.' Beth follows him over to the corner of the room, where she can see there's a selection of black and white photographs framed on a wall. The first thing she sees is an image showing the bombing of the Vickers factory in Brooklands, which is something she already knows about, because she's taken the kids to the Brooklands Museum a few times.

'Yes. Awful that,' says the man. 'Happened in broad daylight, you know. So many people killed. Many women among them.'

Beth agrees, and then works her way around the other photos. There's a crashed German plane in a field, surrounded by locals keen to arrest the pilot, if he actually survived, but that happened in October 1940. Then there are photos of Land Girls working on a farm near Godalming, dated June 1942. And then her attention is taken by another photo of a bombed factory, but this one isn't Brooklands.

'Where's this?' she asks.

'Oh, that's the Millward factory. It used to be on the outskirts of Dorking. It started out as something to do with car manufacturing, but after the war broke out the government asked them to make parts for the new Spitfire fighter there. Actually, come to think of it, this one may be relevant to your search, you know. Everyone who worked there was told to keep quiet about what they were making, of course, because they didn't want to draw Hitler's attention to it. Someone blabbed, though, obviously, because it was hit by an incendiary device one night. Killed a watchman. Put the site out of action for a good couple of months. I've seen articles which blamed it on a potential spy in the workforce.'

A spy! Beth is about to get excited, thinking that this must be relevant, but then she sees the date the bombing occurred – April 1941. Not August.

'Yes, it's not the right month,' says the man, seeing her looking at the date on the photograph. 'But definitely important, locally.'

Beth wonders why there's no reference to this incident in any of Nita's files. If she was so obsessed with finding this spy, why hadn't she clipped up stories about this bombing, something which clearly showed that a traitor might really be in their midst?

What had drawn Nita's attention away from her quest in April 1941?

25

NITA

April 1941

It's been a month since Nita opened that telegram in the hall of the house in Chelsea. She can recite all the words exactly, because she's read them so many times.

```
Regret to inform you of notification
received from the British 7th Armoured
Division that Frank Ernest Bineham has
been reported wounded in action on 3rd
March. Letter follows shortly.
```

First, the extraordinary relief that he was injured, and not dead. And then, that relief becoming concern. How injured was he? They had waited several days for the promised letter, which hadn't told them a huge amount more. 'Considerable injuries', it had said, but that he was stable and being treated at a hospital in Cairo.

And then, a week after that, a letter from Frank, although

written in the hand of a nurse who'd apparently taken dictation from him. This had been disconcerting to say the least, but its touches of humour and the language he'd used had sounded a bit like him, so Nita had chosen to find it comforting.

She is in a great need of comfort. It has been a very difficult month.

First, there was the bombing last week of the Millward, the factory the police had insisted wasn't taking part in war work. Well, that had clearly been a lie, Nita thinks. The spy who'd broken in had obviously found something there that threatened Germany's progress in the war. The bombing had killed a watchman. A man in his sixties, a veteran of the Great War, who'd had the misfortune to be on the night shift. The whole of the local community, Nita included, feels violated by this invasion of their rural idyll, and she feels frustrated that, despite her best efforts, she hasn't yet been able to find out who they are. But the fact is, she is absolutely, unequivocally distracted by her own personal worries. She has no bandwidth for anything else.

Because something must have happened to Joe.

She still hasn't heard from him. Perhaps he's been injured during training, she thinks, or maybe he's got in trouble, somehow, and he's been detained by the army? She can't imagine why, but she is absolutely certain that he'd write to her if he could, and so she is forced to consider a variety of very worrying options. She plans to talk to Simpson at work about it tomorrow, even though this will mean explaining their relationship. Simpson's brother works in the Military Police and may be able to get answers for her. And that's worth giving away their secret for, she thinks.

'Your father is home from London, Nita,' her mother calls from downstairs, and Nita knows what this means. It's time for the discussion both Jane-Anne and Ernest have been telling her they need to have, after what had happened the previous weekend.

Her father's favourite undertaker, Peter Sanders, had visited Melham Manor, keen to learn why his letters to Nita were going unanswered. She had hoped, of course, that the fact she'd fled in a taxi when he'd been trying to invite her out to dinner (which had, apparently, been his intention) would have been enough of a hint that she wasn't keen, but it seems he'd found her 'nerves' charming, and he had persisted. And persisted. And this had culminated in a proposal on one knee in the rose garden.

She had refused him.

This had not gone down well, with him or her parents.

'Right. I'm coming,' says Nita, walking down the stairs towards the drawing room. She's a bag of nerves. Not because she's going to have to explain why she refused Peter – that bit is relatively easy – but because of the other thing she is going to have to tell them. The thing that will undoubtedly change everything.

The conversation with her parents begins as she had expected it would, with chastisement and frustration. Mostly on her mother's part. Her father remains relatively silent, except for a couple of minutes of explaining to her the importance of good business relationships and maintaining a family legacy. She suspects they are both worried that, even if Frank survives, he will not be well enough to produce an heir. *Oh, the irony of what I'm about to say*, thinks Nita.

When her parents have run out of Peter Sanders' related ranting, Nita takes a deep breath.

'I have something to tell you both, actually,' she says, making an effort to look them right in the eye. 'And you're not going to like it.' You could hear a pin drop. 'For some time now, I've been in a relationship with a lovely young man.'

'A... relationship?' her mother asks, aghast, as if she'd just said she'd done a deal with the devil.

'Yes. With another journalist at *The Bugle*.'

'I said you shouldn't have let her work at that place,' says Jane-Anne, shooting Ernest a look of extreme disapproval.

'What's his name?' asks her father.

'Joe. Joseph Miller.'

'And is Miller... an honourable man?' he asks, not unkindly.

'He is. But he was called up recently.'

'I see. When will he get leave, so we can meet him?'

'Are you mad, Ernest? He's a journalist! Not the editor of the paper, or a business owner, or someone with a title. A journalist!'

'Be that as it may, I am prepared to accept that Nita has her own mind and that she should be able to at least express an opinion as to whom she should marry,' he says, and Nita wants to hug him. Except, of course, she hasn't finished delivering her news.

'Thank you, Father. And yes, I would like you to meet him. But first, I need to tell you something very important. Something you will not like. Either of you. I'm... expecting a baby.'

The response from both her parents is dramatic and immediate.

The cigar her father had been smoking drops from his mouth. It tumbles onto the rug below his seat, and he doesn't retrieve it. The rug starts to smoulder.

Her mother's hand, meanwhile, flies to her mouth, and then she stands up and runs out of the room, sobbing.

'I... I'm sorry. I know this must be a shock.'

Ernest Bineham is looking at his daughter askance.

'This is far more than a shock, my dear. This is... unbelievable. I trusted you, Nita. I let you go and work there. I fought your mother tooth and nail to let you go. I believed you were mature enough to get the best out of it, to learn from it. I trusted you. I can't believe I did that... I...'

'This was my choice, Father. Joe is a wonderful man. He will certainly marry me when he can...'

'Has he set a date?'

'Well, no... He has been out of touch for a while... but he will certainly marry me, he promised me he would.'

'Dear child... Oh for heaven's... Nita, this will not do. You are a sweet, innocent child and I can see that you have been taken in, but I understand men. I know men. When we introduced you to Peter, we only had your best interests at heart, you know. We wanted you to be protected, to be secure, with a respectable man. No, he will not come back.'

'He will,' Nita wails.

'He will not. You are now tarnished goods. Unwanted, tarnished goods. No, there's only one thing for it.'

'What?'

'I will speak to your mother and we will arrange for you to be taken to a mother and baby home, as soon as we can. There, you can have the child, away from society and from people who know you, and then they will arrange to find a good home for the child. Then when all of it is over, you can come back home to us. No one else will need to know. We'll just say you're staying with family on the coast.'

Nita doesn't think, even for a second. She had known this was a possibility, of course, even though she'd hoped it wouldn't come to pass. But she has a plan, of sorts, and she realises she must act on it.

She stands up, walks out of the room and runs up the stairs, without looking back or acknowledging any of her father's calls for her to come back. When she's in her room, she grabs a small holdall from beneath her bed and begins to pack, flinging her most treasured items – letters from Frank, her newspaper cuttings, her special pen, her notebooks – and some of her most practical clothing in it.

This takes her only a few minutes. When she's finished, she walks across the landing and down the front stairs. From here, she can hear her mother weeping in the drawing room, and her father murmuring, obviously trying to calm her down.

When she reaches the bottom of the stairs, Nita pauses for a moment outside the door, wondering if she should go in and say goodbye. But then she realises they might try to restrain her and stop her from leaving. She can't risk it. Rather than walking down the front drive, where she might be seen – the moon is bright tonight – she turns left and walks around the side of the house and into the darkness of woods.

* * *

Nita knocks hard on the door, twice. It's starting to rain. She wishes she'd packed a headscarf or a cloak with a hood.

A key is turned in the lock, and the door opens.

'Oh, it's you.'

'Yes, hello, Irene. I'm sorry to turn up unannounced.'

'Don't worry. Come in. It's horrible out there.'

Nita does as she asks. She sees Irene eyeing the bag she's carrying, but neither of them says anything.

'Take a seat on the sofa,' says Irene, as they enter the lounge. 'Can I get you a cup of tea? Something stronger?'

This show of automatic kindness is all Nita needs to lose her composure. She begins to sob. She has spent the entirety of the long walk here running through what had just happened, what she'd said, and what her parents had said. And also, of course, what she has just done. In fact, her brain is only just beginning to process the fact that she's left the family home with only a small bag, no money and a baby on the way. It's almost too much to take in. *And what, oh please God, what*, she thinks, *have I done*?

'Just wait there and I'll get you some brandy.' Irene rushes into the kitchen, but Nita barely notices, until the other woman is thrusting a tumbler of amber liquid into her hands. 'Drink it. It helps, for shock.'

She takes a sip and feels the warmth spread through her mouth and down her throat.

'Thank you,' says Nita, between her sobs, which are subsiding slowly.

'When you're ready, tell me what's up. I'm presuming you're not here about a newspaper story.'

Irene's attempt at humour causes Nita to manage a small smile.

'No,' says Nita, pulling out a handkerchief to wipe her nose. 'No. I'm here because I need your help.'

'What is it?'

Where do I begin, Nita thinks, before deciding that she had better start from the most life-changing news of all.

'I'm expecting. But I'm not married.'

'Oh, I see.'

Nita waits for Irene to say something else, but she doesn't.

'The father is a man I work with. We are going to get married but he's been conscripted and I can't communicate with him at the moment... and my parents want me to marry someone else, but I've refused him, and so I told them about the baby and they wanted to send me away to have the baby adopted, and I can't do it... I can't... Joe will come back, and when he does... we will be... a family...' Nita is rambling now. She knows that. But it feels good to say it all, anyway. 'So I've left home. And I can't go back.'

'I see. But why have you come here?'

'Because I was so impressed by the way you and the other women supported each other with childcare, helping each other work. And I realised that's what I need. I need someone to help me. Oh dear God, I've done the wrong thing, haven't I? I shouldn't have come here...'

In her head, Nita had imagined Irene embracing her, and telling her everything would be all right, that she could stay with her in her house, use it as a base until she manages to find out what's happened to Joe. But she is realising quickly that this was a fantasy. Irene is kind, certainly, but she's not her friend. Nita feels both ashamed and embarrassed by her presumption.

'Do you want to stay here? Is that why you came?'

Nita nods. She's too wrung out to lie.

'Oh, I see. Well, I would never turn you away tonight, of course – you can stay on the sofa, I'm afraid that's the only space I have free – but I can't help more than that, lovey. I'm sorry. You see, I know who you are.'

Nita takes her head out of her hands. 'What do you mean?'

'You're the boss's daughter, aren't you? You're a Bineham. My boss is Ernest Bineham. He's your father.'

'Yes.' What else can she possibly say?

'If he finds out I'm harbouring his daughter, he'll sack me. In fact, there's a good chance he'll sack all of us. The former child-care collective, I mean. And none of us can afford to lose our jobs. But of course you know that.'

'Oh.' *Why didn't I realise she'd work out who I was*, Nita thinks. *And why, even when I've left home, does my family's influence seem to tarnish everything?*

'My heart goes out to you, love. There's a lot of women like you in this war. They spend time with a man on leave, give him what he wants, and then he hops off back and leaves them to deal with what he's left behind.'

'Joe's not like that...'

'Maybe not,' says Irene, sitting down next to Nita and rubbing her back. 'But he's not here, is he? And you say you can't contact him? I'd say you're in a similar position to those other women, anyway.'

Nita sits back on the sofa and stares at the ceiling.

'So, yes, you stay tonight, my lovey. Stay here tonight, and then we can talk at breakfast and see if we can find somewhere else for you to go.'

'Thank you, Irene. Thank you. I appreciate that.'

'Oh, goodness, it's fine. Honestly. We women need to do what we can to look after each other, you know. We really, really do.'

* * *

The next morning dawns brightly. Nita awakes to the sun penetrating the net curtains in Irene's front room. She has slept surprisingly well, given the small size of the sofa and the unfamiliar environment. She realises the extreme emotion she felt yesterday had absolutely worn her out. Plus, of course, she is pregnant, and is starting to feel incredibly tired a lot of the time. She suspects this is something she's going to have to get used to.

She can hear Annie, Irene's baby, babbling upstairs, and Irene tending to her. *It's time to get going*, Nita thinks, pulling herself up and running her hands through her hair. *I can't stay here much longer. My presence here is too risky for both of them.*

She is fully dressed and presentable by the time Irene arrives downstairs with Annie on her hip.

'Oh, goodness, I didn't expect you to be up and about so early.'

'I woke with the sun. Anyway, I have to be going.'

'Don't you want to stay, to talk things through? I was thinking we could try this new women's hostel that's opened in Guildford...'

'No, it's all right. I need to go. I know what I should do.'

'You're not going back to Melham Manor, are you?'

'No. I'm not.'

'Then where?'

'I don't think I should tell you. Just in case someone ever asks you. But I'll be safe.'

'Do you promise?' says Irene, her eyes full of concern.

'I promise.'

Half an hour later – the delay due to Irene insisting she stay and eat a proper breakfast – Nita walks towards Melham's outskirts. She takes care to stick to the back roads, aware that her parents might have people out looking for her. Although whether they'd do that and risk people discovering a family scandal, she's not sure.

After a slightly circuitous walk of about two miles, Nita arrives at her destination, weary and uncertain. She'd felt confident in her plan earlier, buoyed by an unusual feeling of calm when the idea had occurred to her. However, she is far from calm now. *What*, she wonders, *on earth will I do if I can't find refuge here?*

She pushes the gate open, walks up the path and knocks on the door.

'Ah, Nita,' says Harriet Morgan, when she opens the door, her smile welcoming and her face showing no hint of surprise. 'I knew you'd be back.'

26

BETH

February 2009

Beth is drawing up outside Melham Manor when her phone bleeps. She pulls the handbrake and casts her eye at the screen. There's a new message from her father. It's the most recent of several messages she's received today, all insisting she call him.

She has no intention of doing that, though, because she knows what he wants to discuss. He's sent her three separate emails this week telling her he needs to talk to her about the sale of Melham Manor, which he now describes as *very pressing* given *the state of the family finances.*

Beth knows what this means. The collapse of Stellar means the shares they all had in the company are likely to be worthless, and so Robert's income has stopped abruptly. Beth has lost money too, of course, although she had far fewer shares, resulting in a dividend which most quarters had paid her enough to cover the family food bills. It had been a great thing to have, certainly, and she'd planned to sell a portion of them much later to pay for the kids' university education, but the loss doesn't feel as personal to her, even though her current state of unemployment is causing her some panic. Not compared to her father, whose entire life, and in fact, Beth suspects, entire self-worth, has relied upon Stellar and the income it produced.

Beth glances into the rear-view mirror and is momentarily taken aback by the sight of her newly dyed hair. She'd done it last night from a packet, finally enacting a much-postponed teenage rebellion now she no longer has an employer who'll care. Her hair has been transformed from a dull shade of brown to a glorious hint of deep purple. She can't help but smile. Then she shoves her phone in her pocket and sets about removing the children from their car seats. Talking to her father about the sale of the house seems pointless, she thinks. He'll have more jobs he wants her to do, probably involving letting house clearance firms in to do their work. In previous years, perhaps even in previous months, Beth might have said yes to these orders – for they were never, ever requests – but something in her has snapped, and she doesn't want to say yes to them any more. And yet she can't quite find the strength to say no, so instead she's just not replying. She knows she'll have to, eventually. But not today.

'Right, both of you. Coats, hats and boots on,' says Beth, opening the boot and pulling out their winter weather gear. There has been a hard frost overnight, and despite the clear blue sky overhead, the temperature hasn't risen much above freezing. She helps Ella into her coat, mittens and wellies. She has to restrain her as she does so, because her daughter's desire to run wild is tangible.

'Can we go, Mummy?' asks Raphie, who has dressed himself in double-quick time.

'Yes. But don't go too far,' she says, and they scream with delight and run in the direction of the woods and the swing they know awaits them there.

Beth pulls on her own coat and gloves, locks the car and follows them. She's glad she decided to bring them here for the weekend. They could have stayed at home – David had promised he would absent himself, if that made her feel more comfortable – but she's known she'd still have spent every minute thinking about him with his new girlfriend. The house feels wrong, too. Bought with such excitement before the children were born, it now feels like a tarnished school trophy that should have gone back years ago.

No, she feels better here at the Manor. Beth enters the woods and follows the path to the swing. When she gets there, however, she's disconcerted to find the kids aren't there. She's about to shout for them when she hears them chattering to each other, clearly interested in something. She follows the sound, wending her way down a narrow path forged by foxes, past ancient gnarly trees and dense ground foliage, before seeing flashes of the kids' colourful coats.

Ella and Raphie are in the centre of a clearing surrounded by oak trees, and Rowan's with them. That's not a surprise, of course. Rowan is often in these woods. What is a surprise, however, is what she's doing there. She's standing beside a rudimentary table made from what look like trestle supports and a couple of long planks of wood, and on it are a strange mix of objects: a bowl, a candle, and a rudimentary cross in the middle. Rowan is letting the children pick these objects up and examine them.

'Oh, hi, Beth. Love the new hair.'

'Thank you,' says Beth, glowing with pleasure.

'I didn't know you were coming down this weekend,' Rowan says before returning her attention to the children. 'Yes, Ella, there's water in that. Be careful not to splash it or you'll get wet and that's not nice when it's so cold.'

'What's this?' Beth asks, both curious and slightly perturbed by what she's looking at.

'I'm sorry, I should have asked your permission before putting up my altar. My mistake. Nita didn't mind, of course, and my brain is refusing to accept she's dead. I need to get better at asking. Sorry.'

'No, it's fine,' says Beth, her guilt at the impending sale of this whole estate overruling any feelings of ownership she might have had over the woods and what happens in them. *After all*, she thinks, *these trees may be uprooted in a few months.* The thought makes her stomach lurch.

'Are you OK?' says Rowan, noticing.

'Oh, I'm fine. Just... you know, the divorce, and everything,' she says, and Rowan nods, understanding that she wouldn't want to say more in front of the children. 'So tell me... an altar?' Rowan's strange activity is a welcome distraction from having to talk about Melham Manor's dubious future. She assumes, given the cross, that it's some kind of Christian ritual.

'Oh, yes. Well, I'm a Wiccan. It's my faith,' she says, as the children get bored with the altar and run off back towards the swing. 'I'm a witch.' Rowan says this as if she's just told Beth she lifts weights at the gym. She clearly sees no reason to be embarrassed by it.

'Oh,' replies Beth, wrong-footed. She had not expected this at all.

'I know, that's how people usually react. It's fine,' says Rowan with a smile on her face. 'Wicca is incredibly misunderstood.'

'Sorry, I think that came out wrong. I didn't mean to be rude.'

'You're not being rude. Look, I'll try to explain as simply as I can. Wicca is a pagan religion. It's been around in this form since the forties, started by a guy called Gerald Gardner, but actually we believe there have been witches since the beginning of humankind. I'm what's known as a hedge witch. We believe that everything has a soul, even the trees around us now, for example. We want to live in harmony with nature and the cycle of the year, the seasons, are incredibly special for us. We grow a lot of what we eat and we also make potions from herbs and other plants.'

'Potions?'

'Oh, nothing dangerous. In fact, all witches, whatever kind they might be, share a general principle, which is to harm none, and do as you will.'

'And you have been holding... some kind of service here? On this altar?'

Beth realises as she says this that most people would be feeling uncomfortable or incredulous in her position, but she realises she feels neither of these things. On the contrary, she's interested.

'Yes. Today is Imbolc. It's a special day for Wiccans, where we celebrate the stirring of spring. We honour the Celtic goddess Brigid. That reed cross there is Brigid's cross, and in a bit, I'll recite some prayers, asking her to bless my year ahead.'

'Oh, I see.'

'Do you?'

'Yes,' says Beth, realising as she says it why all of this feels strangely familiar. 'Nita was a witch too, wasn't she?'

Rowan smiles.

'You remembered! I knew you would, in time.'

And then it all comes back to her, a flood of memories, of her holding Nita's warm hand as they'd recited what she'd thought were poems in the woods, as they'd lit fires and danced around them, as they'd picked herbs from the back garden and made strange-smelling drinks with them in the kitchen.

'I do,' says Beth. 'Yes, I do.'

'Nita told me she knew you had it, the gift, from just about as soon as you could speak. Children are often magical, you know, but most grow out of it. But Wicca runs in families, you see. She saw it in you. You came alive out here, she said, in the woods, just like your children do.' They stand in silence for a moment and listen to Raphie and Ella laughing as they play hide and seek among the trees and bushes. 'That's why she was so incredibly sad when your parents stopped you visiting.'

'Why did they do that? I've always wondered.'

'Well, I think it's time you knew,' Rowan says, running her hands over the cross on the altar. 'Nita told me that your mother is a devout Catholic.'

'Yes, she is.'

'Well, Catholicism and Wicca are not good bedfellows. She told me Marisa came to visit once and, rather unusually for her, had come out into the woods to try to find you. She was wanting to leave and wondered where you were. She found you and Nita out here, dancing around a lit candle, reciting an incantation. You were taking part in a ritual. Marisa was furious. She believed Nita was communing with the devil. Of course, that was pretty much the worst crime Marisa could imagine. So that was it. She took you away and you never returned. Until you made the journey just before she died, of course.'

Beth looks around her and feels a strange mix of profound sadness and immense peace. It all makes sense now. Her strange affinity for Melham Manor, her desire to escape here. She hadn't been with her sister or her parents in those memories of this place. She had been with *Nita*.

'So were you and Nita in a... coven together?'

'Oh, nothing as formal as that. But there are a group of us in this area who meet from time to time to discuss our faith, and to celebrate big festivals like Beltane, in May. And of course we all love to garden, and that's how Nita and I became close.'

'That's wonderful. I'm so glad she had friends. I was worried she'd been lonely.'

'Oh, no. Nita was never lonely. She was very content,' says Rowan with a smile. 'And she had the animals too, of course.'

'Yes. Good.'

'By the way, have you got any further with finding out more about your list of August plants?'

'Oh, no. To be honest, I've kind of gone off the boil on that. David and I are trying to find a reasonable way through this divorce. I've agreed to mediation.'

'Oh, good. I'm so glad.'

'Yes. We've had separate sessions with the mediator already. We have our first joint session this week. So yes, I've been trying to get my head around things and I've also been applying for jobs, unsuccessfully, and so... No. I haven't had time and I haven't thought about it really. It doesn't feel important. I think I was using it as a displacement activity, you know? Something to distract me from what I really needed to think about.'

'Completely understandable. You can get back to it when you're ready.'

'Yes, exactly.'

'Onto more immediate matters. What plans do you have for this afternoon?'

'Oh, none. I thought we'd grab some lunch at the pub, maybe, and then come back here and play a silly board game or something.'

'Ah, well, if you're at a loose end, I wonder if you might all like to help out at an event I'm running? It's a Bring and Buy sale in the village hall, in aid of the food bank. I need people to help sell cakes and tea and to help me set up and remove the tables and stuff. I'm sure we can watch the kids, between us?'

'Well, they never say no if there's cake involved,' says Beth, deciding that, given what's about to happen to Melham Manor, the very least she can do is to help out at a fundraiser for the locals who are struggling.

* * *

'Just put those cakes out over there, if you could, Beth,' Rowan asks.

Rowan is definitely in her element. She seems to know everyone, and they all seem to know her. Beth hadn't realised how much her new friend was embedded in Melham's community, although of course, being a former headteacher at the local primary school would help in that regard. Beth's prep school, on the other hand, had been an incredibly expensive, small establishment in Kensington. Her friends there were mostly the children of either landed gentry or diplomats and they had lived all over central London, so she had never bumped into one in the corner shop or in a local park.

'Of course,' she replies, checking that Raphie and Ella are still sitting in the corner of the room playing with one of the teenage girls who have turned up to run the Guides' stall. She sees that they are, and they seem to be having a very good time. Beth turns back to her task. She lays the butterfly cupcakes out in neat rows, and places their price, seventy-five pence, at the front for all visitors to see. Then she turns around to open one of the boxes, which she's told contains polystyrene cups for the tea.

'Oh, hello again,' says a voice she recognises. She turns around and sees it's James Connors, the local councillor who had taken her out to visit the site he wants the council to develop as social housing.

'Oh, hi,' she replies. 'Nice to see you again, too.'

'So you bake as well as write news stories, then?' he asks with a smile.

'Oh no. I can't take responsibility for these. I can't bake at all. But I reckon I'm probably OK at sales.'

'I'm sure you are! Look, I meant to drop you a line to say thank you for the story you wrote, but I forgot. And I'm very sorry about that. So, anyway, thank you. It was a very well-written story, and it got the council's attention. In fact, the leader has scheduled a debate about my idea for later this month. I wondered if you might come and report on it?'

Beth has no idea whether Steve will want her to cover it, but she has no intention of saying that now. There's something about James she likes. He's a nice, hard-working, caring man, and if she can do something to help him, then all the better. If anything, it makes her feel a bit better about her family selling Melham Manor. The Bineham family have essentially milked this village for not particularly well-paid labour over the last century and a bit, and she would feel a little better if she could play even a little part in trying to improve things for local people. More affordable housing would definitely help, she thinks.

'Of course. I'll be there,' she says, with a smile.

'Brilliant. I'll be back when you're up and running for some cake and a cuppa,' he says with a wink, before walking away in the direction of a table run by a local Women's Institute. She watches him joke with the women there, who are all over seventy. *He's a nice man*, Beth thinks. *Nice. Definitely*.

As she carries the large metal urn over to the kitchen to fill it up with water, Beth realises she has a smile on her face.

27

NITA

May 1941

'Are you sure you'll be all right?'

'Of course I will.'

'Right. Well, I'll be staying at The Midland Hotel. I've written the phone number down on the pad. You can ring and leave a message for me there if you need to.'

'I've been telling you, I'll be fine. I've got writing to do.'

In the absence of any other employment, Nita has been writing short stories, encouraged by Harriet. To her surprise, the editor of a monthly periodical loved her very first one, and she is now writing them once a fortnight. It's not exactly what you'd call a steady income, but it's something, a contribution to her keep.

Harriet is heading up to Manchester for some sort of educational conference. It's the first time she's left Nita alone overnight since she'd turned up unannounced, begging for somewhere to stay. Since then, Harriet has cared for her without question, as something had told Nita she would, despite the fact she can't work at the paper any more and therefore has no proper income.

In fact, their friendship – for that is undoubtedly what it is now – has shown her just how wonderful human beings can be when they support each other, which is something her previous life had given her precious little evidence of. She's also learned a great deal in the past month about Harriet's Wiccan and feminist beliefs. Her eyes are now fully open to a whole world that she'd never previously realised existed.

'Fine. Right then, I'll be off. I'll be back by supper time tomorrow.'

'Right you are.'

'Look after yourself. Don't answer the door.'

'Don't worry, I won't.'

'And put the wireless on if you're nervous.'

Nita has been feeling increasingly paranoid that her parents have sent people to spy on her. She'd heard what must have been a fox or a badger in the garden hedge the previous day and had shouted for Harriet in panic. But she needs her friend to leave her alone, so she's not going to dwell on her fears.

'I'm fine. Honestly. Go. I'll see you tomorrow.'

'Yes. Don't spend too much time worrying. Keep yourself busy.'

Harriet knows that Nita is given to worrying, not just about Joe, but also about Frank. Being separated from her parents was something Nita had anticipated, but she had overlooked the fact that leaving Melham Manor would mean losing access to any information about how her brother's recovery is going. She aches to write to him in Cairo, if that's where he still is, but she doesn't know how he'll react to her current predicament, being pregnant and unwed. She's worried he'll tell her to have it adopted, like her parents, and this is what's stopping her from writing. She doesn't want her feelings towards him tainted, and she doesn't want to disappoint him in any way. And she knows that being pregnant and unmarried *is* shameful and that he probably *would* think less of her. But even so, she misses their communications dreadfully, and worries about him every day.

'I will.'

Harriet carries her suitcase down the path, pulls the gate open and waves a quick goodbye before striding purposefully towards the railway station. Nita waits until she's out of sight and closes the door behind her but doesn't lock it. She normally does lock it when Harriet's at work, because they can't risk anyone walking in and finding her there, but there's no point today. She's going on a trip of her own. One that Harriet has no idea about.

* * *

Nita is incredibly tired, more tired than she had expected to be. The journey here has exhausted her. She wonders whether all pregnant women feel like this. Maybe that's why expectant mothers are always being told to put their feet up, she thinks. She wishes she could do that now, because her feet hurt and she could murder a cup of tea. She decides to find a tea house afterwards, to replenish her energy levels before she travels to Waterloo for the journey home.

She adjusts the strap of her leather satchel. Whitehall stretches before her, the historic avenue's grand facades now bearing the scars of war. Sandbags flank the Admiralty building and scaffolding covers the Ministry of Defence, a visual reminder of the bomb that had ripped through it last year.

Nita is standing still in what feels like a sea of people, all apparently with somewhere to go and something important to do. She feels tiny and even more inconsequential here than she has ever felt at home. She won't stay long, she thinks. She just has to do this one thing. She presses on, falling into step with the crowd around her, her heart pounding.

'Can I help you?'

'Yes, please, I...'

'Sorry?'

The hall of the War Office is cavernous, and the Portland stone on its floors and walls has turned it into a gigantic echo chamber. Nita raises her voice so the receptionist can hear her.

'Yes, please. I'm trying to find out where my... fiancé is.'

They are not technically engaged, of course, but Nita decides not to tell her this.

'Oh, I see. Is he a prisoner of war?'

'No. No... look, it's difficult to explain. He's training, actually. He was conscripted. But I've lost contact with him and I...'

The woman behind the desk, who is in her forties and has her hair cut into a neat bob, now has a resigned look on her face, suggesting she's heard this request many times before.

'Look, I'm sorry to hear that, but we can't force soldiers to correspond with their sweethearts. Sometimes, men just aren't good at communication, I'm afraid.'

'No, it's not like that. Joe... Joseph... he wouldn't do that to me. I know he wouldn't.'

'Look, I know this might be hard to hear, but this is common. You might have to accept he simply doesn't want to contact you, my dear.'

'But I'm pregnant.' The woman behind the desk's expression changes. Nita is painfully aware that there is a queue of people behind her and they can all hear the conversation she's having, but she realises this might be her only chance to get the information she needs, so she doesn't care. 'I'm pregnant and I've written to him so many times and he hasn't replied at all. He wrote to me once when he arrived, and he seemed absolutely fine, but I haven't heard from him since and I am sure something dreadful has happened to him. I just know something has. And I need to find out what it is...'

'Goodness,' says the receptionist. Nita wishes the ground would swallow her up. 'I see. Well, look...' says the woman, beckoning Nita to lean in closer, which she does. 'Look, I can't promise anything, but I can send you to the administration team who deal with training. Maybe they might be able to tell you something. But as you're not married, I don't know if they will. But say Diana sent you. And don't tell anyone else, all right?'

'I understand.'

The receptionist writes something down on a piece of paper and hands it to her.

'Follow those instructions. And good luck.'

'Thank you.'

Nita leaves the queue behind with some relief. The receptionist has written down: 'first floor, room 102a' on the piece of paper. Nita shows this to a guard standing at the bottom of the enormous winding staircase and he lets her through. She climbs the stairs slowly, taking pauses to get her breath, and follows signs on the landing above, which take her down a series of labyrinthine corridors towards a room with a frosted door labelled with the corresponding room number. She knocks and a female voice tells her to enter.

The room is long and thin and there are fifteen men and women seated at a series of wooden desks, all piled high with paper. They are all either typing or writing, and none of them pay any attention to her as she enters, except for a young woman seated at a desk immediately to her right, who she assumes was the person who told her to come in.

'Hello,' says Nita. 'Reception told me to come up here. I'm searching for someone who's in training...'

'Searching?'

'Yes. Diana sent me.'

Nita does her best to explain, as simply and convincingly as she can, why she's here.

'I see,' says the young woman when Nita has finished telling her story. 'The problem is...'

'I know this is a big ask. I know that,' says Nita. 'And I wouldn't ask normally but I've been kicked out of home and I'm having a baby and I just need to know he's all right...' She crumples again. 'And I'm so tired.'

'Bless you,' says the woman, who can obviously see that Nita is exhausted. 'Take a seat. Look, I don't have any power in here really, I'm just a clerk, but I'll ask my friend Mary over there, and we can see if she can check his record. See if there's anything on there that would be concerning.'

Relief floods through Nita. She hands the woman her precious copy of Joe's only letter to her, which includes the details of his unit.

'Thank you so much. Thank you.'

It takes about ten minutes for the clerk to return. Nita tries to work out whether she's about to deliver bad news, or indeed any news, but her face is inscrutable. She returns to her seat and leans into Nita, so they can hear each other over the clatter of type-writers.

'Mary and I had a good look,' she says, returning to her seat and handing Joe's letter back to Nita. 'And I'm afraid we couldn't find anything.'

'So no record of him getting ill or being disciplined or shipped off somewhere?' says Nita, every straw she's been grasping at since Christmas tumbling out of her.

'No. But that's the strange thing. It's not that there wasn't any record of him hurting himself. There weren't any records of him at all.'

'What do you mean?'

'I mean, I thought perhaps he'd written the wrong unit number down by accident, so we searched the lists for all units with similar names and numbers, and there's no record of him there either. Are you sure this is how his name is spelled?'

'Yes, definitely.'

Nita's head starts to spin. This can't be right, she thinks. It simply can't be. He wouldn't have lied to her. And he'd written it down for her, so she could write back, and the writing was clear.

'I'm so sorry, Miss Bineham. I really wanted to help you, but I can't. There's simply no record of him. You could try the Navy or the Air Force record offices? Perhaps there's been some confusion about which force he's with?'

But Nita knows there isn't. She might be exhausted, but her memory is clear. He said he was joining the Army. Definitely the Army. There could be no confusion about that.

'I must go,' is all Nita can think to say. *She'll think he made it all up to escape me*, she thinks. *Made it up so he doesn't have to marry me and become a father.* Her face burns with anticipation of the pity this woman must be feeling. She stands up hurriedly, wobbles slightly as her inner ear struggles to come to terms with where it is in space and time, and then opens the door and walks out, calling out a hurried 'thank you,' before it closes.

As she stumbles back down the maze of corridors, a horrific thought invades her mind. What if that is right? What if Joe never loved her at all?

28

BETH

February 2009

'After you.'

'Thanks.'

David holds the door open for Beth and she walks past him and into the mediator's office. It's a tidy, functional space with white walls decorated with prints of abstract modern art and three high-backed armchairs flanking a small walnut table. A window at one end overlooks a small car park and a railway line. The mediator, a woman in her forties called Sue, walks into the room behind them and tells them to take a seat.

'Thank you both for coming today,' she says, pouring them all a glass of water from a jug on the table. 'As you know, I am unable to give legal advice, but I do promise to listen to both of you and I won't take sides. I'll do my best to help you to remain calm, so you're able to reach an agreement you're both happy with. And if necessary, I can give you practical ideas of how to make things work, based on the experience I have of working with hundreds of other couples.'

As Beth sits, she wonders how on earth she's supposed to remain calm. She hasn't felt calm around David since he announced he wanted to separate. She's constantly on high alert, wondering what he's thinking about, whether he's annoyed that she's still around, and what he might be doing when he leaves early for work, or comes home late.

'David, I wonder if you can start things off for us,' says Sue. 'Can you tell me what your ideal outcome from our mediation sessions would be?'

'I want... I want us to reach an agreement without her parents shoving their noses in, as usual.'

This isn't at all what Beth had imagined he was going to say. In her darkest moments, she'd wondered whether he might say he wanted her to agree to him having full custody of the children, due to her lack of a proper job and her emotional instability.

'What do you mean by "shoving their noses in"?' asks Sue.

David shuffles in his seat.

'I suppose I mean taking control. Like paying for an expensive bulldog lawyer to try to bully me into a particular divorce settlement. They try to control everything. They always have done. They've been controlling Beth since she was in her pram. I'm sick of it.'

Beth realises she should probably leap in and try to defend her family here, but she finds she doesn't know which words to use.

'Can you give an example?' Sue asks.

'Yeah, I can give you lots.' Beth realises she is holding her breath. He has never been this honest with her about this, not in their entire marriage. 'So, they told her what universities she should apply to. Then they expected her to work in the family firm when she graduated, even though she'd been thinking about taking some time off to write a novel and she had thoughts about journalism. And when we got married, they insisted that she shouldn't change her surname to mine. I mean, I'm no misogynist, it should be up to a woman to decide what surname she has. But it wasn't her choice. It was theirs. And she just,' he says, refusing to meet Beth's eye, 'lets them do it to her.'

Beth's breathing quickens and she feels her stomach tighten. She feels like fighting back, but she realises with a flash of irony that it's not David she wants to fight. It's herself. She's suddenly deeply, deeply embarrassed and ashamed that she's failed to stand up for herself for so long. *What kind of woman am I?* she thinks. *What kind of person? What kind of mother?*

'I see. Beth, do you want to come in here? What do you have to say to that?'

Where the hell do I start, she thinks.

'I... Honestly, I'm... David, why have you only just said this?'

'I've been saying it for years, Beth. Ever since we met. You just never want to hear it.'

It's true, certainly, that he's said all of these things individually, in different arguments over many years. But he has never presented them to her as a whole before, and the impact of this is significant.

'Is that what all of this is about? Are you leaving me because of... my parents?'

'God, Beth, no. I have always remained with you *despite* them. They've never liked me, have they? They made that very clear. But I stayed because I loved you.'

'Did you? Love me?'

'You know I did.'

'But not any more.'

'No. I've changed. Things have changed. I don't know why. Maybe I just kept hoping you'd change, and you didn't. But that doesn't mean I hate you. Even though you think that it does.'

'I think that's an important point to make,' says Sue. 'I don't sense hatred in this room, and I didn't get that feeling from either of you in our separate meetings. But there is a lot of sadness, and a lot of pain. Both of which is entirely normal to feel, of course. Beth, can you tell David what it is you want from this process?'

'I want... the kids to be OK. I want them to have parents who can talk about their needs and share things. I feel... have always felt... that David has left too much of the caring for the kids on my shoulders. His work takes him all around the place and it's always been me who's been left picking them up and dropping them off, and I would like that to change. I've realised I need... something... something more for myself. David's right, I think. My parents have pulled my strings like a marionette for far too long, and I genuinely have no idea who I am. I need to work that out, and to do that I need to be more... free. But I adore my kids. I can't lose them...'

'I never wanted to take them away,' says David. 'Don't be daft. I was never going to take them away.'

Sue leans down to a box of tissues beside her chair, takes one out and hands it to Beth, who dabs her eyes with it.

'OK,' says Beth, sniffing. 'That's good.'

'David – do you agree with Beth that she has shouldered too much of the caring responsibilities?'

There's a pause. Beth wonders whether David is about to say something incredibly hurtful, like the fact that she's so incapable at work, he didn't feel her career would suffer much from taking time out to care for children. But he doesn't.

'I've never really thought about it, you know. Not until now. My mother stayed at home and looked after me and my sister, and I suppose I was subconsciously following that. I just assumed Beth would want to. But yeah, I think maybe I've always just assumed she'd be there. Her work at Stellar was usually in London, so I knew she wasn't far away.'

'So you would be prepared to accept more responsibility for childcare in the divorce settlement? Regular days, perhaps, where you do the wrap-around care? And certain weeks in school holidays?' asks Sue.

Beth waits with bated breath. She knows this would mean David getting his office to agree to flexible working, a suggestion he has always resisted in the past.

'Sure. Yes. I can do that,' he says.

* * *

'Are you getting the bus, or shall we find you a cab?' David asks.

They've just emerged from their hour-long mediation session. After his agreement about childcare, it had gone relatively smoothly. Well, more smoothly than she had anticipated. There hadn't been a slanging match, at least, and they have a meeting scheduled for next week to discuss finances. At least now Stellar is being wound up, Beth's stake in the company is no longer even on the table. Her parents also seem far less motivated for her to use their own lawyer now their own business interests aren't on the line.

'Oh, I'll get the bus. It'll give me more time to work out what I'm going to say to Mum and Dad.'

'Are you sure you should go now?' David asks. 'You must be feeling exhausted after that. I definitely do.'

'Yes, but I've been putting it off for too long already. I need to speak to them.'

'If you say so. In which case, I'll see you later.'

For a moment she thinks David might be about to kiss her on

a cheek like a well-tolerated aunt, but instead he pulls her in for an unexpected hug.

'I meant what I said in there,' he says, into her ear. 'I really do think they've ridden roughshod over your life for far too long.'

'Yes,' she says, pulling away. 'I think so, too.'

'Oh, and by the way, I think your new hair colour suits you,' he says, with a smile.

'Thanks.' Beth smiles back and walks towards the bus stop. She feels light, as if a huge weight has been lifted from her shoulders. David doesn't hate her. She doesn't hate David. *There's something we can work with here*, she thinks. *Thank goodness.*

She manages to find a seat at the top of the double-decker bus. This has been her favourite seat ever since childhood, when she'd imagined she was the driver and she'd experience a thrill at every tight turn of near miss with a low hanging branch. She watches the populace of this particular pocket of London go about their daily business: walking dogs, lugging groceries home, heading to meetings, holding hands with children and lovers. There's something immensely comforting about this apparent normality, when her own life is falling apart. *Mind you*, she thinks, as she spots a woman remonstrating with a tantruming toddler, *who knows what's really going on in that woman's world? She might have just received a life-changing diagnosis or a ground-shaking piece of news from a friend, and still have to be outside in the world, acting as if all she cares about is that child's demand for an ice cream. You can never really tell, not really, what agonies someone is carrying around them.*

The bus eventually wends its way into Chelsea and Beth gets off and walks the short distance to her parents' house. She takes a deep breath and knocks. This time, her father answers quickly, probably, she thinks, because he doesn't have an enormous amount to do at the moment, now he no longer has a business to run.

'Hello, darling,' he says, kissing her warmly on both cheeks. She's taken aback. The last time she'd seen him, just before Christmas, they'd parted on dreadful terms.

'Hello, Dad.'

'Come through. I've made us lunch.'

Beth raises an eyebrow as she follows her father into the kitchen. He rarely cooks.

'Where's Mum?'

'Oh, she had a meeting with her publisher to discuss her next book. So it's just you and me. Do you want a drink? There's some of that elderflower cordial stuff your mother loves in the cupboard.'

'Oh, just water, thanks.'

'Of course. Sparkling?'

'Tap is fine, Dad.'

She watches as he finds a glass and pours her water – not from a tap, but from a water filter jug in the fridge. Naturally. Her parents would never drink tap water as others drink it, would they? They love filters. Not just physical ones, of course, but mental ones like the clothes someone's wearing, the accent they use, the way that they hold their cutlery.

He places the glass in front of her. The table is already laid. She's sitting in front of a place mat that is decorated with a scene from Eton, her father's old school.

'Thanks.'

'I'll just assemble the food. It's just some nice bits from the Waitrose.' He sets about opening the fridge and the cupboards, decanting olives into a bowl, plating prosciutto and slicing sourdough bread.

'So you wanted to talk to me about Melham Manor,' says Beth, deciding she's had enough of social niceties. So much of their communication is subtext, and it's ridiculous.

'Yes, I do,' he says, carrying the bread board over to the table. 'Do you like Camembert? They had quite a nice raw milk one from Normandy.'

'Dad. Stop it. Talk to me. What is it?'

'Honestly, Beth, you are so abrupt at the moment. Why can't we just have a nice lunch?'

'Because the last time we met I shouted at you and we haven't had a conversation since. Come on, Dad. Why do we always pretend everything's OK in this family? It's exhausting. And I know you're trying to butter me up, because if you weren't you would have said something rude about my new hair colour.'

There's an awkward silence while her father brings the remaining bowls and plates to the table and sits down opposite his daughter.

'I think it's a habit I learned from my parents,' he says, finally. 'They didn't want to talk about anything "unpleasant", as they put it. And so I don't, either. I know it's a failing.'

Beth is taken aback by her father's frankness. It's like he's finally removed his mask.

'Oh,' she says, helping herself to cheese. She feels she needs to pretend she's not taken aback by this new side to him. She doesn't want to put him off.

'And then they sent me away to school, of course, and no one talked about how they really felt there, so... Here we are. I am as I am. And you were right, I think, in some of what you said at Christmas.'

Beth remembers her tirade well. She'd accused her father of distance, of being addicted to work, and failing to acknowledge the unhappiness of his marriage to her mother.

'I shouldn't have said that. I know it was hurtful. I was angry...'

'Yes. It did hurt. But as I say, some of it was true. Your mother is still angry, in fact. She has not... will not... see her alcohol usage as an issue. As you know.'

'Yes, I know.'

'But you were right about me. I have used my work as a prop all my life. And now look at me. It's all gone. In an instant. It's unsettling. I'll definitely say that.'

'Dad, I...'

'It's all right, Beth. I am not now magically a touchy-feely person, and I think that's all I want to say on the subject. But yes, let's just park what you said and try to move on. Shall we?'

'All right,' she says, picking up some servers and placing some salad leaves on her plate. 'So, Melham Manor?'

'Yes.'

'What job do you want me to do there now?'

'Ah, yes, I did tell Marisa that she's been expecting too much of you, vis-à-vis the house and clearing it et cetera. You have the children to care for and...'

'Yes. But honestly, I've liked it. Loved it. I love it down there. Melham Manor feels more and more like my home.'

'Ah. Would you like some balsamic dressing?'

'Yes, thanks.' He passes it. 'So, what is it you need me to do? Are you sending in cleaners? Architects? Bloody bulldozers?'

Robert winces.

'No, darling, we're not ready for that yet. The thing is,' he says, chewing on a piece of prosciutto, 'Aunt Nita's will has thrown up a bit of a complication.'

'I thought it wasn't hers to leave in a will? That there was a family trust that administers it?'

'Yes, that's what I was always told. But I've recently been made aware that it's a little bit more complicated than that. What the will actually says, you see, is that following Nita's death, the three of us, you me and Phillipa, will each inherit an equal share of the house.'

And then it all makes sense. Beth had wondered why her father had been going to so much effort. She'd thought for a wonderful ten minutes or so that it had all been about trying to make amends, about forging a new connection with his child. But it hadn't been, had it? It had been about buttering her up so she would acquiesce.

'I see,' she says, taking a big swig of water and swallowing hard. 'So I own part of Melham Manor?'

'Yes, once probate is completed, you'll own part of it. But it should all be fairly straightforward. We can all agree to put it on the market and the great news is that you'll be in for quite the payout when we sell. It should be a tidy sum. You'll be able to get a great place for you and the kids with it.'

'But what if I don't want to sell?'

Her father's cutlery clatters onto the table.

'Beth, we have to sell. I told you, I... we, the family... We need the proceeds, as we have plans to launch another business.'

'We? You and Mum?'

'Goodness no, she has no interest in the business. Me and Philippa.'

'Oh, right.' Beth is not surprised by this at all. But what she is surprised by is that she feels absolutely no jealousy. She realises she also has zero interest in any new incarnation of Stellar. 'Well, I hope it works out.'

'Thank you. I hope it will, too. These are tricky times. But we have a new idea and we hope it'll fly...'

'What is it?'

'It's an internet platform that'll let people rent out rooms in their houses on an ad-hoc basis.'

'Oh, right. Well, good luck with it.'

'So can we make a date for you to come and sign the papers for the house sale?'

Beth takes a deep breath. She's about to do something she'd never previously have considered doing. But times have changed, and so has she. She is going to do her own thing. She is going to be true to herself.

'Not yet, Dad. I need time to think about it.'

Robert's head snaps up and his eyes bore into hers. 'Think about what?'

'Selling the house. As I just said – I don't know if that's what I want to do.'

'But you can't keep it, Beth. Don't be absurd. It's a wreck. You don't have the funds to do it up.'

'But you can't force me to sell it, can you?'

Her father gives her a withering glare. 'Are you doing this just to be difficult?'

'Dad, I...'

'You are, aren't you. You're trying to get back at me for starting a new business with your sister, and not you.'

'I'm really not.'

'I'm not responsible for you becoming suspended, Beth. You are. You made the gaffe live on television. And we all know you haven't ever really put your back into the business...'

Beth puts her knife and fork down and pushes her chair back.

'Right, that's it. Enough. *That's enough, Dad,*' she says, standing up and throwing her napkin down on the table. She notices that a piece of cheese has fallen off her plate and landed on top of Eton's chapel. She doesn't wipe it. 'I'm going now. I'll be in touch when I've made up my mind.'

'But... Beth darling...'

She ignores her father's protestations. She's out of the house and walking down the street before he even makes it out of the kitchen. *How* dare *he*, she thinks. *How dare he assume I'd just bend over backwards to give him what he wants?*

As she pounds the pavements back to the bus stop, reality begins to dawn on Beth. She now owns a part of Melham Manor. And although she knows that it would be a huge battle to stop the house from being sold, this news does at least put her in a position of power.

She pulls out her BlackBerry. She needs to send a message.

29

NITA

May 1941

'Please eat something,' says Harriet. Nita shakes her head. *'Please. Please try.'*

It's been two days since Nita's visit to the War Office to try to find out more about Joe's whereabouts. She has been feeling utterly dreadful ever since.

'I can't. I feel nauseous.'

'But you must. You're expecting a baby.'

They've been having a version of this conversation since Harriet came back from her conference yesterday and found Nita slumped on the sofa, sobbing. Nita doesn't even remember how she got home from London. She had been far too absorbed by this new living nightmare. Because she realises now that if Joe had lied about where he'd gone, he was most likely also lying about loving her, about admiring her, about finding her attractive. She wonders whether it had all been one huge game to him. Some kind of bet?

'I... just need to sleep.'

'No, you need to drink some water, and you need to eat. Come on, Nita, you need to snap out of this. The baby needs you to.'

Harriet had left her that morning to go into university, as she always does on a Wednesday. She'd left some ginger nut biscuits – good for nausea – on a plate next to Nita's bed in the spare room, but they remain uneaten. Nita hasn't been doing any of the writing she's supposed to be doing. In fact, she's barely been awake. She is so exhausted she's slept almost all day, only being woken once by the postman and the second time by the bats in the roof.

'What's the point?' wails Nita into her pillow. 'I can't work, I've got no money, my parents have disowned me and Joe lied to me. The man I love lied. He gave me a false address and ran off to war without a second glance. I'm never going to see him again, am I?'

'Nothing is made better by just lying in bed all day,' replies Harriet with forced jollity, dodging having to answer Nita's question. 'Come on, let me help you sit up,' she says, and Nita allows her to place another pillow behind her head to raise her up a little. 'Now have a few sips of water.'

Nita sighs, turns onto her back and complies. She is actually very thirsty, and she knows she must be annoying Harriet. She really can't risk alienating the only friend she currently has.

'How was work today?' Nita asks, hoping this will stop Harriet haranguing her.

'Oh, it was fine. Listen,' says Harriet, sitting down at the bottom of the bed, by Nita's feet. 'I need to tell you something. And it's something I really shouldn't be telling you. And I've debated telling you about it, for other reasons which will soon become apparent. But I must now, I think. I simply have to.'

Nita pulls herself up a bit more in bed.

'I see,' she replies, wondering what on earth her friend is about to tell her. Harriet is an interesting woman with many layers, and Nita knows she's only just getting to know a small part of her.

'You know I work at King's College?'

'Yes, I do.'

'Well... that's a sort of half-truth. I do lecture at the university, but since the war broke out, I've also had another job. Also in London.'

'Oh.'

'I can't talk about it in much detail. But you might have an idea what I mean.' She means she works in Intelligence, Nita thinks, her mind spinning. So she's... actually a sort of spy. 'Now, I don't want to give you the wrong idea. I'm not at all important and I'm a tiny cog in a wheel. But I do know someone... very well, actually... who knows things. And today, I asked him about your Joe.'

Nita is rapt. She pulls herself up to a proper sitting position and focuses on her friend's face. She feels more alert than she has done in days.

'Oh, did you? What did... they say?'

'I'm so sorry, Nita. I don't think you're going to like it. But I do think it's important you know.'

Nita doesn't reply for a moment. She wants to enjoy just another minute of innocence. Another minute where she doesn't know whatever awful thing she's about to hear about the man she loves. Because she does still love him, even if he doesn't love her still, or never loved her at all. She listens to the grandfather clock next door ticking, the leaves and branches of the dense trees at the end of the garden rustling in the breeze and a dog barking in the distance.

'Tell me,' she says, after a deep breath. 'Just tell me. I need some kind of answer. Whatever it is. Does he already have another wife? Has he deserted?'

'No. Nita, listen to me. No one else can ever know what I'm about to tell you.'

'All right,' she replies, nodding her assent.

'There is no record of anyone called Joseph Miller being conscripted by the army, or any of the forces, from this area for the duration of the war,' says Harriet, her hands brushing the woollen blanket.

'Oh. He must have changed his name, then?'

That's a minor thing, changing your name, thinks Nita. And that would explain why she can't find him. She realises he must be in the army under his original name. She feels relief flood through her. Here is the explanation she's been waiting for.

'Yes,' Harriet replied. 'In fact, there is a man called Josef Muller who we think may be your Joe.'

'So Joe is... German?'

Harriet pauses.

'We suspect so, yes.'

Lots of people with Germanic names had changed them to English-sounding ones after the First World War, so this news isn't too upsetting for Nita.

'Well, that's not too bad. I can understand why he wanted to keep that hidden,' she says, thinking of Mr Brown and his handicapped daughter.

'I'm afraid that's not all of it,' says Harriet, who's staring at her hands and not meeting Nita's eye. 'The reason why his name popped up particularly is that the security services are searching for him. They suspect he... Oh goodness, this is hard. They suspect Joe was... is... a German spy.'

Nita catches her breath. She had imagined all manner of horrific, upsetting things Harriet might have been about to tell her, but none of them had been as insane as this. She doesn't know what to say. Her mind is spinning. *This simply can't be true*, she thinks.

'Do you remember when I warned you, when we first met, about someone close to home who was spying?' Harriet continues. 'That was because I'd had a warning from work about it, to be on my guard around here. There had been some break-ins at key sites in Surrey and we suspected the Nazis had someone around here, doing some digging for them. I hoped that by telling you, you'd chase the story and you'd put pressure on whoever it was to stop their operations. I had no idea that it might be someone you were working with, someone you might become close to...'

Nita can hear Harriet talking but she is not actually listening. She can't bear it. This is too awful for words. She can't believe that Joe, her Joe, could be the spy they had been looking for, and fearing. The man who had fed information back to the Germans, leading them to bomb the Millward factory, killing that poor man. She can't believe that Joe could actually be a Nazi. Because Nazis are unspeakably evil, she thinks. The newspapers are full of dreadful reports about them killing Jews and handicapped people and anyone they decide isn't worthy of life. She feels sick, even more sick than before.

'No. *No*,' says Nita, shouting now. 'It can't be him. Joe wouldn't do anything like that. He's a socialist, not a Nazi. He was passionate about helping people, about workers' rights and women's rights and...'

How could Joe be the mysterious Mr X, the man she, *they*, had been searching for, she thinks, full of rage and indignation. How could he have stood in the room at that news conference with all of those police, if he had been the very person they'd been looking for? The idea is simply ridiculous.

'I'm so sorry, Nita. I'm so sorry,' says Harriet, reaching out to try to stroke Nita's arm, but she snatches it back. She's too furious to be consoled. 'I debated telling you, but I really think it's best you know...'

'So he was never called up?'

'No, I don't believe so. Having a false identity probably explains why he wasn't called up earlier, in fact.'

'So where did the letter come from? The one he sent me when he arrived?'

'The German security services are very adept. It's possible someone forged that post office stamp on the envelope for him, to convince you it came from a training camp. He could actually have posted it in London, or even locally.'

'So... if he's not training, where has he gone? And why did he just suddenly disappear? Why couldn't he keep sending me letters?'

'We don't know where he is. I'm told that all chatter about him has dropped off German channels. This might be because he's returned to Germany.'

'So he's gone... back to the continent? He's left England?'

How could he have left me, Nita thinks. *How could he? After everything we did?*

'He might have, yes. They think that the huge police presence here might have spooked him and his handlers enough to pull him out. And it might be that he'd got all the information he needed. Perhaps the Millward factory's secret Spitfire project was all he was sent to find.'

'But he must miss...' she says, and then she realises the subtext of what Harriet is telling her, and she sinks back down into the bed and under the blankets, willing the mattress to swallow her whole. Because of course, Joe had taken a job at the newspaper office in Melham for a reason. It would have been a handy job to have, going in and reporting on the war effort in

local factories that were busy churning out parts for new aero-
planes and tanks. And who better, she realises, to form a relationship with than the daughter of a local factory owner? Had he
hoped, she wonders, to gain more access to the secrets her father's
business and his contacts might have held? She realises then,
with a sinking feeling, that he'd had a clear motive to get close to
her, to pretend to fall in love with her. It's quite possible he was
fooling her all along.

Nita lets out a cry of both despair and rage. And Harriet says
nothing, knowing, Nita suspects, that nothing she can think of to
say will make any of what Nita's just been told, anything that she's
currently feeling, any better. Instead, Harriet pulls back the covers
and wraps herself around Nita as she weeps.

30

BETH

February 2009

The car thermometer says it's minus two degrees outside, and Beth can believe it. The village pond she just passed was frozen solid, and the minor roads are treacherous. She doesn't want to think about how cold it will be at Melham Manor tonight.

She pulls on her thick winter coat, grabs her laptop and her bag, locks the car and walks up to the entrance of the council offices. She's a bit nervous. This is the first council meeting she's ever reported on and she realises she has no idea what to expect.

'I'm here for the meeting about the proposed Hazel's Field development?' Beth asks the receptionist.

'Oh yes, that's up the stairs, to the right.'

Beth enters a crowded room which, despite the plunging temperature outside, is stuffy and far too warm. She spots James and he points to a spare chair in the audience. She makes her way to him. 'I'm going to be sitting up there,' he says, pointing to the other end of the room, 'but I made sure I saved you a seat.'

'Thanks.'

She sits down, peels off her coat and takes out her laptop so that she can take notes. She spots Rowan sitting a few rows in front. She hadn't realised she'd be here, but given how involved she is with the community, it makes sense.

'Thanks so much for coming,' says James. 'I told the chairman that the local press would be here. I think it helps to let them know their words will reach the voters. There's an election in a few months,' he says, with a wink. Beth notices that he's picking his nails. It must be strange, she thinks, to be a local councillor, and therefore someone with decision-making power, but not enough to be able to influence something as important to you as this.

'Welcome, everyone,' says a man standing up on a small platform at one end of the room, and James rushes back to join two people seated either side of him. The large audience quietens down. 'And thank you for coming to this meeting on such an inhospitable night. As you all know, this is a meeting to discuss the proposed Hazel's Field development. This is for about forty homes, a mix of apartments and small houses, on greenfield land on the edge of the village for either social rent or affordable joint-ownership. We understand that the landowner has told Councillor James Connors – who is seated up here with me – that she's prepared to sell it at a reduced rate. I'm going to invite him and two colleagues to talk you through some issues first, and then we'll take questions.'

James is the first to speak. He has a presentation projected onto a screen behind him, and explains, passionately, why he believes the area needs decent social housing, explaining the state of the sort of accommodation he'd taken Beth to see.

When he's finished speaking, Beth sees that there are nods all around the room. *This is feeling promising*, she thinks.

'I'd now like to invite Councillor Michaela Lee, who's on the planning committee, to speak,' says the man in charge. 'I believe you've been canvassing opinion?'

'Yes, thank you, Mr Chairman. You'll all have seen the stories about this in the local press – it's getting a great deal of positive coverage as it's a modern, efficient design. There's also a suggestion of some planning gain, with a playpark and a central, green square to be built as part of the design. I think you'll all agree that it's a lovely looking design, and clearly sensitive to the local area. We have done some polling of local people and despite the fact it would mean giving up some green-belt land, there does seem to be majority support for it.'

'Finally, before we take questions, let's hear from Councillor Marcus Trimble, who's on our finance committee. Marcus?'

'Thank you, yes. I want to start by saying that I'm a huge fan of the project. I think it's genuinely unusual for there to be a broad consensus for a project like this, but I do understand why. Unfortunately, there is the usual huge stumbling block, and that's money. The financial team at the council have been running through some figures and they've produced a report for me. I believe a digital copy has been made available on our website. The original plan, put forward by Councillor Connors, was that the council would borrow from a pot of money held by central government specifically designated for this sort of project. However, I'm told that this fund has been closed early due to the credit crunch. There just isn't the money available any more, both to buy this land, and to build on it, even if we sacrificed some of the units allocated for social rent and put some on the open market to subsidise the scheme. There's a huge financial hole here and I think there's just no way of filling it.'

Someone on the other side of the room gasps. Beth sees James' head sink down.

'That is disappointing indeed,' says the chairman. 'I think we all know how much this area needs a project like this. I want to take the opportunity to tell Councillor Connors how much I admire his vision for this project. Now that we've heard that summary, and that rather depressing financial picture, from these councillors, I want to invite members of the public to ask any questions they have.' Several hands shoot up immediately. 'Yes. The man in the third row.'

* * *

The questions and answers last for a good hour, and by the end of the session, Beth can see that James' energy is sapped. The financial report has taken the wind out of his sails. She knows how much hope he had for this evening. She packs up her bag, picks up her coat and is about to walk over to commiserate with him when Rowan comes to talk to her.

'Hi! That was such a shame, wasn't it,' says Beth.

'It was, yes,' says Rowan, her voice strange, distant. And maybe, Beth thinks, even... angry?

'Are you OK, Rowan?'

'I'm disappointed.'

'At the financial report? I know... But maybe it's not the end of the line? Maybe more funds will be made available from central...'

'No. I'm disappointed in you.'

Rowan's face is almost transformed by her mood. *What on earth have I done?* Beth wonders. *What can I possibly have done to make her this angry?*

'What do you mean?'

'I mean, I'm very disappointed that your family is planning to sell Melham Manor, and you haven't thought to tell me.'

'But I...'

'Hello, Rowan. Hi, Beth,' says James, unaware he's joining their conversation at such a difficult moment. He looks tired and a bit beaten. Beth is about to open her mouth to say how sorry she was about the way the meeting had turned out, but Rowan gets there first.

'Hi, James. Look, don't bother denying it,' says Rowan to Beth, clearly determined not to be derailed. 'My friend works for an estate agents' in Dorking. She tells me that you've had a couple of different agents out to Melham Manor to value it.'

'You have... something to do with the Manor?' asks James.

'You haven't told him?' says Rowan, looking askance at Beth.

'No. I... It didn't seem relevant. I met James when I was reporting for *The Bugle*...'

'You're... Oh, why didn't I think about that?' he says, clearly not wanting a response from Beth, who sees that in an instant, the rapport they've built up over the past few months has vanished. 'You're a Bineham! I'm a fool. I should have realised you were one of the Stellar Binehams.' James rubs his hands over his forehead.

The *Stellar* Binehams. Yes, she thinks. The reputation of the company has always gone hand in hand with her reputation, hasn't it? Even in school, where her father's place on the *Sunday Times* Rich List had been commented on each year. She'd hated it. At least Stellar is gone now. At least there's that.

'And hang on... The family is selling Melham Manor?'

'Oh, they're not just selling the house,' says Rowan, her eyes wide with fury. 'I'm told it's being sold with plans for more houses to be built on the land. Houses that will involve cutting down some of the woodland.'

'How many houses? And what kind of houses? Not for social rent, I bet?' asks James, so fast he can barely get the words out. His cheeks are glowing red.

Beth's eyes dart between both Rowan and James. Both decent

human beings, she thinks. Both rightly angry with her. She could tell them she hasn't given her permission yet to allow her father and sister to do this, and that she plans to try to hold them off for at least a while, even though she knows she won't be any match for her father's lawyers when it really comes to it. She could try to explain this, yes, but she simply can't find the words. She's far too mortified. Because she knows she should have been honest with both of them, and her own stupid pride, her pathetic attempts at disassociating herself from the family business which she was until recently both employed by and a shareholder of, is unjustifiable.

So instead of trying to explain, she picks up her bag and coat and walks away, staring hard at the floor as she goes.

I need to be alone, she thinks. *I need some time to think.*

Neither James nor Rowan follows her.

* * *

Beth is incredibly relieved to shut Melham Manor's front door behind her. Her cheeks are still burning after that intensely awkward encounter and she needs to be alone. She also needs to think about what on earth she's going to do about the three-line whip she's received to sell her share in the house. She knows her father will make her life very difficult if she doesn't do what he wants.

The hallway is pitch black. She turns the light on, walks through to the kitchen, fills a glass with water and then walks up the stairs to her bedroom. She's decided to get a very early night. She's had enough of today.

It's so cold in the bedroom, she can see her breath. She sets about building a fire, starting with kindling, some balls of newspaper and a firelighter, and topping it with a couple of small logs she had brought in from the garden that afternoon. She watches as the paper catches and the fire meanders and licks its way through it, eating the words. And yet when it reaches the logs, there is just a hissing sound. She realises it's not going to work. The wood's too wet. She sits in front of it, cross-legged, willing it to help her body thaw, but it refuses to take. Eventually, she retreats to the bed, which is cold and damp. She wishes she'd had the foresight to pack a hot water bottle.

As she lies in the darkness curled up in a foetal position, she tries to distract herself from the cold by running through her options. First and foremost, she will have to apologise both to James and Rowan as soon as possible, and try to explain to them, properly, the situation she's found herself in. Technically, as part-owner, she can stall any efforts to sell Melham Manor, but she knows that a good team of expensive lawyers will find any number of ways of making her life uncomfortable if she refuses. Her share of the insurance and running costs of the house alone will probably swallow her savings within a few months, and of course, her family will absolutely expect her to pay her dues. That will be their leverage. Added to that, there are no shares in Stellar to fall back on any more, and her financial settlement from the divorce will only stretch to a small house near the school. The reality is, she simply can't afford to hold the sale back, however much she might want to. She also knows that there's almost zero chance of persuading them to keep a house they neither love nor spend time in. She seems to be the only Bineham alive with an affinity for Melham Manor.

Eventually her bed warms up enough for her to stop shivering, and her exhausted and disrupted brain begins to let go. She falls asleep about an hour after she first climbed into bed.

* * *

Beth wakes up in the middle of the night. This is unusual for her and it takes her a while to come to terms with where she is, and crucially, what she's seeing. Because the fire that had refused to light before she went to bed, the fire with logs too damp to catch, is now blazing away in the grate. The room is full of flickering firelight and blessed warmth.

Beth wonders how on earth this happened. Perhaps a very small flame had remained in there, alight somewhere, even though she couldn't see it, she thinks. Yes, maybe. But then she checks her watch. She's been asleep for three hours, and she was in bed for at least an hour before she fell asleep. How could it have taken that long to catch, and then, when it had caught, burn for so long, and so brightly? Normally, a log wouldn't last longer than an hour, tops.

But as she sits up in bed and stares at the glowing fire in the hearth, Beth feels not fear at this strange turn of events, but reassurance. Suddenly, things are starting to make sense. Because her great-aunt Nita had been a Wiccan. A witch. A hedge witch, according to Rowan. Someone who believed that every living thing has a soul.

Beth's interest in Wicca had been piqued after that meeting with Rowan in the woods, and she'd taken out a book about it from the library. And that book told her some interesting things about the Wiccan belief in an afterlife. Hedge witches in particular believe in reincarnation. They believe their energy will live on after they die, in some natural form. Some believe in the astral plane, a place where spirits live on after death. And while some think this is a separate place, a bit like the Christian heaven, others believe the astral plane is still on earth with us, that the dead walk among us. Not in a malevolent way, but in a protective, joyful way, released from their earthly bodies.

And so, as Beth sits there in a room lit only by the flames of a fire she is pretty certain she did not light, she feels her great-aunt is with her. Yes, she realises, there may be some rational explanation for these phenomena – sleep paralysis, in the case of the orbs of light she saw, or a hidden source of ignition, in the case of the fire – but she doesn't feel like accepting that now. She now believes, in fact, that Nita has been with her all along, starting from almost as soon as she'd died. And this thought fills Beth with peace.

'I'll sort it, Nita,' she promises, out loud. 'I don't know how, but I'll sort it.'

31

NITA

July 1941

'She's through here.'

Nita is barely aware of the new arrival, because she is experiencing a whole new world of pain. It feels like her insides are clamped in a vice, and nothing she does – pacing, squatting, lying on her side – is making it feel any better.

'Nita? Nita? My name's John. I'm a... friend of Harriet's. And I'm a doctor.'

'No... doctors!' wails Nita. She's aware enough to know that if any of the local doctors find out she's pregnant, both her current location and her predicament will be broadcast across the county. And then her parents will make sure that this baby – *if* it's born alive, she thinks, aware of the risks her illness brings – will make sure it's taken away from her. She will never see it again if anyone finds out she's in labour. Of that she's certain.

'He's not from around here, Nita, I promise. John works with me in London.'

'At the university?'

'Not at the university, no. Look, John has been giving me advice on how to look after you for a while now, and I had to tell him you were having the baby tonight. I had to. It's coming a month early, Nita. And you've been poorly. We need help. The baby needs help.'

Nita is in no position to argue. She's too focused on the heat rising in her as each contraction hits. She tries to distract herself by thinking of plot lines for the novel she's been writing, of names for her characters, and that works, partially, until the pain is at its peak, at which point all bets are off.

'Try to breathe slowly,' says John. 'Nice and slowly and deliberately. That's it. Could you lie down on the bed for me, Nita, and I'll take a look at you, and see how far you have to go.'

Nita does as he asks, with considerable difficulty.

'I haven't overseen a birth for several years,' he leans over to Harriet and whispers as Nita shuffles into position, obviously hoping she can't hear. 'You should really call someone else...'

'I can't call anyone else, can I? You'll have to do it.'

'Fine. I'll do this for you.'

Nita opens one eye, sees a look pass between them and realises she's not the only one who's been keeping secrets. Harriet has clearly been carrying on with this John for some time, without ever saying a word.

'Let me wash my hands.'

While John disappears to the kitchen sink, Harriet sits on the bed next to Nita and holds her hand.

'He's lovely, John. He'll help you.'

'As long as he's... actually a... doctor... I don't care.'

Nita is frightened. Really frightened. She's worried she's too ill to have this baby and survive. For either of them to survive, in fact.

She has been unwell for some time now. Initially, she'd tried to hide how she was feeling from her friend, but it had become harder and harder to do. She has been incredibly tired. So tired, actually, that some days Harriet had got back from work and found her still in bed. But it had been her unusual thirst and appetite that had set bells ringing.

'Right. Let's have a look at you,' says John. He proceeds to assess her, feeling her pulse, checking her temperature, and then he asks Nita's permission to examine her internally. She nods.

Nita screams. The pain is excruciating.

'Sorry... just... one... more... second...' he says, before withdrawing his hand. Nita exhales hard. The relief she feels is palpable. 'You're progressing well, Nita. Really well. But the baby is early, Harriet tells me. That's not unusual in cases of gestational diabetes.'

That's what Nita has. Diabetes, which is something she thought people were only born with. It turns out, however, that pregnant women can get it too, and it's incredibly risky for the baby, who might be too large, or jaundiced, or have dangerously low blood sugar. Or it might... not survive. But she is trying not to think about that. Every nerve in her body, every synapse in her brain, is focused on delivering this child safely. Nita has been on a strict low-sugar diet for some time now. She's hated it, but done it without question, because Harriet has told her – apparently, advised by John – that it's the only treatment available that will help. She hopes it has been enough.

'You're doing so well, Nita,' says Harriet, back at her side, holding her hand. 'Really well.'

'I really... don't think I can do this.'

'Of course you can. Look what you've done so far! You've left your home, your family, you've hidden yourself away here for months, you've been working hard, writing. You're amazing.'

'No, I'm not. I'm not amazing. I'm just doing what I have to do, to keep this baby safe. I won't let my parents take it away. I want it to know who it is. Who its mother is.'

'And it will.'

'Arrrrrghhhhhhhh.' Another contraction hits.

'Try to breathe deeply. It helps with the pain,' says John, who's standing a few feet away, apparently giving the women space.

'Nothing... is... going... to... take... this... pain... away.'

'Yes, it will,' says Harriet. 'The baby will come, and the pain will go.'

Yes. This is pain with a purpose, Nita thinks. Not like the pain she feels when she's thinking about Joe and his apparent betrayal, his double life. That's a pain that has no purpose, and no end. She knows she will feel it forever. But this moment, this agony, *does* have a purpose. The thought gives her strength. She concentrates on taking deep breaths and exhaling slowly. The next contraction comes, and although it's still incredibly painful, the breathing definitely helps.

An hour passes. John spends most of this time sitting in an armchair in the front room, occasionally coming up to check Nita's pulse. Harriet, meanwhile, barely leaves her side, except to fill a hot water bottle to help with the pain in Nita's back. She's slumped on the bed beside her, possibly napping, when Nita screams, '*I feel like I need to push. I feel... pressure.*'

'Right, right. Let me see you,' says John, running into the room. He lifts the blanket that's currently covering her lower half. She's dreading another painful internal examination, but this time he doesn't even touch her. 'Yes, yes, baby's coming,' he says. 'I can see the top of its head. That's good news. It's coming out the right way.'

There's a wrong *way?* Nita thinks. *How can I not have known that?* But then, aside from Harriet, she's had no one to tell her anything. She hadn't really even known she could get pregnant so easily.

'What... do... I... do?' says Nita, feeling a burning sensation emanating from down below.

'I just need you to pant for a moment. Don't push. If you push you could... do damage.'

I feel pretty damaged down there already, thinks Nita, trying to take short, harsh breaths instead of long ones.

'Right,' she says, in between breaths.

'Your baby's nearly here, Nita,' says Harriet. 'Keep going.'

'That's the head out,' says John, doing something down below that Nita can't see. 'Keep panting.'

Never mind panting – Nita isn't even sure if she's still breathing. She's not in control any more. It feels as if her body has its own plan, and she's just letting it do it.

'And that's the shoulders... one more push...' Nita takes a deep breath and bears down. 'Yes... here we go...'

Nita feels an emptying. She knows the baby is out. She is expecting euphoric cries, either from the doctor or from Harriet. But they aren't saying anything.

'What's wrong?' she wails.

'Baby is just a bit shocked, Nita. It hasn't taken its first breath yet. I'm just going to give it some help.'

John lifts up a tiny blue and red object and rubs its back vigorously with a bloody towel.

'Come on, little one. Come on,' he says.

It feels like time is frozen. Nita is still not sure she's actually breathing. Harriet is holding her hand so hard, she has pins and needles.

And then there is a noise.

A very quiet noise. It's more a mew than a cry, but it is coming from the baby.

John lets out a half-laugh, half-exhalation.

'Thank goodness. Nita, you have a baby girl,' he says, quickly wrapping the baby up in the towel he's just been using.

A girl, Nita thinks. *A girl*.

'Is she all right?' she asks.

'She's breathing now, at least. But she's tiny and she seems a little weak.'

'Weak?'

'That's quite common in babies of mothers with diabetes. Harriet, could you bring the bowl and teaspoon in from the kitchen? The ones I left on the side?' he says, bringing the baby over to where Nita is sitting.

Harriet races off to get it. Nita is still in a lot of pain, but she takes hold of the baby without question, pulling her close and staring at her face. She is now pink, not white, and has long brown eyelashes and a smattering of brown hair.

Harriet returns holding the bowl.

'Thank you,' he says, taking it from her. 'Nita, this is honey water. I made it while you were in labour. If you can hold baby still, I'll pop a little in the baby's mouth. It should help raise her sugar levels a bit.'

Nita nods and turns her new daughter towards John, so that he can administer the treatment she needs.

When it's done, and he's satisfied the liquid has been swallowed, he says, 'I'm just off to wash my hands. I'll be back to keep an eye on the baby, and deliver the placenta, of course.'

Nita doesn't really hear him. She's vaguely aware that the whole messy business of birth isn't quite over yet, but she no longer actually cares. Because she has done what she wanted to do. She has given birth to a living baby, a beautiful little girl, despite everything. It's a bit of her, and bit of... Joe, as hard as it is to think of him now. This baby is part of them both.

'What are you going to call her,' asks Harriet, who Nita sees is also staring at the baby intently.

'I'm going to call her Carole,' she replies.

32

BETH

February 2009

There's ice on the inside of the window when Beth wakes, creeping up the glass from the corners. Beth can see from here that Nita's garden is also frozen, the bare roses and empty cane wigwams standing like enchanted sentries, waiting for the warmth of spring to bring them back to life. She wonders whether it's worth trying to light the fire again, the fire which, against all odds, had been ablaze last night. *No*, she decides. *I've spent enough time in this room, hiding. I've got work to do.*

She quickly dresses, packs up her things, makes the bed and goes down to the kitchen for tea and toast. She's standing at the window with her hands wrapped around a warm mug when her phone bleeps. She pulls it out of her pocket and checks it. It's a message from her father, another one insisting that she calls to discuss the terms for the sale of the house. She puts her phone back in her pocket. She needs time to think.

On impulse, she decides to walk through the house's increas-

ingly empty rooms, trying not to think of it as a valedictory
gesture.

Beth begins in the sitting room, thinking of the awkward wake
they'd held there after Nita's funeral. Then down the hallway into
the library, where she remembers spending hours leafing through
books; then into the dining room, where she recalls oddly formal
evening meals at which Nita had always seemed more a visitor
than a resident. She stands in this space and takes in the elaborate
embossed wallpaper she'd run her fingers over as a child, and the
polished parquet floor she'd enjoyed skidding on when no one
was looking. She smiles at these memories, grateful now to
acknowledge the happiness she has always felt in this house.

Then she walks over to the boxes that remain on the table.
They're all things she'd identified with the auctioneer in
November. The two art deco Clarice Cliff vases are on the top,
encased in bubble wrap. And when she lifts them up, she sees
that the Royal Doulton figurines are underneath them. What had
the auctioneer said? Yes, that they each represented a month, that
was it.

A bolt of energy and inspiration runs through her.

One for each month.

So there will be one for August.

It's a long shot, she thinks, *but it's worth investigating, surely?*

She lifts the figures out one by one and checks the month
that's glazed into the bottom. May first, a woman decorated in
bursts of bright colour; then September, painted in autumnal
hues; and then December, all greens and reds. And then, on her
fourth try, August. It depicts a woman with auburn hair wearing
an elegant yellow gown. At first glance, there's absolutely nothing
unusual about it. But then she notices something sticking out of a
tiny hole in its base. Her heart quickens. She takes a moment to
calm down, wary of panicking and dropping it. When she's taken

a few deep breaths, she pulls and discovers that it seems to be paper. She sits down on one of the dining room chairs and tugs at it gently with two fingers. Bit by bit, it emerges, until she is staring at a roll of yellowed paper. *It* could *just be a receipt*, she thinks. *Or a shopping list. But what, if it isn't?*

She picks it up and unrolls it with great care.

What she sees when she unrolls it changes everything.

33

NITA

July 1941

Carole is now two weeks old. Nita can neither believe a fortnight has passed, nor comprehend how she has managed to get this far, with both of them still alive, and in fact, thriving.

Nita is exhausted. Her daughter is voraciously hungry, feeds almost constantly and doesn't like to be put down. Harriet is wonderful and helpful when she's home, of course, but she's often at work and when she isn't, Nita feels too guilty to ask for her help during the night. After all, she and the baby are now taking over most of the house and she's only paid a pittance towards their board. Nita knows this situation cannot continue forever, particularly because it seems John Ringwood, the doctor who'd saved them both, will become a permanent fixture in Harriet's life in the near future. Despite knowing this, however, Nita is too frightened and overwhelmed to talk to Harriet about it. She has filed this situation at the back of her brain as something to deal with later.

Nita is about to attempt to put the baby down for a nap – in the main, a largely fruitless exercise – when there's a knock at the door. She freezes. No one is allowed to know she's here. They've managed to keep her presence hidden for so long because Harriet's cottage is so isolated, on the edge of the woods. And no one ever walks up the path, except the postman. And he almost never knocks, unless there's a parcel. That's what it must be, she thinks. It must be a parcel.

Nita stands stock-still, praying the baby still stays asleep, waiting for the postman to give up and continue on his rounds. But she doesn't hear footsteps. Instead, she sees something being pushed under the front door.

It's an envelope. Nita tiptoes towards it and picks it up with her right hand, still holding the baby tightly with her left. The envelope doesn't have a stamp or a post office frank, and it simply has 'NITA' written in capital letters on the front.

Oh goodness, Nita thinks. *Someone knows I'm here.*

Panic runs through her. If someone knows she's here, she wonders, why are they writing to her? Why haven't her parents just turned up at the door? Are they hoping to blackmail her, perhaps? She opens the envelope with trepidation, knowing this cannot be good news.

When she sees who it's from, however, she gasps. She reads it twice, just to make sure she's understood it properly.

My darling Nita,

I know that receiving this will come as a shock, and for that I apologise. I have wanted to write to you many times before this but for reasons I hope to be able to explain, I simply couldn't do it.

If you are willing to meet with me, despite everything, please reply by leaving a note under the loose tile on the front doorstep tonight.

Always yours,

Joe

A few minutes later, Nita finds herself sitting on the sofa, still clasping the baby in her left hand and the note in her right.

She has no idea how she got there. She's not quite sure, in fact, that she's even awake. She runs her fingers over the paper, as if by doing this she'll be able to absorb the words, to really understand them.

The first thing she feels, when the shock subsides, is relief. *He's still alive*, she thinks, and that's something.

But then relief is replaced with rage and fear.

Because if Harriet's right, Joe is a German spy. He's not the man Nita had thought he was. It seems likely he was lying to her all along. And here she is, clutching a baby that is both the most extraordinary thing that has ever happened to her, and the absolute cause of her undoing, and that's entirely his fault. He was a man of the world, she thinks. He must have known she might get pregnant, and he clearly hadn't cared enough about her to prevent it.

She wonders why he's decided to make contact now. Is he still hoping she can provide him with useful information about her father's business dealings, perhaps? The thought of this makes her feel ill. And then she realises that if he knows she's here, it's likely he also knows she's had a baby. The thought of him witnessing her predicament and her struggles and not making himself known, not helping her, is utterly infuriating.

That's why she's angry.

But her fear? Well, Harriet doesn't speak about her secret work in London at all, but Nita has absorbed enough from the newspaper and the wireless to know there is much more going on in this war than the headlines might suggest. She's no fool. She knows people disappear all the time and leave no trace. There's a reason why local people went into a frenzy when the police told them there was a spy in their midst. They are dangerous people, the Nazis, Nita thinks. They kill.

Nita puts the note down and strokes baby Carole.

And it's not just about me now, is it, she thinks. *It's about me and her. And I have to protect her at all costs.*

Nita stands up and walks over to the phone. She needs to speak to Harriet, urgently.

34

BETH

February 2009

The document is written in old-fashioned, curly handwriting, and it takes Beth a few minutes to work out exactly what she has in front of her.

It seems to be an informal adoption agreement between Nita Bineham and a woman called Harriet Ringwood, for a baby called Carole.

Carole Bineham.

Nita had a child.

Beth is shocked. There had never been any hint of this when she'd been growing up. She wonders if her father knows. If so, he's hidden it well. Although he rarely spoke about his aunt, of course, and if he did, he'd restricted it to referring to her as a 'crazy old lady' who 'lived like a hermit'. Beth does have an inkling as to why Nita's pregnancy was covered up, though. She was clearly not married, and this was a matter of great disgrace in the early forties. Particularly in 'society', and Beth knows her great-grandparents were intensely protective of their place within it, which, as a family with 'new money', had been hard won and would have been incredibly easy to lose.

But, oh, Nita, she thinks. *The absolute pain of giving up your child. No woman should have to endure that.*

Beth sits back in her chair and stares at the document. It's interesting, she thinks, that it is a private agreement. It's written on ordinary writing paper, with no sign of any formal authority taking part in it or being notified of it.

Who is this woman, then, Beth wonders – Harriet Ringwood? She's never heard of her, but then of course she must have been of Nita's generation, and probably long gone.

But something about the name is familiar. Why is that?

And then it comes to her.

Ringwood.

That's Rowan's surname, isn't it? She has a memory of her telling her that it was, right back when they'd first met in the garden last autumn.

Beth stands up, grabs some bubble wrap from the box and encases the precious roll of paper within it. Then she pulls out her phone and dials Rowan's number.

* * *

Beth pushes open the little wooden gate and walks up the paved path towards Rowan's cottage. She's never been here before, but unsurprisingly, the garden is gorgeous. Even in February there are splashes of colour. There are snowdrops beneath the trees and purple crocuses peeking out of flower beds.

She rings the doorbell and waits, taking in the pots of herbs that proliferate across the porch.

'Hello, Beth,' says Rowan when she answers the door. 'I'm so glad you phoned me.'

'As I said, it's a complicated story, but I thought you might be able to help,' says Beth, slightly flustered, because only last night, Rowan had chastised her for not telling her about the sale of Melham Manor. She had thought she might even refuse to see her, but Rowan had sounded completely normal on the phone, as if those cross words had never happened.

She looks at her friend's face now, examining it not only for anger, but also for... similarities. *Am I leaping to conclusions?* she wonders. *Am I adding two and two, and making five?* Because ever since Beth read the document, and she'd realised Rowan shared the same surname as Nita's daughter, her mind has been running wild. She wonders whether she could actually be related to Rowan. And if so, might that explain why she's always felt so at ease with her? The idea seems at once fanciful and entirely believable. Now she just needs to find out if it's true.

'Well, come on in,' says Rowan, standing back to allow Beth inside. The cottage is warm, both physically and metaphorically. A log burner is ablaze in the corner, and the living room is decorated in reds, oranges and yellows, with cushions and blankets slung over every seat. 'It's good to have you round at my place, at last.'

'This is a lovely house.'

'It is, isn't it. It's been in the family for quite a while. We all love it. I'm surprised you haven't been here before, actually. It's part of the Melham Manor estate.'

'Is it? God, I had no idea.'

'Yes. We've leased it for two generations.'

'Oh,' says Beth, feeling guilty, as she always does, about her family's determination to milk every last penny from every property they own. She imagines the 'lease' for this house isn't cheap. And she also realises why Rowan is so upset about the sale of Melham Manor. It will, of course, put her own house in danger.

'Would you like something to drink? Tea? Coffee?'

'I'd love a coffee.'

'Coming up. I'll just be a sec. Take a seat.'

Beth sits in an armchair beside the fire. Her attention is immediately taken by a small black cat who, sensing the activity, has just opened one lazy eye, stretched and sauntered over to her. Beth strokes her, and the cat's reaction is immediate; she's purring so loudly, her whole body is vibrating.

'Ah, you've met Alice, then,' says Rowan, walking towards her carrying a tray with a large cafetiere and two mugs. She places it down on a small table next to Beth and sits down on another chair.

'She seems friendly.'

'Yes. She's the gentlest of cats. She spends almost all of her time asleep, unless there's a lap nearby to sit on.'

'I like her.'

'Good. Do you want your coffee white or black? Sugar?'

'White please, no sugar.'

Beth watches her friend plunge the cafetiere, before pouring some milk into one of the mugs from a jug and filling it with coffee almost to the brim.

'Here you go,' says Rowan.

Beth accepts it with relief. She didn't sleep very well last night.

'Look, I just wanted to say... I'm so sorry I didn't tell you myself about the sale of the Manor,' she says, deciding to bite the bullet and apologise first. 'I... didn't know how to do it. It's not my choice, at all. The house is in some kind of family trust, so when Nita died, it was left to my dad, and my sister and me, in equal shares. They're putting a lot of pressure on me to sell. And I know I can theoretically hold them off, but as you know, I'm getting divorced and I don't have loads of spare cash and they will throw all sorts of costs at me to keep the house running, and I just won't survive that, financially...'

'That's OK. I know all about that.'

'You knew about the trust?'

'Not in great detail. But I knew you would inherit a share. Nita told me how it would be split between you all, afterwards.'

'You and she really were close, then? She told you everything?'

Rowan takes a sip from her coffee and raises an eyebrow.

'Yes. We were very close.'

'Rowan... I want to ask you something. About Nita. About something I found.'

'Oh, right.' Rowan's expression is serene, unbothered. Beth wonders if she knows what's coming or not.

'I found... an adoption agreement. Not a certificate. It was more informal than that.'

'Ah. Right.' Rowan doesn't look at all surprised.

'It was between Nita and someone called... Harriet. Harriet Ringwood.'

'Yes. She was my mother.'

'She was?'

Beth can't quite believe it, even though that's what she'd been hoping for all along.

'Yes. She died two decades ago, unfortunately, but yes, she was my mother. She was an amazing woman. Quite extraordinary. Fiercely intelligent. An academic, you know, but also a woman at peace in nature. She was a Wiccan, too. One of the first, in fact. She passed it on to me.'

'And she...'

'Adopted Nita's child. Yes.'

'Oh.'

They sit in silence for a moment. Beth listens to the crackle and wheezing of the burning logs and the distant sound of the wind whistling through the trees that run behind the back of the house. She realises that if she entered that woodland and kept walking, Melham Manor would only be a short walk away.

'I knew she was adopted, of course, but I had no idea she was Nita's daughter until just before our mum died,' says Rowan, cradling her coffee.

'She? So... it wasn't... you?'

'Oh goodness, no. My father, John Ringwood, was definitely my biological father. He gave me his arthritic toes, for a start.'

'So her daughter... was she... is she... called Carole, still? That's what the document says.'

'Yes. She's still alive, if that's what you're hinting at. She's still working, actually, as a nurse. She likes it too much to retire. She lives in Dorking.'

35

NITA

July 1941

It's 10 p.m. Nita is staring out of Harriet's kitchen window, watching the bats swooping over the small pond in her garden, diving for insects, and the leaves on the trees swaying in the gentle summer breeze. It's always a calming view, but it's not working its magic tonight. Her heart is still thrashing around in her chest.

Because she's waiting for Joe.

After her conversation with Harriet, they'd both agreed that she needed to know, *deserved* to know, in fact, why Joe had abandoned her. But more than that, they'd both realised that an opportunity to help locate a German spy in the middle of this filthy, godforsaken war, was an opportunity neither of them can pass up, no matter how much the thought of handing him over makes Nita feel utterly wretched.

They did disagree on one point, however. Harriet had wanted to make it all official, to alert the people she works with and have them on standby near the house, waiting to capture Joe at the first opportunity. Nita, on the other hand, had railed against this. If she's to go through this, she reasons, if the man she loves is going to end up in the hands of the British Secret Service and goodness knows what fate, she wants to be able to speak to him properly first. Her plan, the one Harriet has now accepted with great reluctance and with two mandatory fail-safes, is to persuade him to give himself up. But not before she's had an opportunity to tell Joe how his lies have made her feel, what they've done to her.

And so, the scene is set. The sun has taken its lingering leave from a glorious English summer's day, Carole is asleep in the bedroom next door, and Nita is gripping the wooden kitchen so hard, her fingernails are leaving a mark.

There's a knock at the door.

A jolt of electricity passes through Nita. She takes a deep breath and walks slowly towards the front door, pausing for just a second before she opens the latch, a small part of her wanting to freeze time, to never know what awaits her on the other side.

Despite this, she opens it.

Her first thought is that he does not look like himself. It is undoubtedly Joe who's standing in front of her, of course, but he's changed. He's thinner, dishevelled. He makes no attempt to touch her, to kiss her, to hold her. What passed between them before, whatever that had been, is clearly over. They are almost strangers again. Neither of them says or does anything for a moment. Her anger and fear and frustration and worry and love are all mixed up together, and she struggles to separate them. But then the anger lashes out.

'I knew it was you,' she says.

* * *

They are in the kitchen. Joe has eaten the sandwich she's made him. Nita has almost stopped shaking. But then he hears the noise from next door. Carole has woken up.

'Don't...' Nita says, fruitlessly, as Joe stumbles past her, out of the kitchen and into the bedroom. She surges after him, but it's too late. He's standing over the baby. 'Joe, I...'

'She's so beautiful,' he whispers, his voice soft and full of wonder. 'I've only seen her at a distance before. But she's... perfect.'

He knows about the baby, then, Nita thinks. And he even knows she's a girl. Then she remembers the strange noises she's been hearing, and the odd movements in the corner of her vision, phenomena she's been attributing to bats, mice, or foxes in the garden. And suddenly, she knows the truth.

'How long have you been watching me, Joe?' she says, rearranging her daughter's blankets. She has already fallen back to sleep.

'I...' His eyes dart towards hers. 'This sounds wrong, but I've been watching you for a long time, Nita.'

'We can't talk in here,' she says. Nita doesn't want to wake her again. 'Let's go into the sitting room.'

'All right.'

'Did you ever actually go? Did you ever leave to go to... Yorkshire?' she says as they leave the bedroom, her voice dripping with both sarcasm and pain. He walks towards the armchairs. As he does so, she grabs a knife from the kitchen and stuffs it up her sleeve. As she approaches the chairs, Joe sits down with the sort of sigh she'd expect from an old man. She sits down opposite him.

'I did leave Surrey, yes, for a short while. They told me I had to, that I was risking being discovered. But then I found I couldn't stay away. And I... Nita, you are a clever woman. And so is Harriet.

I suspect you know what I'm going to tell you, but... I need to tell you, in my own words. I need to explain. Can I do that?'

'All right,' she says.

'I'm so sorry,' he says, looking her straight in the eye. She tries to decide whether he means it. Given how accomplished he must be at lying, she's really not sure. Before all of this, before the lies, she'd have thought this was truth. 'I really am. I never meant any of this to happen.'

'Which bits?' she asks, raising an eyebrow. 'Seducing me, getting me pregnant, abandoning me, or stealing secrets for Nazis?'

He winces visibly. He doesn't deny any of it.

So it's true then, she thinks. Harriet was right. He *is* a spy. Nita's blood runs cold. The part of her that ached to be loved had been so relieved to see him again. But the Fascists have almost killed her brother, and hundreds of thousands of other young men, not to mention the hideous rumours of their treatment of the Jews on the continent. Anyone who spies for them deserves punishment. However much she may have loved them. She clasps her hands together and fingers the knife.

'So you *are* working for the Germans? You've always been working for them?' she says, not making any attempt to hide her disgust. 'I know your name isn't Joseph Miller.'

'No. No. It's Muller. My parents changed it a while back. Look, Nita... Look, I know you're angry. I know nothing can ever go back to the way it was between us. But before it's too late... I need to tell you how it is. How it was.'

'I see. Go on, then.'

'I spent a lot of my childhood in England, but yes, I was born in Germany and my parents always took us back there every summer, to visit my grandparents. And when I was there, they sent me to a local summer camp for young men. It was run by the

Hitler Youth. And that group, they told us a lot of things. Things I believed. They were very persuasive. And I don't know. I suppose it appealed to my... ego. I was stupid. Very young and very stupid. And anyway, I was singled out because I was bilingual, and that's where... it started.'

'Your training to be a spy?'

'I'm not... a spy! Is that what you think? I wasn't an Abwehr officer. I was more of an... informant.'

'Was?'

'I went AWOL not long after I told you I had been conscripted. I *had* been conscripted, you know, in a way. The Abwehr said there wasn't much more for them to learn here, and that I'd been too clumsy, putting the authorities onto the scent. Instead, they wanted to change my posting, and send me to London, to infiltrate some right-wing groups there and encourage them to take part in sabotage. But that's not what I signed up for. All I said I'd do over here was to give them some information about military hardware. I never wanted to get involved in causing actual damage.'

'You didn't think giving them that information might cause damage? For goodness' sake, Joe. They bombed the Millward factory after you'd broken in there and found out they were building Spitfires. That bomb killed a man! I thought you were intelligent. I was clearly wrong.'

Joe puts up both of his hands, not to silence her but to acknowledge the truth of what she's just said.

'Yes, yes. I know.'

His voice is shaking. She can see that he's tiring. He sits back in his chair, his voice now quite shallow. She knows they don't have much time, but she really needs to know everything first.

'So... you left? You stopped being an... informant?'

'Yes. I had been regretting my promise to them for a long time.

But meeting you, falling in love with you... It changed everything...'

'Oh, don't talk rubbish, Joe. You never loved me.'

Joe suddenly pushes himself out of the chair and comes at her. She reacts instinctively, pulling out the knife to defend herself. He sees this, and then he falls at her feet, weeping. Part of her aches to reach out to touch him. The other part, meanwhile, is so angry she wants to pummel him with her fists.

'Oh, Nita. You think I'm going to hurt you? I would never hurt you,' he says, sobbing. 'I never meant... if I could change things I would.' He sits there at her feet, his body racked with sobs, for a few minutes. And then, finally, he continues. 'Of course I love you. I loved you almost immediately. You are funny, you are clever, you are... mine. That was, in large part, why I decided to leave them, the Abwehr. But I didn't know what to do. We all know that handing ourselves in to the British government would be like signing our own death warrants, and going back to Germany would mean the same. They can't bear deserters. So I did the only thing I could think of... I came back here. I just wanted to be near you. But I didn't have anywhere to stay, so I've been sleeping rough.'

'It was you who broke into the cricket pavilion, wasn't it?' she says, with a sudden realisation. 'And the post office?'

'Yes. They had water in the pavilion, and it was warm. And of course cash at the post office. I tried not to do too much damage, except for the windows...'

'How have you survived? What have you been eating?'

'Scraps. Food stolen from pantries. Raw vegetables from gardens...'

Nita thinks about the break-ins local people have reported. Joe's painfully thin face tells her all she needs to know.

'Why didn't you tell me you were here, watching me, all this time?' she asks.

'Because I didn't know if I was being watched, too. The Abwehr are clever. They want me back, and they want to punish me for leaving. Literally no one is allowed to leave. If they knew about you, they might have used you to get back at me, to make me obey. So I just... stayed here. Close to you, but not with you. I did plan to tell you in time, when I was more sure I hadn't been followed. And then I saw you were pregnant with our child, and I realised I couldn't risk anything at all.'

'So why have you decided to risk it now? And risk my life, and Carole's?' asks Nita, her eyes burning.

'I... I can't live like this forever,' he says. 'I will be found out eventually, I know that. But I wanted to see you and... the baby, before I go. I needed you to know what really happened. Who I really am.'

'Did you seduce me because of my father? Because of who he is?'

Joe stares up at her blankly.

'No! Once I found out who your father was, it made me question myself, to be honest. I was brought up in a very socialist family. My father despised individual wealth and he said all wealthy industrialists were destroying society. But then I found myself falling in love with someone from a family like that, and, well... So, no. I found out all I needed to know about his businesses from the factory break-ins. I needed nothing from you.'

Nita feels herself soften. She believes him, even though she knows she shouldn't. He is the enemy, after all. But he is also her Joe. The only man she has ever loved. And so she reaches out for him, and when she does this he turns, and before either of them is really aware of what's happening, they are embracing.

They stay like that for quite some time, their arms locked

together, their hearts inches apart, their cheeks sharing their warmth. Behind them, the logs spit and crackle in the grate.

'How long until they come and take me?' says Joe, finally, into her ear.

'What do you mean?'

He pulls back.

'I know you will have called MI5. I know where Harriet works. I'm not a fool, you know.'

Then Nita sees a flash of metal. She realises Joe has taken the knife from her.

'Joe, no...' she says, her fear of him returning.

'Oh, I'm not going to hurt you with this, Nita. I'd never do that. I'm going to use it on myself.'

Nita's stomach lurches.

'Don't be ridiculous... I want you to give yourself up.'

'I assumed Harriet would have put something in the sandwich you gave me, but whatever it was doesn't seem to have worked quickly enough,' he says rapidly, not even acknowledging what she's just said.

He's right about the sandwich. However, the drug Harriet told her to put in it doesn't seem to be working as intended. Joe's eyes are wide, and the flames from the fire are reflected in the black pits of his pupils. If anything, he seems hyper-alert. He's hyper-ventilating. He's holding the knife a few inches away from this neck.

'*Please*, Joe, don't do this. We weren't trying to kill you with the sedative we gave you. It was only supposed to make you sleepy. Don't do anything rash. We'll think of something. We will talk to the security service. Maybe you can provide them with information in return for...'

'No. No. It's over, Nita. We will never be able to be together. We can never be a family. I will never be able to live anywhere in safety ever again. I made the most terminal of mistakes.'

Nita realises with a jolt what he's about to do.

'Help!' Nita screams, no longer capable of pretending she doesn't care, doesn't want him to survive. 'Help me, Harriet! Help!'

'But I do want you to know that I love you. And that I'm sorry. So, so sorry.'

Then everything happens very quickly.

Harriet bursts through the front door as Joe swipes the knife across his neck, and Nita throws herself at him, wrenching the knife away and screaming at him to stop, to stop this nonsense, even when it's far, far too late. Then Harriet and John are suddenly next to him, on top of him, trying to stop the bleeding.

In the end, every single white towel they use is scarlet.

But it's not enough.

In just a few minutes, Joe is dead, and Nita's life changes irrevocably.

36

BETH

February 2009

Philippa opens the door to her double-fronted, detached Victorian villa and says, 'You look tired.'

'Thanks,' replies Beth, so fired up by what she's discovered about Harriet and Nita's daughter Carole that she's prepared to ignore her sister's passive aggression on this occasion. She walks past Philippa and into the large kitchen at the back of the house, where she knows her father will be waiting.

'Darling. Thank you so much for coming,' he says, getting up from the large marble kitchen island and dispatching air kisses over her unwilling cheeks. Beth ensures she doesn't give an inch. She is not in the mood for playing at happy families.

'It was me who wanted to see you,' she replies, taking one of the wine glasses her sister has placed next to a chilled bottle of Chablis, and filling it with water from the over-engineered tap behind her.

'Yes, well. But we have wanted to speak to you properly about this for days.'

'I know,' says Beth, taking a seat on one of the high-backed, glossy black bar stools. Philippa sits down opposite her and pours a very large glass of wine. Now she's looking properly, Beth thinks her sister also looks rather tired. 'How's Nick? How are the kids?' she asks, realising with a jolt she may have missed her youngest niece Hope's recent birthday. It's not her fault we don't all get on, she thinks.

'We're going to have to pull Olivia out of her school,' says Philippa, staring into her glass. 'The teachers say they can't cope with her.'

Beth is completely blindsided by this. She had been vaguely aware that Philippa and Nick's eldest daughter had been having speech therapy and various other tests, but she has been so consumed by her own emotional turmoil, she hadn't probed further.

'Why?'

'Well, she's still not speaking, and she's prone to... outbursts. She's frustrated, you know, not being understood. They say she's not learning, and that they aren't a... special school, so they can't deal with it. And because they're a private school, we can't force them to keep her. Obviously.'

'I'm so sorry, Pip,' says Beth, meaning it. 'I didn't know.'

'Nick doesn't want people to know. I think he's embarrassed. Or overwhelmed, perhaps, if I'm being generous...' She slurps down most of the wine in the glass and pours some more.

'It's understandable,' says Robert.

'What is? That Pip's husband is embarrassed by his own daughter?' says Beth, enraged.

'No... that's not what I meant... I meant it has been a difficult time for them both.'

'Nick's hardly been here. He has left me – and the nanny, of course, God bless her – to deal with it all. He says he's too busy at the moment with an acquisition.'

'Is there anything I can do to help?' Beth asks. 'As I say, I'm so sorry. I think I've been far too caught up with my own issues and I really shouldn't have been. We could share childcare for a bit? Or I can come with you to... meetings.'

'No, it's all right. We have plenty of money and we'll find a solution. We'll pay for a private teacher here if we need to. I'm sorry, too. I didn't mean to hijack this meeting with my personal woes,' she says, running her finger around the rim of her wine glass.

'We don't have to do this now, if you'd rather not,' says Beth.

'No, we do,' says Robert. 'We need to get the house sale sorted. But let's not take too long about it. We all have other things on our minds. So, as you know, Beth, I instructed several agents to value Melham Manor. The plan Philippa and I have in mind is to sell to a developer we know well. They've done several of these projects before. The house itself will become flats, and the land around it will be parcelled off into plots for individual houses. As you know there's quite a lot of land on the site, so the estate is surprisingly valuable. The woodland is scrappy and not protected, so at least some of it can be cleared and used. Your share of the sale, a third of the estate, will be considerable. It'll pay for a home for you and the children and set you up with a savings pot that will last you a long while. I've actually got the paperwork here in my bag, to save you the time...'

Robert leans down and picks up a briefcase and pulls out a stack of papers marked up with Post-it notes, a clear sign that his solicitor has been at work.

And then the doorbell rings.

'Probably a delivery,' says Philippa, leaving her seat to answer the door.

'So, as I say, all you need to do is check you're happy with this agreement, and sign wherever it says to sign,' her father says, his smile pasted on like a ventriloquist's dummy. Beth reaches over and pulls the stack of paper towards her, but she doesn't start reading it, because at the same moment, David walks through the door.

'Thanks, Pip, lovely to see you. Hi, Robert,' he says, walking over and taking a spare seat next to Beth. 'Beth told me you were meeting and she invited me along.'

'Did she, indeed.'

Beth sees her father and her sister exchange a quizzical look, and she doesn't blame them. After all, she and David are getting divorced, and they know they haven't been on friendly terms for quite some time. And yet recently, that hasn't been true. Something shifted during their mediation sessions, and they have been talking recently, actually talking and finding solutions to problems. And so when she'd realised she'd inherited part of Melham Manor, she'd been in no doubt at all about who she needed to call.

'Yes. She explained the situation with the family trust, and she knows that I've dealt with a couple of sales of large family estates. So she asked for my advice, and I'm here to help her talk you through a plan she has.'

'A plan?' says Robert, his eyes wide.

'Yes,' says Beth. 'Dad, I know you need the money from the sale. I know the loss of the family firm is... horrible for you. For you and for Pip. But I've been spending a lot of time at the Manor in the past few months, and I've realised that the estate is far too precious to just rip apart. It's just as important to the people of Melham as it is to us. More important, in fact. They all walk, camp and rest in those woods. We shouldn't just pull up those trees for profit...'

'There are thousands of trees there, Beth. We're not suggesting all of them are cut down...'

'But you'll fence it all off and stop access to the public, won't you? And that will really affect everyone in that area. There will be a huge outcry.'

'They're not supposed to be in those woods at all.'

'Oh, Dad. How much of that land did we ever use, as a family? A tiny percentage of it. Don't you think clinging onto it is greedy?'

'It's not greedy. And we're not holding onto it. We are selling the land, aren't we? For more houses.'

'No, I don't think we are, Dad. I own a third of the estate, and I simply won't let it happen.'

'But you won't be able to afford the ongoing costs of running the estate if we don't, Beth. My lawyers have laid down the expected annual amount in Annex B of this document...'

'Oh yes, I knew you'd do that,' says Beth. 'But it's all right. I do agree we should sell the house. David, do you want to explain?'

'Yes, OK. So, I've worked on a couple of deals with the National Trust recently, and I think there's a good possibility that they would be interested in the woodland surrounding Melham Manor. It's a beautiful area and there are several NT estates nearby. As you know, you will have a significant inheritance tax bill to pay on the house, and you will be able to avoid a great deal of that if you donate that land to the Trust.' Beth sees her father shift in his seat, as if it's suddenly become uncomfortable. 'In terms of the rest of the estate, there are also, I believe, several properties on the edge of Melham, at the edge of the woods, which have been leased to local people for decades. Often in this situation, tenants are given the opportunity to buy their homes first, before any open market sale. We could also talk to the NT about buying any that remain as an ongoing concern, if you like. That would leave the house for you to dispose of as you wish, most likely, I'd have thought, to a developer to turn into apartments.'

'And I'm fine with that,' says Beth. 'As long as the gardens at the back can continue to be used to grow food for the community.'

Her father's eyes widen.

'We'd get much less for the estate without the land and other houses parcelled with it,' says Robert.

'Didn't you listen to David? We'd save a huge amount of tax if we agree to give the woods away,' says Beth.

'I'm telling you, your share will be much smaller. And you can't afford that, given the situation you're in with… David.'

'I will make sure, whatever happens, that Beth gets a fair settlement from our divorce,' says David. 'We have already arranged for—'

'So you say,' interrupts Robert.

'*Oh for God's sake, Dad, why don't you just tell her,*' says Philippa, shouting down everyone else.

'Tell me what?'

'Tell her about the other money. You've played enough games.'

'What other money?'

They all stare at Robert in silence. But instead of replying, he pours himself another glass of wine.

'Fine. I'll tell her,' says Philippa. 'Beth, you may be wondering why you haven't seen the actual will yet. There's a good reason for that. The firm that's acting as the executors would've had to tell you eventually, but it suited Dad at this stage not to tell you that although Nita couldn't control who inherited the house, she has left you money, separately. Quite a lot of money, as it turns out. We had no idea she had much personal wealth, but it turns out she was keeping quite a secret. She'd been earning a fortune over her lifetime as a novelist. She was, quite extraordinarily – Josephine Rees.'

Beth remembers the bookcase packed with novels by Rees upstairs in Melham Manor. Nita hadn't just read them, she now realises – she'd *written* them. She'd written novels that Marisa Bineham, the relative who'd approved of her the least, adored on the sly. This is delicious, delicious irony.

'And she also left you a note.'

'A note?' says Beth. She's astonished. She'd come to this meeting hoping to wrong-foot her father, but this news has done exactly the same to her.

'Yes. Dad? Why don't you give it to her? I know you brought it.' Philippa puts down her glass. 'He was showing it to me before you arrived, Beth.'

'This is not the order we agreed to conduct this business in, Philippa,' says Robert, reaching into his bag again and pulling out a tatty envelope, which he hands over to Beth with what appears to be reluctance.

She takes it, sees her name handwritten on the front, and turns it over. It's open, of course. Her father and sister and probably a huge number of lawyers have both obviously already read it. She opens the flap, pulls out the folded piece of paper inside, and reads.

My dear Beth,

   Firstly, I want to say how sorry I am that we have been unable to see each other for so many years. I have missed you. I feel such an affinity with you, you see. As I'm sure you know, we Wiccans believe that all children have magic in them, and I am certain I saw it in you, and, moreover, that you retained it long after it would have left most children. I hope you still feel the magic around you. It is the greatest gift. I am also certain that your magical soul has led you to feel the same way about Melham Manor and the nature that surrounds it as I do. And that is why I am writing to you. I know that important decisions will be made about it after my death, and that your position as one of the three beneficiaries of the trust gives you some decision-making power over the Manor's future.

Before you make your decision, I want you to know some important things about me. If my spells and prayers have worked, you will have visited me before my death. And if you did, I will have told you about a box in the attic containing my secrets. Knowing your instincts as I do, and, coupled with the assistance of my wonderful friend Harriet's daughter, Rowan, I think it's likely that those documents will help you to not only learn more about my past but also lead you to find out about my child, Carole. I have kept her existence a secret for many years. When I had finally shed all care about what society might think, and after my parents died, I could and perhaps should have told everyone about her. But I was so insular by then, and it seemed like too many years had passed. I was wrong, I think. That's why I'm keen you should find out now. Far too late, I know, but better late I think than never.

I am sure you will have questions to which the box of documents does not immediately provide an answer. You will be wondering who Carole's father is, I think, and what happened to him. These are things I have been unable to risk writing down, for fear of discovery, but please ask Rowan to tell you about them. Harriet made sure she knew the truth.

I also need to address my other secret – my writing. It's been source of great joy and solace over my lifetime. My lawyers will have told you all by now that I have been writing popular novels under a pseudonym, Josephine Rees, for many *years. To my astonishment, I've had considerable success. I gave Rowan, and through her, Carole, as much of my earnings as she was prepared to accept – nowhere near as much as I would have liked – and have made anonymous donations to important local projects, but there is still a great deal of it left. While I am leaving the rights to my novels to Carole and am giving her and Rowan significant cash sums, I am leaving you half of my savings, to do with as you wish. I trust you absolutely with the future of the Melham estate, and I know you will find great things to do with the funds you have been given.*

Finally, you may be wondering why I didn't simply write to you during my lifetime to tell you all this; why I didn't invite you to Melham Manor to explain. Some of the blame for this lies in my habitual solitude, I'm afraid. I am now far more comfortable with animals than people. I worried also that you had been in London too long, out in the business world, to really understand what Melham Manor means to me and to the wider community. I hope that learning about me and my past has helped you understand yourself more. I hope you know how precious you are. You have so much left to give. Please forgive me for deliberately setting you off on this path of discovery. I wanted, you see, to lead you back home. Back home, to Melham Manor.

I must finish this. I'm growing tired now and need my sleep.
With much love, darling girl,
Great-Auntie Nita

Beth sits back in her seat and stares hard at her father. Her mind is spinning. She thinks about her great-aunt, alone in her crumbling old mansion, crafting her romantic stories. She wonders whether Nita had ever experienced her own romance, whether the man who'd got her pregnant had been someone she'd loved. And how must it have felt to have to live her life apart from her child, never to be identified as her mother?

'So you knew she had a daughter?' she says, her nostrils flaring.

'I had no idea, frankly,' he replies. 'If my father knew, he never told me. I only found out when I read Nita's will. Looking at her financial records, she was giving money to a woman called Harriet Ringwood, who I presume was the adoptive mother, for years. For her daughter's upkeep, I expect. Anyway, as she says in the letter, she's left all the book rights to her daughter, along with quite a lot of money. She will be a very wealthy woman. And Rowan, whoever she is, is also getting a large chunk of cash.'

Robert Bineham seems to have trouble forming the words for the last couple of sentences. He clears his throat. 'Anyway, at least some of the money has come to our side of the family.'

'Have you contacted Carole, to introduce yourself, Dad? After all, she is a relative.'

'Not yet. Your mother and I are worried it might open us up to more claims, financially. I mean, who knows what she might decide she deserves...'

'Don't be ridiculous,' says Philippa. 'If you could just stop thinking of your bloody business plan for five minutes and start thinking about how other people might feel, the world would be a better place.'

Beth lets this extraordinary statement sink in for a moment, before leaning over and embracing her sister, who she suspects she's really *seeing* for the first time in decades.

'I'm sorry you aren't getting any of Nita's money,' Beth says, as she pulls away. She realises Philippa may feel Nita has been unfair in only giving the money to her.

'Oh, honestly, don't worry about it. I'll be fine. Nita was right, anyway, wasn't she? You were always the one who loved Melham.

And loved her, too. It makes a lot of sense to leave the money to you. And I'll still inherit a share of the estate, anyway. Don't give it a second thought.'

'Thank you,' says Beth. 'That means a lot. Now tell me,' she adds, ignoring her father, who has just got up and left the room. 'Tell me more about Olivia.'

37

NITA

August 1941

It is a fortnight after Joe's death, and Nita is taking Carole to visit him. It hasn't rained for weeks and Surrey's open fields and heaths are crisp and brown, but here beneath the leaf canopy the ground is a lush green and there's a cooling breeze to wick away the beads of sweat on Nita's brow. She is taking careful steps across the uneven terrain because she's carrying the baby in her arms.

She reaches the clearing. It wasn't planned this way, to her knowledge, but there's almost a perfect circle of oak trees here, and a space in the centre where she often came to read when she was a girl.

In the corner of the clearing is a large area of fresh, disturbed earth. They have placed a few twigs and some fallen leaves on top to disguise it, although Nita has never seen anyone else in this part of the woods. She suspects that by the time anyone stumbles across it, nature will have reclaimed Joe's final resting place. Soon, he'll be part of the leaves, the roots, the tree trunks and the grass in this special place. She will always be able to come here and be with him.

'This is where your daddy is,' she says to Carole, who at one month old is getting more and more interested in the world around her. 'He was called Joe. Joseph. I loved him. And he loved me.'

Nita sits down in the clearing to rest and to think. She has much to think about. Harriet has just become engaged to John, and this means her time lodging with her friend will soon be over, despite Harriet's protestations that she and the baby do not need to leave. Harriet is trying to persuade her to go back to her parents to ask them to provide her with enough money to find somewhere to live, but Nita knows this would never work. They will insist she surrenders Carole to a stranger, and that's something she will never do. She loves her daughter with a passion she had never thought possible, and she is determined that whatever happens, she must be safe and happy. That is the most important thing of all, Nita thinks; safety and happiness.

It has taken her some time to come to this conclusion, because the shock of Joe's violent death has knocked her sideways. For a couple of days afterwards, she had been unable to take care of herself, let alone Carole. Thank heavens, she thinks, for Harriet, who had stepped in and looked after her as if she was her own. Nita knows she hasn't even begun to grieve, although she knows she must try. That's why she's here.

With Carole gurgling in her lap, Nita reaches into her small shoulder bag and removes a pink candle, into which she has carved her name with a knife. She pulls out a small holder, places it on the ground in front of her, inserts the candle and lights it. It flickers in the breeze before becoming secure and strong.

And then she recites an incantation she has learned from memory:

> *Angels,*
> *Please help me heal after this separation.*
> *Melt my pain like the wax of this flame.*
> *Restore peace to my spirit.*
> *And so mote it be.*

Nita sits for a moment with her eyes closed, absorbing the sounds of nature all around her, and feeling the warmth of Carole's little body nestling in her arm. She's spent a great deal of the past two weeks in terrible pain, but right here, surrounded by God's creation, she feels something approaching peace.

'Nita? Oh my God, Nita...'

Her eyes fly open.

In front of her is her brother, Frank.

For a moment she thinks she might be hallucinating, that he can't possibly have made it home from Cairo in such good health, but then he speaks again.

'Are you... all right? And who... is this?'

Nita places Carole down onto the soft grass beside her, stands up and throws herself into her brother's arms.

'Oh goodness, Frank. I'm so glad to see you again. I have been so worried. So, so worried...'

'Don't be silly, Nita. I've been far more worried about you,' he says. 'Mother and Father said you had run away and I simply couldn't believe it. I thought maybe you'd been tempted away by some sort of scoundrel but now I see...' he says, looking down at the baby, who is currently trying to pick blades of grass.

'This is Carole. She's mine. They didn't tell you?'

Frank shakes his head.

'We've got a lot to catch up on, haven't we,' he says, and they sit down together on the grass.

Nita begins by telling him, as concisely as she can, why she left Melham Manor and that she's been living with her new friend Harriet, who has been an absolute Godsend. She tells him she became engaged to a man called Joe, but that he was killed in action before they could be married. This is, of course, a lie, but she knows that telling the whole truth about Joe would change the way he thinks about both her and the baby, and Nita desperately doesn't want that. Because she now believes that Joe was, in his heart, a good man. He had not gone back to Germany. He had stayed around and risked his life, no, lost his life, for them both.

'Enough about me, I think,' she says, exhausted from telling her story, which is still so raw, it feels like she's reopening a wound every time she tells it. 'When did you get back? I thought you would still be in Cairo. Your letters were so sparse, we were worried...'

'Yes. I'm sorry about that. I didn't much feel like writing. It was a hideous time, out there. I saw things I never want to think about again. And it affected me, badly.'

'What injuries did you have?'

Frank takes a beat to reply.

'I was injured in the leg and chest when a shell exploded near me, but that's mostly healed now. It was my... brain that was the main issue.'

'The shrapnel went into your brain?' Nita looks all over Frank's face and head but can't see any scars.

'No. It's... I don't know how to explain it. The thing is, I actually came back to England from Cairo more than two months ago, but I didn't want to tell you all. I was receiving treatment at a hospital near Weybridge. A place called May Day House, on its own little Thames island. It's for service men who... have illnesses in their minds.'

Nita pauses. 'I see,' she says.

'Do you?'

'I think so. I have been feeling a great deal of darkness since Joe died, and I am not myself. Do you feel as if you're not yourself?'

'Yes, that's exactly it.'

'I wish you'd told me. I'd have come to visit you.' Nita picks up Carole and cradles her, as she can see that her eyes have a fixed stare, which means sleep is not far off.

'They don't allow visitors at May Day.'

'Still, we could have written. I could have told you my troubles. We could have shared how we felt,' she says, noticing the baby's eyes are closing.

'Yes, I think that would have been much better.'

'Are you going back to the war now? Are you... better?'

Frank sighs.

'I'm well enough, so they say. But I think my record may mean they won't send me back out to Egypt. I'm told they're seconding me to a job in Whitehall. I'm going to be waging the rest of the war from a desk.'

'That's great news,' says Nita, before she realises Frank isn't smiling.

'Well, it is, in terms of me living to see the end of this damn war,' he says. 'But the guilt of not being there with the men I was serving with is... significant.'

'I can imagine that. But, Frank, you *were* there. You *did* fight.'

'Yes. I did,' he says, picking a blade of grass and running it between his fingers. 'So that's what I'll be doing next. What about you?'

'Well, it's been a difficult time and I haven't been at all certain, but I actually came here to help me make up my mind. And it's helped. I think I know what I'm going to do now, about Carole.'

'Oh?'

'We can't both stay with Harriet, that's for certain. She's to be married, and I have no means of supporting myself, aside from some stories I've been writing, and I haven't made much from them so far. And I can't arrive back at Melham Manor with a baby. Society will reject me. I'm an unmarried mother. Our parents will insist Carole is adopted. And I just can't be parted from her, Frank. I just can't.'

He doesn't reply immediately. Instead of talking, Nita listens to the sounds of the wood. The melodic song of a blackbird soothes her.

'The thing is, Harriet is really good with the baby,' she continues. 'And she lives in a house rented from the estate, just on the other side of the woods. I think I'm going to ask her to take care of her, Frank. Adopt her, even. Would you be willing to help me? To find enough money to help Harriet take care of her? So I can keep Carole close?'

Nita has been thinking about this possibility for a while. In her darkest moments during the pregnancy she'd even considered putting the baby up for formal adoption, as her parents had originally urged her to do. But this option, this chance of keeping her daughter close to her, is appealing. Harriet is wonderful with Carole, and she knows that she and John would like children.

'I can see the appeal. But how on earth would we get this idea past Mother and Father?' says Frank.

'Well, we could lie and say that she's been adopted far away, or even that she died? Anything that will put them off the scent.'

'Yes, that might work. They're making noises about moving back to London permanently, anyway. We could ask them to let you live in the Manor by yourself. I would make sure you're provided for, if you need it. I'm going to inherit the estate eventually anyway, aren't I.'

In the distance, a robin whistles. Once; twice; three times. It's just enough time for Nita to make up her mind. She needs to stay here to be near to Carole, she thinks. And Joe.

'Yes. I'll ask Harriet,' she says.

38

BETH

February 2009

The sky is a steely grey when Beth pulls up outside a seventies semi-detached house on the outskirts of Melham. She checks her watch; it's just gone 9 a.m. She's slightly early, but she hopes that won't matter. She's been thinking about this moment ever since the meeting with her father and sister a few days previously, and she's keen to get on with it.

She sticks her BlackBerry in the back pocket of her jeans, locks her car, walks up the garden path and rings the front doorbell. James Connors answers it almost immediately.

'Hello. Thank you so much for agreeing to see me,' she says.

'That's OK. Come in,' he replies, his expression unreadable. She knows he must still be angry about the impending sale of Melham Manor, not to mention the fact that she failed to own up to her own connection to the house on their three previous meetings, something she now sincerely regrets.

'Thanks.'

Beth follows him down a hallway lined with photos of two

school-aged kids, a girl and a boy, into a living room furnished with a sofa, an armchair, two bookcases and a TV on a pine unit in the corner.

'Would you like a cuppa?'

'Yes, please. Milk, no sugar.'

'Coming up.'

While James makes the drinks in the kitchen, Beth walks over to his bookshelves. There's a strong mix of non-fiction and fiction on display, with Ian Rankin, Agatha Christie and Anthony Horowitz all appearing several times. There are none of her mother's books here, she notices, despite the fact they are best-sellers of the genre. Beth is just about to read the back of Horowitz's *Magpie Murders* when James walks back in with two mugs of tea.

'Ha, you've found my hobby,' he says, handing her a cup. 'I love to read.'

'Me too, when I'm not wrangling kids.' She hopes this will raise a smile. It does, albeit a small one. 'I have always loved words.'

'Hence the journalistic hobby?' he says. She notes the barb.

'Actually, I'm hoping to turn it into something much more serious than that,' she says, putting the book back on the shelf. 'But that's not why I asked to come and see you.'

'OK,' he says, raising an eyebrow. 'Fair enough. Take a seat.'

Beth sits down in the armchair, diagonally opposite James.

'The first thing I wanted to do is apologise for not being straight with you about... my family connections. I know I should have been honest from the start, but frankly I'm... embarrassed about them and when Steve at *The Bugle* offered me work, it felt like an opportunity to relaunch myself, to be someone different. I suppose I didn't want anyone to know. And then, of course, when I realised you worked with people living in substandard rented accommodation, I knew you wouldn't take kindly to finding out who'd been paying my salary for almost two decades.'

'I must admit it was a shock when I realised who you were. I can't deny that. But I've been thinking about my reaction and I realise I was committing that horrible sin of tarring people with the same brush. It's the sort of thing I abhor, because of course people are generally derogatory about, oh, you know, asylum seekers, or travellers, and I hate that. And there I was, basically treating you as if you were single-handedly responsible for the housing crisis. And that was unfair of me.'

Beth, who has been almost hiding behind her mug of tea, decides it's safe to put it back on her lap.

'Honestly, I really don't blame you... I stopped working there a while ago, actually. Before Christmas. Before they went under. You probably know about that horrific gaffe I made. Anyway, I no longer work in property. Or anywhere, actually.'

'I see. I'm sorry you're unemployed. I really am. Nobody deserves to lose their job over a mistake.'

'Oh, I resigned. I'd had enough of all of it. More than enough. I'm getting divorced, too, so this feels like a proper season of change. I'm trying to tell myself it's that, by the way, rather than a full-blown crisis.'

There's a ghost of a smile on James' lips. A smile, she thinks, of solidarity.

'Oh God, poor you. That's tough. I went through that myself a few years ago. I wouldn't wish it on my worst enemy.'

'Thanks. It's been a grim time. But I feel like I'm pulling through it. My ex, David, and I, we're finally talking. We're hammering out an agreement and we're sharing the childcare a bit more equally now. All in all, it's not... not a disaster, you know? Not as disastrous as I'd felt it would be.'

'That's great to hear. Ours wasn't quite as amicable, but we've managed to make it work for the children, sort of.'

'Oh, I saw some pictures in the hall?'

'Yes, my two. Sophie, she's thirteen, and Dylan, he's ten. They live with their mum most of the week in Guildford, but they come over most weekends.'

'It's weird being without them, isn't it? David took them on holiday for a week and I felt bereft.' There's an awkward pause, and she realises there are lots of unanswered questions hanging in the air. 'By the way, I'm so sorry I didn't tell you that Melham Manor was going on the market. As you know, I didn't even tell Rowan, and I've found myself telling her pretty much everything else. I just didn't know how to break it to her, to everyone in this area, that the estate was going to be broken up, and built on. I knew it would upset people. I wasn't brave enough to tell you all, but I should have.'

'Look, there's no reason at all why you needed to tell me. Rowan, maybe, because I know she's been working on the gardens and stuff over there, but not me. I have no part to play in any of it. What your family does with that house is your business.'

'Yes, but the woodland... I'm not happy about that, either.'

'No. I know that's definitely going to upset people, and I have to say I'm not sure you, or whoever wants to develop the site, will find planning permission easy to obtain on that basis. Cutting down ancient woodland is never a good look.'

'I agree,' says Beth, sipping her tea. 'That's why I've talked my father and sister out of it.'

James is about to take a sip, but he stops as soon as she says this and puts it back down.

'Oh?'

'Yes. We're in talks with the National Trust, who we hope will take on the woodland. The house will still be sold, mind you, and turned into flats. But the woods will become fully accessible to the public, and I've also got my family to commit to keeping Nita's vegetable and herb gardens for community use. I'm also going to find caring, suitable new homes for the cats. Rowan, by the way, is going to take Roger the cockerel. She insisted. Anyway... I think all of this is frankly the least my family can do, given the way they've lorded it over Melham for more than a century.'

'Goodness. That's all wonderful news.'

'I'm really glad,' she says, smiling broadly, her relief that he's pleased showing on her face.

'So was that what you came to tell me?'

'Actually, no. Although that was part of it. No, I wanted to talk to you about something else entirely.'

39

NITA

May 1945

'Push me higher, Auntie Nita.'

'Oh, all right then.'

'Weeeeeeeeeee,' says Carole, her legs stretched out in front of her, her head thrown back, her smile infectious.

'So, what was London like, then? After the Germans surrendered?' Nita asks Harriet, who is sitting down on a log nearby. Harriet is six months' pregnant and her feet are hurting.

'It was manic. Absolutely bonkers. I saw the crowds beginning to build on the way home from work the day before, but on the day of the actual announcement it felt a bit like everyone had taken some kind of drug. People were dancing with complete strangers, hugging complete strangers, kissing complete strangers... It was bedlam.'

Harriet, unlike most married women, has managed to retain her job at the university. This, Nita realises, is because Harriet is simply extraordinary; one of a kind. There is even talk of her returning to work after the birth. Nita admires her greatly, for these and many other reasons.

'I can imagine,' says Nita, still pushing Carole on the swing that John has recently hung on the largest oak tree. It gives Harriet an excuse to bring Carole up here regularly to play, something which both women enjoy. It's a chance to chat, and for Nita to spend time with her daughter.

She had wondered at the beginning, after the initial pain of separation, whether she could bear this way of life, this decision she'd made to be so close to her child, and yet, not close at all. She had wept for days after she had moved back to Melham Manor and left little Carole in Harriet's care. But when that initial pain had subsided, she had begun to see that this was absolutely the right thing for her daughter. She has a secure, loving home with John and Harriet, who care for her brilliantly and love her dearly. Nita knows she would never have been able to afford to keep them both, and a life of terrible poverty would have hurt Carole immeasurably. No, this was the right thing to do, Nita thinks, as she pushes her daughter higher, then higher still. This was the right thing for her, and it is not goodbye. It will never be goodbye. She is settled back in Melham Manor now, living happily without any staff and with just the occasional visit from Frank, and she knows she will never leave. She knows Harriet won't leave the area either. They are part of this place, part of the trees and the grass and the weeds and the flowers and the wild fruit; part of the birds and the wind and the rain and the field mice and the squirrels. They will never leave here. Not even in death. They are women of the woods. Women of nature. Wiccan women.

'Weren't you tempted to take the train up and come and see for yourself?' Harriet asks.

Nita laughs. 'You know me too well to suggest that,' she says. 'I don't travel any more.'

'Oh, come on. You'd never have seen anyone you knew. It would have been fine.'

'No. As you know, Frank and my parents have told everyone I'm unwell. No one expects to see me in London ever again, and honestly, I don't care one jot. I have everything I need here. Frank visits, and I have Carole, you, John and… Joe.'

Her eye turns towards the corner of the clearing. His grave is now fully grown over and looks like every other patch of woodland. *You would never know*, she thinks. *You would never ever know.*

'Fair enough. I know how you feel about this place. It's special, there's no doubt about that. Are you still all right with us having the meetings here, by the way? I know you were fine with the Beltane celebration here last week, but I didn't want to presume. Our cottage is a little small now for the coven.'

'Not at all. I love it, in fact.'

It had been a warm, cloudless spring night when they had marked Beltane, a celebration of the peak of spring and the transition into summer. Newly liberated from the blackout by what they knew was Germany's imminent capitulation, they had lit a large bonfire in Melham Manor's back garden, and they had eaten, drunk and danced around it until the early hours. Nita had been consumed by it. She hadn't experienced joy like it before.

In fact, the joy and peace that the discovery of Wicca has brought Nita is something that she would struggle to measure. Harriet's gentle induction into her beliefs has brought Nita new friends, new purpose and new meaning. And reassurance, too. Because she has experienced a few strange things in the house over the past couple of years. Things that have made her feel a bit uneasy. But Wicca has given her tools to deal with them, and she's immensely grateful for that.

'Wonderful. So we will be here this evening, then? About ten?'

'Yes. Thank you. Yes.'

* * *

'Are you sure you're ready for this?' Harriet asks.

Nita takes a deep breath and inhales the delicious scents of nature's perfumiers, stock and jasmine.

'Yes. Let's get on with it.'

Earlier in the evening, at Harriet's instruction, she had gone into every room in Melham Manor and opened every window. Some of them hadn't been opened in decades. She turns to look at the old house, and imagines decades of frustration, sadness, repression and anger bursting out of the casements into the night sky. Even if this spell they're going to do this evening has no effect, she thinks, she'll feel better just knowing that so much negative energy has had a chance to leave the house.

'Do you really think this will work? That Joe will... leave me in peace?'

'It might not be Joe's spirit, you know, Nita,' says Harriet. 'It might just be... the old house. Houses creak. They move. And you're alone in there. I keep telling you, you should allow your family to pay for a housekeeper. It would be better if you weren't completely alone.'

'I'm not alone. I have the animals.'

It had started soon after Carole had gone to live with Harriet and John. Harriet's cat had given birth to a surprise litter of kittens at dawn one morning, and Nita had fallen in love with them. She had adopted two: Oliver and Max. Then she had started to feed the badgers that she'd spotted in the garden; the hedgehogs, which to her delight had begun to breed; and the myriad birds who come to gorge themselves on juicy fat balls on her bird tables daily. And then some weeks ago she'd found a young fox caught in a hunter's snare in the woods. She was furious when she found it. She does not agree with trapping, and moreover, whoever it was had been trespassing on Melham Manor land. She had acted instinctively. She had prised the trap open, picked up the young animal, which had barely registered this turn of events, and carried him, braced to her chest, into the house. Then, on the advice of a vet in town, she had fed him a mix of water and puppy kibble in a specially constructed outdoor enclosure until he was strong enough to walk on his leg which, despite a nasty cut, had healed reasonably well. She had let him go as soon as she could, mindful that he was a wild animal, and he had padded away into the woods without glancing back. She had thought she'd never see him again. But she'd been wrong. She sees him most nights now. She often looks out of the window at bedtime, before she pulls the curtains closed, and she sees him by the treeline, looking at the house. She's taken to putting food out for him, too, and it is always eaten in the morning. She spotted several other prints around the bowl last night, in fact. She suspects there may be a family of foxes who are paying her a visit.

'I know. And I'm glad we all make you happy,' says Harriet. 'Right. Shall we get going?'

Eight Wiccans – Harriet, Nita, four other women and two men – gather by the door that leads off the kitchen, each holding an incense stick. Then Harriet lights a match and goes around the group, lighting each stick in turn. When they've all taken and the heady scent and smoke fills the air, Harriet issues her instructions. They all nod and head off.

Nita is last. She watches her new friends walk in single file, counter-clockwise around the house, chanting an invocation which is familiar to them but new to her. This spell is designed to tell Joe's spirit – or indeed, any others that are currently inside the house – to depart. As they move away and their chanting fades,

Nita hangs back. She says, 'Thank you so much for this. Honestly. This gives me such comfort.'

'You don't need to feel guilty about Joe's death, Nita. You know that. He made his choice. He chose to die on his own terms rather than at the hands of our government, or even the German government. It really was his choice. I honestly don't think he's angry with you, or unsettled. It doesn't make sense.'

'Then why? Why do you think he's been haunting me?'

'I don't know. I'm not even sure he has. But if he has, then perhaps he's just... worried about you?'

Nita looks up at the sky, where Polaris is shining brightly.

'Yes. Maybe. But he needn't be, you know. I really am happy here. Honestly.'

'Honestly? You don't regret letting me have Carole...?'

'I don't regret that at all. I know how happy she is. And she will never be far from me. It's a huge comfort.'

'We could tell her, you know. We could tell her that you're not just a family friend. Sometimes I feel so guilty, being called her mother, around you...'

'It would confuse her, and I don't want that. I really don't. She needs stability, and you're giving her that. But you can tell her one day, if you like. When you feel the time is right.'

40

BETH

February 2009

A milky dawn is casting ethereal light over the village as Beth dresses, ready for a day she had never imagined would come.

She's still sleeping in the guest bedroom she'd been directed to on the night Nita died, but she's recently started spending time in her great-aunt's old bedroom. There's something about the view from here, of the houses below and the woodland on either side, that grounds her. She takes immense comfort from the fact that even when the house is sold, this view will remain the same, thanks to the agreement she's struck with the developers who are buying it. She reckons Nita would be pleased about that.

She pulls a jumper over her head and turns, taking in the bed where her great-aunt had taken her last breath. The sight of it used to make her feel uneasy, but that's changed now. Whatever the cause of those strange incidents with the noises, the fire and the strange lights – Beth is well aware that she might have been dreaming them all – they have served to bolster her belief in something she cannot rationalise, something that inhabits a space just beyond her comprehension. And instead of frightening her, this belief in something much bigger than herself and her petty concerns gives her comfort.

* * *

It's mid-morning when Beth arrives at the offices of *The Bugle*, sufficiently late that she's fairly confident Steve will be fully dressed and at his desk. She hasn't actually seen him in person since just after Christmas, when he'd helped her read some shorthand. The occasional articles she's still contributing to *The Bugle* have been filed remotely, something that has worked well for both of them. For Beth, because she can write while looking after the kids, and for Steve, because he doesn't have to put up with having anyone in the office.

Beth uses her key in the front door, walks up the steps and pushes open the door to the newsroom. She can see that Steve is in fact in his office, which is a good start. She walks through and realises there's someone else in there with him – a young man this time.

'Ah, Beth, how lovely to see you,' says Steve. 'This is' – she can see he's struggling to remember the poor boy's name – 'our new intern. It's...'

'Dan,' says the intern.

'Yes, Dan. He's just joined us and he'll be learning the ropes for a couple of weeks.'

Beth smiles the biggest smile she can manage, knowing he'll need as much encouragement as he can get when he discovers what he's expected to do for absolutely no remuneration.

'I was hoping to have a private chat, actually...' she says to Steve, who looks startled.

'Yes, of course. Right, yeah. Could you go and do a quick vox pop on the high street about the proposed new licence for a pizza van on Fridays, Dan? Take a pic of each with the digital camera and get their ages and jobs and stuff. Thanks.'

Dan looks like a startled rabbit, but he clearly decides not to ask for further clarification – he's probably going to google it as soon as he leaves the office, Beth thinks – and he leaves quickly.

'What can I do you for?' Steve asks. 'Would you like something to drink, by the way? I should have asked Dan to do it, sorry...'

'I'd love one, actually. But it's OK, I'll make it. Do you want to follow me into the kitchen, and we can talk?' Steve nods and follows her. Familiar with the kitchen from previous visits, Beth fills the kettle and gets on with making herself a cup of coffee. 'Do you want one, by the way? I should have asked.'

'Yeah, thanks. Coffee, two sugars.'

Beth nods.

'What is it, then? What do you need to speak to me in private about?'

He looks concerned. *He thinks I'm going to report him for living in the office*, she thinks. Time to put him out of his misery.

'It's about this place,' she says. '*The Bugle.*'

'Oh, right,' he says, and she sees the weight visibly lifting from his shoulders. 'Yeah, well, I was going to message you about that. I don't think I can put much more work your way, I'm afraid. As I thought, the owners are going to sell, and I know how it goes. Each time this place changes hands, costs get cut even further. This time, they'll probably find a way to get the content all written by computers, ably assisted by a chimp. I mean, if they could, they would. Put it that way.'

'I see,' says Beth, finding a jar of instant coffee in the cupboard and spooning it into mugs. 'How are things with you? With the kids, and your ex, and everything?'

'As good as can be at the moment. I'm still kipping here, before you ask, but I'm managing to save a bit for a deposit on a rental flat. I reckon I'll get there in about another decade. So that's all good.'

She looks over at him and sees his fixed grin is under severe strain.

'I might be able to help you there.'

'Really? How?'

'Well, there's no easy way to say this, so I'm just going to put it out there. I'm the new owner of *The Bugle*. Well, I will be, when we sign on the dotted line.'

'Errr... How?'

'Well, my great-aunt Nita turned out to be a fairly wealthy woman in her own right, and she's left enough money for me to buy this place. I knew, because you'd told me, how much financial strain the paper was under, and I also know, because I've experienced it, the amazing work great local journalism can do. I really believe in it. And so did Nita, it turns out. It just feels right to do this. We need a proper new strategy – my sister Philippa says she'll help with that – and it'll be a lot of work, but I reckon we can save *The Bugle*. And it'll be a new start. For me and for you.'

'Am I getting the sack, do you mean?'

'Ha! No. I can't do the day-to-day running of this place. I've got young kids and I want to do a proper journalism qualification, too. No, I want to keep you as editor. But we need to get rid of this office. You're right. There's so much space we don't need here. Actually, I reckon we don't need an office at all. I've been working remotely for you for months, and as long as we both live near here, there are plenty of coffee shops and a library we can meet in if we need to. No, I reckon we could save money and have you working from home.'

'But I haven't got a bloody home.'

Beth pours hot water into the mugs, grinning to herself.

'That's the thing. I'm going to rent you one. One with enough space to work, and with a spare bedroom for your kids to come and stay. We can offset some of the costs as a business expense.'

'But why would you do that?'

'It'll be cheaper than renting this office, I reckon.'

'Christ on a bike. This is amazing.'

'I'm so glad. I hope you don't mind the awkwardness of having me as your new boss, though?' she says, putting milk into the coffee.

'If they were going to put me up for free, I'd tolerate Genghis Khan,' he says. 'But sod that cheap excuse for coffee for a bunch of soldiers. Shall we hit the pub? I feel like celebrating.'

* * *

'What are you having?'

'A gin and tonic, please,' replies Beth. She doesn't usually drink at lunchtime, but then, it's been an unusual sort of day. One for the ages, in fact.

'Right you are,' he says to the barman. 'One for the lady.' The man smiles and sets about his work. 'So are you going to stay up in London, then, while we work on saving the paper together?'

'No. Well, it'll take me a while to move, but I'm planning to rent locally for a bit, and then when Melham Manor is converted into flats, I'm going to buy one of the units there. David and I have agreed to share parenting really flexibly, and he's happy for the kids to attend the local primary school here. He rather likes Melham, actually. He came down last weekend with his new girl-friend. It was... not too hard. Surprisingly.'

'Oh really? That's great. I'm pleased somebody's managing to stay friends with their ex.'

'Yeah. We are, I think. Friends.'

'And they'll like living up in the Manor, won't they, the kids? It's nice up there. In fact, we should do a story about the new development, boss.' Steve winks. Beth knows his manner will never stop being slightly jarring, but she also knows his heart is in the right place.

'Yes. And we need to get an interview with the National Trust about the woodland.'

'On it.'

'Actually, will you excuse me for a minute? I need to freshen up.'

'I'll find us a table,' he says, receiving the drinks as Beth heads to the Ladies'. She follows the signs around the bar towards the far corner, beside a chalkboard announcing the lunchtime specials and a blazing log fire. And, to the right of it, to her complete surprise – James Connors. He's sitting with a couple of people she doesn't recognise, and they are clinking glasses, smiling broadly.

'Talk of the devil!' he says, spotting her, standing up and pulling her in for a brief kiss on the cheek. It's the first time he's done this and she's slightly taken aback, although not at all upset about it. In fact, it might be just the fire, but she can feel warmth spreading all over her face and down her neck. She hopes the light is dim enough at the back of the pub for him not to notice. 'This is Beth Bineham, everyone. She's the person I was just telling you about, who's single-handedly saved the housing project from disappearing into obscurity.'

The two people he'd been sitting with both raise a glass to her.

'Absolutely wonderful news,' says one of them, a man in his fifties who's wearing a red checked shirt. 'It's going to make such a difference.'

'Yes. We can really get going on this now,' says the other, a woman in her forties. 'I can't wait to tell the families I've been supporting in temporary housing.'

'Oh, honestly, it's...' Beth is about to say that donating a large chunk of money from her inheritance to help buy the land for James' social housing project is nothing, but then she realises how ridiculous this sounds. 'It's... a joy. An absolute joy to be able to do something so positive with my aunt's money. She'd have approved, I know.'

The two people take a sip from their glasses of sparkling wine and return to their earlier conversation, leaving James and Beth standing in the firelight, looking at each other awkwardly.

'I know I told you so earlier, but I can't thank you enough,' he says. 'You could have done so many other things with the money.'

'Oh I did, actually. I sent the vicar a cheque yesterday to go towards the building work on the new tower. I think he's a lot further forward with his fund-raising now. And I'm also the new owner of *The Bugle*. The business plan I've drawn up suggests I'll make a small profit. And I also kept back a little bit to tide me over while I'm getting things going. It'll be OK.'

'Well, most people wouldn't have ever thought of doing any of it. I know that for certain. So, from the bottom of my heart, on behalf of everyone who will benefit... thank you.'

Beth sees that James' eyes are a little red and that a tear has formed at the corner of his left eye. She almost reaches out to dab it with a clean tissue from her bag, before she realises how overfamiliar that would seem. And yet she feels so comfortable with him.

'Thank you. That means a lot.'

'Will you join us for a drink?' he asks, gesturing towards his friends.

'Oh, no, that's a lovely invitation, but I've got a seat waiting over the other side of the bar with Steve, the editor of *The Bugle*.'

'Ah, I see. Fair enough. Well if that's the case, how about' – he looks away towards the fire for a moment – 'dinner? Sometime soon?'

Beth's heart leaps. She's quite shocked by this, as it hasn't leaped for a very, very long time.

'That would be lovely,' she replies immediately, not caring at all that she probably sounds very keen. Because obviously she *is* keen, and she's old enough now to know that playing games in situations like these is utterly pointless.

'Excellent. Excellent,' replies James, also with pleasing speed.

'You've got my number.'

'I do. And I intend to use it,' he says, his face one enormous grin.

Beth grins too.

She has so much to look forward to, and not just an impending dinner with a very lovely man. Right now, she feels more herself than she has ever felt. She has thrown off her old mantle of self-loathing. In fact, she has taken a conscious decision to love who she is. She is creative and caring. She is a mother, but also a woman with talents and needs. She is independent, but not alone. She has a community here. She has a tribe. And she has a new understanding of the natural world, and her place within it. Because, she realises – *because* – she is home.

* * *

It's late afternoon when Beth hears the sound of tyres on gravel. Her guests have arrived. She leaves the library, the location she's chosen today to carry on writing her as yet unfinished novel, to answer the door.

'Thank you so much for coming,' Beth says, taking a deep breath.

'Our pleasure,' says Carole, smiling at Rowan, who's by her side.

'Come in,' says Beth, shocked by how familiar Carole looks. She regains her composure quickly, however, and steps back to let them pass. 'Do you want to come through to the kitchen? It's warm in there, and I've bought us some pastries.'

'Lovely,' says Rowan, and the three women make their way to the back of the house.

'I wanted to...'

'I think I...'

Beth and Carole both try to speak at the same time. They look at each other and laugh.

'I'm sorry. I'm a bit nervous,' says Beth.

'Me too,' says Carole.

'Shall I help get the ball rolling, then?' says Rowan. 'I'll make the tea, while you two ladies chat. Let me suggest you start with your memories of Nita.'

Beth smiles gratefully at her friend.

After a stilted beginning, they soon find that their stories about the woman they both loved – great-aunt to one and birth mother to the other – flow freely. They laugh a lot, and at one point, when Beth's relating the story of how her parents took her away from the Manor, apparently never to return, Carole reaches across the table and takes her hand. Although she hardly knows this woman, Beth finds this gesture incredibly moving. She realises too how many of her great-aunt's features are present in Carole's face. Her expressions, too; the skin between her eyebrows wrinkles when she laughs, just like Nita's used to.

'So when did you find out that Nita wasn't just a friend of the family?' Beth asks, as they make their way through their second pot of tea.

'I've known for more than twenty years,' says Carole. 'And so has Rowan. Mum told us together, before she died. She said she wished she'd told me sooner, but that she was fulfilling Nita's wish to keep it a secret.'

'How did you feel about it being kept from you for so long?'

'I was shocked, initially. I had to reassess all of my childhood memories, to look at them, and at her, from a new angle. But when I'd done all that and the dust had settled, I think I mostly just felt compassion. She did what she thought was the best thing to do, in the social context of the time. And I had such a happy childhood. Mum and Dad were amazing, and Rowan and I are sisters, there's no question about that.'

'Yeah, you'll do,' says Rowan with a grin. She tears off a piece of chocolate croissant.

Beth decides this is her moment to ask two nagging questions.

'I wanted to ask you, Rowan – both of you, I suppose – about a couple of things I didn't find the answer to in Nita's documents. She told me in her will that you'd be able to fill me in. The first thing is – I saw in there that she'd been searching for a spy, a German spy. She called him X. She seemed quite obsessed about it. I'm desperate to know. Did she ever find him?'

Rowan shoots a look at Carole.

'Yes,' says Rowan. 'Yes, she did.'

* * *

It's an hour later, and the three women have decided to take a tour of Melham Manor, taking each room in turn. They know they are running out of opportunities to do so before the sale, and Beth is grateful for this opportunity to stop talking for a while so that she can process what she's just heard.

She tries to imagine, as they walk into one of the downstairs rooms and leaf idly through the few boxes of Nita's possessions that remain, how it must have felt to discover that the man she loved was working for the enemy, lying to her for all that time. And to lose him in such a terrible way, too. Rowan and Carole have told her about the circumstances surrounding his death, and Harriet and John's role in it. They've made her promise not to disclose to anyone where his body lies, too, and she has agreed. Everyone involved in the incident is gone now, anyway. She sees no need at all to dig up the past, quite literally. Far better, she thinks, to let it rest. She is more grateful than ever now that the woodland surrounding Melham is going to be left undisturbed.

As they make their way through the building, the sun begins to set. Beth turns on lights as they go, but several of the ancient bulbs refuse to work, and the house remains stubbornly in partial darkness.

'It's a bit creepy in here, isn't it,' says Carole, as they climb up the creaking staircase. 'I've always thought that it is, at night.'

'I know what you mean. I've heard things, you know,' says Beth. 'After dark. It sounded like people walking around. But when I looked, no one was there.'

Carole stops suddenly, halfway up the stairs.

'Oh goodness. That might have been me. I'm so sorry. I came in a couple of times after work, after Nita died, just to feel close to her. I borrowed Rowan's key. I walked through the woods to get here from Rowan's place – I wouldn't have seen your car. I didn't know you were here.'

Beth laughs with relief.

'Thank God for that! That's one less mystery,' she says, and they keep on walking up the steps.

'How you do feel now, Beth? Now that you know everything?' asks Rowan as they reach the first floor, and head into Nita's bedroom. They stand side by side looking out of the window, down towards the village, which is gradually lighting up as darkness falls.

'Happy,' Beth replies. 'I know it's a sad story. Terribly sad. But I can't help but feel happy that she's brought us together, the three of us, and that you're going to be able to stay in your house, Rowan.'

'Well the money Nita left me more than covers it.'

'I'm so glad it's finally yours to keep,' says Beth. 'I'm looking forward to making Melham my home, too.'

'I'm very glad you're staying,' says Rowan. 'Those vegetables won't grow themselves, you know.'

'Ha, I'll need some lessons.'

'I'll be happy to provide them. And to your kids. They love the garden, don't they. I'm so glad they're still going to be able to run about in it.'

'Me too,' agrees Beth, delighted that Rowan will remain a part of their lives. At the bottom of the hill, the church bell chimes. 'You know, Carole,' she says, when it stops tolling, 'I can't believe you didn't say anything to me about who you were, when we met just before Nita died.'

When Beth had laid eyes on Carole on the doorstep of Melham Manor two hours previously, she had realised instantly where she'd seen her before.

Because Carole had been the nurse who'd been looking after Nita in her final days. She'd been the woman who'd greeted Beth at the door on that fateful night.

'Ah, yes. Well, Rowan and I agreed it would be better if we did as Nita wanted, and let you find out for yourself,' says Carole with a smile. 'And anyway, I wanted to spend that time with Nita, without distractions. I had something I needed to tell her.'

41

NITA

October 2008

'She's here, Nita.'

Nita wakes with a start, her mouth dry. It takes her a few seconds to work out where she is. She's relieved to discover she's in her bedroom at Melham Manor, and not in a ballroom in London, or at the War Office, or any of the other places her vivid dreams have been taking her. She wonders how long she's been asleep, and who it is that's come to see her. No one ever comes here, she thinks. No one except Rowan and Harriet these days. And then she remembers, with utter sadness, that Harriet is dead.

'Auntie Nita?'

Carole used to call her Auntie Nita, she thinks, remembering as she does so the doughy softness of her beautiful, tiny hands, the hands that had so often clasped hers, both before their separation, and afterwards.

'You will have to speak up. She's gone quite deaf. And please do sit down.'

'Auntie Nita. It's me, Beth. I've come to see you.'

Beth... Frank... So many names, so many faces, so many words spoken and unspoken. Nita is too tired. Too tired to live in the real world any more. She is much more interested in what has gone before and what will come next. But she does decide to open her eyes a crack, just to see who it is. She turns her head very slightly in the direction of the voice.

'Ah.'

It's Beth! Nita knew she'd come.

'Dad is very sorry he can't come. He's so busy with the business. He says he'll try to come this weekend.'

Beth's father is... Robert. Yes, Robert, Frank's child. Such a selfish boy, she thinks. Nothing at all like his father. She remembers how Frank had fought with their parents and won for her the right to remain in Melham Manor for the rest of her living days. She wishes now she'd fought harder for her own independence, for her right not to marry a much older man and for her right to keep that precious, precious child.

'I... don't want... this,' says Nita, to her mother Jane-Anne, who has appeared suddenly in the corner of the room. This has been happening a lot in recent days. She has got used to it. Her mother is always bossing her around and telling her who she's supposed to be, which is generally everything that she is not. She is enjoying biting back now she's old enough to know her own mind. It's about time, really, she thinks. About time.

'It's not you, don't worry. She's been saying a lot of strange things. That's quite normal for people when they're close to the end. She hasn't been interested in food or drink for a while now. It takes its toll. She's in her own world a lot of the time. But she can definitely hear you. And sometimes she's really present. Just be patient.'

Yes, I can hear you, child, thinks Nita. *I can hear you quite clearly.*

Then she finds herself back in the ballroom during wartime.

This is another place she's spent a lot of the past few days. At this moment, Jane-Anne is trying to cajole her into dancing with that utter buffoon of a man. He was nothing compared to Joe, Nita thinks. *Nothing.*

'I am not... ludicrous... dancing... Mother, no. I will not,' says Nita, her face now a scowl.

'Lots of people seem to talk to their mothers at this stage,' says the nurse.

Then Harriet is there. She's cajoling, reassuring, suggesting. Consoling.

'Yes, if you think so... the woods... so cold.'

'Auntie Nita...'

And then Nita is suddenly back in the room, and very, very awake. Because Beth has come. She came in the end. Lovely, beautiful Beth, who has no idea she is either of those things.

'Beth? Is that you?'

'Yes. It's me.'

Thank goodness there is still time to tell her, Nita thinks. *I don't have much time on this earth left.* 'You came then. Good. I wanted to say... There is a box in the attic. It has... secrets.'

Nita smiles, because she knows what will happen now. She knows everything.

'Secrets?'

And then, as quickly as she entered the room, she leaves it. She's back in the ballroom now.

'No! I will not, Mother. I will *not*.'

She heaves with all her might, determined to escape this infernal room and this infernal marriage market where they treat women like cattle.

'Help. She's...'

Then the ballroom fades, and Nita feels the child putting a pillow beneath her head. This relaxes her, but then her eyes start to roam the room. She is looking for Carole. She has something to tell her. Something she should have told her long ago.

'I always wanted to tell you. *Always*.'

The effort exhausts her. She sinks back into her pillow, her eyes closed.

'I think she needs a rest. She's unsettled this afternoon, as you can tell. And you need a break, too. You've come a long way. Why don't you go and get some food? There are some sandwich ingredients in the kitchen and the guest room across the landing is made up, I think. I'll come and get you if she takes a turn for the worse.'

'OK then. I'll do that. Thanks,' says Beth. Then she pats her on the arm, and even when she walks away, her warmth lingers. Nita hears her walking to the door, saying thank you and then heading down the corridor towards her room. Nita feels a pang of sadness, because she knows she will never see Beth in this life again. But she also knows that she has done the right thing, and that Beth will save the woods and the garden for her. She has every faith in her. She was a magical child, and the magic is still in her, Nita thinks.

'She's gone now. But I'm here, Nita,' says Carole, sitting down on the bed beside her. 'I'm just going to check your pulse, OK?'

'Carole...' says Nita, every word making her chest ache. 'Carole... I always wanted to tell you... That I gave birth to you.'

'It's OK, Auntie Nita. I know. Mum told me before she died. I've known for a while, but I didn't know how you'd feel about it. I knew you could have told me at any time, but you didn't, and I didn't want to upset you by coming up here and asking about it. I didn't know how you'd feel about me just coming out with it, to be honest. So I didn't. And I'm so sorry about that. I shouldn't have left it this long.'

'But... you aren't angry?'

'Goodness no. I'm not angry at all. You are a very special woman, Nita. The best. Mum always said so. And I have always loved you.'

'So it's... all right?'

'Yes, it's all right,' says Carole, gently sweeping Nita's thin white hair away from her face with her hand. 'It's absolutely all right.'

When Nita feels the warmth of her daughter's hand on her forehead, and the warmth of her forgiveness and love pulsing through her, she knows it is time to go. She takes one last look at her beautiful face, then closes her eyes and allows herself to be pulled upwards, into the light.

AUTHOR'S NOTE

Nita Bineham was a real person. She was married to my grandfather's cousin, Gerald, a man who was really my grandfather's brother in all but genetics. Nita and Gerald were unable to have children of their own, and when Nita died in the early 2000s, it fell to us, her really quite distant relatives, to clear out the house she'd lived in with Gerald from their marriage until the end of their lives.

Although I'd met her several times throughout my childhood, it was, ironically, only after her death that I began to feel I knew her. Like Nita in this novel, the real Nita had been a journalist during World War II, albeit for the *Manchester Evening News*, and not *The Bugle* (which, of course, doesn't exist). Looking through her things, I found lots of cuttings she'd kept, and several complete newspapers and magazines from key points in history. In fact, I have her copy of the Radio Times from May 10, 1945, a special VE Day edition, framed on the wall in my study.

Nita wrote right until the end. My parents have kept the typewriter we found in her living room. She left behind many letters and works of non-fiction, including a wonderful account of her wedding day, part of which I read at her funeral.

It's important to note of course that Nita Bineham's character and experiences in *The Storyteller's Daughter* are entirely fictional. The Nita I knew didn't search for a Nazi spy, as far as I'm aware, but I do hope she might be pleased to find a character inspired by her in this story. According to the rules of the time, she gave up work when she married, and never returned to the newsroom. It feels special to have been able to send her back there again, albeit in fiction.

Furthermore, although I invented the Wiccan coven in Melham, this element of the story is also rooted in truth. As outlandish as it might sound, a coven did genuinely hold a Cone of Power ritual in WWII to try to keep Hitler at bay. Gerald Gardner wrote in 1945 that a coven of Wiccans gathered in the New Forest on England's south coast on August 1 1940 and carried out the ritual. This involved marking out a circle in a clearing and dancing around a shuttered lantern, rather than a traditional fire, due to the blackout rules of the time. The cone in question was a large wooden one, and it was pointed towards Berlin. According to Gardner, this ritual had also been performed by witches to ward off both the Spanish Armada and Napoleon.

Finally, while Melham Manor and the village of Melham do not exist, I took inspiration for the house's design from the real-life Leith Hill Place, the childhood home of composer Ralph Vaughan Williams. It's located in roughly the same area as the fictional Melham and managed by the National Trust. It's a wonderful, atmospheric place with great views, and it also holds some excellent concerts.

If you'd like to find out more about me and the four other novels I've written, you can visit my website, www.toryscott.com. I also spend far too much time on social media. Do come and say hi!

Facebook: VictoriaScottJournalist

Instagram: victoriascottauthor

Twitter/X: @toryscott

Tiktok: victoriascottauthor

ACKNOWLEDGEMENTS

Firstly, I'd like to thank the wonderful Donna Lansdale, a very experienced senior hospice nurse, for the advice she gave me when I was writing the scene describing Nita's death. Donna exudes warmth and care, and I know she's devoted to her patients. In fact, she's a lovely person in general and I'm very lucky to have her as a neighbour.

I'd also like to thank my agent Elizabeth Counsell at Northbank Talent for her support and my editor Rachel Faulkner-Willcocks at Boldwood Books for her insightful editing and brilliant vision. Boldwood are a fabulous publisher and every single member of their team does a wonderful job. You rock, guys.

Lastly, I know Wicca is a multifaceted belief, but I hope I captured at least some of it in this story. I'd like to thank the authors of these two books for their part in helping me understand it:

Wicca, Leanna Greenaway, Orion

Wicca Magic, Agnes Hollyhock, Wellfleet Press

Thanks also to the journalist India Rakusen for her podcast *Witch*, which you can find on BBC Sounds. It explores modern Wicca and also explains the history of witchcraft. It's beautifully made and definitely worth a listen.

ABOUT THE AUTHOR

Victoria Scott has been a journalist for many media outlets including the BBC and The Telegraph. She is the author of three novels as Victoria Scott, including her Gothic timeslip novel *The House in the Water*.

Sign up to Victoria Scott's mailing list here for news, competitions and updates on future books.

Visit Victoria's website: www.toryscott.com

Follow Victoria on social media:

x.com/Toryscott

facebook.com/VictoriaScottJournalist

instagram.com/victoriascottauthor

tiktok.com/@victoriascottauthor

ALSO BY VICTORIA SCOTT

The House in the Water

The Storyteller's Daughter

Letters from
the past

Discover page-turning
historical novels from
your favourite authors
and be transported
back in time

Join our book club
Facebook group

https://bit.ly/SixpenceGroup

Sign up to our
newsletter

https://bit.ly/LettersFrom
PastNews

Boldwood

Boldwood Books is an award-winning fiction publishing company seeking out the best stories from around the world.

Find out more at www.boldwoodbooks.com

Join our reader community for brilliant books, competitions and offers!

Follow us
@BoldwoodBooks
@TheBoldBookClub

Sign up to our weekly deals newsletter

https://bit.ly/BoldwoodBNewsletter